HUMAN

Arca Book 2

KAREN DIEM

Copyright

★★★

eBook version 1.0, published May 5, 2017.

First Paperback Printing: May 30, 2017.

ISBN: 978-0-9975740-3-6

To contact Karen Diem or subscribe to her newsletter, go to http://www.karendiem.com.

Dedication

This is dedicated to the readers who enjoy my work; my family, who puts up with me and a lot of peanut butter; and my editors, who I wish the best of luck in their valiant battles against my rampaging comma army.

Table of Contents

Chapter One

Once again, a cookie doomed her.

"Save the animals! Sign our petition and get a free giant cookie," a girl's voice chirped over a speaker.

Pues, if I had been able to sit still on the bus long enough to reach the auditorium, I might've missed out on this treat. After all, the sugar will help me stay awake during the concert, and I would have signed the petition before becoming a teleporting shapeshifter, anyway. Though crossing the grounds of the large university on foot would take up most of the time left before her blind date, Zita Garcia spun on her heel in an abrupt right turn into the wide plaza.

Her muscular legs moved in short, swift strides toward the stately edifice anchoring the opposite side of the plaza. Beneath the broad stone portico engraved with "Biology" and "Psychology," her target, a table at the base of the entry steps, beckoned. Stretched across a white plastic tablecloth, a maroon and gold banner announced: "Testing Animals Stops Today."

No students lingered near the protesters. A girl with curly brown hair hoisted a microphone and uttered her siren call again as a gaggle of other demonstrators revolved around the table, waving clipboards in a rainbow of primary colors. For Zita, who enjoyed guessing the sports played by fellow athletes, they held little interest as their movements had the zest of youth, rather than any physical conditioning. The only unusual-looking activist, distinguishable by his wild, ungroomed beard and the two giant tufts of hair that stood out above his ears, glowered and shook his walking stick at those who did not sign. Eyes all but closed in boredom, a campus security guard loitered nearby.

As always, Zita assessed the area and the people in it as she marched toward the promised treat. Like a squished spider, leggy pathways led in every direction from the bare, round center of the plaza. Senseless sets of little stairs erupted up and down along and on the paths. Tall deciduous trees dotted the spaces between the trails, granting irregular patches of shade to black metal tables with attached benches. Evergreens nestled close to the buildings. Scattered throughout, students socialized more than studied, unsurprising given fall classes had yet to start. The occasional bird skittered from branch to branch overhead, and squirrels congregated on the tree trunks a safe distance from humans. *When my date ends, I can free-run through here on my way to catch the bus, even if I have to re-wear the dirty workout clothing in my satchel.* She smiled, pleased at the promise of fun for later, and planned a challenging route.

With a guilty jolt, she remembered she had promised to give Luis an honest chance. Her brother Quentin had said that her date, a prospective client of his, met her standards. Though Zita hoped that meant he enjoyed climbing and extreme sports, she suspected he was just a gym regular. Her traitorous sibling must have needed to divert inquiries about his own frenzied social life; both her mother and her other brother, Miguel, made her promise to be sweet to that "nice Catholic boy" (from her mother) who "lacked a criminal record and maintained steady employment" (Miguel's contribution). She wondered if the poor guys her brothers set her up with knew how much Garcia attention they received with each date. Since Miguel's last pick had required rescuing from thugs and preceded a short coma that landed her in months of quarantine, she reassured herself that tonight's date could not be worse. If nothing else, a decent meal might soothe the sting of having to abandon her plans for Friday night: aerial acrobatics, followed by practice for an upcoming capoeira roda.

As Zita approached, a group of twittering coeds with athletic legs bounced up to the table. Lacrosse sticks and gym bags hung from their shoulders. With eager smiles, the student activists greeted them and proffered clipboards. When the lacrosse team set down their belongings to accept the forms, she hurried as much as her red and lime-green skirt suit would allow without flashing anyone. *Oye, don't take all the cookies!* She blessed her own decision to wear her dressy sneakers (she had bejeweled them herself). The sports bra hidden under her clothing kept her generous chest under control enough to risk a higher speed.

A chubby man barreled down the building steps and grabbed the arm of the curly brunette with the microphone, snarling something at her. Clad in a baggy polo shirt and jeans, he lacked the coordination or form of a dedicated athlete. His posture and the hard shove to return his glasses to their position shouted his annoyance as did the unhappy lines of what little face was visible above a prodigious ginger mustache. Despite the ball cap worn backward on his head, he seemed older than most of the activists, closer to Zita's own twenty-six years. *Graduate student, perhaps?*

Unimpressed with whatever he had said, the curly-haired girl jerked her arm away and jabbed his sternum with her finger as she responded.

The way the other members of the group, except for the surly, cane-waggling bearded guy, pretended not to notice made Zita slow. *Ay, looks personal. Cookies aren't worth getting near that kind of drama.* The promised treats with their telltale chocolate chip dots flirted with her from a plate next to a pile of pamphlets. *They're probably store-bought anyway,* she assured herself, veering toward a tiny fountain surrounded by thornless honey locust trees.

Eager to circumvent the argument, she almost missed the first mental flicker as a male voice called out, the words too garbled and distorted by static to understand. Stopping, she scanned the area, her shoulders tensing at the intrusion. *Wyn? It doesn't sound like her, and Andy and I don't have telepathy. We can only talk that way when she links us together.*

Huge edifices towered on three of the four sides of the plaza. One was a library for undergraduates; her bookish friend Wyn, who worked at a graduate-level library on campus, had pointed it out on Zita's last visit. The others were fancy campus classroom buildings, complete with pillars and overdone stonework hiding the plain windows and doors of repurposed historic structures. Everything appeared innocuous enough, and no one had stirred. A breeze, a relief from Maryland's late August heat and humidity, teased the leaves into periodic murmurs and carried the scents of crushed grass and cooking food. The rise in volume of chittering alerted her, and a glance up showed that the handful of squirrels had multiplied, and now every tree had several. The birds had fled. She rubbed the short, choppy black hair on the top of her head as unease grew, and she sped up to reach the side of a building.

Is a male telepath poking around heads? Zita ran through the exercises Wyn had taught her to close her mind and make it harder to read. Noise broke her concentration.

The curly-haired activist's voice ascended to a screech as she accused the chubby graduate student of bowing to the will of his professor. The name meant nothing to Zita, and she blinked as the bearded fellow moved behind the quarreling pair with a speed belied by his average physical tone and coordination. He joined in berating the graduate student.

Her stomach clenched.

When the security officer sensed the disruptive trio's imminent altercation and tried to intercede, her disquiet receded. The aggressive bearded man withdrew a few paces, and the mental muttering increased. Although the words were unintelligible, they held notes of command.

She cursed inwardly. *Let campus security handle it,* she told herself. *He's trained for it. You're a dilettante with a couple of powers, and telepathy isn't one of them. If there's a mind reader hanging out around here, I need to go before he learns my secrets.* She stomped away, sans cookie, settling her clothing satchel on her shoulders. Zita had only managed a few more steps when shocked shouting made her look back.

The security guy and graduate student were sprawled on the ground, and the bearded weirdo stood over them, cane raised. With a dramatic flourish, he slipped off the tip of his walking stick to reveal a sword. The activists and lacrosse girls had taken several steps away but stopped when he unsheathed the blade. He pointed to the curly-haired girl and held out his hand in demand. One or two of the students had their phones aimed at him.

Eyes wide, the curly-haired girl handed him the microphone.

A melodic basso transmitted through the scratchy speaker as he spoke. "I have been patient. I have gone through channels. No more. You will all bow and present Professor Clarise Weppler to me! She must answer for her crimes against squirrelkind!" He wove a dramatic pattern in the air with his sword, a move that would have gotten him skewered in an actual fight.

Squirrelkind? Is that a real word? Zita shoved away the incongruous thought. *Right, so he's the guy mumbling in my mind, even if I have no idea what he's saying or why I can hear him since I am happily not telepathic.*

He continued ranting into the microphone, waving his naked blade. "Should you think to silence my voice, know that I have placed at least one bomb on campus. Should I fall today, my people shall be avenged! If you bring me the foul evildoer, I will remove the bombs!"

Oye, someone took extra drama pills instead of their medication. Zita ducked behind the corner of a building, one that looked as if a giant toddler had glued multiple medium-sized houses together and then tried to cover up the mess with columns and classical ornamentation. Slipping into the shadow of a trio of evergreens, she pulled her satchel closer to her body, freeing it from a squat holly. *The police can handle this. They have negotiators who have to be better than me at talking. De verdad, the police likely have janitors who are more diplomatic*, she tried to convince herself. Much to her discomfort, the muttering in her mind grew louder but no more understandable.

The reply to the call came in a susurration of sound, like distant thunder, growing louder as it approached. A throng of squirrels (and their probable accompanying horde of fleas) poured down the path between buildings, fearless. Rather than going around people, the rodents swarmed over them. One girl, frozen in shock at the sight, disappeared beneath the tide of tiny bodies. When they passed, she began a broken wail despite seeming unharmed. The animals headed toward Zita's hiding place.

"Oh, hell no," she said and teleported to the top of the building she hid beside. As the roof was a collection of odd angles where pitched rooflines met, it hosted a plethora of small, hidden areas invisible from neighboring buildings and from below. Safe from the rampaging rodents, the athletic Latina climbed over the rough, tarry shingles to a spot where three sharp, angled peaks rose from a relatively flat surface. Though no one would be able to see her there, she couldn't see anything, either, but as she pulled her flip phone from her satchel, screams sounded. Zita clambered up the closest peak and observed the chaos below through gaps in the trees.

Squirrels eddied up and down the tree trunks in the plaza, several clustering by the now-abandoned table. All humans had fled, save for the bearded bomber and those who had been standing or lying closest to him: the security guard, the graduate student, the curly-haired girl, and one of the other female activists, who held a phone. The two men sat on the pavement, the graduate student holding his head in one hand. The mad bomber (Zita named him Squirrelly) punctuated words with his sword, coming close to puncturing his hostages multiple times. Abandoned bags, lacrosse sticks, and clipboards littered the ground by the table.

"The time of the rodent is upon us," Squirrelly intoned, the microphone amplifying his words as he produced a thick sheaf of papers from nowhere. For a moment, he performed an awkward juggling act with his sword, microphone, and papers. When he managed to get everything else in one hand, he pointed his sword at the girl with the phone and spat, "Keep filming."

His furry audience stopped moving and sat motionless, every tiny nose directed at the man speaking, save one. That squirrel ran up his leg and perched on his shoulder, its brown fur so perfect a match with the man's hair that Zita wondered if he had chosen the animal for that reason.

Zita pressed a number on speed dial.

The girl with the phone—Camerawoman—held it higher and nodded, her trembling noticeable enough that Zita could see it from the roof.

With a smile, Squirrelly licked a finger and turned a page. He pontificated into the microphone. "Mankind is not our friend. Its so-called science imprisons and tortures us. The kindest feed us only leftovers. We must rise, my rodent brethren, and begin a glorious revolution!"

"If squirrels are your brothers, your mother's got a nasty kink, buddy," Zita mumbled as someone picked up the other end of the call.

"What was that? Zita, is your date over already? Is everyone unharmed? It's Friday night, so of course, a professor sent me additional requirements for a special project, but if you want to talk, I'm here," her friend Wyn said. Concern warred with amusement in her dulcet voice.

Descending back to the flat spot on the roof and ignoring the continued blather coming from the square below, Zita frowned at sunbaked asphalt shingles. *People can easily eavesdrop on phones, so I'll have to be indirect when I ask Wyn to use her telepathy to talk privately. Nobody's learning about that or her magic from me. Great, subtlety and conversation, two things I suck at. Quizás, I could reference the party-line joke, about how her telepathy tied us together like a shared phone line, to cue her in to use it.*

Zita cleared her throat and took off her satchel, holding the phone to her ear with her shoulder. "My dates don't get injured that often—well, depending... Never mind, you need to get off campus. Some loco, I mean, crazy man, put a bomb somewhere at the university. If you find a party line, you can call me back on it." She let her bag drop to the roof.

"Here?" Wyn replied incredulously, her Southern accent thickening. "Wait, you're on campus, and you didn't mention it? Weren't you too busy to get together with me today?" Her questions held an odd tone.

Zita paced the three steps her hiding spot allowed. "Yes to all the questions. Get to safety. Party after."

"Oh, but the Hades project... Fine, I'll go, but we need to talk," Wyn said and hung up.

Crashing chords, like a marching band at a football game, underscored by a shrill, unintelligible chorus, rose whenever the tirade below paused.

Squirrelly brought music to rant to? Zita wondered as she tucked away her phone.

As expected, a few seconds later, Wyn's voice spoke in her mind. Unlike the man below, her tones were clear and her words sensible. *I do hope this is all a tasteless joke*, she sent.

No such luck. Can you find out from Squirrelly's head where he put the bombs? Given the amount of special sunshine he's sharing with everyone, he should have a distinctive brain.

Exasperation trickled through the mental connection. *Even if I locate him in the crowd, what would we do with the information?*

Zita rolled her eyes, forgetting her friend could not see her. *Call the police and leave an anonymous tip so they can take him out of action as soon as the bomb's disabled. If possible, warn them he's a squirrel hypnotist telepath because he's controlling them somehow.*

Since she suspected what she would need to do, Zita sighed and shapeshifted into a South American pipe snake. If she had to switch to a large animal later, the last thing she wanted, given her tight budget, was to destroy one of her few viable work outfits. Slithering out of her clothing, she transformed into a different human form, the one she thought she'd never have to take again. Since taking any human form other than her own made her feel off balance, always bad in a fight, her disguise was identical to her natural body, except for the different face, pointy ears, and the mass of long black hair that hung like a cape to her thighs. She reminded herself to carry a tie to keep the hair under control in case she ever had to do this again. After a moment, she altered her fingers to hide her prints.

Silence greeted her words. When Wyn replied, surprise laced her tone. *That seems unusually prudent for you. If I could find him, I would read him for the bomb locations, but I can't locate him. All the staff, including myself, just got orders to clear the library, thanks to a student who ran in shouting about bombs and terrorists. People are going mad.*

Carajo. Can you use me to find him? If I look at him, would that help? After rummaging through her satchel, Zita withdrew her exercise gear, wrinkling her nose at the clammy touch of the still-sweaty material as she slid it on. *At least I have my ancient and boring black stuff today if it gets wrecked in a shapeshift.*

Dubiousness tinged Wyn's reply. *I'll try it. Why are you contemplating changing shape? You're staying back, right?*

Despite her disgust, Zita tried to tie a used hand towel around her lower face, but the fabric was too small. She dropped it. After worming her way up to the peak, she checked below again. *Try now.* For a second, her vision doubled, and she felt crowded, as if someone stood too close. *How about now?*

No, sorry, Wyn replied. The claustrophobic feeling receded.

Frustrated, Zita pushed loose hair out of her face and propped herself up on one arm. *How can the brain of a man controlling hundreds of squirrels and reading from something he calls the "Squirrel Manifesto" not stand out?*

Irritation colored Wyn's reply. *Which one of us is the telepath? Right now, I can't find him. I'd have to see him myself, or you'd have to get closer so I could use your sight.*

How close? Zita asked, hunching down to avoid being seen.

If I used you to triangulate, you would have to be within... Wyn's mental voice broke off. In a sharper tone, she said, *Zita, what are you planning? Don't approach someone who has a bomb.*

A shriek, followed by terrified screaming, made Zita climb back up the pitched roof and peek below again. A group of squirrels swirled near the hostages then withdrew, revealing the graduate student lying in a fetal ball. Myriad tiny red circles expanded to larger ones, drowning out the white and blue of his clothing. *He's hurting people.* Revulsion filled her, twisting her focus. *Not the time to relive Brazil,* she thought, sweating as she forced the memories of a friend's death away before they leaked into her communication with Wyn.

Squirrelly gestured to the bloody man. "Do not try to run. The monkey will fall beneath our rodent might," he intoned in his sonorous voice. "You! Tie up the transgressors." He tossed a roll of duct tape to the feet of the curly-haired activist, who had a hand touching her mouth. Turning, he smiled into Camerawoman's phone.

Both of the hostage women stared at him, their mouths agape. Music rose. The one with the phone almost dropped it as she fell to her knees and vomited.

"Now!" he thundered, with a theatrical gesture toward a clump of squirrels.

With uncanny synchronization, the selected rodents swarmed up the stairs, a churning mass of fur. They fixed their beady eyes on the captives.

All the hostages flinched at their proximity.

Once the animals were in place, Squirrelly tucked the sword beneath his arm, stroked his unruly beard, and flipped through the stack of papers as if he had lost his place. He glanced over at Camerawoman's phone. With a scowl, he gestured for her to raise it.

The frightened young woman, pale beneath umber skin, wiped off her mouth and held the phone higher.

Although most of her attention was on the people, Zita noted that the squirrel audience grew restless as the selected rodent soldiers menaced the hostages. A few even scampered away between buildings.

The curly-haired girl (Zita named her Curly) picked up the duct tape and obeyed, beginning with the security guard. After taping his arms behind him and his ankles together, she did the same to the graduate student, propping him against the guard to keep the student sitting upright. He turned his face from her as she worked, unwilling or unable to do more. When she finished, she gestured toward Camerawoman and asked a question.

The bearded bomber shook his head and gestured for Curly to come nearer. As she drew near enough, he swooped down, pressed a kiss onto the back of her hand, and murmured something. He waved at his feet.

Her eyes glassy, Curly complied, sitting on the steps at his feet.

After clearing his throat, the man spoke into his microphone again. "You see before you the King of All Squirrels and their kin. Today, I shall judge the vile creatures who would perform horrific experiments on my noble people. Rise, my rodents, and speak! No more will we be victimized! Bring me Professor Clarise Weppler!" The group of squirrels split to stand like rodent bookends at either side of the stone steps, and the chittering increased enough to be audible.

Zita teleported to her chosen spot, behind one of the decorative columns and Camerawoman. She crept closer to the security guard, keeping low to remain unseen. Using his bulk as cover from the madman, she worked to release him. "Shh," she whispered, "I'm here to help."

Shoulders stiff, the security guard inclined his head an inch. This close, the sour perspiration staining his uniform reeked, and the movement of his throat was visible as he swallowed. Although he recoiled when he saw her there, the graduate student hunched closer to the other man. To their credit, both men stayed silent and leaned together, shielding her from view with their larger bodies. More bitter fear mingled with blood and sweat in their scents. The bellowed demands for the professor and the bombastic music (now repeating itself) hid the noise of duct tape ripping.

How can you not appreciate the glorious utility of duct tape? Assuming you're not as inept as Curly when you use it, Zita thought.

Duct tape? What? Don't do anything stupid, Wyn warned.

Too late for that, Zita sent. *Can you read the nut job now?* Although she had braced herself for the double vision, the sensation of a person standing too close had her fighting her instincts to defend herself. Her fists curled, and she inhaled and exhaled slow, controlled breaths to even out. She snuck peeks at the self-proclaimed monarch.

Her friend's unhappiness rang through their mental link even as the feeling receded. *No, he's on a bizarre mental path, like you,* Wyn sent. *Also, that pun was terrible.*

Andy would have appreciated the nut job pun. What do you mean bizarre? Zita thought, tearing off the last of the tape from the guard's wrists. She kept a wary eye on the posturing Squirrelly— the erstwhile Squirrel King—as she switched to working on the graduate student. The security man curled his legs back and began scraping at the tape on his ankles.

Wyn explained. *When you're in animal form, you don't register as human.*

Zita paused for a second. *I am always a person, no matter my shape.* Hoping to sever the tape fast and avoid inflicting any more pain than necessary, she dug her fingers into the bindings on the graduate student's wrists and gave a sharp yank. "Sorry," she said, her voice almost inaudible. He winced but continued blocking her from view. Her respect for the rotund student increased; this close, the vicious bite marks covered so much of him that blood hid much of his visible skin. Her determination to help grew.

Frustration vibrated down the mental link. *You are? Just kidding. You're like a website that never appears in search results, or the more distant radio station between two louder stations that drown you out; a person has to know what channel to search for. When Andy's a giant bird, he's the same way, although a different frequency. Neither human nor animal. That's part of why it's so restful to focus on the two of you.* Wyn apologized, *I'm sorry, I'm trying, but I can't find your bomber, which might be a mercy if his mind is as horrendous as his hair. I can see him through your eyes, but all the squirrel brainwaves are hiding his mind. Every now and again I pick up a weird chitter telepathically, which I'm guessing is him, but I haven't been able to follow it to him yet.*

"I am weary of the delays!" the Squirrel King declared. "The death of the transgressor who assisted the vile Weppler was foreordained, but you shall watch it now." When Camerawoman fumbled her phone at his words, he directed his sword at her. "You will continue to film. They must know the truth." He murmured something to Curly, his tones softening.

Her eyes glued to him, Curly folded her hands in her lap.

Zita worked faster, unbinding the student's hands. She seized the ball cap from his head, revealing a small bald spot. After putting on the hat, she pulled the bill low to hide her face from the cameras. Even transformed, she preferred to leave as few clues as possible. Apropos of nothing, she wondered if she should name her disguise. *I should just call it Arca,* she thought, *as that's what the media thinks my name is. Miguel would call it my death-wish shape given what I do with it.* "I'll distract him. You get to safety," she whispered.

The synchronized squirrels bounded back up the stairs, one group encircling Camerawoman, and the other following Squirrelly. With a flourish of his blade, the Squirrel King turned to approach his captives. He had taken only two steps before he caught sight of Zita hiding behind the men.

"What is that?" he bellowed, lowering his weapon. The squirrels at his feet flashed their tails and made repeated "kuk" alarm sounds.

Beyond them, the horde of squirrels fled up tree trunks, even scampering over each other to escape. Many escaped the area entirely. In comparison, until emotion got the better of their "King," the controlled squirrels seemed like zombies or robots. *Tiny, furry ones.*

When he recovered, the Squirrel King pointed his sword at Zita.

Chapter Two

Zita rose to her full, menacing five feet of height and waved. "Hi there. Are you talking about me? If so, I'm definitely a who, rather than a what," she chirped, suppressing a twitch at the sound of her assumed voice. The only sign of her nervousness was the fake Mexican accent, a habit she had picked up during the tumultuous events following her receipt of powers. At least this time, her brother was safe from anything more dangerous than an STD. "I'd like to register a complaint on behalf of the squirrels. Is this the right location?" *Is this close enough? I need to lure him from his hostages in case I piss him off.*

Wyn replied. *In case? You mean when, don't you? No, I can't find him. Get rid of his entourage, and it might happen.*

Whatever the Squirrel King had anticipated, that was not it. He blinked. "What? I suppose you may speak regarding my subjects, although I am ending the torturous experiments today." His sword dipped.

Keep trying. Stepping out from behind the guard and the graduate student, Zita strolled away from the captives. The doubled vision, expected this time, did not cause even a hitch in her stride. To avoid the squirrels now chattering their teeth at her, she chose a circuitous route as she approached the steps. She contemplated the plaza, the rodent-covered trees, the table (stupid cookies of temptation still in place), and the abandoned belongings on the ground. When she reached the bottom, she faced him again. "Yes, animal testing is bad. I wanted to discuss a different issue facing your, ah, people."

Tension eased in her shoulders as the Squirrel King lowered his weapon and turned his back on his prisoners. He trailed after her. His rodent bodyguards shadowed him, though the other animals remained by the unwilling camerawoman. "You may speak."

"You want what's best for the rodents?" Zita said, trying to seem sympathetic. *Any time now would be good, Wyn. If I need to ask him a question to help you, I've got his attention.*

The Squirrel King stroked his beard. "Of course. I am a loving monarch." He puffed out his chest and almost strutted.

As she reached the table, Zita met his stare with her own. "Then prove you love them."

"Am I not here? Do I not act to end and avenge the terrible wrong that has been done them?" He narrowed his eyes and came close enough that his pungent sweat assailed her.

From her peripheral vision, Zita saw the security guard helping the graduate student to his feet. Broadening her motions, she let her natural inclination to speak with her hands keep the Squirrel King's focus on her. "It's fall. They should be hoarding food, lining nests, scratching at their fleas, and leaving pellets and disease everywhere. You know, happy squirrel things. Is it right to have this many abandon their territories and the caches they need to survive the winter, just to hear you talk?" *And talk, and talk, and talk. They probably want to slap you, too.* She edged toward the table and made a mental note to say another Hail Mary later. "Set your rodents free."

The Squirrel King seemed stricken for a moment but stepped forward, his face twisting. "You're a pretender who cares not for the rights of animals."

Zita laughed. *If only he knew.* "Hombre, I'm all about saving them. If you truly considered them people, you wouldn't enslave them unless you're an utter and complete dick," she replied. *Wyn? Close enough?* She planned her escape, judging his cadre of bodyguard squirrels to be the real threat due to their proximity. By the time the larger mob descended from their trees, she could shift and fly away.

He stiffened, face contorted with anger, and waved his sword at her.

When masculine muttering in her mind began again, Zita inched closer to the table. "What's that? Forcing your people to do your dirty work against me and all my mighty armies? So, you're choosing tyranny then, and showing you can't handle one woman on live TV. Or phone. Or whatever." She waved at the empty plaza.

"Streaming video," Camerawoman suggested. Some of the fear had faded from her face, and she seemed either bemused or shocky.

"Gracias." Zita dipped her head in thanks, hoping the cap hid enough of her features from the camera.

Camerawoman replied, "You're welcome."

"A monarch of my power needs no aid to handle a mouthy girl," the Squirrel King shouted. The squirrels at his feet parted and moved back, closer to Curly.

Zita cleared her throat. *Right, attempts at diplomacy failed, but I got distance between him and his pets. Time to be me.* Setting one hand aside her mouth, she stage-whispered, "Awesome woman, you mean. You don't want to piss off the feminists. I'm only a smartass; they're all badass." *Wyn? You done in there yet?*

He charged, all fury and furry, no finesse or skill.

He's very disorganized, Wyn answered in a prim tone.

Zita stepped to the left and let him continue past her. *Tell me about it. On the bright side, I can stay human for this. Between my capoeira and free running, and his lack of stamina, fighting him is pan comido, a piece of cake.* She jumped onto the table, snatched two handfuls of cookies, and threw one bunch at his face.

Alarm rang in Wyn's mental voice. *Never say that!*

Acting on instinct, the Squirrel King batted the food away with his sword, his next swing losing momentum.

Zita danced aside to avoid the thrust of the blade, tossing the rest of the treats she held at the group of squirrels by Curly. The table rocked and groaned underfoot.

Focused on skewering her, the Squirrel King made another wild jab.

She leapt onto the stair rail nearby, balancing for a moment before flipping off and backing toward the trees. The table clattered down, flyers and any remaining cookies cascading to the ground.

As she had hoped, the closest squirrels went for the food while the preoccupied Squirrel King pursued her. Maddened musical chords crashed around them, as if half a high school band played one song, and the remaining musicians played another from a different universe.

The drummer knows his beats at least, but I can't tell where the music is coming from. Zita backed up, forcing him to chase her around the tree trunks as she led him farther from his captives. She permitted herself a small, tight smile when she saw the camerawoman, security officer, and graduate student (with assistance from the others) run toward the rear of the building.

Curly continued sitting on the stone steps, watching.

"How can you claim to love the squirrels if you're willing to blow them up?" Zita barked at him, evading a telegraphed swipe with ease. *Why isn't Curly running? I can keep this up for hours, but we don't know when the bombs will explode, so concentrate, Wyn.*

Overhead, the entire horde of squirrels quivered at a mental screech from the Squirrel King, one that echoed in the back of her mind, but she could guess what he said when the squirrels poured out of the plaza in a furry stream of bodies. They parted to avoid running over their king or Zita, a nicety she appreciated. Distant shouts broadcasted their progress.

When the animals were gone, the Squirrel King grew a foot taller and gained a massive overbite and even more body hair. His now-fuzzy ears poked up through his hair, and his eyes turned dark. "I have sent most away to safeguard them," he declared. With inhuman speed, he crossed ten feet in a single lunge, and his sword almost nicked Zita's side.

Ew. Disgusting, Wyn opined. *Got one. It's in the undergraduate library, in the biology section. The second is in the den of iniquity, whatever that is.*

Less amused now, Zita fell into a capoeira ginga, her mind spinning as she flowed through the moving fight stance. When his sword swished again, she rolled to the side. She peeked around a bush at him and stuck out her tongue. "One bomb's in the undergrad library by the biology books?" she yelled, hoping someone would tell the cops. *Can't teleport in front of witnesses. That brainless Curly is still on the steps. Run, idiota, so I can get away. If I shift, my clothes might end up in evidence, and I don't want that.*

His next charge embedded his sword in a tree when she ducked. Pressing a foot against the trunk, the Squirrel King pulled it free and chattered his teeth at her. "Yes. They'll never discover it though. How did you find out?"

"Little squirrel told me." An idea coalesced, and Zita sprinted for the collapsed table, sliding to a stop by the abandoned gear. Catching sight of movement out of the corner of her eye, she seized two lacrosse sticks and threw them up in time to block another blow. Not only did the force of the hit reverberate through her, but a gym bag, still attached to one stick, smacked her in the face. She rolled, taking the sticks and bag with her. *Stronger and faster when he already had height and reach? Not fair. My turn to cheat.* With a firm grip on her Arca form, she reached for a gorilla shape but did not allow the full change. She had been practicing taking animal attributes without a complete transformation, but the results were still unpredictable. *Please let me get useful skills instead of just fur,* she prayed.

As she pulled at the straps on the bag, frantic to release it, he rushed at her again.

The stick and duffel separated, and Zita threw the bag at his face, derailing his assault and sending him staggering back. *Strength's boosted,* she noted as she danced away. Her weapons glinted pink and purple and blue. *Shiny.* She sprinted to a tree, did a short wall-run up it, and used it to vault away from another wild swing. "They might have squirrels in the den of iniquity, you know," she panted at him, his speed forcing her to exert effort to dodge.

The Squirrel King sneered, his oversized incisors making the face grotesque as he gasped his reply. "No, I let them all out. You waste your time trying to guess."

It's in a laboratory, Wyn sent, *where they were experimenting on squirrels.*

Can't be many of those, Zita thought. *No lo creo, Curly is still sitting there. I don't want anyone to die, but she's too stupid to live.* "You're bombing the lab where they were doing the squirrel experiments? Did you free everything in any adjoining rooms? Extra squirrels might be captive there." As she danced away from another swipe, the memory of an averted methadone lab explosion a few weeks ago reminded her of another risk. "What if it has chemicals that increase the damage radius? You know those scientists be playing with unstable shit and giggling over their energy drinks."

I'll try to find an unguarded phone and call it in, Wyn sent; then Zita was alone in her mind again.

Zita flexed her shoulders, continuing to move.

The Squirrel King swung again. Fear mingled with rage on his face. "I would have known!"

"The second bomb is in the squirrel experiment lab," Zita shouted. Then she could talk no more as the effort of dodging his blow stole the last of her breath. She crouched low, swept out with one leg, and felt it connect.

He teetered but remained standing.

While he was off-balance, she rolled behind him and smacked the back of one knee with a stick.

The Squirrel King stumbled, and she bashed him on the head with her other stick. With a grunt, he collapsed, returning to the shape of a normal man, or at least as normal as he had been before taking on the hybrid man-squirrel form. The weird music hiccupped and switched to a vaguely familiar march.

Where is that music coming from? Breathing hard, Zita called out, "Quick, get the duct tape!" After setting her weapons beside her, she checked his pulse. *Steady. Excellent. My tía's training aside, I'm not killing anyone if I can help it, especially someone with as many problems as this guy.*

When she checked on everyone else, she saw Curly approaching and the security guard talking on his walkie-talkie as he returned from behind the building. Camerawoman and the graduate student followed him. "Make sure they know where the bombs are." She twisted away to begin searching the unconscious man for a detonator before he woke.

"Watch out!" a man yelled from behind her.

Zita lifted her head.

"How dare you attack such a hero?" Curly shrieked as she tossed away a canvas purse and lunged with a boxy black Taser in hand. Music swelled theatrically.

After rolling away from the inept assault, Zita swept out one leg, tripping the other woman.

Curly fell, landing on her rear and bouncing. The music stopped. Her tearful gaze moved toward the others. "Ah! You broke my ankle! Won't someone take care of this awful creature and help me?"

The guard squinted at them and continued conferring with his walkie-talkie, but the graduate student stared at Curly, his eyes wide and face going blank. After picking up the duct tape, Camerawoman started toward Zita.

"Oh, please. You landed on your ass," Zita said. She grabbed the Taser and tossed it away from Curly.

The rapid, agitated flap of feet on pavement alerted her as the injured graduate student rushed her from behind, hands outstretched.

"What is in the chingado cookies around here?" Zita shouted, dodging him.

Curly sobbed.

The graduate student waved his fists at her. His eyes were glassy, and his movements were jerky and even less coordinated than before. He interposed himself between Curly and Zita. "Don't you touch this poor woman again, or I'll make you regret it."

Zita held her palms out. "I've got no intention of doing so," she said, trying to sound soothing as she stepped back. *I can take him, but I won't beat up an injured man if I have a choice. Not even if he begs me. Especially if he begs me, now that I think about it. Eww.*

Curly sniveled, still sitting, "Why are you doing this?"

"What is your damage?" Zita asked the crying woman.

"All that brave hero wanted was to save the squirrels. In the name of science, they manipulated squirrels into forming pair bonds. Once they were attached, the researchers separated them to study the effects," the curly-haired girl wailed.

The statement took a second to parse. Zita gawked at her. "Seriously? This was all about squirrel breakups? Rodents?"

Camerawoman stared at Curly. "You said they were probing them and destroying their organs. Aimee, so help me..." Her whole body tightened.

"The researchers were breaking the squirrels' hearts. They have a right to love, Raquel." Curly—Aimee—screeched back, tears streaming again.

Camerawoman—Raquel—punched her in the face.

Aimee crumpled with a cry.

Nonplussed, Zita clapped.

The graduate student sat on a step with a thud and a pained groan. "What happened?" he asked, bewilderment on his face.

Sometime during the brief scuffle and dramatics, Squirrel King must have woken. Once again in his half-man, half-rodent form, he limped to Aimee and raised her to her feet. One arm supported her. While staring into her teary eyes, he said, "I will remember you."

Aimee's eyelashes fluttered, and a smile trembled on her lips. In a quick move, she ripped open her own T-shirt. Beneath her now-tattered TAST top, she wore a second, this one with Save the Squirrels emblazoned above the image of a black squirrel. Music stirred, swelling with a slow rock ballad.

With a flash of his reddened eyes, the Squirrel King moved a step closer to Aimee. He tugged one of her curls and caressed her cheek with one furry hand. "Oh yes," he whispered, "you will be mine."

"Wait, are they flirting? Now?" Zita asked, disbelieving. She ran for the Taser. "Did somebody order cheese? Because it's gone bad and is stinking up the joint."

Distracted from his so-called wooing, the Squirrel King bared his teeth and chattered. Before he could do more, he bent double, choking and clutching his groin. Glass may have shattered with Aimee's shrill shriek. The song cut off.

Behind him, Raquel held a lacrosse stick, her phone no longer her weapon of choice. "I don't like your lines, either."

Before he recovered, Zita tased him. Even as his form collapsed back down to his human shape, his shoulders drew upward as all his muscles tightened and he toppled. His surprised expression morphed into a pained grimace.

"I was saving it for Aimee, but that works better, I guess," Raquel said. She lowered the stick, disappointment written on her face.

Zita blinked at her in disbelief, a slow smile coming to her lips. "You got problems, but I like you. This time, we tie him first." She shoved her hair back. *I'm definitely going to start packing hair ties to keep the stuff in line. Hey, did I manage to do this without wrecking my clothing? Sweet.*

"You got my vote," the security guy said, kneeling and taping.

Before Zita could finish her search of the Squirrel King for a detonator or weapons, Aimee threw herself on his unconscious body. "Leave him alone," she ordered. The music restarted, the rock ballad battling with a dramatic march this time.

"Stop it! That freak needs to be tied up," the security guard said, pushing Aimee away.

His gaze captive in hers, Aimee said, "You should let him be. Why don't you go arrest those two dreadful women?" Her lower lip quivered. "Save me from them?"

The guard's eyebrows shot up, and he shook his head. "They're not the problem here."

Puzzlement crossed Aimee's face, and she turned her attention to the graduate student. "Chris, help! They're going to hurt me," she implored him, reaching out both arms. Her voice broke, and a single tear rolled down her cheek. The ballad soared, and the march faded.

His face emptying of emotion, the graduate student—Chris— struggled to rise. "I won't let you harm her."

"Are you kidding me?" Zita said, all patience lost.

Aimee gave a crocodile's smile, all teeth through the water of her tears. "Start with her," she hissed as she pointed at Zita. She picked at the tape on the Squirrel King's wrists, her actions tentative, as if afraid to break one of her pastel pink, manicured nails.

Zita clicked her tongue and tased Aimee. *Her against me is sad.*

The girl fell. The music stopped, and her top changed to a plain, unripped, TAST T-shirt.

Aimee does special effect illusions? Zita thought.

Raquel applauded, shifting her weapon under her arm.

Chris stopped, blinking as expression leaked back onto his face. "What am I doing?" he asked.

"I guess Aimee here hypnotized you, possibly with that awful music she was playing," Zita said, jerking her thumb at the girl in question. "Somebody clever tased her dumb ass, and you snapped out of it."

After pushing his glasses up his nose, Chris gave a confused nod.

The guard finished his taping job on the Squirrel King and then did Aimee. "Police can sort it out," he said. "I'm not paid enough for this."

Raquel sighed and set her lacrosse stick on the ground. "I was kind of hoping to hit someone again," she complained.

Zita cocked her head at the young woman. "Have you ever considered martial arts? You know, a healthy outlet for that anger? Exercise can work out emotions and reset everything back to happy."

"I like my anger where it's at, thanks," she replied.

Crap, Andy's puns are contagious. Exercise works out, indeed. Once you tell one, you can't stop. A flicker of movement caught Zita's attention. The stealthy approach of heavily armed police reawakened her heartfelt desire to remain anonymous and unpunctured by bullets. "Make sure the cops check the Squirrel King for a detonator. Adiós." She darted around the others and ran around a corner.

Once alone, Zita shifted into a golden eagle, scooped up her discarded clothing, and flew back up to her rooftop. After another shapeshift back to herself, she dressed in the date clothes now redolent with tar and asphalt. *Maybe Luis won't notice.* Once she verified she would be unseen, she teleported to the base of the college arena, just visible from her vantage point. She brushed off her skirt suit and continued on, ignoring the sirens in the distance.

Chapter Three

The next day, Zita stood with Wyn as their friend Andy opened his door, puzzlement in every line of his body. Curiosity shone in his chocolate eyes, and his straight black hair hung wet and loose. The scent of his shampoo lingered, and he held his brush like a weapon. "Come in and have a seat, I guess? Can I get you anything?" he said.

As Zita trooped into the main room of his basement apartment, she spotted a dusty set of weights and a treadmill even older than her own. A desk and computer were crammed behind an overstuffed sofa, with multiple bookcases slanting at precarious angles against dark, wood-paneled walls. Surrounded by weird electronics and alien remote controls on an avocado shag carpet, a television reigned over it all. Credits rolled on-screen. Doors gaped open; a minuscule bathroom, an untidy bedroom, and a laundry room faced each other down like a trio of bulls. The only closed door was at the end of the hall. She reasoned it was likely the stairs up to his father's house. Graduate students couldn't be picky, or so he had told her, but at least the suburban Maryland home wasn't too far from the university where he and Wyn held jobs.

Wyn moved with the grace learned from long-ago ballet lessons and seated herself on the sofa—knees together, hands in her lap—and smiled. She toyed with a chestnut ringlet, coiling it around one pale, elegant finger. A shimmer of lavender glinted on her nails, matching the tiny floral motif in her lacy top and her sneakers. Around her swan-like neck, a pentagram with an amethyst center glinted on a delicate chain. "No, thank you, we fed Zita before we came. So, this is your place! It's charming," she said, the gentle lilt of the South in her musical voice.

"Thanks." Shaking his head, Andy continued, "Aren't we supposed to meet up in a few hours before my train to Boston? Did I mess up the time?" He checked his phone.

After setting aside a basket of unfolded laundry, Zita plopped onto the other end of the worn sofa, swinging a leg over the arm. Up close, the bold purple, orange, and cream plaid upholstery pattern that age had faded to an indistinct blur of stripes and color sprang out at her. *Probably was sweet when it was new other than the poop brown background.* "That's what I thought, too, until Wyn told me otherwise. We had oranges after yoga, but more food later would be great, thanks. It was delicious, though, the fancy kind with no seeds." She gave the fruit double thumbs up in approval.

Wyn narrowed her hazel eyes and gave Zita a warning look. *No getting distracted by your stomach,* she sent mentally. Her face smoothed back out, other than that little mark between her eyebrows that appeared when she was in pain or annoyed.

Andy grinned. "So, you've had a second breakfast, and now you have your sights on elevensies?"

What? He offered, Zita replied. *Plus, Andy's half Italian and half Kwakool—whatever.*

Kwakwaka'wakw or Kwakuitl, Wyn corrected. She rubbed her forehead and groaned. "That joke never gets old for you, does it, Andy? Don't encourage her."

"Oh, I don't mind so long as I get fed," Zita said, leaning back. *Sí, that's the name. How do you know his tribe doesn't have a deep-seated hospitality thing? Or the Navajo, I mean, Diné, he lived among? Between those and his Italian dad, he may have to feed guests or risk exploding. Just look at him. Even now, he's trying not to giggle with happiness at the idea of feeding us. Real friends snack for others. I'm a giver like that.* "A nibble would rock later."

Wyn rolled her eyes.

"Sure, Zita," Andy said with apparent amiable amusement, and then he snapped his fingers. "Hey, the internet is buzzing about a woman fighting a bomb-throwing were-squirrel on a university campus the other day. At first, I thought it had to be you, but when she threw cookies, I figured it was someone else. You would never do that." He shot a sly grin at her.

Zita clutched at her chest and laughed. "Verdad, that was me. They were a noble sacrifice to stop him from hurting the people he had captured. And technically, he didn't throw the bombs. He had planted a couple before I showed up. My job was just to keep him busy so Wyn could do the hard part, digging around in his brain to find out where the explosives were. Oh, and the cookies were totally store bought."

Deftly tying his hair back into its usual braid, fastening it with a brown hairband, Andy mumbled agreement. "Ah, so you had to do something."

"You didn't call and tell him about it?" Wyn squinted at Zita.

"No, Andy and I only talk when we've got stuff to say. I would've called him to tell him about the free food on campus, but then the Squirrel King ruined it," Zita said.

Andy smiled. "Thanks, Z. You got my priorities straight." They did a fist bump.

Wyn folded her arms over her chest and crossed her legs. The furrow deepened between her brows. "You spoke to me about it."

"You were sort of there. Plus you call every day, multiple times, when you're not already visiting. I have to say something." Zita shrugged.

His smile fading, Andy looked between them and pursed his lips. "Maybe you can fill me in later. So, you decided to stop by hours early for dinner because?"

Wyn replied, "We're here to help you get ready for the momentous, first in-person date with your girlfriend. You and Brandi have been together online for what, a year? I'll ensure you impress her now that you're in the same time zone again." Her eyes lit and her forehead smoothed out as she smiled.

"Wasn't my idea. Far as I know, you've been dressing yourself for a long time. Grab clothes appropriate for the activity and go. They gotta be clean, though. You don't want Brandi to think you're nasty," Zita volunteered, swinging her leg back and forth. Her attention strayed to one wall, decorated by four odd outfits, complete with wigs, boots, and jewelry. Two even had knives, but the designs made the weapons impractical. *I could check their balance to see if I'm wrong, plus they need sharpening, anyway. Is that a plastic breastplate?* With a frown, she waved her hand at the garments. "Or too weird. Are you wearing those?"

Andy shoved his hands in his pockets. "Those are cosplay costumes, Zita. You wouldn't understand. Thanks, Wyn, but guys don't do the whole picking out clothes for each other thing." His gaze turned downward, and he smoothed his baggy jeans and black tuxedo T-shirt. Paired with his olive-bronze skin and braided raven hair, the little red rose on the faux lapel inserted much-needed color.

Zita interjected, "She's here to dress you. I'm here because I'm your wingman. I got your back." She glanced at Wyn, honesty compelling her to admit another reason. "Also, Wyn threatened to turn my martial arts dummy into a stuffed puppy if I didn't come with her." Her feet hit the floor with a thump, and she leaned toward him. Lowering her voice, she asked. "I think she was joking, but do you think she can do that?"

He cleared his throat. "We're going on a walking tour of Boston Harbor and dinner after. I shouldn't have to dress up." His eyes darted toward Wyn, his uneasiness with witchcraft obvious for a moment before his countenance changed to what he probably assumed was a neutral expression.

Zita lacked the heart to tell him that it made him seem constipated.

Wyn tilted her head up and down, considering him and ignoring their byplay. She tapped a finger on the sofa for a minute and rose, strolling to him. Stopping, she set a hand on his shoulder, which was only an inch lower than her own. Given that she had nine inches of height on Zita, both loomed over her. "Andy, you're my friend, and I love you. You care about this girl, so I can't in good conscience have you going on this important date without assistance. Since I know how most women think and how to make the most of your appearance, I'll pick out a few pieces for you. If you lack the right apparel, we have time to purchase it today."

"What?" he asked, raising an eyebrow.

Zita eyed him. He seemed more startled than afraid, but perhaps he was trying to show no fear in the face of a threat to go shopping. *Brave man.* Andy always wore jeans and one of an unending supply of T-shirts with strange logos or equations on them. *Why wouldn't his girl, assuming this internet person is female, like him as is? It wasn't that long ago that he was a backup judoka for the Olympics, so his body's decent enough for most people. She wouldn't have dated him for so long if she didn't like his personality. And if you like shy geeks, he looks okay. He's like a dorky third brother and so not my type, but I can be supportive. Somehow.* "Wear what you want to wear." She nodded and smiled to encourage him. "Don't let her bring you down. What you have on now with those red socks in the basket should work, or something similar. Only if they're clean, of course."

Andy's mouth snapped shut, and his shoulders slumped as he turned to Wyn, who twined a curl around her finger and arched an eyebrow at him. "Right. I appreciate the help, Wyn."

With a double pat on his shoulder and a triumphant expression, Wyn began to speak, but cut herself off when her phone rang. After a glance at the number, she bit her lip and said, "I'll take this in the other room while I go through your closet." She ran into the bedroom. The door creaked closed as she spoke in a quiet voice, the thumps and creaks of rummaging drowning out the words. Familiarity let Zita identify Wyn's tone; the person on the phone was not telling her friend anything pleasant.

Zita rolled her eyes and tossed the crimson socks from the basket at Andy. She kept her volume low to avoid disturbing Wyn's call. "Seriously? Does the word of your wingman, wingwoman, mean nothing? I mentioned the clothes had to be clean. I had your back, and you caved."

His eyes shifted left and right, and Andy rolled his shoulders. "Wyn's got a lot more experience. Tons more. On successful dates with men, not like the kind you have."

Waving her hand dismissively, Zita cast about for a defense. "Mano, if the goal of a date is to determine if someone is relationship material, I'm a genius at that. Maybe a super genius. At this point, I know within one or two dates. Wyn takes longer."

He snickered. "Definitely veering toward super genius, Wile E. Coyote. That's not what I meant, and you know it. Why does it bother you if I let her play fashionista? It's not like you care about clothes."

Zita sighed, her shoulders slumping. "I don't. If the clothing doesn't have holes and suits the activity, I'm good. What I care about is the ritual that unleashes the dread monster. How do you think my brothers got to alternate picking one blind date for me each month? I never asked them for their help. My family has this idea that I need to be seeing someone to be happy, despite knowing me."

"I had wondered about that," he admitted. "Still, it's only the once."

"You don't get it. You give in just once to please them." Zita held up a single finger and shook it. "Then BAM!" Her hands smacked together.

Andy flinched.

From the bedroom, Wyn's voice rose in anger. "What do you mean they're taking me to court?"

Zita glanced toward the other room and exchanged concerned looks with Andy. *Not much I can do to help Wyn with a lawsuit, but I could slip a business card for that one attorney in her purse. I'll need to add a note telling her not to tell him I sent her, or she'll end up paying double. In the meantime, I'll let her have her privacy until she asks me for something.*

She continued her conversation with Andy. "The reason I reacted like that is because when you let people start interfering with your relationships, they don't stop. Pattern established. Try to wiggle out of it, and you're breaking their hearts, so your only hope is to try to limit them. Wait and see. Wyn will get all uppity now and insist on butting in every time either one of us has a date. She won't stop with you. I was already holding her off. My family is more than enough unwanted help in that area, and she'll want me to buy clothes I can't afford, too. Thanks so much, mano." Waving a hand in the air, she slumped back onto the formerly glorious sofa. "Think I'm wrong? She's going to come out and say you have to go shopping."

Andy rolled his eyes and made a derisive sound. "You're overreacting, Z."

"Am I?" Zita grinned. *He'll learn soon enough, so I should try to be a helpful wingman now. I'm bored with sitting, anyway.* She rose and punched his arm gently. "Oye, though I'm certain Wyn will make you be all flash, you don't need anyone's help. All you need is to relax."

"Easier said than done." Andy sighed, any remnant of humor disappearing from his face. He stared at his hands.

Zita poked him in the stomach with a finger. It hurt her more than him, she assumed, given his invulnerability power. "Man up. Clothes are props. From what you've said about your girl, you need to be you. Brandi likes that for some reason. You're doing well controlling your super strength, and if you stick to dates in public places, the whole sex issue won't come up. Well, it might come up. Theoretically, you're a dude and all, but you can always handle that in advance to reduce the chance, so to speak. You'll deal." A snicker escaped her.

Andy crossed his arms over his chest, but he lost the hangdog expression. Sarcasm laced his voice even as a flush spread over his face. "Thanks, Zita. Can we stop having this conversation now?"

She flapped her hand at him. "You want a friend to pat your hand and be sympathetic, talk to Wyn when she's done with your wardrobe. If you want a pal to help you move in with your girl or tell you straight out when you're wrong, call me." Zita paced to the door and back to the sofa.

From Andy's room, Wyn called out, "Don't you have any dress slacks? Where do you keep your pants?"

With a nervous glance toward the bedroom and back to Zita, Andy retorted, "Like you can give relationship advice? At least I have a steady girlfriend. All jokes aside, your last date was the government shrink you alienated so much that he wanted to quarantine us forever to annoy you."

Zita lifted her chin in the air and continued wandering. "For your information, I had a date yesterday, thank you."

"And how'd that go?" He eyed her, his eyebrows rising.

She grimaced. When the Squirrel King incident canceled the university concert that had been their original date, Luis had moved things to a nearby club. Slow jazz had proved an irresistible sleep inducement after her adrenaline faded.

Andy's brows lowered, and he gave a small smile. "Thought so." Despite his words, he patted her shoulder.

"It happens." She shrugged and bumped him in passing.

He snorted, but his grin broadened. "It happens a lot." This time, he ruffled her hair.

Zita batted at him. "Hands off the hair. I swear almost everyone I know does that, including my coworkers."

"That's the peril of being so adorable you could be one of Santa's elves from south of the border," he teased. "Don't worry. Your real friends know you're just a socially inept adrenaline junkie."

Before she could reply, Wyn bustled out of the bedroom, beaming and gushing. "I have wonderful news! You have a shirt that will do, but none of your pants will work. We need to go shopping and fix that for you right away." Her eyes were a bit too shiny and her movements more frenetic than her usual graceful sway.

Zita held up a hand when Andy gaped at her, surprise on his face. "Not saying anything."

"Excellent," Wyn declared, "because while we're out, we'll get something for you, too, Zita. I saw the remains of your outfit from yesterday when I picked you up today. It smelled like an eatery fell into a tar pit, and bore close resemblance to a moldy watermelon. Not to mention that delightful black stain across the bottom. It doesn't matter how much you scrub, it's a loss. You might lose the grease, but the tar will never come out. This trip'll be fun for everyone." The last few words sounded as if they were spoken through gritted teeth.

Andy had the grace to appear abashed.

Zita waved in dismissal, forcing her voice to remain light despite her trepidation. "No, I'm good. I'll get something from the thrift store that'll work if the stain is permanent." She mouthed "Monster" to Andy and tilted her head at Wyn.

Wyn gave a tight half-smile. Her hazel eyes glinted. "Oh, it's not up to you. I'm doing the world a favor, given what you're wearing now." She gestured toward Zita's outfit and winced. "Now, Andy, why don't you show me where your ties reside?" she said as she turned back to the bedroom.

"Ties?" Andy moaned. "For a walk and dinner?"

Zita crossed her arms over her chest. "Should have listened to your wingman. At least you've got a nine-hour train ride to ditch the tie tomorrow." *What did Wyn mean about my clothing? Doesn't she appreciate comfort? Between my two jobs, only the tax preparation office requires fancy business outfits. Quentin's locksmith and security company has me in the standard uniform work coveralls. I could wear a suit of armor under that, and nobody would know. Not that I'm getting enough hours at either to worry about their dress codes right now anyway.* Shifting position, she smoothed her favorite T-shirt, an orange one with a fat surfing unicorn and the word "Awesome" in neon colors. It had blue waves on it, which meant it matched her navy cargo capris with the red and white star trim.

With a gulp, Andy trooped into the bedroom to meet his fate.

As her friends discussed Andy's attire, Zita wandered to the neglected weights. She stooped and picked up an envelope knocked down by her passage. *Pues, I got the same one yesterday. The Department of Metahuman Services must be harassing him, too, under the assumption he's another quarantine patient with no powers. These DMS letters are all just invites to go in so they can dissect us. Wouldn't it thrill them to know we do have powers? Wouldn't it suck to be their experimental subjects if they found out?*

When she straightened, she set his mail back on the desk. Plucking a hand weight from the set, she did absent-minded biceps curls with one hand and thought. Tension leaked out of her with the activity. *Bet none of these work with his strength, and since we're all keeping our powers on the down low, he can't exactly ask anyone for permission to lift their mobile home for a workout. For his birthday, I should figure out how he can exercise and maintain his anonymity.*

As she returned the dumbbell to the rack, her fingers left impressions in the dust. Zita frowned. Nothing could tempt her to join the discussion in the next room, but she could dust for him. While she hunted for a suitable cloth, the television began playing a jazzy tune far too reminiscent of her date. *Quentin should have told me that Luis aspired to be a music critic. I might've tried harder to be more diplomatic about the music and not dozed off. Since that serial killer kidnapped him a few weeks ago, Quentin's been so distracted that he didn't even try to sell me on his blind date choice like he usually does. Not to mention if I did have a love life, he'd put a crimp in it by sleeping on my couch almost every night. Does he even realize how often he's been at my place since then?*

Unhappy with her thoughts, Zita grabbed strange remotes at random and pushed buttons until she found one that changed the channel. An ad came on, and she set the controller down. "Hey, Andy, they're advertising the Water Balloon Death Run 3000. Did you get your registration in or do you want me to do it for you?" she shouted.

"If you'd register me, that'd be great," Andy called back.

Wyn's voice lifted in an enquiry in the other room.

Zita continued searching for a duster and added registering Andy to her mental to-do list, which reminded her that she'd promised to help her friend Claire with a rather smelly project. *After Wyn and Andy go shopping, I'll call Claire and plan a road trip to deal with the skunks under her porch. I hope she bought some of those humane traps she mentioned. Otherwise, it will be rough keeping the little stinkers out from under there while we seal up the openings. If she has peanut butter, we might be able to lure them elsewhere. Where to put them once we've got them is the question... With any luck, I'll figure out something on the ride there. As much as I love Wyn and Quentin, a few hours in the mountains without one or both of them hanging around would be awesome. Claire's not much of a talker, which is probably why we've always gotten along well, even when we were teens in the cancer ward.* Although she had expected to ignore the television, a whirl of agitated words caught her attention instead.

Voice brimming with suppressed excitement, an anchor broke into the weather report. He announced, "In horrifying breaking news, a human supremacist group is live-streaming their execution of a handful of so-called parahumans." As if to underscore the gravity of the situation, he paused and gazed into the camera, his expression sober.

Zita's breath caught. "Guys, come here!"

Wyn's laughter preceded her friend into the room. "Whichever Zita doesn't like. You try those on," she called back into the bedroom. Andy's reply was unintelligible. "Goddess. Andy, you need to see this." She moved closer to Zita.

The anchor continued. "Police say they are aware of the problem, but their location is still unknown. We bring this appalling spectacle to you live." Although his tone tried to be serious, his voice quivered like a dog shown a treat.

Andy emerged, buttoning a blue dress shirt over his T-shirt. His eyes went to the screen as the scene changed.

Holding a ten-foot-long prod tipped with silver, a masked man stood in front of three giant cages, ranting about fiends seeking world domination. His belt hung low, straining under the weight of a holster that held a large-caliber handgun and a gray baton. As the width of the room prevented the camera from displaying everything at once, the view panned horizontally every few minutes, allowing glimpses of windows on either side.

Two burly men with shotguns bookended the cages, standing out of reach of the bars and wearing handkerchiefs to shroud the lower half of their faces. A huge black wolf with mad eyes snarled in the enclosure on one end; he or she had to be three hundred pounds, far too over-muscled and large to be anything but a shapeshifted person. On the opposite end, a red velvet cloth hid the occupant or occupants. Based on the different miserable noises emanating from it, almost inaudible beneath the constant mechanical drone of an engine nearby, Zita would have bet multiple. The middle cage, mostly hidden by the spokesman, held a bleary Kodiak bear, wobbling to his feet and banging his head against the roof of the too-small prison. Although large, he could have passed for natural had it not been for his thoughtful, too-intelligent eyes.

Behind the prisoners, rotting wooden slats showed through where once-white walls had abandoned the fight against age. Paint in multiple bright hues peeled from support columns that held up a patchy, decaying ceiling. As if in sympathy for the imprisoned people, deciduous branches reached through empty windowpanes into the room. A woman's shoe hung incongruously from a branch outside one window, the buckle glinting in the weak sunlight that squeezed through the screen of greenery. Darker ivy snuck in at the bottom of another. Most of the illumination came from an unseen source that cast jagged shadows behind everything it touched. Debris clogged the edges of the room, and the cages rested on even more trash. The wolf's cage was not flat with the floor and lurched with his angry movements.

After turning to gesture at the metal prisons behind him, the masked spokesman closed in on the prisoners. He twirled the pole, aimed, and stabbed the bear.

It roared, any hint of grogginess fleeing.

Wyn made a choking sound behind her.

Zita ignored her friends' shocked exclamations, her focus riveted to the screen. *Active, but not into anything serious or martial arts, unless cruelty is a sport,* she thought, assessing the spokesman. Memories of another hostage situation closed her throat with horror and dismay.

"Change back and show them the faces you hid behind! You will be executed soon. For the sake of your family, wear your human disguise so they know your stain has left them," the spokesman said. He went to jab the wolf but yanked the prod back when the great canine snapped at it.

The wolf snarled.

The bear snorted.

Still covered, the occupants of the third cage made only muffled, mourning sounds.

Zita forced herself to breathe and scrubbed her hands on her pants. *Brazil was years ago. Unlike then, I can stop this. They don't have that many people. At a minimum, I can find out where they are and tell the police.* Resolve formed. Pulling her wallet, keys, and phone from her pockets, she set them down on the arm of the sofa. More reluctantly, she removed her multitool and positioned it beside her other belongings, fingers caressing the metal. She stepped out of her shoes.

The spokesman continued ranting, pausing in his abuse of the captives. "Humans of the world, unite against these creatures! Even if they are only tokens compared to the beasts of yesteryear, they endanger us all and must be destroyed. Remember how the world trembled after Shining Woman destroyed the Chernobyl nuclear plant? Libya and Egypt still avoid areas of their own countries at the mere chance of the Dragon surviving the destruction they had to pour down to stop him. How many innocent students died at Tiananmen Square at the paws of the infamous Fu Dog before Chinese tanks brought him down? The previous generation of monstrosities taught us what to expect. They've been breeding in secret, and they must be stopped. If you will not do it, we will." He waved the prod.

Indignation sounded in Wyn's voice. "No one ever proved those deaths were their faults. Up until the explosions that killed them, Shining Woman and Fu Dog stood for the USSR and China respectively, not against them. That homicidal idiot has his history all wrong." Left unspoken was any defense of Dragon, whose atrocities had even penetrated Zita's consciousness.

Stripping off her beloved top, Zita grabbed a shirt from Andy's laundry basket and the simplest mask from the costumes on the wall. *My shirt's distinctive, and all I have left of my time dating Paolo. Andy's is almost plain and must be far more common, plus black is easier to hide in.* "What is wrong with people?" More loudly, she called out to her friends, "You're my alibi." She watched the screen, waiting for her chance to come again as she dressed in the borrowed clothing.

"Why are you putting on my Avengers shirt and Batman mask, Zita? You know they don't go together, right?" Andy asked. "Wait, I forgot who I was talking to. Please wear clothes, any clothes."

Zita heard a pair of gasps from behind her as she assumed her Arca form.

Andy swore. "Oh man. You only pull out that shape when you're going to do something stupid."

Without taking her eyes from the television, Zita said, "I'm saving their asses. Stay here and be my alibi. Please." *Better my friends keep safe here. I won't risk their lives or identities if I can help it. Now, pan back across that tree with the shoe. It's distinctive enough that I shouldn't end up scaring anyone somewhere else.* When the camera panned over the cages, it displayed the window she wanted to see.

"Zita, don't you dare. Not again," Wyn warned. "It's too dangerous, and you don't have your brother as an excuse this time. Don't you leave me—"

Ignoring Wyn, she teleported.

Chapter Four

Zita reappeared in the tangle of foliage she had seen outside the briefly visible window. Prepared for the unknown height, she bent her knees to absorb the impact as she fell two and a half feet in the thicket and rolled upright again. Years of decaying leaves on the ground blunted the sound of her movements and oozed between her bare toes, interspersed with painful chunks of building and... more rotten women's shoes? *Bizarre.* Slipping behind the thick trunk of a London plane tree, she put her back against the aged brick wall and crouched in wait, heart pounding. Silently, she prayed the plants that crowded each other and created a green-tinted twilight effect would hide her presence. Slime dampened her spine as she pressed against the building. Next to her, and new enough to show no age or grime, a thick black cord escaped the window and met with an extension cord four feet off the ground that snaked through the trees to connect to a black and red generator.

Inside, the spokesman continued without pause, except to take a breath. His voice was the only sound other than the growl of the generator. A shadow darkened the window above her and then disappeared.

After two minutes and no uproar, Zita relaxed. The warm August breeze ruffled the leaves of her hiding spot and teased her with the odor of brine, dead fish, crushed plant matter, and mold. *We're near water. I'm here. Where is here and what can I do?*

Zita, where are you? Wyn shrieked in Zita's mind, breaking her concentration.

I'm trying to figure that out, Zita replied. *Shush. I need to pay attention to what's going on.* Andy's presence lurked in the background of the link, but he remained quiet.

Leaping up, she grabbed a thick branch, not trusting the crumbling wooden window frame to hold her weight, and did a pull-up to see inside. Adjacent to her, the three cages lined up along a back wall, with the velvet-covered one closest. In the middle cage, the bear jiggled the door, loosening the bolts. The wolf glowered. While the two gunmen and the spokesman remained where they had been on camera, others were now visible. At the far end of the room, a skinny man worked a laptop, a cameraman filmed, and a fair-skinned woman touched up her makeup with a hand mirror. Photographer's lights glared at the cages, throwing shadows like knives and intensifying the odors of sweat, wet fur, and urine.

As she watched, Computer Guy held up a piece of paper bearing a large number and a word, "Higher?"

The man speaking bobbed his head in reply and continued cajoling viewers to contribute to his filthy cause, said goal being death to all the "monsters."

Computer Guy returned to tapping at his keyboard.

At that, Zita had to stop herself from a derisive snort at the greed.

How could you leave like that? Wyn sent. *Of all the asinine and irresponsible actions—*

I'm busy right now. Yell at me later. They're waiting for something, which gives me a few minutes more to figure out how to save those people. I need to scout and plan my strategy, not talk, Zita sent. She tried a trick Wyn had taught her to lower her mental volume, visualizing a door, and closing it on her friend.

Hurt vibrated through the mental link for a second before Wyn sniffed and cut off the link herself.

Alone again, Zita let herself drop and considered her surroundings. Shaped like a large U, the building she hid against had familiar trees and bushes surrounding it in a natural jumble. Ivy warred with the moss in an uneven pattern across the dull bricks. Weeds poked out through a thick layer of decomposing leaves underfoot. *Foliage seems to be East Coast or Midwest, likely coastal with the salty tang in the air. Not arid enough to be farther west. Can't be too far south as it feels cooler than Maryland, unless this is in the mountains. Doesn't have the pressure of a major altitude change though.*

With a cautious glance back toward the window, she followed the extension cord thirty feet to the portable generator. The canopy of a black cherry tree shaded both the generator and a gas can. Leaves had been sloppily cleared in a rough circle around the machine, showing stained, cracked asphalt. She guessed the larger gaps between the trees hid the remains of an old road. *I can work with that and maybe take out one of the men with guns.*

The acrid stench of gasoline and something very dead assailed her nose as she moved from the embrace of the greenery, and she shuddered, mood plummeting. Her shoulders tensed and her stomach curdled. She followed the road toward where the woods thinned, and the source of the decomposition odor strengthened, as did her fear that she would not like whatever she found.

The trees ended at a broad, cleared area. Bare where heavy machinery had crushed and cut out rectangular sections, regular furrows and undulations (fill dirt, she suspected) marred the ground. Equipment tracks crisscrossed the stripped land, and only a few brave weeds survived the trampling. *Someone's been digging.*

Less than a mile away, another sparse tree line began. Geese yakked in the distance, though none were visible.

She crept forward, keeping low, trying to scope out the area. When the surface underfoot turned hard and crunched instead of squelching, she glanced down to see gravel-covered plywood and a long trench. Peeking under the wood, Zita gulped, recognizing the unadorned pine boxes stacked three high and wide. *Please don't let this mean those maniacs have killed that many people.*

From there, she caught sight of movement at a pier, surrounded by a wooden barricade. A long gun silhouetted in his arms, a man stretched, facing away from her. Signs lined the rocky, barren shore every few feet, but the words were unreadable from her angle. She retreated behind a tree and surveyed the little dock. Two shallow-bottomed motorboats, one much larger than the other, bobbed in the water. Camouflage netting covered both boats; it would have been more convincing if any real foliage had remained near the docks. Buildings covered the entire shore opposite and were just perceptible across the water. *Can't be that far. So, an island or peninsula on the East Coast with a mass grave. An island would make more sense. Now all I need is a phone and to stop those executions.*

While she refined her strategy, she dashed back to check the building again. Her eyes returned to the generator sitting in its cleared spot. Zita rolled her shoulders to loosen the tension gathered there and reached for a jaguar shape, but stopped the change before it completed and replaced her Arca form. Colors dulled and details sharpened in the shadowy forest. Scent exploded around her, the charnel and dead fish no longer offensive. The forest developed layers of information she lacked time to explore. She grinned and began working.

When she unplugged the extension cord from the generator, the building went dark, and exclamations sounded from inside. She returned to the window to unplug the other end (teleporting to speed the process). As the spokesman ordered a guard to find out why the lights had died, she teleported into the higher branches of the black cherry over the generator and waited.

Two or three minutes later, a gunman trudged over to the generator and nudged it with his foot. It continued running. He frowned and set his shotgun down beside it.

When he knelt, one hand reaching out to the plug lying on the ground, Zita leapt onto his back.

He fell face first onto the asphalt, and his exclamation was lost in the noise of the generator and the ground meeting his face.

Zita straddled him, pinning his arms with her knees, and put him in a chokehold. Counting seconds, she released him when his thrashing stopped. He passed out before she hit a number high enough to be risking permanent brain damage, a fact she said a silent prayer of thanks for. Once she rolled him over and confirmed he would live, Zita grabbed the extension cord and dragged him a few yards, to where the plywood covering the trench was visible. She teleported both of them to it, then under it. *That trick sure saves time carting his heavy ass around.* Her mind refused to dwell on the boxes that shared the trench.

Even though her jaguar sight had been a blessing in the dimness of the woods, details blurred in the harsh sunlight of the exposed zone. Her plan had not required any attention to detail that touch or scent could not compensate for, so Zita soldiered on. *Partial shifts are chancy enough; I can keep my outward appearance the same, but I can't control which senses or other attributes get a boost or a downgrade. I don't want to risk losing the enhanced vision now that I've turned off the primary light sources inside. Need to hurry.* With the cord as a rope, she looped it around the unconscious man.

He started rousing.

Ripping off one of his boots, she removed his sock and stuffed it into his mouth. After tying him as tightly as possible with the extension cord, she searched him. His gun, a wallet, a knife, a phone, and keys rewarded her efforts. *With any luck, one of these is to the cages.* Zita left the wallet in his pocket and took everything else. She tapped his forehead when done.

He squinted up at her.

"Listen, hombre, you stay quiet, and you stay safe, right? The stench here will hide you. The bear and wolf will be free soon, and they seemed upset about your whole plan to execute the monsters. I'm not thrilled about that myself."

His eyes widened.

After verifying the dock sentry was still oblivious, Zita clambered out of the trench and darted back into the thick brush. Teleportation got her into a fork in a sturdy tree trunk where she could watch the windows and the generator. Even though the phone showed a weak connection, she dialed while she hid.

A nasal voice answered. "Nine one one, what is your emergency?"

Zita used her fake Mexican accent and whispered. "Trace this call. These haters got people in cages, and they're getting ready to kill them on camera. I don't know where we are, but it's an island or peninsula with a crap ton of signs and a mass grave. A city area is on the other side of the water, a mile away tops."

The person on the other end paused. "Who is this?" Keys clicked so fast that Zita assumed the operator used at least four fingers to type instead of two. *Lucky duck.*

"Doesn't matter. They've got a lookout with a shotgun or another long gun. He's on a dock with all these weird wooden barricades. You want the U-shaped building in a tiny forest, ground floor for the cages. They've got at least one man inside with a shotgun and the guy being filmed has a large-caliber handgun. Another man is tied up in a trench. His Mossberg 500 shotgun will be in the tree near the generator."

The emergency operator did not sound surprised, excited, or even all that interested. "Got it. Can you remain on the line so we can track your call? You need to stay hidden and safe." More keys clicked.

This must be New York, Zita thought. *No way would the operator be this blasé anywhere else on the East Coast. It can't be Baltimore. They haven't called me hon.* "No, I have to stop the killing, but I'll leave the phone on by the gun for you to track." After dumping everything but the keys in the tree, she considered the brick building, now dark inside, except for the natural light that filtered through the windows. *One guard down. Maybe I can get the captives under the blanket free before they notice me there.* She teleported again, this time, to the tree by the window. Perching on a branch and hanging down to peer inside was easy.

Without artificial lighting, the interior of the building was dim, and her vision took a moment to adjust. This close, her enhanced nose told her both shapeshifters were male. The remaining gunman hovered near the other side of the cages, his attention on the wolf, who glared back, violence in his eyes.

Zita had to stop herself from clucking her tongue at the staring contest. *Doesn't he know anything about canines?*

At the opposite end of the room, Computer Guy attacked the keyboard with his fingers, as if the amount of violence he directed at the keys would resolve his problem. The spokesman, woman, and cameraman were all missing. A flash of movement through a doorway suggested their whereabouts.

Metal rattled. Using his bulk to shield his actions from the gunman, the bear pried the sides of his cage apart at one corner with his hooked claws. Two of the three hinges on that side were already busted. He huffed and sniffed the air, turning his head toward Zita. Beady black eyes squinted at her, but experience had taught her that his nose was his real source of information.

She put a finger to her lips, anyway. Zita had no intention of sitting there until the bear gave her away or she was discovered by another means. *None of the would-be murderers show any indications of martial arts training, so the guns are the big threat. If I free the captives in the covered cage, we can gang up on the others. Or they can run while I figure out how to free the shapeshifters.*

The gunman broke off the staring contest with the wolf, swore, and stormed over to Computer Guy. "Isn't that fixed yet?"

The wolf smirked.

While the gunman and Computer Guy conferred, Zita slipped inside and under the velvet cover, pushing the front of her body up against the cage to avoid being seen. Her enhanced eyesight picked out four forms inside, dressed in dark, overelaborate clothing. If her nose and ears had not alerted her to the misery and fear in the cage, she might have recoiled and given away her position.

At first, it seemed as if the cage occupants were poised to strike at anyone entering the cage; closer observation showed they were tied, hand and foot, into menacing poses. Horror movie restraint masks covered their mouths, and blindfolds hid their eyes. One man quaked and whimpered. Another slumped in his bonds, almost catatonic. A woman, the only female in the group, leaned against the cage as if too tired to fight, though a moan escaped her with every twitch. Clad in the remnants of an ornate dress, now ripped to the waist, her modesty was saved only by an excess of lace. The last of the group, the one closest to Zita, had been rubbing his face against his shoulder repetitively, but he turned his head toward her. His eyes glinted red for a second beneath a half-off blindfold, and the restraint mask over his mouth was askew. He watched her, calm despite her unexpected presence and borrowed Batman mask. A red viscous liquid covered what she could see of their necks and chests as if they had indulged in an orgy of—Zita sniffed the air—ketchup? Someone's stomach grumbled. With a jolt, she realized it wasn't hers for once.

Zita risked a whisper as the gunman continued harassing the man on the computer. "I'm here to help. Don't give me away."

Reaching up, she pulled the restraint mask away from the calm one's mouth.

He licked cracked lips and nodded to her. Oversized canine teeth flashed in his mouth.

For a moment, Zita stilled. At the odor from the floor of the cage, her nose wrinkled and reason reasserted itself. *They're all breathing, have heartbeats, and smell... Ugh. Not dead. I doubt real vampires wet themselves or sweat. The killers staged them to look like dangerous vampires and to hide their obvious fear.*

"No killing," Zita whispered, using the knife she'd taken off the trenched gunman to cut the calm vampire free. She passed him the blade through the bars. "Free the others."

The vampire shook out his hands before taking the tool, inclining his head at her words. He turned to the others, a half-cape flaring with the motion, his movements angry and clumsy with returning circulation. Though fast, it was an unenhanced human speed, and she breathed easier for it.

After inching to the front of the cage, Zita reached around to try the stolen keys on the lock. Her movements were slow and careful to avoid moving the cloth any more than necessary. When the first key failed, she went to the second. She could hear the soft scrape of her co-conspirator freeing the others.

"My fangs are implants," one of the other men sobbed. "I'm only a normal person with tooth implants. I thought they were cool." Something thudded behind her.

Footsteps slapped against the hard floor. "What's that? Who's there? Is a creature loose?"

Fear raced through her, and Zita slipped out from beneath the cloth. *If I leap outside, he might chase me, and the vamps will have their chance to run, if nothing else. The bear is almost out, too, so he might help soon.*

When he spotted her, the gunman raised his shotgun and advanced. He had gotten far closer than she expected, too close for great accuracy, but shotguns did not require precision. "Don't move, freak," he barked. Marching toward her, he walked past the first two cages, stopping when he reached the covered cage.

Zita raised her arms in the air and tried to seem unthreatening as she edged toward the window. "Hey, how's it hanging?" she asked, as if sneaking around in a Batman mask during a terrorist video was an everyday event. *Given the squirrel supremacist the previous night, this is almost boring in comparison.* Her pulse rate soared anyway.

Just then, the bear heaved his bulk against the weakened cage joints. One clasp stood no chance against the full weight of a gigantic ursine, and the entire front panel of his cage smashed into the gunman.

Hit from behind, the gunman stumbled forward, almost falling into Zita.

She struck him in the diaphragm and followed up with a fast strike to his jaw. He fell, wheezing, his eyes glassy. She seized his gun and held it on him.

"Gracias," she said to the bear.

The bear grunted.

Something clunked, and she turned to see Computer Guy fleeing. Zita swore in Spanish and Chinese, then in Portuguese in case any of the imprecations was strong enough to unlock the cages. She nudged the fallen gunman with her filthy bare foot. "You. Get those open and be fast," she ordered, pointing at the prisons.

"Free me first," the uncanny wolf growled. *He gets to talk in animal form? Wait, he seems familiar. Was he the one who wanted to eat Jerome when the quarantine hospital was invaded? Nobody eats my friends when I'm around.*

After a glance at the wolf cage, where sharp white teeth flashed in an evil smile, the gunman shook his head. Rising to his feet, he opened the vampire cage instead, shaking. "No, you can't make me.

I'd rather be sucked to death by the undead whore. The female. I'm not gay."

"Maybe not, but you are an idiot," Zita said. "Nobody here wants to sex you up. Probably nobody anywhere else, either."

As she spoke, the calm vampire carried his barely conscious male companion out of the cage. The other two staggered behind him, rubbing their arms as circulation returned. The vampiress stopped by the gunman and kneed him in the crotch.

He fell to his knees, keys clattering to the floor.

With a deep rumble that might have been a laugh, the bear moseyed to the wolf's cage. He ripped the door off.

In a single, liquid movement, the wolf flowed from the cage like incarnate darkness.

Zita tilted her head at the bear. "The keys are right here," she told him. "You could have waited." In the hopes to avert bloodshed, she moved, breaking the line of sight between the gunman and wolf.

The bear huffed.

Zita considered the bruin's size and weight, comparing them to her own petite frame. "Right, whatever the one-ton bear wants."

The wolf spoke. "We should kill him and the sniveling would-be vampire who told the human scum our mission."

The man with the tooth implants blanched further and cowered.

"No killing," Zita said, using an authoritative tone copied from a dog-training show. *Mmm, sexy Cesar.* "They suck, but nobody's dying here today." She had the urge to bop his nose with a rolled-up newspaper but managed to stop herself.

A dull thud and moan made her turn her attention back to the vampires. As the angry vampiress raised her foot to stomp on the gunman again, Zita stepped forward and caught her wrist. "Let's toss him inside the cage. You're better than this. Consider how much fun he'll have in prison."

Although her eyes narrowed, the vampiress acquiesced. She licked dry, split lips and glared at the gunman. Tearing herself away from him, she shivered. She said, "I'm grateful they were too afraid of my powers as an unholy succubus to do more than ruin my clothing. Did the God Kings accept our petition? Have you come with their gratitude for our work finding Lord Hades' Key?"

Zita released her and picked up the keys from the cracked cement floor. "The who accept what? Oye, I saw them hurting people. That's not right, so I did something about it."

The vampiress made a face, and her shoulders slumped. "I should have known better than to trust a recruiter. It would have been nice to have protection from the humans. My thanks, anyway." After pulling her torn dress closed as much as the tattered fabric allowed, she lashed out with another kick, knocking her former guard into the soiled cage. Her shoulders straight and stiff, she walked to where the other vampires stood (or curled on the floor in one case).

The calm one removed his cape and settled it on his female companion's shoulders.

She snaked an arm around him and closed the cape over herself. In the sunlight, their tattered black finery, smeared makeup, and sunken eyes told a pitiable story.

"The God Kings will remember who aided them and who wears the mantle of the monster well," the wolf said. His eyes glinted, glowing red as his glare singled out the man wedging himself behind the real vampires. "And the pretenders who told the enemy what we seek."

Under the scorching gaze of the wolf, the man with the implants shrank against the wall.

Am I going to have to lock up the guy with the fake teeth to keep him safe, too? A moan distracted Zita as she locked the door on the gunman's cage for his own safety. Leaning the shotgun against the wall, she gestured to the shivering man on the floor. "He okay?"

"Diabetes," the calm one told her.

Zita winced, pressed her lips together, and dug in a pocket. "Here," she said, pushing her trail mix at the sensible vampire. "Try this?" *Gracias a Dios that I usually carry snacks. That's the problem with shifting. When your clothes bust, not only does everyone freak like they're not all naked underneath their outfits, but you lose your food, too.*

He nodded and knelt by his friend, extracting a chocolate candy.

As Zita finished locking the cage, an exclamation came from the doorway.

Framed by the sagging wood, the spokesman drew a .357 Magnum revolver, clenching it tightly in both hands.

Zita dove for the captive gunman's shotgun, hoping to intimidate him into lowering his handgun.

With a snarl, the wolf launched himself at the hate group's spokesman.

His target aimed and fired.

The great body of the wolf stopped. The gun boomed again, and he staggered. On the third shot, he fell.

As a unit, the vampires drew back, crowding into the small gap between the cage and the window, with the diabetic dragged by the others. The bear snarled.

Zita seized the shotgun, rolled to her feet, and shouldered it in a move. She aimed it toward the door, moving between the former prisoners and the spokesman. "Drop it, pendejo. You're well within range of this no matter what load it's carrying," she said. *I'm so never telling Miguel how all that firearms drilling paid off. My brother would never let me forget it. Also, he would have a coronary if he knew why I needed to do it.*

From behind her, the bear rumbled, an almost contemplative sound.

In the doorway, the spokesman smirked. His aim was now either on her or the bear.

Zita prayed she wouldn't have to use the gun. Her stomach roiled at the idea, but she held herself still and targeted the shotgun on his legs. *Por favor, Dios, don't make me have to shoot him. And if I have to, let me miss anything vital. I don't want to kill anyone.*

Horror replaced smugness on the spokesman's face.

He's going for my bluff. I finally scared some sense—Zita realized the massive black hulk of the wolf was stirring, head shaking.

A snarl rippled out of the monstrous beast. *Oh.*

The man bolted as the wolf tried to regain his feet.

After another unsuccessful attempt, the wolf struggled upright. Though his fur hid most of his injuries, flattened metal bits and drops of blood dripped to the floor when he shivered. He launched himself in a staggering run as he continued to heal.

Zita swore.

Outside, a woman screamed.

Chapter Five

Zita raced after the wolf, through a room with blackened tin ceiling tiles, and burst outside through an arched door. After a pause to allow her eyes to adjust to the bright sunlight, she scanned the area for her quarry.

The quiet green scent of the trees and salty rotting fish of the nearby water mingled with the odor of metallic blood and corpses. The cameraman and woman huddled to one side, the female still shrieking. Both bled, but neither seemed in danger of dying. The camera had a new dent, as if it had been hit in passing, and the cameraman cuddled it like a child. The midnight coat of the wolf disappeared beyond the trees, gaining speed as he ran toward the docks.

Ignoring the people, she followed the wolf into the flattened zone. Zita shouted after him. "Stop! Don't kill anybody! How hard is it to remember not to murder people? It's a commandment and everything. I'm here to fucking stop any killing, not change who kills who." *I need to be fast and tough. Steroid Dog there isn't making me a murderer, either.* Her clothing (and Andy's) ripped from her as she shifted into a common wildebeest and galloped after him. Scent magnified even more than when she had partially jaguar-shifted, particularly that of the water. An indignant, guttural sound, somewhere between bleating and honking, escaped her. Several times.

Despite his size, bulk, and still-healing wounds, the wolf reached the boats before she could stop him. As he went to pounce on his prey, he glanced back and stumbled when he spotted her barreling toward him. He recovered, but his aim was off.

Even off-center, the impact still threw the spokesman into a wooden barricade. The silver baton flew from his hand.

A litany of swear words came from one boat, where the pale Computer Guy pounded on the boat console.

Abandoning his frantic attempts to remove the camouflage netting, the sentry pulled his shotgun and aimed.

With a snarl, Steroid Dog crouched near the fallen man, lowering his shoulders and tensing for another attack, his tail horizontal behind him. He opened his mouth and crept forward.

Ignoring the instinct that made fur prickle along her spine, Zita rammed the wolf. The force drove both shapeshifters into the water as the shotgun boomed and boomed again. As she staggered back to land, the odor of blood rose over the dead fish and river scents, and she felt flaming pain lick along her back haunches. Another ridiculous grumbling bellow escaped her. *I should have chosen a kangaroo. They're too adorable to shoot until they whip out the boxing gloves.*

"Quick, before the cow or the wolf gets you," Computer Guy bellowed. He seized the baton and tried to drag the downed spokesman into the larger and better-appointed of the two boats. Based on the number of ripped vinyl seats, his chosen boat was meant to be a commercial tour or large family boat. He ignored the smaller boat, a rust-striped runabout with dirt-splattered, hard-plank seats redolent of fish.

The spokesman staggered to his feet, assisted by Computer Guy, and fell into the larger boat. After planting himself face-first into the deck of the vessel, he showed no interest in further consciousness.

Zita disapproved. *I would have chosen the smaller one for maneuverability and because it reminds me of Paolo and happier times, but he must need soft chairs for his squishy butt. Cow, indeed.*

Muttering complaints, Computer Guy rifled the spokesman's pockets, roughly rolling the bleeding, insensible man over. "Where are the keys?"

"Stay back," the dock sentry warned Zita as his nervous gaze raced over her, then darted toward where the wolf had disappeared under the water. She was just grateful he stopped at shooting her. "Where's the wolf-man?"

After shifting back to Arca, Zita called to the creeps in the boat. "Oye, no idea. You should run and lock yourself in the cages before he gets you, though. He doesn't seem crate-trained." As usual, no one listened to her excellent advice.

Computer Guy swore again and addressed the sentry. "I need the keys, and you have to drive this thing." Sweat glistened on his forehead.

The man blinked. "I don't have the keys, and I can't drive a boat."

For a geek, Computer Guy had an exceptional vocabulary of swear words. When he was done cursing, he said, "Dave drove us here, and he never came back from checking the generator. Don't tell me he still has the keys?"

A massive black form arrowed out from behind the runabout and onto the bigger boat, mouth open, teeth gleaming. The wolf charged the sentry, who fired at him and tried to duck.

Zita shifted into a polar bear and ran toward the boat. As she set her paws on the boat, she gave a massive roar. The vessel groaned and tilted under her bulk, throwing Steroid Dog off balance long enough for the sentry to scrabble over the side of the boat with a splash and a wail.

Finding himself the only man standing near the angry wolf and massive bear, Computer Guy emitted a high-pitched shriek that would have done any irate toddler proud. "I just want to go home. You won't take me without a fight," he bellowed and squeaked, his voice breaking as he batted at the shifters with his silvery stick.

You lack the upper body strength for a melee weapon, Zita critiqued, as his blows landed on her: harmless, but annoying.

To her surprise, Steroid Dog yelped and flinched away when one lucky flail hit him. He growled, but his hatred seemed to have found a focus in the wailing technician, who still waved the baton wildly in the air.

Zita jerked her nose out of the way of another blow and interposed her body between the wolf and Computer Guy.

"Stay out of this," Steroid Dog snarled at her. Darting around her, he swiped at the technician's arm with one paw, and the baton flew.

Scarlet furrows appeared, and Computer Guy squealed, this time with pain. He grabbed at his arm and chest and fell to his knees.

I can't, Zita thought. *Nobody's dying here today if I can help it.* She lumbered over the wounded Computer Guy, drew up on her haunches, and struck the wolf with a solid blow. Even though she pulled her punch, it knocked him off the boat and into the water.

After taking a deep breath, she followed. The water seemed balmy to her polar sensibilities. When the wolf surfaced, she seized him with her front paws and pushed him down to pin him. The buoyancy of the salty water proved to be her ally; it prevented her full weight from accidentally crushing him, and he was unable to squirm to full effect.

The wolf bit and clawed one of her arms, and she reared up in pain.

In that position, she discovered, as a polar bear, she was tall enough to have her head out of the water. Taking a deep breath, she held him underwater. *Just until he stops struggling. Dios, that hurts.* She sought out Computer Guy and the sentry and was relieved to see both had taken off toward the U-shaped building. *Finalmente. Dumbasses.*

As soon as the wolf stopped fighting, she hauled him out of the water and tossed him on the shore. *If a bullet can't keep him down, a few pointy rocks will only be an inconvenience.*

Steroid Dog turned and snapped at her as he flew, proving her supposition had been correct; he had been pretending unconsciousness to lure her in. He landed on the stony beach with a yelp. Mud hung from his soaked fur, and he snarled at her. At least his time in the water had mellowed him; his eyes held rational thought, or at least calculation, and not just anger.

Zita waded toward the shore, stopping when she thought her human form could stand with her head out of the water, but not so close as to put her escape at risk if he tried to attack. She shifted back to Arca. The muddy water made the long hair of her disguise swirl on the surface like kelp, covering her shoulders and hiding the damage to her arm. For once, her lack of height helped. "Hombre, you need to chill. Killing them won't help, and the cops will be here any second. You need to suck it up until they arrest those creeps and drop them into whatever hole terrorists rot in these days."

"What kind of were are you?" Steroid Dog snarled, "They're prey. We're predators. At least, I am. I'm not sure what you are."

Happy to have averted any further murderous attempts for the moment, Zita waved her uninjured hand above the water. "I'm a fun and interesting individual who will not hesitate to smack you upside the head with that silver stick if you try biting again." *Please agree before my adrenaline wanes and I feel these injuries more.*

Motors buzzing in the distance alerted her, and she glanced over her shoulder to see distant blots in a triangle formation converging on the island.

"You're a naïve fool," the wolf said. "They'll kill us all if they get the chance. You could be so much more. The day of the God

Kings is coming, and you will have to choose where you stand." With that, he plunged into the water, and Zita readied herself for a fight, but he paddled away toward the distant buildings on the other shore.

She waded to the funereal shore and over to the boat, checking on the spokesman. He was curled into a ball that quaked when she checked his pulse, so she assumed he would live.

As weariness and pain replaced adrenaline, she stood by a chair on the boat and watched the boats in the distance come closer.

The scent of the woods, fur, and hamburgers preceded the heavy footfalls of the bear. He considered her and grunted, a querulous sound, around the packet of rags in his mouth.

"Yeah, I'm fine. I needed a second. Stupid-ass everyone attacking everyone else," she answered, guessing at the question. Zita made her way off the boat, her assorted injuries making themselves known with the movement. Her arm and rear were strident with pain, but she pretended nothing was wrong in case the bear turned belligerent as well.

The ursine shapeshifter spat the pile of clothing scraps, an empty plastic baggie that still bore a trace of her trail mix, and a broken mask at her. "All the humans, including the one from the trench, are caged, and the vampires are quoting emo death poetry. Dunno if that's punishment for the humans, comfort for the vamps, or a bit of both. The smart one has the prod. Police are almost here. You want to be here for that?" His growling voice was gruff but clear. He faced the water; by the way his ears flicked, she knew he must be relying on his hearing to track the approaching police or military boats.

"Carajo, can everyone talk in their animal form but me? I gotta learn that trick. And what's with 'the humans?' We're all people," Zita shook her head. Her fingers dug into the fabric scraps, albeit painfully as her adrenaline had faded and her injuries demanded attention. She pressed the fabric against her arm to stanch the bleeding.

The bear shrugged. His nose pointed toward the civilization on the opposite shore. "Dunno, haven't spoken to that many others. Don't have your flair for words."

Zita chuckled at his description of her and realized he had angled his head that way to avoid appearing to stare at her nudity. *Polite, but not really necessary.* "No, I'm not staying around, especially without clothing. Will the diabetic survive?"

"If the cops bring a medic, yeah."

Relief had her closing her eyes for a second. "You going to wait, take the last boat, or do you want a ride to the next island? I can haul you, but it would be easier if you were in human form." *An orca might work. Wouldn't that be fun, an orca towing a bear, like the weirdest water-skiing event ever?*

Something that had to be a smile spread on his face, so he must have imagined something similar. "Kodiak bear. Strong swimmer. They're getting close."

"Right," she said, "You go. I'll fly off in a minute." *I knew that. Should have remembered. High end of the scale for his subspecies, but not grossly oversized like Steroid Dog.*

His nose dipped, and his head turned toward her mauled arm, before he rumbled and plunged into the water. He paddled toward the opposite shore.

Zita got to her feet and trudged back to the building. After checking inside to ensure that everyone behaved, she held her bundle against her chest and waited at the tree line. When the boats swarming with police reached the shore, she stepped back behind a Norway maple and teleported home.

***

An hour later, Zita paced in her apartment, because pain left few alternatives. She had showered, rinsing carefully. The scrounged, almost floor-to-ceiling mirrors in her home gym (formerly the master bedroom) revealed truly nasty bites on her one arm and a long, shallow graze across both of her buttocks. *Lucky me,* she thought, *Steroid Dog didn't get any arteries, and the bullet was a graze. That arm is toast, though, until Wyn heals it.*

After coating both sets of injuries with a thick layer of antibiotic pain ointment, she bandaged them as best she could. Loose terry shorts covered her legs to her knees, and a long-sleeved, purple T-shirt advertised a zip line with a suggestive comment in Spanish and hid her arm. If Quentin showed up on her doorstep before Wyn arrived, Zita did not want to explain her injuries. Ibuprofen had not dented the pain, and she contemplated taking another.

When a knock sounded, she verified it was her friends, then undid the three deadbolts and let them in. Zita smiled, relief overriding the pain for a moment. "Hey, guys," she said. "Thanks for bringing my stuff so quickly."

Wyn stormed in.

Andy entered behind her with a mild expression that belied his body, which was tensed to fight. He closed the door behind them.

That's not good. Maybe I'll wait until after she calms down to ask Wyn to heal me. Discomfort from her arm protested that plan, but survival instinct had Zita trying to deflect the anger. "Can I get you a snack? If you prefer, you can get your own. After all those weeks in quarantine here after the hospital got attacked, you know where everything is. Do you need to rush off to buy pants?"

"Don't try to distract me with trivialities! What were you thinking?" Wyn raged. Curling tendrils of brown hair haloed her angry face, and pink stained her cheeks. She threw the canvas bag she carried at Zita.

Clumsy with only one usable arm, Zita caught the bag, feeling cloth and the outline of small objects within. She bit off a whimper, and tears sprang to her eyes as the movement launched another round of agony. "They needed help," she said. Clearing her throat, she sought support from Andy as she set the bag on her little white dinette table. *Mano understands, right?*

He folded his arms across his chest and sniffed the air. "What is that smell? And what happened to your arm?" His tone was cold.

Carajo, he's mad, too, Zita thought. "I'll get you a new shirt, and I fixed the mask." She gestured to the table where the mask lay, the disguise repaired with paracord. *Wish I could fix my bra that easily. That's another sixty dollars I can't afford to spend.*

"What? Smell?" Wyn stopped and sniffed. "That's the awful ointment she slaps on every little... Zita, you're hurt." She scowled. "I can't do this while you're injured. Sit, and I'll heal you, and then... then we are going to talk. You know, in most of the books I've read, shapeshifters change shape to heal injuries."

"Are these the romance novels with the heroes that can go for days? I should be so lucky. Shapeshifting doesn't work like that for me, either. If I knew how to change either, I would." Zita delayed. She cast a glance at the chair and leaned against the counter. When a cabinet handle brushed her derriere, she rocketed to an upright position. "I'm good here, thanks."

Andy watched, and his mouth twitched, breaking the icy expression on his face. "Zita, did you get hurt somewhere other than your arm?"

"No importa. Not important," she answered. "You sure you don't want food? I can eat." For once, she wasn't hungry, but if it would stop the argument, she'd eat.

"Tell me, or I won't heal you," Wyn said.

With reluctance, Zita admitted, "My arm is pretty ripped up, and I have a minor bullet graze, too."

"Where?" Wyn prodded her.

Zita rolled her eyes. "My culo. They shot me in my ass."

A snicker escaped Andy, smothered when Wyn narrowed her eyes at him. After a second, his body relaxed, and he went past Zita to rummage in the kitchen cabinets.

"I'd like to shoot you there, too, right now," Wyn muttered. Her lips pressed into an unhappy line, and she reached out to touch Zita's unwounded arm. Despite her anger, her touch was gentle. Hostile silence reigned while she cast her healing spell.

Breath escaped Zita in an appreciative rush when all of her injuries disappeared in the glowing green cloud of Wyn's sparkling magic. "Thanks."

Wyn waved off the gratitude, releasing Zita's arm. "You're welcome."

Shaking the remaining tension out of her shoulders, Zita was amazed as always at the efficacy of the healing. After she had removed the now-useless bandaging from her arm, she started to drop her pants to remove the other bandage and then stopped. Neither of her friends had spent the bulk of their lives disrobing in crowded locker rooms and living quarters, and Andy had a thing against nudity, she reminded herself. "Be right back," she said, jogging into her bathroom to remove it. Task completed, she bounded back into the kitchen in time to see Wyn putting a wad of bloody bandages into the trash and shaking her head at Andy.

Both of Andy's hands were in his pockets, and his face wore an expression of intense unhappiness. His gaze dropped to the floor.

Did something happen in my absence? "Thanks again. I would have gotten that in a second," Zita said.

Wyn fussed with her purse, then wrapped her arms around herself. "You're welcome. Is that all we're good for? Healing you after your escapades and bringing you your things?"

"Don't be ridiculous," Zita said, but something in those three words set off her friend.

Wyn's eyes flashed, and anger wiped away any sorrow. "By the Goddess, I don't know if you're that stupid or you have a death wish or both! I thought your crazy behavior before was because you were so concerned about that killer holding your brother prisoner, but it seems not." She tapped her fingers on her hips and glowered.

Anger rose in Zita. She turned to face Wyn full on and held up a hand. "Hey now, where do you get off busting my ass? Quentin was kidnapped. Miguel couldn't find him even with his FBI connections. The police were clueless. If Quentin had died because that murdering pendejo had a grudge against Miguel, I would have lost both brothers. I did what I had to. You were there. Was I supposed to sit wringing my hands and waiting for him to die?"

"Do you ever park yourself for more than five seconds?" Andy queried from behind her in the kitchen. Plastic rustled.

"Mass, most Sundays," Zita snapped. Wyn began to speak, but she blazed on, cutting her friend off with a curt wave of a hand. "We found Quentin and rescued him and all those others, too. This time, I saw a problem and solved it. I'm not going to sit in safety if I can help and nobody else can. No, my family wasn't involved, but more people got rescued by the shapeshifter rescue brigade of one. Big deal. Nobody died despite their best efforts. And believe you me, a couple of them were really trying. Dumbasses." She took a few deep breaths, reining in her temper.

"You took off, alone, when you knew they outnumbered you. You didn't even take Andy, and we know guns don't hurt him. We were right next to you, and you just left. Didn't ask us for help or anything," Wyn snarled, her voice rising in both pitch and volume.

The microwave beeped, then hummed. Andy remained silent.

"Lower your voice, my neighbors don't need to be all up in our business," Zita said, following her own advice. Her gossipy neighbors probably could not hear them, but she preferred to be cautious. "All I wanted was for you to be safe. You know, protect you two from injury or being found out. None of us wants to end up as a research subject, and neither one of you likes dangerous stuff. Oye, Andy hesitated to join a water-balloon obstacle course race."

Wyn's face darkened further.

Andy cleared his throat from behind her. "Like doesn't enter into it. I would have helped if you'd bothered to ask. They needed help. Even if I thought otherwise, I would have gone for your sake. It was foolish."

Squeezing Andy's shoulder, Wyn turned her angry face back to Zita. "With Quentin, the police lacked key information, and he's your brother, fine. I understand you obsessing over that. You never talked about it with me afterward, though, and I gave you multiple opportunities. Earlier today with the people in cages, the police likely had more information. They're trained for it. You're not, no matter what bizarre escapades you've been up to on all your trips. Like whatever happened in Brazil that you keep not thinking about when we're around."

One hand ran through her short hair, and Zita exhaled. "Eavesdropping on my brain again? Can't you get a real hobby that doesn't involve invading my privacy?" She held up a hand, pacing a few steps back and forth, as she bit back what she really wanted to say about the telepathic prying. "You two are even less trained than I am. The difference today is that the police couldn't find them, but I could. So, I did."

Wyn glared, her jaw tightening.

In comparison, the cold anger from earlier had deserted Andy. He came closer, scrubbed the back of his neck with a hand, and sighed. "Z, we're not helpless. You know that. Between my strength and other shape, and her"—he swallowed, broaching a subject he generally avoided— "magic, neither one of us is a pushover. Even if you're in bear form, I'm still stronger and tougher. Why wouldn't you take me?" Popping sounds interrupted the steady hum of the microwave.

Zita grabbed an apple and winged it at him, fast and hard.

Andy flinched and batted it away. The apple exploded with his blow, splattering her white table, chairs, and the nearby lemon-colored wall with mush and chunks.

Wyn squealed and brushed at her clothes.

"Explanation right there," Zita answered, rubbing her eyes. She took a deep breath. The air was fragrant with apple and popcorn and antiseptic salve. "It's not about who's the biggest badass. That's definitely not me. Powers should make life better, not be used as an excuse for behavior you'd condemn under other circumstances or to force people into situations they'd otherwise run from."

Andy tilted his head. "You think we'd run or go to the Dark Side?"

"No, I know you wouldn't. But you don't want to do it, and you would have been in danger. That's why," Zita said. She jogged to the sink, retrieved cleaning supplies, and began wiping up the mess while she struggled to explain, hating that she had to. For once, Wyn stayed out of her mind. *As far as I know.* Fear, love, and guilt warred within her, and she scrubbed harder at one patch.

Before Zita managed to articulate anything else, Wyn spoke up again, stepping away from the destroyed fruit. Curling tendrils of hair escaped her bun, and she polished her glasses, a useless affectation, on the hem of her blouse. "The question is why are you running into danger alone? Is it the adrenaline?" she said. She paused. "If not for yourself, can you stop it for people who care about you and worry?"

"Not if someone's going to die if I don't help," Zita replied. *I hate this conversation. My family nags me enough about my hobbies, now my friends, too?* When glittery white paint came up from the chair with the vigor of her scrubbing, she lightened her touch and exhaled. She promised herself an extended workout after they left, one that would last until she felt like herself again. *Maybe I need fewer people worrying about me and assuming I can't take care of myself. Simpler for them, too, if they can go back to their normal lives.*

"Pues, you won't have to fret about it much longer. This zip line company in Brazil might need me if they get approved for an expansion loan. I'll be out of here until December if things work out, and I won't have access to much television to find out about things like today."

The microwave beeped, and crunching sounded from behind her. Popcorn perfumed the air.

Another crunch had Wyn directing her gaze past Zita. "How can you eat right now? I'd expect it from the walking stomach," she said, waving a hand at Zita, "but I expected better of you."

"Hey," Zita protested. "You try hitting my required calories in a day and doing it healthy. You'd be eating all the time, too, especially if you tried flying." She paused in the cleanup and turned to the others.

Andy tossed a piece of popcorn in his mouth. "I put the food in my mouth, chew, and swallow," he replied to Wyn, tone dry. "You and Zita have the fighting handled. Popcorn seemed appropriate. So, the upshot is that Zita's ditching us and running away after being stupid?"

Wyn folded her arms over her chest. "Yes, she's running away to Brazil, like when we were teenagers. We should expect to have all of our correspondence ignored again, but at least this time, none of us is still in chemo."

Zita tried protesting, but no one seemed interested in listening. "I didn't get any letters, they whisked me out of the country too fast, and my family moved."

"We didn't move. You could have written us or called," Andy pointed out.

Zita sighed. "I did. I wrote Wyn, and the letter came back with *deceased* handwritten on it. My tía doesn't have a television or personal phone, let alone email, so I couldn't reach Andy. Not that it would've worked there, anyway, but I lost my phone, too." With a grimace, she rubbed at another patch with her sponge. *Once I got*

Wyn's letter back, I didn't want to know if cancer got Andy, too, like so many others from our gene therapy group. I certainly wasn't going to try to get the phone back from the gang who stole it, either.

Her mouth falling open, Wyn stopped, and her shoulders slumped. "It did? You did? Why didn't you say something when we met again as adults?" Wyn said, her tone softening.

"What would it have changed? Forget about it." Zita shrugged, surveying her work. *It would only have made you depressed about your evil, crazy-ass parents.* She wiped apple off the wall, keeping her touch gentle to avoid ruining the paint. "How about some popcorn?"

Wyn's shoulders stiffened, and her head snapped up. Her eyes narrowed. "Oh no, you don't get to divert this conversation the way you run out on any meaningful discussion. You're too terrified of anything serious to even call Remus for that date he asked you on."

"Really? Remus asked Zita out? Remus and our little Zita?" Andy asked. From the corner of Zita's eye, she saw the steady transfer of popcorn to his mouth stop. His eyes widened, and he shook his head.

He doesn't need to sound so incredulous, Zita thought, annoyed both by his disbelief and the accusation of cowardice. "I'm not scared. It just wouldn't work out. We've got different styles."

"She's writing him off before even trying," Wyn explained to Andy. "It's symptomatic of her general refusal to connect at a deeper level with anyone, even people she claims are friends."

"I'm standing right here," Zita said, tossing her sponge into the bucket in exasperation. "How am I refusing to connect? You and I have talked and texted every day since the quarantine ended. We had lunch four times in the past two weeks, plus the times you stopped by. Between that and Quentin sleeping here most nights, I'm better connected than most gangsters."

Andy repeated himself, snorting a laugh and missing (or more likely, ignoring) everything else. "Remus? My hospital roommate from quarantine that had almost all the women and the guy in 543 drooling? The one who broke the sound barrier running to California?"

Wyn narrowed her eyes at Zita and shook a finger at her. "Yes, but you refuse to talk about anything in depth except exercise and food."

Zita slashed a hand through the air at Andy. "Mano, leave it alone already. Yes, he gave me his number after I helped him and Jerome against those kidnappers. Maybe a pretty man goes for cute chicks who are useful in a fight." She rounded on Wyn, "Why you got to be hating? I've totally talked feelings with people. Deep, meaningful, blow-your-mind shit." Even if she couldn't recall the last time she'd been subjected to such a conversation, she was almost certain she spoke the truth.

At last abandoning his fixation on Remus and Zita as a couple, Andy admitted, "We did have one conversation where she tried. It was sad and included a lot of suggestions of brownies." He tossed another piece of popcorn into his mouth.

Suspicious silver moisture glittered at the corners of Wyn's eyes until she turned away, hiding her face behind the curtain of her hair. "You two did?"

Zita panicked, and her foot bumped the bucket of cleaning supplies. The soiled sponge fell out. "Hey, now, no need to be getting all upset. How about a snack? Or some tea? I got those leaves you left here last weekend."

Wyn's back stiffened. "Those were a gift for you. You haven't even tried any, have you?"

Adrift, Zita attempted to recover. "Oye, I don't drink a lot of tea, but if I ever wanted to, I'd drink yours. So, did you want a cup?" She pled silently to Andy for help, but he shook his head.

"I believe we have activities to complete today before Andy has to catch his train to Boston, and remaining here clearly accomplishes nothing," Wyn said. She collected her purse and glided to the door, her gaze fixed straight ahead. "Perhaps when Zita deigns to communicate and not simply rush off on suicidal missions, we will be able to have an adult discussion." She flipped the deadbolts open and stepped through to the hallway.

"Hey," Zita protested. "How many times do I have to tell you? That was to protect you."

Andy gave her a hug before he went out the door, carrying the popcorn bag. "At least think about not being a dumbass next time, Zita. I'm here if you call, or, you know, on a nine-hour train trip. Wyn's really upset, so I'll go calm her down. Plus, she was my ride here."

Zita hugged him back, pounding his back once or twice. "Yeah, go on. Ties like being crumpled under a video game in a bag once you're out of her sight. And good luck with the girlfriend, too."

A smile touched his mouth. As he headed out, his parting words drifted over his shoulder. "Don't worry about me. I speak the international language of love—physics!"

Chapter Six

Sunday was peaceful, perhaps too much so. The priest gave a sermon that had Zita squirming more than usual in her pew. When she returned home, a shiny new fourth deadbolt adorned her door. Quentin must have been the culprit; he had the only copy of her keys other than the emergency ones hidden in the towering jungle of magically enhanced plants on her balcony. Her brother himself was nowhere to be seen.

Wyn did not call, text, or visit. It was the first time in weeks they had not spoken. To her surprise, Zita missed the contact. *Not all of it, especially the rummaging through my brain bit, but it wouldn't be so bad to chat with her.*

Monday sucked, as they often did.

Her tax preparation boss called early to reduce her hours to a single long day later in the week. *She's still afraid I'll spread the sleeping sickness despite the fact that it's been gone for months, or that I'll scare off clients by being one of the newly powered, even if I did hide all my special abilities from her when we last met. If I ever do tell someone else about my shapeshifting and teleporting other than Wyn and Andy, it won't be her. I should dig out my résumé because I can't live in the US much longer without more money. My savings will cover the apartment and electric for a while yet, but only if I've got other income covering food and expenses.*

Since she didn't have any work, Zita tried to send Andy information on a park he could practice his giant bird form in, but her email crashed. She took that as an invitation to treat herself to a workout.

A call from one of Quentin's men ended the intensive workout she was enjoying. Her brother had missed his first appointment, and they needed someone to handle that, bill payments, and payroll. Although the money was welcome, groveling apologies and office work were her least favorite portions of her part-time job at her brother's locksmith and security business.

She texted Quentin to check on him, but his reply implied he wouldn't make any visits before noon. No explanation given. Zita glowered as she dressed and left for his tiny office. *He used to only go out on nights when he had no appointments the following morning. Now he spends every night at my place or with a stranger.*

As expected, work was a mix of frustrations. Shuffling the schedule was easy enough, but calming the irate homeowner was more difficult. Zita purchased forgiveness with a discount that would bite into the already slim profit margin. Quentin materialized in time for his third appointment, reclaiming his van with minimal conversation. He wouldn't meet her eyes, but the lingering scent of a fruity, feminine perfume confirmed her guess to his previous whereabouts.

Wading through the morass of neglected paperwork ate up the rest of her day. Quentin's employees had tried to keep things running during his neglect, but only he and Zita could access the bank accounts. Perhaps aware of how annoyed she was to discover his filing system for the past month equated to shoving everything in a drawer, Quentin did not stop by the office again.

Andy texted the image of a silly dancing dog midday. When she grabbed a fast lunch to eat at Quentin's desk, she tried to reply with a picture of an obese pigeon she saw stealing a fish sandwich. She managed to send it but discovered her finger was the centerpiece of the shot after the bird flew away.

Once she'd addressed the fifty million pages of paperwork, she exited the building and found something sticky on her motorcycle, likely soda, based on the enthusiastic ants. Her brother's van sat in its customary spot, silent evidence of his avoidance of her. Zita rode straight home, her mind whirling with vexation and her pants smelling like a mix of industrial cleanser and too-sugary grapes. Cleaning, waxing, and greasing her bike consumed the last hour of sunlight, but at least the purple and orange paint sparkled, and the engine purred when she finished.

Late but unremarkable, dinner gave her far too much time with her own thoughts. She left her brother an annoyed voicemail over the state of his business, but he never replied. When she attempted to squeeze in a quick workout on her treadmill to soothe herself, the machine refused to start. After an hour toiling over it, she determined the fuses had burned out. She special-ordered the parts for her ancient equipment, swore, and went to bed.

Wyn still had not contacted her.

***

A slow smile spreading across her face, Zita rolled over. Curling up against the man who lay beside her so her curves nestled against his strength, she draped a possessive arm over his chest. She watched her hand brush the contours of his perfect, sharply defined muscles.

He rumbled, a low sound carrying both amusement and sensual invitation.

"I need to speak to you," a strange woman said. "Oh, of course. I hunt you across the night, and you're occupied with that kind of dream? Do stop and listen to me," she insisted, a hint of a musical accent and more than a little exasperation coloring a lovely voice, rich and deep.

Ignoring the annoying woman, Zita rested her head on her companion's shoulder, content. She nuzzled his ear and blew a soft laugh at him.

Quiet laughter vibrated under her hand. His voice was hushed. "So, are you just fun or are you something more?"

"What?" she said, jerking back and pushing him away. She squinted in the dim light.

A callused hand captured hers, the touch gentle. His breath stirred her hair as he spoke, his voice breaking into multiple voices and gaining an accent, "You need to choose, and soon." Zita started to raise her eyes to his face.

"You are stubborn," the woman said. "Very well, I will remove distractions."

The man and bed faded until Zita stood alone on bare feet under a starry expanse. She felt powdery, dry dirt underfoot when she curled her toes. "Where did... Where did the man go?" She frowned and glanced around. *Am I dreaming then? I have no idea who that man was, so I must have been. And why did I switch from beefcake in my bed to the middle of nowhere in...* Checking the sky overhead only increased her puzzlement. *The stars aren't right for South America or Australia, but it's definitely the Southern Hemisphere. Africa maybe? I've never been there.*

Across from her, a figure formed, coalescing into a mahogany-skinned woman in old-fashioned Sunday best. She even wore a little circular hat, baby blue, that never budged from its assigned spot; Zita had always assumed such headgear required an esoteric application of duct tape and serious hair spray to keep it there. "He wasn't real, but I am. Don't get distracted. You need to act. They cannot be allowed to use the Key—"

My subconscious must be on something. She risked a quick glance down, relaxing when she recognized the boxer shorts and ragged men's tank top she had gone to bed wearing. *At least it's not a hooker dress and heels or something silly like that. I haven't lost it completely.*

The starscape shook as Wyn's voice echoed through it. *Zita!*

"More interruptions? Why is it so hard to get you into a conversation?" The stranger sighed, her eyes full of reproach.

Had she not been raised Catholic, it might have induced guilt. As it was, Zita assumed her subconscious didn't care enough to put any real effort into a messed-up dream. "I'm more of a doer than a talker. Though apparently, I don't get to do anything fun even in my dreams these days," she replied, waving one hand in the air in disgust.

"Ignoring the irrelevant half of that, we must speak. You must not allow—"

Wyn's voice broke in again. *By the moon and stars of the Goddess, Zita, get up!*

The landscape dissolved. Zita caught a glimpse of the dream woman throwing her hands up in the air, face twisted in frustration.

Zita jerked awake, her heart pounding. One hand sought out the knife behind her headboard. Her eyes fell on the smooth, empty pillow on the other side of the bed and the sheets untouched by anyone save herself. She rolled her eyes; her libido was anything but subtle. *Can't even get laid in a dream. Maybe I should try the one-night stand thing after all.*

Zita, wake up and help me! Wyn's voice in her mind was insistent.

Leaving her knife in its hiding place, Zita rubbed sleep from her eyes. *Wyn?*

Fear screamed through the mental link with her friend, and words tumbled into Zita's brain as if her friend threw them as fast as possible. *Yes, my wards warned me. Someone's in my house, and they mean me harm.*

Zita blinked and shot from the bed. Her pulse racing, she threw on clothing, and a thought slipped out. *Your words warned you? What, they threw a rock with a threat that used elephant-sized dictionary words?*

The distress shuddering through the telepathic connection eased as Wyn processed Zita's questions. *Wards, not words. They're my magical alarm system. I'm hiding in the basement, and I called the cops, but I had to hang up because the burglars heard me. Andy's stuck on a train returning from Boston, so I can't call him. Can you teleport here and get me out? Now?*

Well, that puts me in my place, Zita thought. Her mouth quirked upward despite the sourness in her throat. She forced her breathing into the same pattern she used for capoeira and felt her own emotions settle. *I don't know your house well enough to teleport there. Since we got out of quarantine three weeks ago, you've been coming to my place. Can you get out a window or something?*

They're painted shut, Wyn wailed.

Her mind raced, and Zita paused, her hands frozen above her shoes. The thought slipped out. *You know that's a fire hazard, sí?*

Exasperation preceded Wyn's answer. *Concentrate.*

You got a webcam down there? Zita mentally high-fived herself as she pressed the button to power on her computer; Wyn's annoyance would be more productive than panic. Doing something also helped her focus, anything to help. Shoes on, she paced and cursed her inability to teleport places she couldn't see or visualize strongly enough.

Her friend paused and then proved she had overheard her cursing. *I remember it as it was before they broke in. I'll send you the image.*

A wavering image appeared in Zita's mind, and she realized, with dismay, it was unusable for a teleport. *Not going to work. The spatial proportions aren't working for me, and you've got weird glowy outlines around some objects.*

Those are auras.

Whatever they are, they won't appear to me, and that will throw off my teleport. The walls of boxes aren't specific enough. Breathe, Wyn, we'll get through this. Zita grumbled as she entered her password.

Fine, then. I don't have my computer, but I've got my phone. Get your laptop, and we'll do a video call since your phone is too archaic to do one.

Already have my machine booted.

Wyn demonstrated that it was possible to hyperventilate through a mental connection. *Click that program Andy installed to chat with his girlfriend. Hurry, I can hear them destroying my belongings up there. They'll discover me soon.*

Zita clicked the icon and waited. Her stomach twisted into knots. *Loading took a minute. I'm in. No worries, we can do this.*

The screen beeped and flashed at her.

She hunted around the display until she found the Accept button. Blackness greeted her. *Oye, all I see is darkness.*

I can't turn on a light. They'll find me. The terror had returned to Wyn's voice.

Zita wanted to punch the robbers in their thieving noses or their balls if they had any. One hand dragged over her short hair, and she paced. Striding back to her computer, she started searching for webcams near Wyn's house in another window. *You need to risk it. Your house is too small to hide you for long unless you use your illusions. Can you do that or put them to sleep or throw magic at them?*

I have to see to do a spell or an illusion, and those take a minute to affect anyone. They could kill me in that time.

Can you booby trap the stairs with a cloud of your sleep spell or something, so they have to walk through it to get to you?

I can't see, Wyn wailed mentally.

Then you need to find a light so you can cast, and I can get there. I can't teleport without it, either. Aim the camera at something distinctive, or I'll end up in someone else's basement. And amiga, breathe. We got this. Zita exhaled, praying Wyn would understand the logic before the intruders found her.

Right. Here goes. Light flashed on, revealing a mostly empty space where a bright red cloth, embroidered with silver and gold thread, draped over an old workbench. Near the sinuous curves of a marble woman, a knife, an ornate cup incised with a crescent moon, and a bottle with a half-burned bundle of herbs crowded around a leather-bound book atop the fabric. Shelves above the bench held bottles, crystals, and the odd fairy statue. A paperback novel with a close-up of a naked man's chest sat on a wooden stool carved with moons and stars.

Zita teleported. *Sweet pectorals and six-pack on the book there*, she joked, hoping to calm her friend.

Wyn stood holding her phone, from which a blinding circle of light emanated. Her friend clutched her purse to her chest with her free hand, somewhat incongruous with the silky red nightshirt and overstuffed gray tabby cat slippers she wore.

The light winked out, leaving the room dark and Zita blinking her eyes.

Never you mind the book. Now can we teleport back to your apartment?

Zita let herself shift partially to jaguar, welcoming the influx of information as her senses improved. At this point, she barely noticed the color change when acquiring better night vision, though the flood of scent information always tempted her to isolate and identify each element.

Wyn's house had more square feet than Zita's apartment, but not by much, with two bedrooms, a kitchen, a living room, and a half-basement spread over multiple floors. They stood now in the basement, and she scanned it for anything that would help. The only official exit was via stairs that led up to the kitchen. Four half windows, the kind that tilted out, let in a glimmer of multicolored light from the streetlights outside. The basement was one large room, with the water heater and other utilities in one corner, the workbench in another, and a jumble of boxes taking up the remainder. Odors of incense, the litter box, and herbs hung heavily in the air, overriding the underlying scents of cardboard and the metallic heat. Movement upstairs, accompanied at random intervals by a cacophony of destruction, kept her silent. She kept her steps silent as she approached her friend, who had hidden beneath the window as if the weak light from outside would protect her.

With a belated wince, she realized she had never replied. *I'm right next to you now, don't scream. If necessary, I'll teleport us and figure out how to cover it up later, but I'd rather try to escape this another way. You called the cops from here. They can track and may already be tracking your phone, so if they saw it jump from here to my apartment, I'm outed. If they don't notice that, then you have to explain how you knew people were breaking in here when you were forty-five minutes away, and that outs you since you don't have an alarm system. We can't assume the cops will be stupid. Also, Quentin might be at my place by then, and he sucks at keeping secrets. Don't worry, we'll get out of this.*

Why is your brother—never mind. Blind in the darkness, Wyn gnawed on her lip, brows furrowed, and body shrinking back between two stacks of boxes. Her fingers fretted with the purse slung over her shoulder.

Zita set a hand on Wyn's shoulder and gave it a squeeze. *Breathe. No hay bronca. We got this.*

Wyn took a shaky breath and nodded. Her shoulders straightened. *What are we going to do?*

Letting go of her friend, Zita frowned up at the window, then turned and picked her way through the cardboard maze. She padded back carrying the stool and set it beneath the window.

After clambering onto it, she verified she could climb up on the sill if necessary. *We run.*

Wyn moved behind her, knocking into something. They both froze as the movement overhead paused, and two male voices rumbled. *Goddess! Run, really?*

When Zita tried to peer out, a decorative film masquerading as stained glass hid the world outside. She filed away the problem before she sent her reply. *So much for being able to teleport out. Pues, I should open that window anyway as the cover for our escape. If the goal is survival and keeping our secrets, the best way to ensure it is to not engage the burglars. Did you want to fight them instead?*

No, but I thought you... Never mind.

Zita stopped herself from a laugh, acid bitter in her throat and her stomach churning. *Sparring is fun, but I'm not risking our lives without reason. Contrary to what others may think, I don't have a death wish. Lucky for us you left that knife out.* She slipped off the stool and picked up the knife from the workbench. Returning to the window, she raised it toward the paint, and light glinted off the blade.

A harsh, indrawn breath sounded behind her. *Not the athame. That's a sacred implement!*

Zita considered the oversized, stabby weapon in her hand. Ornamentation made it too unbalanced for throwing, but it was well cared for and sharp enough to be dangerous. *The weight seems off. Is it an unusual metal alloy? It's a fixed-blade knife, and I need to pry the pane open to see out and provide an excuse for how we escaped.*

Wyn's mental voice was sharp, her fear forgotten in the face of her annoyance and faith. *It's consecrated. Would you use the cross from a Catholic altar as a tool? I have an herb cutter in the box under the altar. Can you use that instead?*

With a sigh, Zita replied, *I'll try the herb cutter. And yes, I would if using the crucifix would save lives. Jesus is totally down with helping like that, especially if it avoids violence.* After a second, she realized the workbench was the altar. Hopping down, she padded over and found a crescent-shaped blade in the box, setting aside a sheath and a roll of duct tape. The athame would have been easier to use than the herb cutter, but she didn't argue. Wyn's faith was too important to her.

In case the intruders came downstairs before she finished setting up their escape, Zita quietly slipped the athame into the sheath and taped it to her leg with the duct tape. She slid the tape roll onto her wrist like a bracelet in case they needed it later.

When the intruders' footsteps moved into the kitchen above the basement and increased in volume, both women froze. Zita identified two people: one whose steps were little more than the brush of leather over the tiles in an odd, unidentifiable cadence and one who made up for it with a solid thunder of steps. *Thief and muscle? I hate to generalize, but the one guy has to be huge or wearing clown shoes to be that loud, and most people aren't that interesting in their footwear choices.*

Nerves sang through the connection. *Could you stop imagining a thief in clown shoes? Especially a huge one holding a gun? I'm having Pennywise flashbacks here.*

Her concentration broken, Zita sent, *Penny what?*

Never mind. Wyn shivered.

A hoarse, masculine voice broke the silence, his words almost growled. "Are you certain the woman is here alone? The vanilla woman's scent is stronger near the kitchen. One of the stupid fang babies told the human scum our mission before I escaped, and we wouldn't have to be here if the humans hadn't gotten the librarian's computer first. If there are two women, that's one for each of us to kill, unless you're squeamish." He sniffed.

He can be Sniffy, Zita decided, as she eased the herb cutter along the edges of the window, breaking the seal.

Movement rustled overhead. A deep voice rumbled, "Didn't see anyone else. We don't need to hurt anyone. Take what we need and leave. Since Halja killed the professor, we may need the librarian alive to interpret his work. The humans only have what the vampire knew, and he had nothing outside of the names of the researchers. What vanilla woman are you talking about?" The louder footsteps crossed the floor, and a door creaked open. As much as she hated to stereotype, she assumed the heavier footfalls belonged to the deeper voice. *Basso will do for him.*

Wyn's thought held confusion, laced with distress. *Don't name them. We're not keeping them.*

With her enhanced hearing, Zita caught a loud inhale and exhale before Sniffy spoke again. His voice (*Why does it seem familiar?*) had a malicious bite that made her dislike of him grow, even before she parsed his words. "The librarian knows too much, so we should make certain she doesn't tell the humans. Her scent permeated her office, and she smells of flowery woman musk and books. She's had three guests that I can separate over the damn cats: a male with desert and windy sidewalks in his scent, a female with the reek of patchouli and pot, and another female trailing vanilla sugar, cinnamon, and trees in her scent. The last is the strongest and might be here now. I've scented her before somewhere, but it's hard to tell under the feline stench."

Patchouli must be one of my coven mates, who swore she was off marijuana. The other two must be you and Andy, Wyn sent. Her fingers dug into Zita's arm.

Zita considered. *That's actually a great description of Andy's scent, and my soap is vanilla. If I keep running around in disguise, I need to ensure my Arca scent is different from my natural one. Where have I heard his voice before?*

"Cinnamon and vanilla? Maybe she made snickerdoodles. Let's get the papers and get out. I don't want to leave our sentry too long," suggested Basso.

Sniffy gave a loud, derisive snort. Glass shattered. Zita imagined him lobbing Wyn's fragile flower teacups and was outraged on her friend's behalf. *Even if they are silly floral thimbles that only hold a few drops at a time, that's just petty.* "I'm not surprised. She's not all there. Zeus will cull her if she's not useful enough or powerful enough to stop him. Good riddance."

The heavier footsteps stopped dead, then took off. A meaty thud and the din of breaking glass preceded an animal snarl. The floor creaked and whined as if the two men circled each other. The last bit of paint gave way, and Zita used the racket from above to hide the cracking sound as she finessed the window open.

Voice now lower, Sniffy made a lewd suggestion about Basso and their female sentry, along with a huff of a laugh. Nails clicked against tile upstairs in a pattern that Zita recognized as animal. A whiff of fur struck her.

Recognition crashed in, and Zita's eyes widened. *We are so chingado. His footfalls weren't following an odd pattern; he was walking on four legs. Sniffy is Steroid Dog from the island. We're out of here. He doesn't play nice.*

"You'll talk about her with respect," Basso bellowed from above.

Steroid Dog? What? I thought you were only fighting men with guns. Wait, is that why your arm was so messed up? Wyn asked mentally.

Zita gripped her friend's arm and assessed the outside. Grass spread to the base of the neighbor's house, and an uneven pair of bushes screened the corner of the house. A white picket fence separated the two lots. Hidden by the swirling strands of thick fog, the street was invisible, only detectable by a nearby streetlamp's struggle to light the area through the mist.

Nonetheless, she teleported the pair of them as far as possible into the neighbor's yard. She tugged Wyn's arm. *Talk later, go now. If he gets too close, I'll teleport us to my place. Given that it's so far away, though, I really want to avoid the cops tracking the sudden change in position later and asking questions.*

They had only taken a few steps before a woman's voice called out. "Who's there? Your feet scream upon my ground. Spying feet, lying feet, trying to hurt feet. You cannot fool me! I will not go back, and you shall not go forward."

That's not my neighbor, Wyn sent. Her shiver vibrated from where Zita held Wyn's arm. *And whoever it is, is not well. Her mind is chaos, whirling with its own noise.*

The earth at their feet shuddered.

Zita recognized the sensation and swore aloud in Spanish. She dragged Wyn aside just as the dirt snapped like a bear trap at where they had been standing. "Run!"

Wyn needed no prompting, and they raced down the street toward the next circle of light flouting the dense clouds of vapor. Even if she had dared release her friend's arm, Zita could have tracked the other woman easily; Wyn stumbled over belongings left out in neighbors' yards and failed to hit any kind of consistent stride, less confident when running almost blind. To her credit though, her friend tried, even stifling her whimper when the ground shook under their feet.

A canine howl rose behind them. The fog twisted the sound so she could not tell where the wolf was.

"Hang on, going to get a lead," Zita said. Hampered by the lack of visibility, she teleported as far as she could see, repeating it as soon as she spotted another destination. Within seconds and multiple jarring jumps, the neighborhood had fallen behind them.

She stopped in a strip mall. Although most of the stores had been shuttered for the night, it was still lit enough to burn through the thick mist. The dollar store, vape shop, and tattoo parlor were closed, but a convenience store remained open. Another neon sign and the movement of cars farther down the road suggested a gas station not far away.

Internally, she cursed the need to hide her abilities, as otherwise they would already be safe in her apartment. She paused to consider their options.

Wyn yanked her arm away and staggered toward the glowing haven of the convenience store. Half-bent over, she stumbled to a nearby bush and vomited, the sound eerie in the fog that fought to claim the worn shopping plaza. She moaned. "Never do that ever, ever, again."

Guess she's decided for us since we're now on camera with that, Zita thought, her gaze stopping on the video camera aimed at Wyn's chosen shrubbery. She wrinkled her nose at the addition of puke to the asphalt, marijuana, and reheated hot dog scent of the parking lot as she hurried over to hold Wyn's hair back. "No promises, but I'll avoid it. Sorry." *When you're along, anyway. My stomach is more hungry than upset, or was, anyway, before you started barfing.*

Wyn's expression was less than friendly when they entered the convenience store.

The clerk inside, at first bored, turned helpful when Wyn explained the situation, even shuttering his store while they phoned the police. His eyes had skimmed over Zita to fasten on the troubled, pale, and perfect face of her friend, framed by strands of glossy hair escaping a messy bun. Given the occasional furtive glances he directed at Wyn, Zita doubted the exposed miles of slender leg revealed by Wyn's thigh-length nightshirt hindered his chivalry or that he even noticed the single remaining bedraggled cat slipper.

As they waited for the cops, he finished closing up the business. Six open jars of garlic lined both the front and back doors between burning incense cones. Wyn had insisted that it wouldn't help against a werewolf, as she insisted on calling the massive wolf, but Zita and the clerk set them up anyway. Zita had wanted to muddy their scents; the clerk was convinced the stink would drive away evil creatures. Whether it worked on the wolf or not, Zita's nose was numb.

Any remaining doubts the clerk held disappeared when the external cameras showed an eight-foot-tall man and an enormous dark wolf stalking the outside of the store. The screech as the great beast's claws casually scarred the metal shutters spooked the clerk and Wyn. Zita was torn between concern and annoyance, and poised to teleport away with the others if necessary.

The police arrived not long after to find the three of them barricaded behind the counter. The clerk held a baseball bat (he had a prison record, so no gun). Huddled in a blanket, Wyn clutched hot chocolate that Zita had pushed on her, and Zita had two box cutters and some empty protein bar wrappers. *A woman has to eat, after all.*

***

An hour later, they remained at the now-open store, and paramedics had checked all three. They cleared Zita and the clerk after a minimal check. Wyn, however, showed enough signs of shock to receive another hot chocolate and continued use of the blanket, especially once she admitted to throwing up after "sprinting" here.

Now, a plump, drowsy-eyed detective waited nearby. Her short-clipped hair had far more salt than pepper, and her shoes had more mileage than most used cars. A complimentary coffee rejuvenated her enough to rifle through her pockets for a battered notebook, and now she appeared ready to take their statements.

Stay quiet and let me do the talking, Wyn warned her. *I don't want you exercising your unique diplomatic style and alienating her. If the cops solve this case, we can return to our normal lives.*

I'm not that bad. Zita arranged her face into a smile.

Yes, you really are. Wyn's plan to monopolize the conversation failed, however, when the detective insisted on questioning them separately and sent Zita off to wait for her turn.

An hour later, Zita took a deep breath as she faced the policewoman. Thanks to a running commentary from her friend, she knew what to expect. She recounted the story they had worked out mentally while huddled in the store. "Wyn's office was ransacked earlier today, and one of her coworkers was assaulted. She didn't want to be alone tonight, so she called me. Mostly, we hung out with her being nervous. Anyway, we were talking, and she said she had pictures from when we were younger, so we were in the basement checking boxes when two men broke in."

The cop considered her for a moment and made a noncommittal noise.

Zita suspected she had not believed part of the lie.

That and her suspicion that her friend was mentally eavesdropping were both confirmed when Wyn grumbled telepathically about the cop thinking they were closet lesbians.

Yeah, if I were, I wouldn't be closeted. How did she get that idea? You'll explain the office and coworker thing to me later? Zita sent.

Not what I was complaining about, but never mind. Yes, I'll tell you.

Out loud, Zita continued her tale for the policewoman. "Wyn tried to call 911 but had to hang up when the burglars heard us. We crawled out a window. A woman outside shouted and tried to stop us as we ran away. When we started running, we didn't have a destination in mind, so it's lucky we got somewhere that could be barricaded and had snacks."

Pen scratched on paper as the detective made notes. "Anything else?" she asked, her breath perfumed with hazelnut coffee.

Zita warred with herself.

Don't do it, Wyn said mentally. *Aren't you the one who said never volunteer information?*

Finally, Zita sighed. "The lookout might have been Jennifer Stone. Her dad's in quarries or construction or something like that. She's supposed to be in a hospital taking medication, and no, I don't know for what. I didn't see her, but I remembered her voice." *Also, she's the only loca I know who can make the ground try to eat people.*

Her intent to help only prolonged the interview and weariness dragged at her by the time the detective was done.

After collecting a yawning Wyn, the policewoman sighed and considered the pair. Her eyes were as sympathetic as the early hour allowed. "We're done here for the night. Miss Diamond, you shouldn't stay at your place tonight in case they come back. Do you have somewhere else you can go? Or should we give you a ride to a hotel?"

Wyn nibbled her lip and fingered a curl. "Oh, but..."

"She can stay with me tonight," Zita volunteered. At Wyn's expression, she shrugged and dropped her eyes, fighting the urge to swear aloud. *Why is she surprised? I'm still not certain why she's mad at me, but am I supposed to stop being her friend because of one argument?*

Now the detective is certain we're a couple, Wyn complained. *As if.*

After eyeing Zita, the cop fidgeted with her notebook. She appeared to be searching for the right words. "Should they track her to you..." Her face held a dubious expression Zita had seen too many times.

Zita kicked at a loose clod of grass and was reassured when she felt the weight of Wyn's athame taped to her leg, though she would have preferred her own non-religious weaponry. "My brother's crashing at my place most of the time these days, anyway, so what's one more person? If nothing else, she'll have a Marine and me if they come after her there. No big." *Not that you're not magazine-perfect gorgeous and all, but I think if I were a lesbian, I'd go for a butch chick who looks like a man, maybe a bodybuilder.* She stuffed down the addendum that she would choose someone less high maintenance, too, and prayed her friend had not overheard that.

Wyn's answer gave no indication if the errant thought had registered or not. *The point of being a lesbian is that you don't want a man. Thanks, though. You're not my type, either.*

Tension eased out of the cop at the word "Marine." She cleared her throat with a phlegmy cough. "It's your decision, Miss."

Claro que sí, another one who thinks I'm useless, Zita grumbled to herself.

Well, she does assume I prefer cute-as-a-button, pocket-sized Sapphic lovers. Her preference is chubby, red-haired women, Wyn sent as a mix of emotions flashed on her face, most of them negative. "My cats, I can't let them hurt my cats," she fretted, pulling the black and purple blanket closer around herself. A raven laughed from the fabric.

Zita still wanted to punch the people who put those expressions on her friend's face, unless she was one of them, which was all too possible. She waved her hand, surprised for a moment at the roll of duct tape still decorating her wrist. Fluffy kittens cavorted across it, a detail she had missed before. "Cats, too, if I have to, though I'm betting hers can hold their own here or in a nuclear apocalypse."

Her posture relaxed, the cop said, "We have to borrow your house key and will lock up behind ourselves, but I think we can let you retrieve your pets and some clothes. Will you be okay?"

A ghost of a smile touched Wyn's strained face. "I'll be all right, officer, thank you."

Chapter Seven

"**Don't think this means** I've forgiven you," Wyn said almost an hour later in Zita's kitchen. She took the kettle off the stove and poured the boiling water over the tea ball in a mammoth purple mug. Steam rose, carrying the floral scent of Wyn's favorite concoction.

Zita grimaced. The ride home in the police cruiser had been a quiet one, but she had attributed that to shock and the late hour. *It'd be easier to apologize if I understood what for. Ay, this night grows only longer, and I had hoped to sleep. Well, tea, contact Andy, and then crash.* "Comprendo. Can you let Andy know we're safe?"

With occasional tremors still wracking her slim form, Wyn sloshed liquid into a second mug, this one advertising Quentin's business. "Already done. This has to be related to yesterday on campus." She paused.

Even Zita recognized an invitation that obvious. "What happened?" She pasted an interested expression on her face, expecting another tale of an idiot trying to impress her friend.

A furrow between Wyn's brows eased at the question. "Thugs raided my office yesterday while I was delivering the last part of a report to a professor. As a proud Luddite, he prefers paper documentation rather than emailed links. When I arrived, the professor was bleeding out on the floor in the ruins of his office. That unfortunate man is over seventy and probably weighs as little as you, and yet there was so much blood. They must have visited him first." She shuddered.

That's actually... Wow. She mentioned it earlier, but I had no idea it was that bad. Zita made a disgusted noise as anger and sympathy ignited at the callous treatment of the elderly scholar. "Poor old dude." She plunked herself in a chair, sensing the start of a long explanation. *Maybe she'll feel better if I'm obviously sitting here listening. I hate sitting and listening. Jogging and listening would be way better.*

Wyn continued. "His injury was both physical and magical. The stab wound was serious, but a curse ensured he would bleed until he died or until someone dispelled it. I removed it but didn't get far healing him before he awakened. Help arrived shortly after that in response to my... rather inelegant summons." At Zita's blank expression, she sighed. "I may have screamed. A lot." Perhaps unconsciously, Wyn rubbed her hands together as if scrubbing them.

Uncertain what she could do without antagonizing her friend and ending the fragile peace, Zita rose, then wavered. She settled for giving Wyn's shoulder three light pats and hovering nearby. "You saved a man despite all that. Good job!" *Wow, lame.*

Wyn took a deep breath. One hand gripped her pentagram necklace as her lips moved in silent prayer. When she finished, she continued her story. "I think he was stabbed with the Key of Hades. It's a Greek artifact dagger, but only the blade was donated to the school. The authorities only cared about my possible identification of a missing object and attempted murder weapon. They seemed ignorant of what eidetic memory means and only took the missing blade seriously when I pointed out the presence of the associated tag and case. The professor followed university rules for the treatment of donated artifacts like a zealot."

Zita's memory stirred, and she tidied up behind her friend while she thought. "Momentito... That sounds familiar. I think one of the creepy vampire people on the island mentioned a key. Is there a reason vampires in New York would want it?"

Her friend puckered her lips, then shrugged. "In addition to being unusually well-preserved, the Key is supposed to be a magical dagger with a colorful history. That might appeal to their interests? Researching artifacts is normally out of the scope of my job, but I seized the opportunity to investigate something at least remotely connected to my field, as everyone else without projects has been drafted to scour history records. The librarian in that area is a territorial wolverine. Not literally." As if realizing that she had rambled, Wyn stilled for a moment. She scooped out the tea ball from the purple cup, tipped a spoonful of sugar in, and then adulterated the tea further with an amber liquid from her purse.

The sharp tang of alcohol stung Zita's senses. She wrinkled her nose before adopting a more neutral expression. On automatic, she crossed to the oven and straightened a towel until it hung square on the handle. *How strong is that stuff? She'll be out cold tonight, but maybe extra rest would help her relax. She's been wound super tight lately.* "Is that the two-faced woman who stole a project from you while pretending to be your friend?"

Wyn paused. Her eyes went distant for a second, then sharpened. She turned and stared at Zita. "You remembered that? That was a couple weeks ago, and no, this is another person."

Zita shrugged. "It helps if I can do something while I listen. My ears work fine, but my brain goes to sleep if I sit too long." *Or if you start talking about clothes or unimportant stuff. Your enemies, those I remember.*

After removing the tea ball from the second, unaltered drink, Wyn set it at Zita's place at the table and lowered herself into a chair. Graceful fingers played with the rim of her own cup, which she put in front of herself instead of drinking. Her voice was tight. "Anyway, the police thanked me and instructed me not to discuss anything. Of course, they declined to commit to warning the owners of the remaining pieces of the Key that a group of bloodthirsty malefactors may seek missing components. I hope the police catch them, but their reluctance to listen does not inspire confidence."

"So, we need to warn the other owners," Zita said, seizing on the concrete task.

Eyes downcast, Wyn nodded, and said, "I could only find the location of the haft." She cradled her mug against her chest.

Hope rose. *Maybe the situation isn't that dire, and I don't have to listen to centuries of the history of silverware accompanied by a cup of liquid weeds. I wish she'd taken me up on my offer of horchata at least.* Zita cleaned and rinsed the tea balls, delaying her return to the table and her cup of the evil drink. "Whoever stole your stuff doesn't have that information, right?"

Wyn stared into her tea. "The university stores all electronic versions of research on a network or cloud drive of some sort. So, whoever took my work computer and my personal tablet won't find anything on either. My paper file, however, had a copy of my report with the haft location listed. I remember it, of course. It's in a museum in Birmingham, Alabama. But as for the sheath, I have no information on its owner or location."

Zita swore without any real heat or surprise.

Wyn's shoulders slumped, and she closed her eyes, then buried her face in her arms. "If the right sacrifices are offered, the dagger's wielder can supposedly claim the power of the gods and smite the unfaithful. In contrast to the feeble, fading magic on the dagger's case, the curse I pried off the professor was strong, flourishing, and not at all subtle. What if stabbing the professor with the blade woke the spell? Does the wielder actually gain something? And if one piece is that powerful, what happens if the blade rejoins the haft and sheath?"

They have a knife that's easier to wield and carry? Somehow, I doubt that's what she wants to hear. Zita ventured an answer when her friend appeared to be waiting for one. "Very bad things?"

Wyn murmured agreement, lifted her head, and opened her eyes. "I know you're a skeptic about most magic, less so mine since the results are visible, but it may pose a real danger. The strength of the bloodied blade was greater than any of the fast spells you've seen me cast. If that power were amplified further, I don't know what the limits would be. Given that it's supposed to have belonged to the God of the Underworld, it could even be a weapon of mass destruction. How do we know it won't kill everyone in a certain radius whenever drawn if the pieces reunite?"

After a moment to consider that horrific thought, Zita spoke. "Do we have any idea what we're searching for? I mean, there's got to be a ton of ratty old knives out there." Out of tasks, she sat and stared in trepidation at the steam rising from the tea cooling in her mug. It smelled like a moldy grandma perfume. She faked a sip, hoping to avoid hurting Wyn's feelings. *If I let it cool enough, maybe the cats will drink it once she guzzles down that alcoholic tea and goes to sleep.* Without giving away her interest, she risked a quick glance over her shoulder. The animals were nowhere to be seen. *Those felines are too clever by half.*

The description of the artifact won a wince from Wyn. Lifting her head, her eyes unfocused and she stared into the distance. "That, I can answer. It's unique. The dagger is in three parts, haft, blade, and sheath. They have the blade, stolen from the professor. The second piece is the haft with Cerberus—that's a three-headed dog before you can ask—chasing the dead down the handle. Macabre stuff, but gorgeous. The last part is the sheath, thin-hammered metal with a delicate engraving of a map of the underworld. The whole thing is supposed to resemble a giant key, hence the name." She held out her hand, uncurling the fingers.

"Here, the blade I've seen, but the other two are from pictures." An illusion of the pieces of the Key sprang to life over her palm.

Zita's first thought, not voiced, was that it fell into the pretty-but-useless category, as the ornamentation had to make the balance awkward for throwing or wielding. The only one to display as a three-dimensional image, the leaf-shaped blade had a gold and onyx river embedded in the fuller and undamaged tang. Blunt edges spoke to the years of not being sharpened.

Given the graininess of the last two pieces in the illusion, the images must have come from pictures enlarged to show details in the cloudy, aged material. On the illusory haft, two-dimensional with catalog lighting, inlaid gold depicted Cerberus chasing human figures against an onyx background. A bird form tipped the pommel. Scratches marred the black on both haft and blade, but the gold gleamed as though it had just been polished. *How is this not more damaged after being separated from the blade? Bizarre.*

A black-and-white image of the last piece, a dull metallic sheath that only loosely resembled a key, drifted over Wyn's hand. The length seemed better suited to a short sword than a knife, perhaps to accommodate the map that wove across it, with rivers picked out in chipped onyx. Several gouges marred the surface where damaged pieces had fallen or been pried out.

Wyn continued to hold the illusion.

With a jolt, Zita realized she should say something. "It's shinier than I thought it would be, and a lot less destroyed."

After a moment, Wyn's fingers curled shut, and the illusion disappeared. "Despite the separation of the parts, the excellent preservation is one of the reasons it's a valuable artifact."

Zita ran her hand over her hair, rose, and jogged in place. "But we know what they want and where one piece is? That's far easier than just a first name and a dance club to go on, which is all we had when my brother was missing." She tried a tentative smile at Wyn, hating the awkwardness between them.

Her friend's lips curved upward, but Wyn looked away, smile fading. She sipped her tea, one finger extended.

Things were serious when the pinky finger extended during teatime. Zita tapped her own fingers on the counter as she trotted. "Okay, let's solve this. First, we contact that museum in Birmingham. Write it down so we can do that tomorrow. Then, we tell them about the break-ins and that the haft is in danger of being stolen. If they allow access to it, you can run your magic sniffer by it to see if it's also enchanted. If it is, can you peel the curse bit off?" After grabbing a notepad from a drawer, she dropped it and a pen in front of Wyn.

"Wait, what? I thought we would just warn the owners or the curator at least. If they hide the piece, the whole power thing is moot," Wyn said, setting down her mug with a thud. Her shoulders stiffened. Reaching for the paper, she scratched out the museum information in flowing cursive, even if her eyes held concern.

Zita sighed and peeked at the paper. "It might not be that simple. The thieves were happy to stab the professor; they'd probably be willing to hurt others to learn of possible hiding places. If they hit the museum, they could endanger multiple staff members to find it unless they've got a magic sniffer like you." Her fingers beat on the counter again while she thought.

Wyn snapped, "Please refrain from calling it that. It's more visual anyway, like an aura. And don't pound like that, either." She slapped the pen down on the notepad and pushed both away.

Zita made a dismissive gesture and stopped tapping, inwardly pleased. *Yes, be angry with me again. It sucks, but anger I can handle. Weepiness, not so much.* "Fine. Magic eyeballs. Voodoo dance. Whatever. You can see if the knife pieces are actually a problem or not."

"We have no guarantee the museum will listen to us, and we don't know who the other owner is." Wyn leaned back in her seat and crossed her arms over her chest.

I could ensure the curator's cooperation by staging a failed burglary. Zita tried not to think that too loudly and instead focused on the discussion. "Even if they hide it for a while, they won't keep up a high level of vigilance forever. It's possible Steroid Dog and his gang of super thugs will wait them out. If we remove the magic, they'll have nothing but decrepit cutlery."

Her friend continued glaring. "Other than my own projects and paraphernalia, I've never even seen another enchanted object. There are no guarantees that I can do anything with it."

"You turned something into magic? What did you make?" *Is it shiny? For someone who professes to not like glitter, most of her magic sparkles. I should totally pick up that rainbow sequin belt at the thrift shop for her after the big alarm installation job pays off. That and brigadeiros might make good holiday gifts.*

Wyn flushed, her attention diverted. "Two things. One is a necklace charm that puts my blond-woman illusion on me when I activate it. The second... My purse holds a lot more now, without being heavier than a wallet. It's great for serious shopping or groceries or a used-book sale. That one was almost accidental, as theoretically, it should be impossible, but it worked anyway."

"That sounds amazing. Think of all the supplies you can carry without having your balance compromised. How great would that be climbing? That's the coolest use of magic I've ever heard," Zita enthused in all honesty.

With a visible headshake, Wyn said, "That's all irrelevant. I may be unable to eradicate the dagger's enchantment."

Only partially joking, Zita suggested, "Well, if I steal the haft and get the blade back, we can hide them in your enchanted purse." *It'd be hard to explain in Confession, but if the alternative is a magical nuke, I'll take it.*

Wyn opened her mouth, then closed it, her face thoughtful. An abrupt scowl darkened her face, and she shook her head. "No, I'm not putting a nasty dagger that grows stronger with blood into my purse so it can stab me multiple times a day."

"That might be a problem," Zita agreed. "What if we put it into a sheath or bubble wrap and tape it shut? Duct tape's right here." She held up the roll she had worn during their escape. *Maybe the kittens will terrorize it into compliance.*

Her friend grimaced. Wyn said, "The puissance that I felt today is more than even the mighty duct tape can handle."

Zita frowned. *Puissance? She must mean the strength of the magic.* "How is that possible? I mean, it's duct tape. That stuff's better than gold. Well, dependent on the amounts, I guess, because a single strip may not beat a humongous chunk of gold that you could use to buy more tape."

Wyn's answer was cut off by the clunk of multiple deadbolts.

"Hi, Quentin," Zita said, greeting him before their presence alarmed him. She glanced at the clock and shook her head. *Two a.m.? Guess I was right to move his schedule around to start his first meeting around nine. Also, these two need to go to bed earlier.*

Her brother grinned at her, exhibiting the smile they had both inherited from their father and straightening his shoulders. The rest of his face resembled a masculine version of their mother's imperious Quechua features, softened by their father's grin and his geniality. "Zita, we're both here and awake for once. Hi, Wyn, a pleasure to see you as always." Quentin drew Zita into a hug, finishing with a gentle bump on her arm.

She returned the hug, then sotto voice, she said, "Check your voicemail from me."

He must have already listened to it, because his smile faltered and he lowered his head, letting his fashionably shaggy bangs fall in his face.

Wyn stood and kissed his cheek. "Quentin, it's wonderful to see you again. I hope you're doing well." Other than the pinched line between her eyebrows, her countenance wore its usual serene expression.

"No complaints here," he said, though the dark shadows gathered beneath his eyes belied the truth of his statement. Also, his face had the scraggly brush that told Zita he had skipped shaving for a few days. *Not like him.* His tone was upbeat, even jaunty, but she wondered if Wyn heard the forced notes in it. "How are the cats? I can see you're as lovely as always."

A smile came to Wyn's lips, and the anxiety in her posture eased. "The cats are well, always in trouble. They get smarter every day, and the world is only safe from their domination by their sloth." She seated herself, inhaled the steam from her cup, and drank.

Another of his grins teased one in return from Zita's friend. "So, average cats then. Glad they're doing well. Zita, I've got bad news. Luis called, and his employer has decided against updating their alarm system or at least that's the line he's giving us." Quentin made no comment that the job had been given to a different company because of her flub on the date.

Zita sat back down in her chair and picked up her mug, staring at the greenish sludge inside. *Oye, he doesn't have to say why. I know. Maybe if I get lucky, this fiasco will stop Quentin from messing with my love life. My brothers need to remember I'm a grown woman, not the kid they had to babysit all the time.* "It wasn't my fault. I did try," she blurted. *Crap, that sounded childish.*

Quentin cleared his throat. "Since we lost the sale of the high-end home stuff, I can't use you on Thursday or Friday as originally scheduled. We'll have some fill-in stuff here and there, and I'll throw it your way when I can."

I won't be able to get Wyn that belt. Zita set her mug down so hard that tea sloshed over the edge in a wash of floral-scented liquid. At the splash of tepid liquid on her fingers, she swore. "Not blaming you, but I need the money. I'm still not getting enough hours—from you or the tax preparation office. You should at least have me coming in more to straighten your accounts out if you plan to keep neglecting them." She exhaled, rose, and stomped over to get a dishrag.

Wyn seemed invested in staring at the remains of her tea.

Guilt flashed over his face, but her brother shrugged. "You know what I told you before. If you can't commit to full time, I can only give you so many hours. My other workers are full timers with families to support. I'll see if I can squeeze in a few more for you, but unless business picks up, my hands are tied."

"At this point, anything helps, so thanks," Zita said, shooting him a rueful smile. "Sorry about the thing with Luis."

Quentin waved his hand. "Nobody got hurt. Given your track record, I didn't expect too much from it, but I'm glad you took my advice after the date."

"What advice is that? To not accept blind dates with your clients before they've paid the invoice and had the system installed? You never said anything like that." Zita wiped off the table and the cup. *If I had to spill, it's a shame I didn't lose more*, she thought.

Half-lidded, his eyes showed a subdued twinkle, "Why, to find a real woman to teach you some game." Quentin winked at Wyn.

An evil smile rose to Wyn's rosebud lips. "Her performance does require improvement, doesn't it? I suppose I can give her some tips, but she requires more drastic intervention than mere guidance."

Quentin punched Zita's shoulder, a light touch. "Oye, don't take it so hard. Eventually, you'll learn how to talk to nice boys without injuring them, falling asleep, or showing them up. Do you need some huggies?"

Zita wrinkled her nose and made a face at both of them. "With help like that? No thanks."

With a beatific smile, he hugged her anyway.

Zita gave her brother a one-armed squeeze back, her mouth quirking into a half smile. Even if she was relieved to see both Wyn and Quentin in a teasing mood, she was not about to comment on it and risk shattering the delicate joviality. She wrung out the wet rag with more vigor than necessary over the sink, rinsing it before hanging it to dry. "I got game," she protested, "Maybe I'm choosing just not to bring it all. Neta, don't want to overwhelm the poor things with my awesomeness."

"I'm certain you'll keep telling yourself that," Quentin said.

Wyn giggled and covered her mouth with a hand.

Haters, the both of them. It's a relief to see them smile, though. "If you're done harassing me, make sure you do up all the locks. Someone broke into Wyn's house tonight, so she's here for a few days. We were finishing our tea and going to bed." *Or at least I am.* She tweaked the cloth, so the edges were even.

He made a series of horrified exclamations that Zita suspected were perfect because they soothed Wyn like little else had.

Zita took mental notes. When he was done, and the conversation had stuttered to a stop, she said the first thing she could think of. "Try to remember not to leave your nasty underwear on the bathroom floor again. I don't need to be handling that."

Perhaps something in Zita's injunction to her brother had disturbed Wyn, because she bid the Garcia siblings a hasty good night, dumped out the rest of her tea, and disappeared into the bedroom.

After a check to ensure her friend had really left the room, Zita emptied her full cup of the floral abomination into the sink.

Quentin checked the locks, dropped his keys and wallet on the table, and fetched his pillow from under the futon.

Walking over to him, Zita lowered her voice and spoke in the rapid-fire Spanglish that had been their habit as children. "By the way, Wyn's two cats are here somewhere. Don't shoot them or

Wyn with the gun you've been stashing under the futon cushion. If you want, you can hide it behind the television in the bird armoire, and take the key to lock it. I'd rather not have a gun sitting loose under the cushions like that, especially when others are visiting."

Quentin punched the pillow to fluff it and tossed it on the futon. He wouldn't meet her eyes. "Thanks for the warning."

"No problem, mano. Also, you owe me for a full day's work today. No weaseling out of it, since I worked my culo off getting your accounts back in order and filing."

Her brother smirked and finally raised his eyes to her. "You'd have to have an ass to work it off."

She called him a rude name while he laughed. As she pocketed the paper with the name of the owner of the haft, most of her attention was on a plan forming to take care of the Key of Hades. After another quick hug, she headed to her room before Wyn could claim the entire bed. Zita paused in the doorway, remembering she had to stash the athame still taped to her leg. "Oh, you keep leaving the range light on all night. Please turn it off when you're done with it. My bosses don't give me enough hours to waste money on electric bills."

Chapter Eight

Andy made it to Zita's apartment by eight o'clock, a bag swinging from one wrist and a box in his arms. Wyn had still been sleeping. The alluring scent of donuts rising from the carton made him Zita's most welcome visitor in days. Despite the weariness set into his shoulders like a cloak, he seemed alert enough for someone who had dozed on a train all night. After all Wyn's attention to his wardrobe, he was back in "uniform": jeans and a black T-shirt, this one emblazoned with three howling wolves and the moon.

Quentin stole a cream-filled donut with sprinkles and took off.

Wyn dressed, made another whispered phone call, and "put on her face" (the arcane ritual of makeup). By the time she emerged, Andy had showered and was chatting with Zita over the crumbs of their donuts.

Wyn smiled at Andy. "Andy! How are you? How was your date?"

"She said hello first," Zita commented. "Morning, Wyn. Hot water in the kettle on the stove."

Andy chuckled. "I'm not certain that counts as a hello. Hi, Wyn. It went well."

Preparing herself tea, Wyn drifted over to the table and settled into her chair. "Were you two betting again?"

Zita widened her eyes. "Who, us?" She struggled not to wrinkle her nose at the whiff she caught of Wyn's tea. *I eat a lot of vegetables, but that stuff. Ugh. Best not to look directly at her mug, in case it senses my fear or she offers me a cup.*

"I'm totally bringing Zita a large Gatorade at our next sparring session out of the goodness of my heart," Andy said, trying to suppress his amusement.

Wyn sniffed, but her mouth quirked into a smile. "You two are terrible. Since I'm apparently predictable, please do share details, Andy." She took a small cruller.

He shrugged. "It went really well. We had an awkward patch near the beginning, but Zita sent a picture of her finger and half of a bird. Brandi thought that was hilarious, which broke the ice, then we started talking about her research and things went really well after that."

Once Wyn finished picking apart her donut, she recounted the robberies and the information about the Key for Andy. Following that, Zita paced and described the events on the island. Her friends had not been happy to learn about the fight with the wolf, with Wyn turning bloodless at the memory of Steroid Dog in her home. When the conversation finally turned to doing something, Zita had stopped herself from cheering with difficulty. Her joy was short-lived, however, when a blaring ringtone announced another call for Wyn.

"I'll get an unregistered phone and be back in a minute," Zita said.

Wyn gave a sharp nod, listening to whoever spoke on her phone. Andy grunted from where he bent over Zita's laptop, searching for the haft owner's phone number.

Zita strode down the hall to her exercise room. In any other apartment, it would have been the master bedroom, but she had her priorities. Grabbing an aerial silk hanging from the ceiling, she pulled it along its track until it reached the spot she wanted. The collection of second-hand mirrors lining one wall reflected her short, quick movements climbing until she held her body parallel to the ceiling. She indulged in a quick spin, keeping her body tight to avoid hitting the wall. The room blurred into an indistinct mass of silver and black (her exercise equipment) against the bright turquoise of the walls as she went faster and faster. *I could teleport, but this way is more fun.* Begrudgingly, she quit playing and got back into position. After twining the silks around her legs, she stretched out and moved one of the fake plants on the shelf above the mirrors.

Glancing back at the kitchen, she opened the secret storage cubby she had installed two weeks ago in a fit of underemployed boredom and borderline paranoia. She dug through the contents, selecting one of the two cell phones, a phone battery for it, and two masks. A blue smiley-face sticker laughed up at her from the phone in her hand. After hiding the rest away again, she reluctantly slid down to the ground, replaced the silks, and returned to the kitchen.

Andy still curled over her laptop, scrolling down a screen and making huffy, snorting sounds. A cartoon might have flashed by, but her other friend's behavior distracted her before she could ask.

Wyn's attention centered on her phone, though the screen was dark. Although her posture remained perfect, she had twined a lock of hair around a finger and been winding it. The tip of the finger showed white.

"You okay, Wyn?" Zita said, hoping the answer was yes. She set the phone and battery on the table and stuffed the masks into a pocket, snapping it shut so nothing would fall out. *Cargo pants are one of man's most perfect inventions.*

Wyn's hand stopped moving, and the curl unwound from her finger. She lifted her head, calm sliding over her face. "I'm fine."

Must have misread her. "Okay." Zita moved on to the problem of the Key. "Andy? You with us?" When he glanced up, she continued speaking, "Here's the phone we called the cops on before. You want me to call from the National Mall again?"

Andy closed the web browser and scribbled on a piece of paper. "You're overcomplicating things. Wyn can call as a concerned victim of the other robberies, and then we can back off."

"If an unknown person calls claiming someone is going to steal an antique doohickey, which then gets stolen, any cop with a brain will trace the call. If they do, calling from elsewhere ensures the trail doesn't lead back to where Wyn's staying if the thieves have an inside man," Zita said.

"Don't be paranoid. They're thieves. We have no reason to think they have a corrupt cop abetting their misdeeds," Wyn snapped.

Ay, she's back to being mad at me again. Awesome. Wish I could figure out what her problem is. Zita raised an eyebrow and cocked her head at her friend. "We have no reason to think they don't. Fine, Wyn can call from her phone, but not from here, in case I'm right. I'll put this phone away." *After I call Remus for my plan. Just warning owners won't be enough.*

After a pause, the others agreed.

Wyn's phone buzzed, and she snatched it. Her posture relaxed after reading the screen, and she sent a text. "I need to identify what was stolen, pick up a few more things from my house, and take pictures for the insurance company. Once we finish up with that, we have an appointment at the diner down the street from my place. Jerome texted to set it up. He has a professional contact, a private detective from New York who wants to hear what happened last night. Apparently, his friend is searching for a missing person who might be connected to the thieves."

Zita grimaced, remembering the malevolent glee in Steroid Dog's voice as he suggested killing Wyn. Anger poured through her. *He probably held off killing her right away for the power kick of having her trapped and afraid first. The odds don't favor the missing person's chances of being alive if they made him angry. Oye, if I have to eat out, I'll have to get cash from the machine. This is blowing my budget to pieces.* "I guess you can call from there, too, as they already know where it is. Andy, can you take Wyn to her place? I'll meet you there after I make a stop."

★★★

At Wyn's house, the three friends (and Wyn's insurance agent) waited while a police officer verified they were allowed inside. Approval gained, they entered, with a uniformed cop trailing after them to note missing items.

Wyn's serenity cracked as they entered the living room, where even the overturned sofa had not escaped unscathed, springs and stuffing visible through long rents in the scarlet fabric. Her voice trembled as she spoke, indicating missing or destroyed items. When the small parade moved to inventory another area, Zita stayed behind in the front rooms.

Since the police were finished with the living room and kitchen, Zita threw herself into cleaning and fixing those two rooms. She did a partial shift to canine as soon as the others left, remaining mostly human, but with increased senses just in case. It did take a couple of tries to do so without any obvious external signs, but fortunately, a smashed mirrored platter helped her judge the shifts. To liven up the work, Zita practiced isolating and understanding scents as she sorted, bagged, and cleaned. She marinated in the scent of crime scene techs and cops until she could distinguish every individual who had been there. They all seemed to snack immediately before entering as the scents of five different types of scorched bargain coffee lingered. As an added benefit, the reek of the overturned garbage and spoiled food did not bother her.

Eventually, Wyn returned to the living room. "We need to get going—" She stopped dead, then she moved forward as if in a trance, to trace the gilt edges of a large photo of herself and her aunt. The frame had fallen behind a bookcase and been spared from the damage that had cracked the glass on most of the other portraits in the room. "Zita?"

The insurance agent skirted around her and slipped out.

Zita beamed and packed up her friend's puny little toolbox. *Not bad work for a morning, especially with the limited equipment here.* "Almost back how you had it, sí? Television was ruined, but I thought you'd like your picture while you save for a new one. Trash is outside. The box over there is loot you might want even if it's broken or that might be repairable. You didn't have the right glue for the cups, but I sorted the larger pieces in case they were fixable and put them in sandwich bags for you. Your linens need washing, but they were mostly white so bleach should remove the stains. In the kitchen, most of the stuff that was broken was at waist height or lower, so you didn't lose as much as it seemed at first. Most of your flower cups survived since they were in the upper cabinets. Sofa's fine if you don't check the back. I taped it so the tears shouldn't spread. Let it air out to get rid of the rest of the stench and cleanser, and you're good to go." *Your creepy happy kitten duct tape ended up being useful, if frightening.*

Tears sprang to Wyn's eyes, and she folded Zita in a silent embrace.

With an encouraging pat or two on the back, Zita slipped out of her friend's grasp. Her voice gruff, she said, "Yeah, well. Hope it's okay."

"Yes, it's great," Wyn sniffled.

Andy bumped Zita's shoulder and smiled. "I'm glad to see you using your anal-retentive cleaning powers for good," he murmured.

She punched his biceps, knowing it wouldn't hurt him. "Make a housekeeping joke and die."

He clutched his arm dramatically where she had hit him, and they laughed.

When they finally emerged, blinking into the bright afternoon sunlight, Zita stopped in the vandalized doorway. "I know a guy who can fix this up with a couple coats of paint and putty, and I can do your locks. Momentito," she said, tracing her fingers over the jagged claw marks in the wood. Taking a moment, Zita inhaled deeply. The doorway held other scents, ones she had not expected. Familiar ones, almost buried under the acrid sting of the fingerprint powder. "Bizarre."

"What?" Andy asked.

After a glance to ensure the (very bored) policeman was not eavesdropping, Zita murmured, "I smell a bear and..."

"And?" Wyn prompted her.

Freelance. "SWAT Ninja man, you know, that mercenary I ran into when we were trying to rescue Quentin. Outside only, neither one went inside." Out of habit, Zita scanned the area. Redbud trees, leaves tinting toward yellow, leaned over rows of parked cars and the occasional motorcycle, including her own. Behind Andy's rusty blue sedan, a white vehicle had multiple people sitting inside. Two uniformed patrol officers headed toward the house, wariness in their gazes as they eyed the three friends standing in the doorway.

"The imaginary friend you kept running into everywhere and nobody else ever saw, even when he supposedly shot a truck in front of a couple SWAT teams?" Wyn asked. She moved to the side to allow the police to pass, and her friends did the same.

Zita wrinkled her nose. *Put like that, it makes me sound crazy. Maybe she's jealous. He did have a sweet grapple gun. I still want that toy so bad.* "Nice. Yeah." Farther from the house, the warm breeze carried the odors of wood smoke and baking bread. Her stomach rumbled.

Wyn frowned and fidgeted with the canvas handle of the tote bag she held. "Perhaps you need more practice with your olfactory senses. One of the policemen likely has a similar scent, or it could be the wolf. A whiff of fur is a whiff of fur."

At that, Zita snorted. "Trust me, I may be the new canine on the block, but I can tell a dog from a bear. And no, it really isn't." *And Freelance has his own unique scent.*

Probably hoping to avoid another argument, Andy cleared his throat and jerked his chin at Wyn's car. "Zita's imaginary friends aside, Wyn, would you like a ride to the diner?" He put a comforting hand on Wyn's shoulder and squeezed.

They all surveyed the vehicle. It would be going nowhere until someone figured out how to remove the stone spear that impaled it through the driver's seat and out the roof. Wyn's lower lip trembled.

Ignoring Andy's dig, Zita patted Wyn's other shoulder awkwardly and then withdrew her hand. "You could ride with me to the diner, if you want," she offered. *She's never accepted any of my offers to ride my bike before, but there's a first time for everything.*

With an appreciative smile, Wyn nodded to Andy. "That will be fine, Andy. I hate to make you go all the way to DC, though," she said.

Andy shrugged and let his hand drop. "It's not a problem. You live close enough to the DC border that it shouldn't take too much time, but will it be all right if I leave you there? The glamorous life of a postdoc calls. I've got to meet with a professor about lab lesson plans as he's late giving them to me. You shouldn't have any problems getting a cab or rideshare."

"I'll take her home," Zita offered. "She's safer with me than with an unknown cabbie."

His expression was dubious. "Wyn?"

She gave him a smile. "Don't worry about it. We're both going to the same place, anyway."

"But..." Andy closed his mouth and shrugged. He hefted three large floral suitcases and a bag of cat kibble, taped shut with more cavorting kitten tape. "If you say so. I'll drop off her luggage later. Let's get a move on."

***

A delightful mélange of meaty burgers, pancakes, and a whiff of chocolate greeted them as Zita and Wyn entered the diner, twenty minutes early for their rendezvous. Lined with matching stools, a long silver bar with red neon accents took up one long wall and barred the path to the kitchens. Chairs and tables crowded against all the other available walls, with a narrow opening to the tiny, dark corridor that housed the restrooms and emergency exit. Most of the seats were occupied. Waitresses in sensible shoes and pink-striped uniforms hurried between patrons and the kitchen, too tired to run, too busy to walk. A sign, lined with tinsel, invited them to seat themselves.

Zita chose a chair at a table near the restrooms and kitchen, her back to the wall, and gestured for Wyn to sit beside her. *So far, so good,* she thought, as her eyes darted around the room, assessing it. This close to the kitchen, she could hear the occasional barked command, though the loud hum of patrons talking and eating rendered any words unintelligible.

Her friend obeyed, though her nose wrinkled, and she gazed covetously at the booths lining the cheery windows. In comparison to the partial shadow of their table, the ones Wyn wanted were awash in brilliant sunlight, with the bright colors of the cars outside visible through the window. "Here? There's a cute little table right over there..."

"No, we got the ideal seat in the house for our purposes. From here, we can go out the kitchen or emergency exit if necessary, and it's separate enough that others can't hear our conversations without being obvious." Noticing her friend's unconvinced look, she continued. "Plus, it's got chairs we can get out of fast and use as weapons if needed. Given that you have been the victim of two break-ins in the past week, caution would be wise."

Her friend stared at her. "Who thinks like that in real life? We're not in an action movie. Is this about the people you thought you smelled at my house?"

My family thinks like that, or at least we used to. Young women who enjoy wandering South America on their own do too. Keep quiet, don't attract attention, and plan your exits. A corner of Zita's mouth curled up, even as she fought down sadness and stomped on it. *Past and gone. Keep moving forward,* she reminded herself. "People who want to survive to do the next crazy ass stunt. No hay bronca, I mean, no worries. I got your back. If I'm over-cautious, you can always tease me about it later."

Wyn picked up a laminated menu and hummed. "You can count on that." A placid smile hovered around her lips.

"Yeah, that's what I thought. No love, I tell you," Zita grumbled, but she smiled and scoped out her own meal.

***

Zita had been unobtrusively watching three men seated near the front entrance, trying to decide whether their staring was rudeness and admiration, or rudeness and ill intentions. Movement at the door attracted her attention as a duo entered. One face was familiar. "Is that Jerome and his friend?"

"Can't be. Jerome's tardiness is a universal constant, and we got here early," Wyn said as she stirred obscene amounts of sugar into her iced tea. She had discounted Zita's suspicions about the men nursing coffee by the front door as paranoia.

Zita had ignored the dismissal; she was fairly certain Wyn was in denial after spending the morning at her trashed house. "Impossible and unlikely have been pretty possible since May," she said, waving to Jerome. When she allowed herself to think about it, the coincidence that had reunited Jerome, Andy, Wyn, Zita, and Aideen, all survivors of the same experimental gene therapy group, at the same hospital during the quarantine still bothered her. At least Zita, Wyn, and Andy had been able to finish the quarantine in her apartment following the attack that left the hospital uninhabitable. They'd all awakened from the still-unknown sleeping sickness with powers and had chosen to hide them. Although she knew Jerome's secret power, she doubted he (or Aideen) knew about her, Wyn, or Andy.

"Even blind pigs can find that acorn, I suppose," Wyn murmured from the side of her mouth as she lifted a hand in greeting as well.

"He's a private detective. You'd hope he could find something," Zita pointed out.

Jerome raised a huge paw and strolled toward them. Zita enjoyed watching. Even if he wasn't her type, Jerome in motion reflected his boxing training, quick and light on his feet despite the impressive breadth of his shoulders. Age, as well as considerable athletic training, had pared down the chubby, cartoon-obsessed teenager to a muscular man, made more appealing by his perpetual good humor. White teeth, framed by a perfectly groomed Van Dyke beard, flashed in brilliant contrast to his skin as he smiled at them. A sturdy Asian man trailed behind him.

Beside her, Wyn rose from her seat. "Jerome! Wonderful to see you," she said, holding out her arms and hugging him. She gave him a cursory peck on his cheek.

Standing up, Zita grinned up at six-foot-plus Jerome. "Oye, it's been forever," she said, as they bumped fists.

Jerome laughed and surprised her with a quick one-armed hug. "Girls! How have you been? Wyn, looking fine as always. Zita, have you been beating up all the bigger kids again?"

For a panicked moment, Zita assumed he had deduced that she was Arca. Her pulse racing, she made herself laugh. After a return squeeze, she released him and stepped away. "No, been waiting to kick your butt first before I take on all the others. You know, start with the weak link to lull everyone else into complacency. So, you called? You in a hurry to lose that sparring match you promised?"

He snickered and clapped her on her shoulder. "You wish, Tinker Bell. We'll get to that match someday, and I'll try not to grind you into the dust too hard." Jerome jabbed his thumb toward the silent man waiting beside him. "Listen, my buddy here's working on a case connected to whatever happened to Wyn the other day. Now, we could go and check the official records, but I figured my friends would prefer to tell it how it is. Anyway, Yi Shen, or Hound as the rest of us call him, has some questions. He and his business partner run a detective agency in New York. If they can't find someone, they're not on the planet."

"As usual, Jerome exaggerates," Hound said. "Thank you for taking the time to meet with us." His voice was low and resonant.

Wyn inclined her head and proffered a hand. Although her voice was pleasant as she greeted Hound, her demeanor had cooled to the same gracious reserve she presented to all strangers. "The pleasure is mine. I'm Ellynwyn Diamond, but you may call me Wyn."

While they shook hands, Zita studied the newcomer. Built tall and broad, if not quite so wide as Jerome, Hound moved with the lazy pace of his namesake animal, even down to the slight quiver in his jowls that suggested leashed energy within, held in preparation for a hunt. His movements showed no particular physical prowess or lack thereof, but his shirt had a worn spot in the place where a shoulder holster would hang. Once Miguel had joined the FBI, his clothing showed the same wear pattern. Despite his round, youthful face, quiet manners, and economical movements, Hound's brown eyes were tired and cynical as he studied them. His assessment was detached and did not linger on her breasts or Wyn's legs. A pale, worn band of gold coiled around his left ring finger. She thought she might like him.

When he turned to her, Zita introduced herself. "Zita Garcia, hey. You picked a good place. They make a mean steak and eggs here, and the sandwiches are delicious, too. Lots of meat." She plopped back down.

Jerome grinned. "Trust you to be familiar with all the local eateries."

"Woman's got to eat."

When Wyn settled herself back in her seat, albeit more gracefully, the men took the two remaining chairs. Hound, Zita was amused to note, set his chair at a slight angle to have a better field of view. Jerome dropped into his chair and sat, legs wide.

Both men declined to order lunch, though they waited patiently as the waitress delivered food for Zita and Wyn. Jerome stole a fry from Zita's plate.

"Thank you both for agreeing to meet us here. I regret any inconvenience. Do you mind if I record our conversation for my partner? She doesn't travel," Hound said. He ignored the flagrant fry theft.

Wyn caught Zita's eye. *Do you have any issues with that, oh paranoid one?*

I don't like it, but I can't think of any reason to say no, Zita replied. She gave a nod but narrowed her eyes at Jerome, who smiled back and chomped down.

"We're fine with that," Wyn said. "Though I'm not certain how we can help with your case? If you're from New York, I don't know how our troubles would have a bearing on anything there."

Hound sighed as he set a rectangular recording device on the table between them. "I'm not at liberty to divulge my client, but I'm searching for a missing person. We have reason to believe the individuals who ransacked your office may be holding the young woman prisoner."

Wyn's face softened, and one hand touched her mouth. "The poor thing. Of course, we'll help."

"Thank you. Miss Garcia, were you with Miss Diamond when her office was broken into?" he asked.

Zita shook her head. "No, I have a life."

At the same time, Wyn replied, "No, just for the second time."

Hound's attention sharpened. "Excellent. More witnesses are always better. So, can you tell me what happened, Miss Diamond?"

Wyn raised an elegant shoulder and dropped it. "Did you want the first time or the second?"

"Both, please, and take your time. I understand this is an unpleasant memory for you," he said. Hound settled in as if for a long wait.

In response to his obvious sympathy, Wyn relaxed a little. "I was working on a project for a professor, and he requested additional information. When I went to deliver it, I found him bleeding on the floor of his office." She paused and closed her eyes.

Hound waited with far more patience than Zita or Jerome, both of whom fidgeted.

Wyn took a deep breath and continued. "While I was en route, my office was ransacked, and my computer was stolen."

"What were you working on for the professor?" Hound asked.

She hesitated. "He had asked for background information on the history and mythos of the Key of Hades, a Greek relic. The university recently acquired a blade he believed to be part of the Key, and the professor's research was hampered by his refusal to use electronic resources. The thieves took my computer and the file for the professor's project."

Hound's head tilted. "Why would the Key be of interest to them?"

"Because they're obsessed with an old, broken knife? We have no clue," Zita offered.

"An ancient artifact, Zita. It's interesting and valuable, but the university certainly has older items of greater monetary and historical worth," Wyn corrected. Wielding her utensils delicately, she cut her salad, a concoction of local vegetables, into minuscule pieces.

Zita waved her fork in the air, a chunk of steak on the tip. "Right, a super old knife with a history. They might believe the cutlery is magic because it's got a fancy name and a supposed tie to mythology." She popped the bite into her mouth and chewed.

Jerome tilted his head sideways and gave Hound an amused smile. "Man, I thought you specialized in missing persons, not weird stuff." He stole another fry.

Hound steepled his fingers. "My partner favors the outré cases. Interesting. So, what of the second attempt?"

"I don't even know how you heard about that since we filed our statements just this morning," Wyn said. "Zita stopped by because the university thing spooked me. We were in the basement looking for old pictures when we heard them break in." She stopped, setting down her fork. Her face was serene, but her fingers twisted together in her lap and a minor tremor ran through her.

To give Wyn a moment to recover, Zita snorted. "We're not a couple, by the way." She was gratified when both men switched their attention from her flustered friend. Taking a bite, she chewed slowly to prolong it.

Jerome guffawed. "This could be entertaining."

Hound paused. "I see. Ah, I don't know if it's relevant, but okay."

Wyn buried her face in her hands, shook her head, and gave Zita a dirty look.

At least she's stopped trembling. "What? He has to have spoken to the cop or seen her notes, and she was all full of assumptions," Zita said. She gave a half-shrug, and then addressed Hound. "I wanted to clear things up, so you don't go barking up the wrong trees. If you're a decent PI, you'll know the cops told us we can't be too specific, especially since the house is still a crime scene."

"House?" Hound said. "I was referring to the second robbery at the university."

Well, if he didn't know before... Zita thought with an internal wince. "Yeah. The burglary and attempted assault at Wyn's place last night. What are you talking about?" She menaced Jerome with her fork when he went after another fry. Pointing it at him, she warned him, "Jerome, you're living life dangerously there, hombre. You really want to try me? Buy your own."

Jerome snickered.

"Two separate groups raided Miss Diamond's office," Hound said.

Wyn nearly dropped the weed she was eating. "Wait, more than one band of malefactors violated my office?" she squeaked.

Way to throw down with the thesaurus, amiga, Zita thought. *Couldn't you say asshole like everyone else? Did you actually pay to eat dandelions?* When Wyn's eyes snapped to her and narrowed, Zita concentrated on eating. *And apparently, I'm not alone in my brain. Shutting up now.* She quashed her annoyance.

"The police didn't mention it?" Hound asked.

Wyn shook her head.

Hound pursed his lips, smoothing a finger over his chin as if stroking a nonexistent beard. "University security cameras caught two men entering your office and exiting with your laptop. Shortly after that, three people, including an unusually tall man, went into your office and ransacked your files, then left with a folder."

Staring at her salad, Wyn pushed around a yellow tomato with her fork. "I had no idea. Someone broke into my house early this morning, and Zita and I escaped before they got us. One of them was Brobdingnagian. You can talk to the police for any more as we're not supposed to give out details."

Hound's eyebrows lifted. "Brobding..."

Wyn sighed. "A man of excessive height."

Jerome stole another fry, calling Zita's bluff.

She didn't stab him, but she did kick him.

"Ow." He smirked and ate as Hound continued his patient questioning.

Chapter Nine

An hour later, Jerome and his companion had departed, and the two women stood outside the restaurant.

"Why are we stopping here? And why did we leave our money on the table and sneak out the emergency exit?" Wyn asked.

Sunlight sparkled on the purple and orange paint of Zita's motorcycle, dancing over and reflecting off the silvery metal panniers. Warmed by the sun, the steel saddlebags were hot to the touch as Zita unlocked them. "We're going back to my place, and I'd rather those creeps who were maybe watching us don't follow." She retrieved her helmet and offered the spare to her friend.

Eyeing the helmet, Wyn shook her head. "Somehow, I didn't realize you only had the motorcycle, though that does explain why you let me drive so often. I'll call a cab."

Zita rolled her eyes. "Come on, live a little. It's a gorgeous day, the street's dry, and I'll drive gently for your sake. It's not rush hour yet, so the roads won't be too crowded once we get out of DC." She cast an eye toward the restaurant, down the rows of cars. The only other motorcycles were three crotch rockets, clearly unloved by their owners, given their boring paint jobs and mud-splattered license plates.

Her friend took the helmet, turning it over and over, and her lips turned downward. "I don't think I want to try, Zita."

After lowering the passenger foot pegs into place, Zita gave the grab straps a quick tug to make certain they hadn't been jarred loose.

When she got out her gloves, she spotted their watchers exiting the diner and scanning the area. One nudged the others and pointed to the two women.

"Time's up." She crammed the spare helmet atop her friend's chestnut curls. "We don't have a choice. Our buddies from the restaurant are onto us." A glance over her shoulder confirmed that the men had sped up their walk. A sleek white sedan pulled out, blocking one end of the street, and the watchers began a slow drift their direction. The lunch she had eaten in the restaurant sat in her stomach like a lump as she mounted and started her bike.

Wyn said, "I've never ridden one..." She glanced back at the men, her eyes going unfocused, then stiffened. "They're with a human supremacy group, and they couldn't get anything off my work machine." Gulping, she turned back to Zita, her eyes dilating with fear. "They want to interrogate me, not in a polite way, and beat the 'freaks' to the Key. My survival is not a major factor in their calculations."

Zita pointed to sections of the motorcycle. "It's part of mine. Don't touch those, they'll get hot. Butt goes there. Feet stay on those pegs and don't set them down until I signal you. Keep your visor closed. Sit straight with your shoulders lined up to mine and hang on tight. I'm going to ignore the whole leisurely drive thing. Hurry!" She jammed on her own helmet and revved the bike, listening to see if the engine was warm enough.

"Got it." Game, despite the tremble in her voice, Wyn closed the helmet face shield and gingerly swung a long leg over the bike.

As soon as her friend's arms slid around her, Zita revved the engine again. Hearing the right purr, she turned to avoid the white sedan. The men from the restaurant ran toward her, and the sedan proved its complicity by speeding up. To her dismay, the men made a beeline for the sports bikes.

Zita drove faster, trying to get away from the crowded streets with all their obstructions and debris. She could feel her friend, several inches taller than Zita, trying to burrow into her back.

Zita focused on driving and the feel of her bike vibrating beneath her. An on- and off-road model, it lacked the higher speeds available in a sports bike, not that any of them could go maximum speed in this area. Making use of its advantage on city streets, the sedan seemed to be trying to nuzzle her exhaust pipes. Despite the way her helmet reduced sound and the roar of her adrenaline, she could hear the whiny buzz of the faster bikes catching up. Wyn's grip on her waist was so tight she feared she'd have bruises on her stomach tomorrow, and her friend seemed to lean the wrong direction on every turn.

Zita cut across a lane and made a sharp right.

Tires squealed behind her as their pursuers followed her, but at least she had purchased a few more feet between them.

If the car gives us even a light bump, Wyn and I are hosed, and they'll walk away unharmed. Of course, if I mess up correcting for her, we're both smears on the road as well. So far, so good, but luck never holds. At the sight of a length of unoccupied roadway, she opened the throttle, increasing speed. Inwardly, she kvetched as she cut tight around a corner seconds later. *How is a woman supposed to drive with so many people on the sidewalks?* A mailbox whizzed by so close that she could have tapped it had she wanted. Her tricks won her more space still, but she took a deep breath, watching for a chance to escape the populous streets without being herded onto the highways where she'd be at a disadvantage or having to do too many more rapid turns. Despite her helmet, Wyn's screaming behind her was audible, if not intelligible.

Finally, Zita saw their chance. *Hang on*, she thought, and zipped up a curb ramp onto a sidewalk again, losing speed as she went. As soon as she could do so safely, she stopped short as if trying to avoid hitting a trashcan. Her head jerked forward, and pain stung her as Wyn's helmet clunked the back of hers.

Police sirens went off when two of the bikes rocketed by, and, lights strobing, a squad car pulled out a block down and chased them. Her remaining two pursuers, one bike and the sedan, slowed, no doubt thinking they had her cornered.

She turned, slapping a foot down on the pavement for a tight 180, and then took off back the way they had come, charging down the curb cut and toward the car.

The sedan's brakes squealed, and she darted aside before they could collide, kicking her engine into a higher gear on the straightaway. As soon as she squeezed a street-hugging turn around another corner, she reduced speed, hunched her shoulders, and drove off the road into a park, slipping between concrete pillars. Zita prayed the sweltering heat would keep people off the paths.

From behind her, she heard a lot of honking, and a flick of her eyes at her rearview mirrors showed she had lost all but one, the last of the sports bikes. He had overshot the entrance, however, so she had several seconds lead before he could turn onto the paved path.

Zita roared around a curve, and then turned down the first unpaved path she saw while out of the other motorcycle's line of sight. Exultation filled her, as she automatically shifted position to smooth the ride over the uneven gravel surface. She tried to adjust Wyn's arms, but her friend clung too tightly to do so without hurting her. *Guess I don't need all those ribs.*

In deference to her passenger, any pedestrians, and the rough track beneath her tires, Zita decelerated again once enough trees hid her from the main path. She turned down multiple trails—the rockier the better—before veering off the last one and cutting around a swamp, keeping to the boundaries of the marshy area. Water splashed over her legs as her tires flirted with the edge of a trickle of river, a welcome respite from the heat radiating from her bike, even though she knew it would have consequences. *Try and follow that trail, pendejos,* she thought. When a frog attempted suicide by motorcycle, she jerked the bike out of the way, tires skidding in the slimy mud. She fought the slide and kept their balance.

Another shriek penetrated her helmet from her passenger, who still hadn't figured out how to sit properly.

When Zita was satisfied they had enough distance between their pursuers and themselves, she emerged from the park, deftly slithering between trees into a fast-food parking lot. Exiting at a marked exit would have risked finding their pursuers (or the police) waiting for them. She brought her bike to a stop and signaled her friend.

Wyn hurled herself off the bike, ripping the borrowed helmet from her head and flinging it to the ground. She staggered to the curb and sat, her head cradled between her knees. Her shoulders heaved.

Removing her own headgear, Zita ran her fingers through her short hair, unsurprised to find it damp. She dismounted, grinning like an idiot, and tried to calm her racing pulse. "Sweet driving, right? I mean, the circumstances suck, but what a ride!" After peeling off her gloves, she dropped them on the seat and flexed her hands. *My tía would have been proud. Intense.*

Her friend lifted her head and glared. "We were off the road more than we were on it, and we almost crashed when you swerved around the frog! I'm all for not killing innocent life, but I don't want to die because you can't stand to run over an amphibian," Wyn said.

Some of the exhilaration of the ride curdled, but Zita tried to be reassuring. "Please, we totally had inches to spare. I've driven far worse in the favelas, and that frog had his whole soggy life ahead of him." When she stooped to pick up the dropped helmet, throbbing in the back of her head reminded her. She rubbed it. "By the way, next time you ride two up—behind someone, I mean—sit up straight and keep your head further away."

Wyn choked. "There will be no next time. When I can stand without regurgitating everything I've ever eaten, we're calling the police. We need to report those men. At least as far as those miscreants know, I'm their sole lead on the Key and whatever the wolf's group, the God Kings, is up to."

Zita grimaced. "I'm not certain they'll believe us when we say we were followed, but can we avoid giving any details on my driving maneuvers? American cops are picky about little niceties, like what qualifies as a road." She stashed both helmets and her gloves in the panniers.

Her friend raised her head and stared at her. "Fine. I'll call and mention that they were staking out my house and followed us to the restaurant. We dodged into an alley somewhere while they roared by."

"That works, but we'll need to change our clothing before you talk to them in person. It'd be good if I could clean the bike first, too." She gave it a pat.

Wyn gave a humorless laugh. "The bike doesn't matter. I'm taking a taxi back to your place, as I'm not getting back on that infernal machine with you. In fact, I am never riding anything you drive again."

Exhaling loudly, Zita gazed upward. "Would you have preferred to be kidnapped, questioned, and killed at the humanist group's leisure? I'm not about to let that happen if I can help it."

"No." Wyn lowered her head to her knees, then gave an audible sniff. Her head shot up, her nose wrinkled, and her eyes went wide. She gagged. "What is that awful stench?"

"The super gross one? Swamp mud, cooked onto our clothes. That or fish the fast-food place is serving has gone bad. Might be both." Zita bobbed her head and surveyed her own outfit. "I think it's both. It won't come out either, so toss that outfit."

Her friend glanced down at herself, shuddered, and dragged herself to her feet.

"Pretty awful, I know. Good thing Andy's bringing all those suitcases to my place, right?"

Wyn gaped at her, then marched into the restaurant.

***

The next morning, Zita slipped out before dawn, confident in Quentin's presence to protect Wyn. She returned when she knew her brother would be leaving and made it back before her friend awakened. Well after nine, Zita let Andy in while a bleary Wyn still drooped at the table, nursing a cup of her favorite nasty tea, with an e-reader in front of her.

"You got Wyn?" Zita asked Andy. "I have to get going. After yesterday, I don't want to leave her alone." She climbed up on top of the washer to retrieve a blanket from the top shelf.

Wyn's head shot up. "You're leaving me?"

"Going where?" Andy asked.

Zita cleared her throat and tried to keep it vague and uninteresting. "I have errands to run and a date. She'll be safe with you, and we can always move her to your place if you need to do something there," she said.

Wyn narrowed her eyes, speculation on her face.

"Really? I thought your brothers only got to set you up once a month," Andy said.

Zita coughed. "Ah, this is someone I asked out," she said. She set the blanket on top of her cheap Styrofoam cooler and crossed the room to turn on the laptop.

This proved too tantalizing for Wyn to resist. "Where are you going? And who's the man?" her friend asked.

"Picnic in a park, maybe a zip line, and it's, ah, Remus." Zita waited for the laptop to finish booting. *Load faster, stupid machine, I need to go before she "helps" and we start arguing again.*

Andy mouthed the name.

"Remus! And you're wearing that?" Wyn said, one eyebrow rising.

"Yeah, I have a date with him. It's not like it will work out or anything, but I'll give it a try anyway," Zita said, shifting to her Arca form.

"What makes you think it won't work out? Might it be because you're wearing a domino mask and someone else's face? Or have you finally realized the tragedy of the cranberry cargo shorts and daffodil top combination you have going on?" Wyn asked.

Zita shook her head. "Neither. He's probably used to women being charming and flirty and stuff. I'm not like that. For one thing, I don't care about his pretty face. It's all about his hot body and personality for me. I want a partner in crime, so to speak. However, if the past is any indicator, it's not going to work." She smoothed the fabric of her shorts. *Having tools is useful, and these hold a lot of those. She has such bizarre clothing rules.*

A smile made the corners of Wyn's mouth tilt up. "You practically can't speak to him. Is that the issue? I could do an illusion of him, and we could talk to get you past that."

Leaning over the laptop, Zita shrugged. She typed in her password using both fingers to speed the process, then paced under the interrogation as she waited. "It won't help, and I need to go soon to be on time." *It's much easier to talk to him as Arca, though.*

Wyn swirled her spoon in her tea, stirring up the floral green sludge. "I don't believe I've seen you be pessimistic about anything else before. Is it something in particular about Remus?"

She shook her head again. "No. I've been on enough dates to get a sense of these things, though. Quentin has a dumbass theory that I sabotage the dates and don't give them a real chance." Zita snickered, stopping when she saw thoughtfulness appear on Wyn's face. "What?"

Her friend pursed her lips. "I love you, Zita, but you don't try. You don't even change your outfit."

Again with the clothing. There's nothing wrong with my clothing. Zita waggled her fingers at Wyn. "Not true, I'm going to wear a mask. I got one out special and even brought a backup. It's easier to talk in one, too." She searched through the bag and pulled out the second mask. When she caught sight of Wyn's mien, she realized she must have said something wrong.

Wyn pointed a long, elegant finger at her. "You're making my case for me. You need help."

Stung, Zita appealed to Andy. "Come on, you're my wingman. Back me up, here. Tell her there's nothing wrong with my outfit." *He's just been through this. I explained how it works.*

Andy turned away and fussed with his messenger bag.

Traitor. "Dude. You're dead to me now."

Wyn sniffed. "We are on your side. You're the one who's not. Sometimes, being a friend means rescuing others from their own egregious mistakes, especially those of a sartorial nature."

With a cough, Andy stepped forward. "I might have a solution. My girlfriend Brandi is a biochemist. Well, her doctoral project is a novel type of fabric, and she's even got a startup grant with General Aetherics. They've manufactured samples, and those are now in human testing. Since I mentioned I had sporty friends— mostly you, Zita, but I figure you're athletic enough for a few people—she gave me a handful of outfits for you to test." Beaming, he turned to Wyn as he concluded, "Zita could wear a set, and that would be fine and new and less stressful for everyone. Especially me." He dumped out his bag, sending dull purple fabric tumbling out and onto the table.

Zita sorted through the fabric, separating the bra tops from the exercise pants. She rubbed fabric between her fingers, assessing the heft, weave, and durability of the silky clothing. "I suppose we can still be friends, mano."

He smirked.

With her lips pressed together, Wyn asked, "Isn't that the company that makes the expensive clean-energy balls where the waiting list is years long to get one to power a part of a country? They said that enormous Japanese earthquake would have been devastating if they still had nuclear instead of a Self-Normalizing Aetheric Reactor Core. Why would they bankroll sportswear?" She hummed as she poked through the piles Zita had made.

Andy shrugged, but his mouth turned upward in a small, proud smile. "Yeah, the SNARC ball people. They give grants to promising scientists in most fields, but you can't apply for it. Nine times out of ten, anyone who gets a General Aetherics grant has amazing commercial success, breaks boundaries in their fields, or both."

Zita poked at the clothing. "I like the feel, but my sports bras are all special order because of my size. I could try the capris or whatever, though, even if the color's boring." Although she still mourned her favorite sports bra, destroyed during her wildebeest shapeshift on the island of the dead, free gear was a siren's call, especially considering how strained her budget had been with so few work hours. Replacing her old favorite alone would run her sixty dollars.

Wyn took a set and held them up against herself.

"Actually, they're legitimately one-size-fits-all for adults. Young children might need a smaller set, but everyone else should be fine. See, she based her research off nanofiber polymers used in self-healing hydrogels for drug delivery..." He paused in his enthusiastic description. "You don't care about that, though. The short version is that it uses your body heat to determine how to conform to the set shape, whether that means compressing, expanding, or both. She said the fabric may be able to do limited self-mending if you push the ripped edges together while you're still wearing it. As far as the color, well, they did a limited production run since these are prototypes. Clever, huh?" His eyes lit as he spoke, and an unselfconscious smile appeared.

Zita laughed inside at his fervor. *Someone likes his girls brainy.* As Andy's words washed over her, she frowned. "Wait, prototypes? That sounds expensive. Oye, I can't try them. If I shift..." She clicked the button for the webcam she wanted to use to teleport.

Andy jumped in. "She doesn't expect you to return them, provided you don't sell them to anyone. Can you two please do this and give me any feedback for her? She's got an important fabric exhibition coming up, and the more test data she has, the better." His eyes held hope.

"I don't suppose you know if they're Fair Trade-certified or not? I prefer organic... Never mind," Wyn said. "I'll try them."

Zita took the set she'd picked up earlier, hiding her misgivings. *If necessary, I can always layer another bra on, which I have to do half the time, anyway.* "For you, mano, I'll give it a try." She pasted on a smile.

"You are going to wear more than a sports bra and capris, aren't you?" Wyn asked. "Let me see that travesty of a closet."

"Of course I am. Too many people see the boobage and assume I'm an idiot or easy. I'll throw a shirt over it. I'm good." Not wanting Wyn's eternal mental snooping picking up her plans or what her earlier errands had been, she forced herself not to think about the date in detail. "Give me a second to change," she said, escaping to the other room.

"However evocative, boobage is not a real word!" Wyn called after her.

Chapter Ten

An hour later, Zita congratulated herself as she snuck a bite out of a plastic container and continued setting up the picnic in the picturesque wooded clearing. Tucked off the main path in the park, her chosen spot was perfect. Cheerful yellow goldenrod and coneflowers sprinkled color beneath the thick ring of oaks and hickory that were not yet dressed for fall, and stolid pines, thick with age, lined the edges of the cliff on one side. The entire glade had a gentle downward slope toward the precipice. Below the drop-off, the old house-turned-museum was visible from specific angles, but the exuberant foliage masked her presence.

Her eyes flicked to the white Victorian below, all fancy lines and curves with a little turret arrowing up one of the sides. It sat tucked midway up the mountain, surrounded by trees and a narrow strip of grass. The parking lot was little better than a gravel postage stamp, and red muddy streaks in the verdant green indicated where previous museum visitors had parked in overflow situations. Right now, no cars graced the lot, and the many switchbacks leading up were empty of vehicles. Everything seemed quiet, and she dismissed the atavistic chill that seemed lodged in her spine. *Nothing happened all morning. I am the best date planner ever. Who wouldn't love a combination adventure and picnic, especially in the middle of the woods with a fun hike to get there? The fact that I can stake out the museum from here is just an extra bonus.*

Of course, nobody should break into the place until well after he leaves, but hey, add a thrill. Wyn doesn't know what she's talking about. Dating doesn't scare me, and I sure hope I get to connect naked with a hot guy this year. Speaking of papi chulos, I wonder when... The air snapped.

"Ah, there you are," Remus said, appearing next to her blanket. The handsome Puerto Rican offered her a smile. In the month since she had last seen him, he had grown a small goatee and mustache, close-trimmed to his face.

Zita smiled in return. She approved of the change. *Before, he was too pretty and unapproachable. A touch of man fur on his face, and he's human again. Why did he use his super speed once he got to the park? Was he worried about being late? That's a good sign, right?* "Yes, here I am," she replied.

"Pleasure to see you again, pretty lady," he said in Spanish. It took a couple of seconds to translate as Zita got used to his accent and rapid delivery of cropped words, as if they would get away if he didn't push as many out as quickly as possible.

After admiring his tight runner's body and the easy, self-assured way he moved, Zita answered in the same language, "Same here. Want to eat while it's still lukewarm?" She hurried over to the picnic blanket, cutting in front of him, and sat next to a small rock, placed there to mark the widest view of below. In case he had missed her hard work, she gestured toward the coarse, woven blanket, laid out with the finest grilled chicken and onions, arroz con frijoles, and garlic green beans that her fridge and a convenient food truck could offer.

Remus settled down onto the blanket. "Thanks for marking the trees with chalk. I got lost even with, so I would have been wandering forever without them. Hiking isn't really my thing." He gave her a half-bashful grin.

With studied casualness, she shrugged, hiding her disappointment and her nerves. "Guess I picked the wrong venue then. Sorry. I'm glad you could make it, though," she said. *Qué lástima. The park's only about fifteen miles long, so how long can a man who can run across the country in under a minute be lost? Now, no negativity. This date is not going to be a disaster. We could still work out.*

"Ah, no problem. It's unique and private." He grinned, sitting cross-legged beside her, where he could admire the mountain view, including the museum. "I was going to apologize for my clothes, but I can see we made similar choices dressing today."

Zita tilted her head, examining him. Her date wore skintight Spandex emblazoned with the logo of a better-quality sportswear line. Although not the attire she had expected, she appreciated the view it afforded her. Her own clothing was a half-mask and the new outfit Andy had given her, with a boring, oversized, olive T-shirt tossed on top of the sports bra in an attempt to blend into the copious foliage of the woods and to downplay her chest. Too many previous dates had assumed her sizable breasts correlated to being easy (or more galling, unintelligent) instead of merely being genetic. Under other circumstances, she'd have chosen a more colorful top to counteract all the dark purple. On the bright side, the sports bra was surprisingly supportive, and the pants had pockets that shut with Velcro strips. *Real pockets in workout pants. Andy's girlfriend is a genius.*

Remus turned, stretching to pull a bottle out of the cooler and giving her a glimpse of his rear.

Ay, guapo. She licked her lips and forced her mind back to their conversation. "Why would you have to apologize for your clothing?"

Remus laughed, a surprised bark of sound. "No reason, I guess. If I run too fast in anything looser, it shreds. While I wouldn't normally wear exercise gear to a date, I did have to get here from DC." He slanted a glance at her.

She smiled and nodded. *This is me, doing this date right. Wyn doesn't know what she's talking about.*

At her silence, he continued speaking. "Water, juice, and soda... What, no wine? Isn't that traditional for this sort of picnic?" He grinned at her, his eyes twinkling.

With a laugh, Zita waved a hand. "No, I don't drink alcohol. If I'm loading up on calories, I'd rather they be in the form of a decadent dessert or something that won't also make me act more like an idiot than usual. I'm pretty good at that sober."

Her honesty won another smile from him. "Well, then, we have an excellent vintage of juice or perhaps water for the lady? It makes sense. I probably shouldn't drink and run anyway."

"Might be a bad idea at your speeds, yeah. Toss me a water, please?"

He tossed one, taking a soda for himself.

Zita caught it and twisted off the cap. She chugged, luxuriating in the cool slide of liquid down her dusty throat. Maryland in late August was hot. But Alabama in late August served sweltering heat, with a side of madness. Despite all her time in South America, she still wasn't used to it. *Have to remember to tell Andy that the moisture wicking works well on the clothing.* "Thanks."

Remus watched her drink. "You're welcome, though I should be thanking you for bringing all this. How did you manage it?"

"Bought most of it local," she evaded, praying she hadn't left any telltale receipts in the cheap Styrofoam cooler. *Yes, local to home and at a discount.*

He sipped his own drink and continued to study her. "To be honest, I assumed you weren't going to call after the first few days passed. No other woman has waited a month to call." A smile touched his lips, and his eyes flicked to her legs before returning to her face. "Or worn a mask and given me no name."

Yes, someone's a leg man. The workout capris are a win, attractive and practical. After screwing the top back on her water bottle, Zita returned his gaze, amused and hopeful. "Things have been busy. I thought they'd slow down, but they haven't." *Honest enough.*

"So, do I get to know your name? Or shall I call you mystery lady?" he teased, wielding his smile like a weapon as he stretched his lean legs out on the coarse blanket.

Zita's mind went blank for a moment, and then she recovered. *Remember the advice you gave Andy. Be yourself, without giving anything important away.* "Arca works for now. As far as the mask and my name, I'm not convinced being open about my identity and powers is the way to go, though I admire your big balls for choosing to be out about your own."

Remus coughed up soda, grabbing a napkin and dabbing at his lips, the white paper bright against the warm amber of his skin. His thank-you was strangled. "So even on a private date in a secluded spot in another state, you think the risk justifies wearing a mask and using a fake name?" he asked.

She thought of her mother and brothers, of Andy and Wyn, and the secrets they kept. The risks of being experimented on or enslaved were horror enough. The danger to her family and friends was completely intolerable. "Absolutely. I've got family, history books, and a television. Most or all the Seventies folks with powers are dead or missing. No government's out there searching for them or crying about that, either. Of our group, the ones who showed up with powers in the past few months, we've already seen gruesome deaths, and we don't know how many have disappeared. People are freaked, and that's with most of the known powers being harmless, like the guy who turns any liquid into perfect coffee. Once people with dangerous powers start misbehaving? That'll be a whole different matter. Just watch."

Her date folded his arms over his chest. "I've got family, too. They're safe enough and haven't felt any backlash yet. The executions have all been overseas. If this weren't the United States, I might agree, but the government couldn't get away with systematic oppression like that." He must have read her expression, because he added, "Anymore. They can't do that anymore."

Zita waved a chicken leg at him. "Disagree, majorly. For one, Congress is already trying to add amendments to tax people using powers in pursuit of their business." *Oops, is that common knowledge outside of tax accounting? Well, maybe he'll think I'm a congressional news junkie. I better think of another current event to mention.*

That stopped Remus for a moment. "They are? I didn't know that... That can't pass. It can't be constitutional." He gave his head a shake.

She crossed her legs. "Talk to a civil rights attorney. You've got that association of businesspeople with abilities who would all be impacted. It wouldn't surprise me if the bill passes next time they do budget crap. I won't even get started on the people campaigning to have us listed as a separate species, put in jail, or registered so we can be permanently drafted." *Not that I would have known about any of those things if Wyn hadn't blabbed my ear off about them a few days ago, but it will hopefully cover my tax faux pas.*

His gaze turned to the horizon, going distant and contemplative. "I think I had someone who's an attorney sign up for my organization. It probably won't be an issue, but I'll talk to her."

Zita shook her head. "Plan for the worst. It'd be awesome if the government would let us do our thing, but I don't think they will, considering that ridiculous quarantine. We don't really know how they treated all the changed, do we? I'd rather be loose and unknown, especially if they begin killing, drafting, or throwing people into internment camps. If the government behaves, you've still got everyone else to worry about. In the few months since people with powers emerged again, how many protests against us have there already been? A lot." She took another bite, then set the food on her plate.

Remus frowned at her. "It's better if we're out and openly voicing our opposition to unfair policies. Even if I agreed with you, which I don't, some of us can't hide and may need special accommodations. The winged girl, for example, can't just get on an airplane like everyone else, because her wings don't let her sit in chairs with backs. My abilities would have been difficult to keep secret after my first cross-country run to California, especially since my clothing disintegrated on the way," he commented, toying with a blade of grass.

Lucky Californians. It's cute how he assumes they were all watching his face, even if it is awfully attractive. Zita focused her attention on their discussion. "You could have been any streaker and given them a false name. It's not like you're a huge star like Sammo Hung and would have been recognized. Be careful. Even if you're right and the government doesn't kill, imprison, or force you into service, you've still got regular people to watch out for."

With a frown, Remus shook his head. "Sammo who? Never mind... Cynical, much?"

She drew up her knees to her chest. *How can he not recognize one of the biggest names in martial arts movies?* "Listen, you've announced that you can't transport anything more than paper without wrecking it. Once you figure out how to carry more, people are going to worry about what you can take over borders, or try to control you. They might go the straight hatred route and attack you, though at least you can outrun most of those...if you're awake. Then there's the risk to your family."

Remus exhaled loudly, leaning back. "What a charming prediction. We'll have to agree to disagree. I think the world's better than that. So, how about your family? Do you have kids or siblings? My parents only had the three of us, but I've always

wanted a bunch of kids, the whole massive family thing, someday.
I don't have any yet," he offered.

"I'd rather not talk about my family too much. I'll say I'm single,
though. No kids," she said, changing position again. Her back
muscles tightened at the reminder of an old sorrow; no matter how
her mother prayed, some miracles were less likely than others.
Giving herself a mental shake, she set it aside and concentrated on
being charming but herself, without fidgeting or saying anything to
put anyone else at risk. *Whatever that means.*

His smile wavered at her response. They sat in silence as she
ate, and he surveyed the sunny dell. "So why are we in
Birmingham?" he asked. "The park's beautiful, but DC has closer
ones."

Zita cast about for an answer, then recalled the gear she'd
examined in the early hours of the morning. She grinned,
remembering. "First, we're more anonymous here, and you can
travel without problems. Second, this park has zip lines and rope-
course challenges that sound sweet. I thought you might be
interested in checking them out."

He grimaced, and his body tensed. "Can I tell you a secret?" he
asked. "I'm not a huge fan of heights." His eyes darted to the drop
off and back to her.

"Oh. Well, that's fine," she said, stuffing her disappointment
into a mental box. Zita tried to remember a safe date topic. "So,
what do you like to do for fun? Do you work out a lot?"

His body relaxed at the question. "Running, obviously, though
I also like...this is going to sound a little hokey..."

"You can tell me," she said, hope rising. She leaned toward him.

Remus smiled, took a hit of soda, and moved closer as if
conspiring with her.

She liked that.

He said, "Other than the running, I'm sedentary. Running is my
life, and I'll do a few hand weights, but the coma bulked me up

some, odd as that sounds. Most exercise is boring. I love to curl up with business journals and self-help books, though."

Zita bit back an involuntary protest and scooted away a little.

Unaware of her internal struggle, he continued. His face warmed as he spoke. "Since I'm starting my own company, I'm working to avoid common small-business pitfalls. It's a lot to learn, but worth it. You would not believe the tax liabilities a small business incurs."

Oye, I might, actually. Zita bit into a chicken leg, her interest waning. She kept her eyes trained on the museum as Remus continued talking about his five-year plan for his company and his nonprofit organization for businesses run by people with powers. He was enthused, which made one of them. *At least he has a plan. My own came crashing down when my new abilities showed up. Being unable to submit blood work means no athletic competitions. What will I do with myself once I stop the theft of the knife? I don't think I've been without a long-term plan since that tool Caroline and the cancer derailed my first chance at the Olympics.* When he paused, she murmured something noncommittal, encouraging, and so boring she forgot it as soon as it left her mouth.

After a few minutes, Remus noticed her detachment and followed her gaze. "You keep staring at that building." He picked at his meal.

She chided herself for being closed-minded and told herself that this might save the date. Zita went down her mental checklist. *Even if he wasn't into hiking or aerial activities or the gym, we might still work as a couple. After all, haven't I done everything right by those rules Quentin keeps giving me, save making overt sexual overtures? I planned a unique date in a beautiful venue so romantic it makes my teeth hurt. I asked him about his interests and avoided talking religion or politics or saying anything offensive. Other than when we debated the risks of being public about having powers, of course, but nobody yelled or threw punches, so it didn't count. Plus, I've been sitting still so long my butt is numb, so that checks off the no fidgeting. If this isn't a total win, he may be a dud in the romance department. Or at least, a bad fit. He doesn't seem as into me anymore, either.* "Yes, I'm watching to see if anyone breaks into it."

He paused. "You...invited me to a stakeout?"

As she tore her eyes from the building, she smiled and nodded. "Yes, but it's probably just an excess of caution. Technically, the museum's closed due to a pest problem, and it's been deserted all morning so far. If it's anything like the other robberies, the thieves won't be subtle. The cliff will prevent them from direct runs at us, and you're more than fast enough to escape. I can always fly away."

"It's...something," he said. "Other robberies?"

Was that shock in his voice? How dreary had the other women been who had asked him out before? Poor man. Zita turned to watch the building again. "Yes, so far they've hit three other places. If the same group goes after the piece here, one of the thieves is about eight feet tall, and another prefers the form of a huge black wolf with red eyes. It should be a piece of cake to tell them from museum workers." Another thought struck her, and she rummaged through the plastic bag she had brought the food in. "Oh man, I forgot to bring dessert. Sorry about that. Wait!" She fished out a bag of trail mix from her pockets and plopped it onto the blanket. "That's got chocolate candies mixed in. Dessert problem solved."

Eyes wide, he nodded. "Wait, what about a pest problem?"

She cleared her throat. "They stabbed and almost killed an elderly man who tried to stop them at another robbery. The happy coincidence of an animal infestation at the museum below will hopefully keep anyone from getting hurt or dying here." *And provide a tempting opportunity for them to rob the place when I can be here to stop them. I've got work tomorrow and bills to pay, after all.*

Remus rubbed his forehead. "Is this what you do for fun? It seems illegal."

Zita held up a hand. "It's outside the ordinary, even for me. No worries. We're having a legal picnic in a nearby public park. If something happens, I can delay them, and you can call the cops. If they come after you, run away. Everything is lawful." *Except for the fact that I broke in and switched the haft with one from a different case so if they did reach it, they'd take the wrong thing. Oh, and when I released the skunks in the museum earlier this morning while Wyn slept. On the bright side, Claire has no more pests under her porch, even if her live animal traps now reek something awful.* She gestured toward the cell phone on the blanket, a cheap model marked with a blue smiley-face sticker. "If nothing happens, no harm done. Most of the time, I let the cops do their jobs. In this case, my source assures me that letting the robbers succeed would mean they could hurt a lot of people," she said. She shoveled in another mouthful of green beans and continued to watch.

Her companion was silent a moment. "No, we can't have that," he answered, his voice faint. "So just watching and reporting? No fighting them?" Remus frowned and raised his eyebrows.

Zita snickered and held up her hand. "Please. Do I seem stupid enough to take on an eight-foot-tall guy and his giant wolf friend by myself for no reason?"

Remus was speechless a moment too long. "No, of course not."

She pushed down her irritation and continued. "My plan is to delay, report, and run, assuming nobody else is in danger. If necessary, I'll follow them to their home base and call the cops from there. A fancy-ass neighborhood like this, though, real close to a major public park, the police response time has got to be amazing."

That seemed to soothe him. "Right, observe and report," he said.

Zita shook a green bean at him, and then bit off the tip. "Don't worry. I doubt they'd break in during daylight hours, but I'm trying to be thorough about this. We'll likely have a picnic and nothing more fun than that."

"Yes, a picnic," he mumbled, pushing rice around on his plate.

She had the feeling she had missed something, but before she could ask, an SUV pulled into the museum parking lot. It parked close to the door.

A burly, rectangular block of a man unfolded himself from the driver's seat. He plodded around to a rear door and threw it open, crossing huge arms over his chest.

A little less than eight feet tall, but close enough. Modest musculature, nothing serious, and no martial arts. Favoring his one leg—concealed carry, maybe? Steps aren't right for a prosthetic or an injury. Can reach the moon, though, Zita assessed.

The second out was the gigantic wolf. *Moves like a true wolf, despite the size.* He padded to the front of the car and sat.

"Return of Steroid Dog," she muttered. "Joy. That's them. Keep your voice low in case the wolf hears us, but here, call the cops on my phone." She scooped up the cell and tossed it to Remus, her attention riveted to the would-be thieves below.

The goliath—Basso, she assumed—leaned into the car. As he straightened, he shook his head and closed the door. With no enthusiasm in his posture, he trudged around to the passenger side and opened the door there.

Emerging next was a female, but not that loca, Jennifer Stone, as Zita had half-expected, half-feared. Instead, a blond woman, clad in a sleeveless black dress showcasing sticklike arms and scrawny legs, struggled to descend from the SUV, like a mantis hampered by a short, tight skirt. A matching hat tilted precariously on her head, and gigantic sunglasses glinted in the sunlight. Finally, she abandoned propriety and did an ungainly flop down, teetering and almost falling on spike heels.

The wolf streamed up next to her in time for her to catch herself on his back.

Once the woman straightened, she retrieved a huge black purse from the vehicle, one that gleamed with buckles and the kind of ostentatious initials that made Zita suspect it was expensive. She scowled at the giant, who slammed the door shut as soon as she cleared it.

He stared into space well over her head.

From her vantage point, Zita frowned. *Her arms make Wyn's appear muscular. Why would anyone wear something like that to a heist? At least Wyn's ridiculous costume is an illusion.*

The woman stomped to the door—Zita had to acknowledge her skill at doing that in needle-thin stilettos without falling—and stopped. With hands on her hips, her mouth was in constant motion as she said something inaudible.

Panting in the heat, Steroid Dog stuck close, leaning against her when she stopped.

When the huge man ambled up behind the woman and canine, his body language screamed disinterest. He shrugged at whatever she'd said.

Another frenzy of words launched from the woman.

The wolf keyed off the woman, and his ruff rose in jagged spikes.

Zita was wondering if the heated discussion would devolve into a fight amongst villains when a gold pickup pulled into the museum parking lot, followed by a blue van with a cheerful exterminator logo on the side. Something rattled in the rear of the latter vehicle as it parked. A wizened white woman hopped out of the exterminator vehicle and went right to the back. After she had opened the rear doors, she donned coveralls and pulled out a humane animal trap.

The pickup disgorged a sturdy middle-aged woman with dark skin and hair in a classy cornrow bun. A briefcase dangled from each arm; one was probably meant to be a purse, but Zita could not figure out which. The lady with the briefcases tugged down her suit coat and made a beeline for the exterminator.

Curator, perhaps? Zita thought. *Neither one appears to have combat experience based on their walk.*

The pest control lady waved and called out to the other newcomer as she wrestled another wire cage out of the van.

Zita swore. "Pest removal happens faster if you've got the cash, I guess." *When Quentin called them for the mice in his place, it took them a week to get someone out. All that work to clear the place, wasted.* Her mouth turned downward, and she rubbed the top of her head.

One hand out as if offering the exterminator her help, the curator caught sight of the trio on the sidewalk and came to a stop. She called out something to them.

The exterminator followed the curator's gaze and frowned. With a distracted air, she continued to dig through the back of her van.

The female robber touched the wolf's ruff and bared her teeth in an approximation of a smile at the two women. Beside her, Steroid Dog sat and watched. Basso seemed guarded now.

"What's going on?" Remus asked from behind her.

Zita repressed a flinch. She had almost forgotten his presence. "Exterminator and a curator showed up. I may have to go down there to ensure their safety. Are the cops on their way?" She risked a glance at him.

He shook his head. "No, nobody's done anything illegal yet." The phone sat untouched beside him on the blanket.

She closed her eyes, counted to three, and stood. "Not yet, but the cops need time to get up here... Just call as soon as you can." Flexing her shoulders and opening her eyes, Zita headed toward the edge of the cliff, her body tensing as her mind sifted through animal choices.

In the brief time her attention had been diverted, the tableau below had changed. The giant man now held the exterminator close, a massive hand at her throat. With a glare that rivaled a displeased school principal, the curator was approaching the door, keys in hand. She proceeded into the building, followed closely by the wolf and his female companion.

Zita swore. "So much for the alarms. Are hostages enough motive to call? I can't let them hurt those two women." Behind her, she heard Remus murmuring into the phone. Green fabric crumpled around her as she shifted into a large turkey vulture. The world sharpened, colors tinged away from human, and the forest and picnic scents were a painful pleasure in their strength. As she flew by a huge, gnarled tree at the cliff's edge and let her body drop off onto a thermal, a whiff of gun oil and man caught her attention. *Hunters must have been here earlier. Lucky I didn't pick a deer form.* Something about the scent teased at her memory, but the activity below demanded her focus. Choosing a spot that put the precipice at her back and allowed an unobstructed view of the giant and his hostage, she circled down and landed on a tree branch.

Chapter Eleven

As Zita prepared to act, Basso released the exterminator's throat. He kept a controlling hand on his prisoner's shoulder.

With the canine robber at her heels, the curator plodded back outside and over to stand beside the exterminator, arms folded over her chest. Anger radiated in every line of her body.

Steroid Dog growled, "Do what he says. If you don't, I get to eat your intestines." After depositing his charge with Basso, the wolf veered back to the building, but then paused, staring in Zita's direction.

I hope that threat was a lie, because gross. Zita waited. *Go away, doggie, and let your friend stand farther from the ladies, at least long enough for me to knock him down so they can escape.*

Steroid Dog cocked his head. "Do I smell garlic and onions?" His nose lifted, and he prowled toward her hiding spot. "I do, with cinnamon pastry?"

"Should have had more kibble this morning," his cohort suggested, maintaining his grip on the elderly exterminator.

A snarled obscenity answered his comment.

Zita fluttered to a higher branch, one she hoped was too far for the wolf to jump. She grunted, nestling back into the shadows and forcing shallow breaths. *Note to self: no garlic and onions during the next stakeout. Save it for other dates. Where's he getting the pastry scent from? I forgot the dessert. Maybe my body wash? Add using unscented soap to the list of things to do before sneaking around, though I'll probably never have to do this again.*

An imperious demand came from the depths of the building, and after one more suspicious snuffle through the bushes under the tree, the wolf sprinted inside.

Fifteen seconds later, a white pickup truck pulled up to the lot entrance. Two shapes sat within. Sunlight and shadow hid what little of the driver's face was visible above a bushy beard, and he seemed cramped compared to his smaller companion.

No lo creo, another one? How much traffic does a museum of metallurgical history get? Zita kvetched to herself.

"Not a word. We don't need to pull anyone else into this, ladies," Basso rumbled to his captives. He took the arm of the curator. Both women wore identical rebellious scowls but remained silent.

From the passenger seat of the truck, a lanky woman hopped out, holding a phone in front of her, attention focused on the screen. The largest, floppiest pink hat ever sat atop an explosion of spiraling blond curls. Sunlight glinted off oversized, wraparound sunglasses. "Not to worry, this is the last one. We're close," she shouted over her shoulder, hustling to the center of the parking lot with ground-eating strides that belied the flip-flops flapping on her sock-clad feet. She consulted her device again.

For a second, the thought of the newcomer and the female robber slapping each other with their oversized headwear sidetracked Zita. She shook off the distracting image, narrowing her eyes and inching sideways on her perch. In addition to being military perfect, the tourist's posture was too rigid. Something bulky hid under the cheery Hawaiian shirt covered in fluorescent surfing gummy bears. *Is that a hidden bulletproof vest? It'd have to be fitted, but that would explain the way she's moving. I wonder if it and the cool top come in petite sizes. Why does she seem familiar? Could the police be here that fast?*

The blond tourist revolved in a circle, holding her phone out like a dowsing rod. When she faced away from Basso and his captives, she lifted her sunglasses and winked at the bluff. Letting them drop back onto her nose, she continued her slow revolution until she confronted the building again. She jumped in surprise. "Oh! Didn't see you there." Her head tilted up and down as she eyed the man, and she added, "My, you are a tall one. I love cuddly bears. Are you proportional? Never mind, I just didn't believe my friend when she said they grew them big down here. Let me take a picture to send her." She fumbled to raise her device.

"No. No pictures." Basso freed his captives and took a step or two toward her. His entire body tightened, and his weight shifted to a sloppy fight-ready stance.

Recognition slapped Zita. She peered at the face beneath the pink hat. *Prefers bears... that's not the police. It's Trixie in a wig. Why is a New York doctor pretending to be a brainless tourist at the world's most obscure yet popular museum? You'd think after all that time in quarantine and being kidnapped, she'd be back at work scaring patients back to health.* Her attention piqued as Basso moved again. *He's released the women. If I get his attention, they can run.*

The curator snuck a hand into her purse.

With a worried glance at her friend, the exterminator addressed the tourist. "Ma'am, this area has a pest problem right now. You should be heading on to your next stop."

A bright pink-painted mouth fell open beneath giant sunglasses as Trixie abandoned whatever she had been doing. "For real? Fine, no picture, Mr. Pouty Spoilsport Face. I need one more geocache to win the contest, and my phone says the last spot is around here. I'm feeling lucky, real lucky. Do you see any disturbed gravel or piles of fresh dirt?" She bent and examined the ground of the parking lot, circling around to the cars. After a pause to poke at her phone, she called out, "I'll just be a moment!"

When Trixie ignored him and returned to her bizarre search, Basso withdrew a few feet. His shoulders relaxed. The exterminator edged away, and Basso shook his head in a silent warning.

Trixie waved her phone under the SUV, holding onto the back bumper as she did so. "Nothing. Why can't I find it?"

Basso turned his head to Trixie and frowned. "Step away and move along," he ordered. He reached for the exterminator's and curator's arms. "Behave," he murmured, his voice too low to carry far. "Nobody needs to get hurt today."

Zita prepared to spring down and shift, but the hostages acted first.

The stocky curator stepped back from the colossus, shoving the exterminator behind herself. From one purse/briefcase, she drew an M1911 pistol and aimed it at Basso. "Nobody but you if you don't stay right there. Get on out of here, Lois. The skunks can wait."

Classic Weaver stance, firm two-handed grip, Zita assessed. *Who knew? Most of the criminals I've met have terrible gun stances, but apparently, museum staff practice shooting when they're not dusting old stuff. I should rethink my opinion about people who work in museums.*

Basso stopped and raised his arms. "Guess you got me," he said. "If you were all to run off now, there's clearly nothing I can do." The corners of his lips twitched upward, and his expression was a mix of fear and relief.

From behind the curator, the elderly exterminator, Lois, skittered around Basso and ran for her van. Once inside, the locks clicked.

"Silly me, I transposed those numbers," Trixie sang. Her eyes widened at the gun, and she backed away, clutching her phone. "I'll be going then." When she reached her ride, she threw open the door and hurled herself inside. Whoever was driving pulled out with a screech of tires before the door had finished closing.

Zita watched in bemused fascination, her beak gaping. *I may be superfluous.*

The curator edged toward the exterminator's van, whose engine remained turned off, though a faint clatter came from inside.

Dropped the keys, Lois? Zita wondered. *Hurry up and get to safety.*

Basso continued standing still. He was definitely smiling now. "You should rush and go before my associates return," he advised. "They're not pleasant people. Plus, my arms are getting tired."

The curator took another step toward the van.

A yip and a feminine shriek rang out from inside. As if summoned by the reference to them, the female thief ran into the parking lot, followed by a staggering wolf. Steroid Dog bounced off the doorframe exiting the building. He made it a few steps out the door before he began vomiting into the grass. His eyes streamed.

Zita would have smirked, but all her current form managed was a rumble at the partial success of her plan. *Enhanced senses are not always a blessing, Steroid Dog. If only everyone else had stayed away. Run, curator lady.*

Bent double, one hand over her mouth, the female robber clung to the doorframe. Her face was pale, her huge sunglasses askew, and her gaze furious. "You didn't see fit to mention your pest problem was skunks?" When she caught sight of the tableau, her hand dropped, and she stared. This close, Zita could see she had powers of some sort as one eye was solid blue, the other all black, and neither had pupils or sclera.

"You didn't ask now, did you?" the curator drawled, "As I do recall, I was to do as you commanded and not say a word." She didn't bother to hide her smug expression, but she retreated faster toward the van.

Recovered or out of material to expel, the wolf tilted his head in her direction, his nose skyward. Rougher than usual, his voice growled, "Tiffany? What's going on?" His head turned toward the female robber, but his eyes and nose continued to blink and stream.

With pity, Zita realized one of the skunks must have sprayed his face, and he had to be blind. *At least it's only temporary... I think. Given his reek even from here, I hope his nose is numb for now.* She squashed the empathy; the skunks had been the best option she had been able to come up with to avoid violence. Since it wasn't working as she had planned, she prayed she could still help the two innocents escape.

"This moron lost control of two old ladies," the robber woman, Tiffany, explained.

Basso's smile widened. "They have a gun."

"You're twice their size! How could you lose control of two dried-up biddies?" the irate Tiffany shrieked. "Kill the one with the gun and have the other one get rid of those skunks. Someone moved the haft, and my spell needs to be close to locate it. Make it fast before my potion wears off." She waved an empty bottle at him.

His voice mild, Basso said, "Jen's the muscle. I'm the mindless gofer, remember? You just assumed our roles were reversed when you had her stay back."

"Don't bring her into this. She's insane. I'm not having her screw up my job the way she did the last one. With her power, she shouldn't need you to nursemaid her," Tiffany snarled back.

The humor left Basso's face. "Speak respectfully of her, or you'll have more than guns to worry about, witch. She did her job, and we got what we went there for. Garm's desire to eat the librarian was an unnecessary distraction."

Eat Wyn? Carajo. That is messed up.

With a snarl, Steroid Dog—Garm—tilted his head a few degrees too far to be watching the other man. His eyes and nose still ran. "No witnesses are better than one."

Skunk must have overpowered his sniffer. I don't like that they're throwing names around, Zita thought.

Tiffany folded her arms over her chest. "Agreed, Garm, but the librarian's gone missing, and that's enough to keep the idiot human group from getting her. They've lost the Key's trail and won't be an issue unless they catch her. Now, Atlas, get rid of the old bat or my report will reflect your incompetence."

While they argued, the curator eased the last few steps to the extermination company van. Her weapon wavered as she tugged on the door handle.

During the curator's distraction with the door, Atlas bent and pulled a KA-BAR knife from an ankle holster as he advanced on the curator. Hefting the seven-inch blade in his right hand, all humor died in his expression. "Should have hurried," he said, his mouth settling into sad lines.

Before Zita could move, a whip crack sounded, and Atlas held only air. He cradled his hand to his chest and stood still.

Another snap and Remus stood by the curator, his face sickly beneath the warm color of his skin. He held the knife between two fingers. "Go and be fast," he urged in English.

Lois threw open the van's side door and held out the keys. "Get in and drive the car, Rhonda!"

With a fearful glance, the curator obeyed, slamming it shut behind her.

Garm snarled and hurled himself, either at the handsome Puerto Rican or the fleeing women.

Zita launched herself off the branch and at the canine. She picked the first form that came to mind and charged, howling and oinking. They collided, and the force of her charge plus her swinish weight shoved the wolf back and up against one of the walls of the building. Her eyes and nose stung with the proximity to his skunk-imbued fur. *Feral pig is not the optimal choice when dealing with a skunked dog. Ugh.*

On the island, she had ignored her instincts and gotten shot. Now, when the same feeling warned her, Zita dodged right before a shotgun boomed. She squealed, her ear stinging with the noise.

Already dazed from Zita's attack, Garm took the brunt of the blast. He howled.

Zita whipped around to see Lois leaning out of her van, bracing a short-barreled Remington on the van window frame as the old exterminator prepared to take a second shot. The engine turned over.

Atlas stood behind the van, out of Lois' line of sight, still cradling his hand and watching with a bemused expression.

The gun boomed again, and Garm fell. Lois aimed at Zita.

Running behind the front of the oversized SUV, Zita shifted into human form, remembering at the last second to use her Arca disguise. "Don't shoot me. I'm the pig! I came to help!" She peeked over the car hood, dropping down again when another boom announced Lois' doubt.

The exterminator's demand that everyone hit the ground and wait for the police followed. An ominous hissing sound came from the other side of the vehicle.

Remus appeared next to Zita with another crack, kneeling by the door. The knife was gone.

"Come closer," she said. "The engine's the only thing with a chance to stop a bullet if the exterminator alternated rounds in her gun." She tugged him so the engine block would cover as much of him as possible, even if she lost some of her own protection. Her smaller size granted her better concealment, anyway.

Remus gulped. "I don't know why I'm asking, but why would she do that?"

"If you don't know what you're up against, it covers your ass. If the first type of ammo doesn't work, the second might. That's what I'd do in her job," Zita replied, her attention on the wolf by the wall. Metal clinked as shotgun pellets fell from the shuddering nightmare hulk of Garm. She raised her voice and peered over the truck. "Oye, Lois, get to safety already!"

The shotgun boomed again, and Zita dropped back down. The SUV groaned and tilted on the side opposite where they hid. *Guess I don't have to worry about disabling their vehicle.*

A shriek had her risking another glance. Atlas stood next to the window, holding the shotgun. He bent the barrel, watching the exterminator with a conflicted expression.

Lois gulped as he reached out a meaty hand for her.

Zita started to sprint toward them.

In another explosion of sound, Atlas stood wrapped in a green and yellow garden hose tied in a festive bow. Water dripped out of one end. Remus banged the side of the van twice and shouted, "Go!"

Garm twitched and staggered to his feet, lips drawing back from his teeth in a snarl.

The ladies in the van listened to the advice to flee this time, pulling out in an eruption of stinging gravel. Brakes shrieked as the van braked to avoid hitting a school bus trundling around the curve of the last switchback. Tires squealed for purchase. The exterminator's van skidded, the rear fishtailing, but the vehicle recovered and made it around the bend.

In an explosion of honking, the bus ran off the road and into the deeply rutted grass. It managed to stop before the drop-off.

Remus winced.

Avid faces and camera phones filled the windows as teenagers in the yellow vehicle responded to the fracas. Several lowered the top half of the glass panes and shouted, the words blending into an incomprehensible mess. An alarm sounded nearby.

Zita's words escaped on their own. "Seriously? What's next, a circus?"

A masculine murmur of agreement escaped someone nearby though she missed who had made the sound.

Garm snarled and charged Remus or the bus, she couldn't tell which.

"No!" Zita shouted, shifting again to a feral pig and ramming the wolf a second time.

He howled and skittered sideways.

She blocked the wolf from going after anyone else. The bus engines whined, tires spraying warm mud everywhere, splattering Zita and Garm. Mired even deeper than before, the vehicle remained stuck.

Garm snapped at her, and she dodged. He paced around her, and she turned slowly, keeping her focus on him.

The sound of the alarm intensified as the door to the museum opened. Zita risked a glance. With dainty steps, Tiffany minced outside. "Is everyone in this place incompetent?" she screeched, gazing at the scene. She cradled her purse to her chest. "We're done here, boys. Stop playing and let's go."

Zita returned her attention to the still-circling wolf, catching glimpses of the others in her peripheral vision.

"SUV tires are busted, and I'm tied up," Atlas offered from behind her.

Her voice as petulant as a cranky child, Tiffany commanded, "Then break your bonds unless you want me to report to Zeus that you were useless. You know he enjoys a culling."

He ground his teeth, and his bonds stretched and broke. A shamrock green piece of hose winged by as Atlas shuffled toward the bus. "It seems rude after all the effort he made to tie me up," he protested, his tone mild.

"Must I do everything myself? Commandeer another vehicle." Tiffany sighed and dug in her massive purse.

He shrugged, stopped, and strode to the curator's abandoned pickup truck.

Tiffany pulled a stoppered bottle out, examined the label, and then threw it at Remus in an underhand softball pitch.

With a crack of sound, Remus ducked the bottle and reappeared fifteen feet away.

The bottle shattered harmlessly against the rear door of the bus, or so Zita thought until the black sludge inside dripped down, and then ignited in a whoosh of iridescent ebony flame. In a biting coil of smoke, herbs, old blood, and sulfur mingled with the fumes of melting paint and burning plastic. The jeering shouts from the bus turned to screams. Glass shattered nearby, but Zita's attention was on the bus. *Ay, no,* she thought, horrified. *The kids!*

Remus disappeared. When he reappeared, his speed slowed to that a speeding racecar, and he dragged a long coil of hose behind him. He dropped it by the bus, then took off with a pop of sound. Another pistol-crack of noise and he held the hose in time to aim the first jet of water at the fire. The front doors of the bus creaked open, and teenagers spilled out, pushing and shoving each other as they stampeded from the bus.

A freight train hit Zita from behind, one stinking of fur and irate skunk. Teeth latched onto one of her legs, and she fell to the pavement. It was hard, painful, and unyielding beneath her.

Forgot about Steroid Dog, I mean, Garm, and his healing. Gracias a Dios that pigs have such thick skin or I'd be unable to stand. Grunting, she rolled and bucked until he released her. She whirled to face him.

Tiffany stood not too far off. She leered at the bus. "Pity about the collateral damage," she said. "They're only humans, however, so no great loss. Garm? Do finish this for me, darling."

Garm's mouth hung open, panting. He closed it, his head turning to the bus and the screaming children. His head and tail lowered, and his ears perked up, tilting toward the noise. The wolf's tongue darted out to lick his lips, once, twice, a third time. "Right."

Despite the annoying acrid burn of the smoke, Zita's sensitive nose picked up another scent, buried beneath the skunk and

Garm's basic odor—unhappiness. *At least have the balls to disagree with her,* she thought in disgust. Anger rose within her. She took a step toward Tiffany, who turned her back and strolled toward the gold pickup truck.

Garm flowed between Zita and the witch.

I can't ignore the kids, but I can't help but feel this is a trap. Zita snorted and feinted as if she were going to the bus.

Garm lunged at her.

She rushed him, and he made the mistake of coming to a full stop.

They crashed together. Her leg throbbed and almost crumpled under the pressure.

Six hundred pounds of moving, enraged pig met three hundred pounds of wolf with a thud, a crunch, and a clear winner. Garm flew back from the collision and hit the defunct SUV with a yip and the sickening snaps of bone. His great furry bulk trembled.

Zita interposed herself between him and the panicked teens.

"I can't put it out," Remus shouted.

At his words, Zita squinted in his direction.

With a hiss like nasty, whispered laughter, the unholy flames had spread and now covered the rear of the bus. Runnels of water spread the flames even further in long lines the length of the bus, and plumes of evil gray smoke billowed. Wind carried away most of the smoke over the precipice, but even the small amount that reached her scraped and clawed at her throat. Remus lowered the hose and coughed. Teenagers choked and coughed as they continued their panicked escape from the vehicle.

With a glance to ensure Garm remained down, she limped back to the bus, switching to her Arca form. Her mind whirled. *How do we stop the flames? It's like a grease fire, but the bus wouldn't have been oily. More like napalm? What did Tía say about that? Besides promising my inevitable death for not paying attention... Smother it?*

A portly man, pale and puffing, tried to help a battered girl off the bus, and other fleeing teenagers almost trampled the pair. They slipped and slid, falling, and Zita caught them as they tumbled. Sun-heated mud squelched and oozed over her bare feet. Tires crunched on gravel, and a flash of gold moved into her peripheral vision, but she couldn't spare any attention to see what was happening. An idea sparked.

"Mud!" she shouted to Remus. "Cover it in mud! I'll get the kids off!" She assisted the driver and the injured student to firmer ground. "Get them all away from the bus," she told the man.

The driver grimaced. "What'd you think I was doing?" Without waiting for an answer, he bellowed commands at the teens as he assisted the girl.

Remus dropped the hose, water still pooling out. He stared at her. His lips moved, and then he was a blur of motion. Splashes of red mud bloomed amid the black flames. Her ears rang with panicked cries and the steady stream of pops as Remus moved, the cacophony almost drowning out the squelch of mud splattering the side of the bus.

Zita caught another student falling off the bus and set him on his feet. She concentrated on clearing the bus, though she stole glances at Remus' progress. The man himself moved too fast for her to make out what he was doing. She suspected he shoveled with his bare hands, but it seemed to be working.

When no more students stumbled from the bus, she boarded it to ensure they'd all escaped. Fouled by smoke, the air was so noxious she held an abandoned bandana over her mouth during her search of the vehicle. She bolted into the cleaner air as soon as that was done. Bending low, she coughed, her abused lungs feeling as if they would rip from her chest. When she recovered, she stood up and assessed the area. Zita forced her breathing to even out.

The driver, students, and a pair of adults she had missed in the confusion stood near the museum. Two-thirds of the kids had phones out and focused on the bus and Remus. A few panned over to her. The gold pickup had disappeared, as had Garm and his accomplices. She cursed. When cameras turned toward her, she shut her mouth and went to help Remus.

Shifting to a badger, she began to dig, throwing mud up behind her onto the lower portions of the bus still on fire. The added abuse to her leg sent agony streaking through her, but she pushed it aside and continued.

Remus' cough broke her concentration. He said, "Arca, please don't."

Zita squinted up at him.

"You're slowing me down," he explained before blurring into motion again.

Chastened, she hobbled away. *Fire's almost out, anyway,* she told herself. Since the bus driver and teachers seemed to have the excited and battered teens under as much control as could be expected, Zita bypassed them to sit on the other side of the SUV. She didn't need to be naked on the internet in any human form; she had the suspicion her mother would somehow know.

This close to the museum, the blaring alarm penetrated her sore ears. Guessing what she would see, she shifted into a turkey vulture and flew up to the window of the room in which she had hidden the haft. Even from outside, she could see the smashed case that had held the knife handle. *They got it despite the skunks and the fact I switched it with another handle in a different room. I just wanted to avoid stealing.*

Her spirits sank, and she spiraled back down to land on a low tree branch. As her adrenaline drained and exhaustion overtook her, she sank into a half-doze, leaning against the tree trunk.

Minutes later, Remus stood by her branch. "Are you okay?" he asked in Spanish. Not a speck of mud marred his appearance, but fatigue showed in his posture, and his voice was scratchy.

With a cautious check to see if the teenagers were filming her (mostly not), Zita shifted to Arca form. *I never get naked on the first date*, she grumbled mentally as she smoothed her palms over her thighs. Smooth fabric greeted the motion. *Wait... Did I finally practice enough to shift with my clothing?* Excitement rising, she risked a glance down. Dull purple cloth peeked out beneath the layer of dirt still covering her. "I'm not naked!" she exulted in the same language.

Remus wore an odd expression. "No, you're not."

"I totally thought my clothes would be gone by now, but they're not! This is great," Zita blurted out. Pain reminded her of the suboptimal parts of the afternoon, and a rash of coughing stole her breath. Her brain shied away from her friends' reactions to all this. "Other than the injuries, but I'll heal. Are you okay? You did good."

He nodded. "I'm fine. Listen," Remus said in a cautious tone, "the police will be here any minute now, and then I have an appointment I really have to get to right after I talk to them."

"So, you have to run?" Zita realized what she said and gave a tired chuckle at her own words before she caught his subtext. Her shoulders slumped. "Right. You have to go. No problem. I'll retrieve the picnic stuff and go home for a Band-Aid or something. The cops and I don't need to chat."

Remus considered her. Gone was the steamy, approving assessment of earlier. "Why don't you stay here? I'll pack up everything," he said. With a pop, he disappeared before she could reply.

"My, people come and go so quickly here," the school bus driver said, coming near Zita. The smile beneath his salt-and-pepper mustache seemed both expectant and rusty, as if he did not often bother to use it.

"What?" Zita said. It sounded familiar, like something she'd heard when she hadn't been paying attention. *To be honest, that doesn't narrow down the possibilities much.*

The smile disappeared. "From the *Wizard of Oz?* School curricula these days are clearly missing the classics," the driver grumbled. A burst of noise from the direction of the milling students had him turning and glaring that direction.

"If you say so." She adjusted her position to put less weight on her injured limb. Pressing her pant fabric against the wound, she hoped to slow the bleeding. Instead, she saw the fabric meld back together, the rips mending. *Wish my leg would do that.*

With a cough, the older man rewarded her effort to be agreeable. "Thank you for your help with the kids. We're grateful. Since this isn't over the Mountain where the rich folks are, the police wouldn't have been here in time to stop that woman y'all were fighting with." He narrowed his brown eyes at her.

I didn't scope out the area well enough. I assumed all the trees and the museum meant it was a fancy part of town. He's got to be a parent or Catholic to put that much guilt into a thank you. "You're welcome," Zita replied, her assumed voice hoarse. "We tried to stop them when they attacked people."

"Is that so?" he replied. His tone implied it wasn't an acceptable excuse.

A flash of light and a siren's wail heralded a pair of police cruisers speeding around the sharp curves of the road.

Oye, he might be a Catholic parent. Another conversation I won't be winning. Zita offered him a weary smile. "Here's the police now, so I'll be on my way." Careful to avoid damaging her leg further, she shifted into a turkey vulture and floundered through the air back to the picnic site and her things, now packaged in the cooler.

Remus was gone.

Just as well. Perching on a tree branch, she peered down. Flashing police lights surrounded the place, and excited teenagers swarmed in the road, gesturing wildly in excitement. Another bus labored up the switchbacks.

Zita sighed and then paused, her breath catching. Nearly obscured by fresh pine sap, traces of man and expensive gun oil emanated from the bark, but this time, she caught more of the layered, complex scent. *I must be imagining things. Why would a freelance assassin or mercenary or whatever be here?*

Turning her head, she scanned the tree, her heart pounding when she noted a new notch in the branch near where she perched. After scuttling awkwardly over, she sniffed. The wound in the tree held the odor of a firearm. *Bizarre. So, he watched, maybe through his scope, and then left? I suppose I should be grateful that he didn't shoot me. How could I have missed sensing him earlier? I've been in and out of the clearing most of the day. Bird form is surprisingly soothing for stakeouts because you can watch but nap at the same time, or fly all over and still pay attention. I guess this is the first bird form I've used today with a good sense of smell, though. It's good the webcam I used to teleport isn't visible from here or he'd know about that trick.* Another thought struck her, this one more frivolous. *I stripped to practice shifting. Did he see that?*

Gliding to the blanket, she shifted back to Arca and grabbed her picnic gear. Zita prayed no one would catch her before she could shower and somehow learn the eloquence she'd need to convince her friends not to be upset at her failure. With a deep breath, she teleported to her bedroom.

Chapter Twelve

When she appeared in the room, Andy waved from her desk, where he played on a black electronic device. "Hey, Zita. All quiet so far. Wyn's been doing paperwork all morning, and now she's on a private call that isn't going well, so be warned. She'll be all over your date." Raising his voice, he called out, "Wyn, Zita's back." Glancing over, his welcoming smile faltered, and his face turned grim.

If she's busy, it might be better to get a shower and give Wyn time to cool down before we talk. Zita hobbled over to set down the picnic things by the closet and shapeshifted back to her own human form. A trickle of blood dripped from under her capris, warm droplets gliding down her calf.

Wyn bustled into the room, flicking off her phone and sliding it into a pocket. She stopped, concern on her beautiful face, then circled Zita, her wariness like that of someone approaching a wounded animal. "Errands and a date do not cause that. Remus didn't..."

As Andy poked a few buttons on his game, the screen went dark. "She's limping, too."

"He didn't do anything wrong. We didn't click. No big." Zita tried to wipe mud off her face, stopping when she realized she was just spreading it around, and squared her shoulders. With a sigh at the laundry, she rubbed her hands on her pants, smearing more red dirt on the fabric. "I did have errands to run and a date. If you could spare a quick heal, that would be awesome, but it's not critical. Why don't you do that and then get back to what you were doing? I'll grab a shower and start chopping stuff so we can have alambres for dinner later. I can fill you in at dinner."

Relief had spread across Wyn's face before her expression hardened again.

Andy set down his game with a crack. He picked it back up and checked it, frowning. "You're covered in muck, hurt, and suggesting we go back to playing? Plus, weren't you wearing a shirt earlier? Z, you know we're not that stupid."

Wyn snapped first. "You're the only one in the room with a food obsession. What asinine thing did you do this time?" She strode forward, growling out the words to her spell. As if unable to stop herself from healing the injury, her hand sought Zita's arm, sparkling magic already twining around it.

"Nothing stupid." Zita scrambled to think of a diplomatic way to tell them her brilliant plan of staking out the museum had ended in the loss of the haft of the Key and getting beaten up by an oversized wolf. She grimaced. *Oye, that does sound bad.*

Wyn's eyes widened. "You surveilled the museum, lost the second piece of the artifact, and suffered an ignominious defeat by a colossal wolf? You said you were going on a date! Is anything you say true?" She glared at Zita's leg, even as the cool touch of her magic soothed and healed the bite.

"Would you let me talk without messing with my brain every five seconds? A little privacy would be nice. If I want to tell you something, I will," Zita snapped. She drew herself up to her full height and crossed her arms over her chest, glaring up at her friend. "It didn't go the way I expected, but I did do errands and have a date. The fight was unplanned. I was just going to observe and call the police if necessary."

Andy gave a humorless laugh. "Because that's worked out so well for us before."

Removing her hand when Zita's injury vanished, Wyn took a step back and scowled. "Maybe if it were the only time, but it's not. The first time was with your brother's kidnapping." She extended one finger.

"What? I'm supposed to ignore when Quentin disappears?"

Wyn did not deign to answer other than to have a second finger join the first and continue with her list. "The next incident that I know about, as you never tell me anything of any importance, was the thing with the octopuses a week and a half ago."

Zita waved her hand. "Unavoidable. How could I have known what was happening? I was there for the food. I was hungry, and they just happened to pick the same food truck as me."

"Are you ever not?" Andy muttered.

Wyn ignored both of them and extended another finger. "The squirrel bomber at the university?"

"Literally right in my path. Could not be avoided since those rodents were everywhere." Zita folded her arms over her chest again. *I am way too tired for this, and I am sick of her invading my mind.*

Wyn's eyes were slits. "You didn't have to get closer to an armed bomber and provoke him."

Zita exhaled and tried to keep from getting upset. *Be a friend. Wyn's under a lot of pressure. Try to be diplomatic. She likes logic, so use that to calm her down.* "You couldn't find him unless I was closer, hostages needed to be freed before he could behead them, and in all honesty, I didn't mean to antagonize him. That was a natural side effect of talking to him at all."

"Fair point," Andy said, providing unexpected but welcome support.

Both women turned their gazes to him.

"What? Conversation's not her strength unless you're talking extreme sports or athletics." He shrugged.

I'm not certain if that was a defense or an insult, but I'll take it. At least it's truthful, Zita thought.

Dismissing him with a roll of her eyes, Wyn ticked off two more fingers. "The island, plus whatever happened today. You can't tell me either of those was a wrong place, wrong time coincidence. You chose to go without us, and you lied about it."

Zita made a dogged try. "No, I left out some details."

"Omission of salient details is lying."

"I didn't lie. I was trying to keep things simple." *And that was a mistake. I don't need another failure to repeat that particular painful lesson. It's sheer luck those people weren't killed today, that and Remus being present. Gracias a Dios, I underestimated him. Time to woman up.* Zita took a deep breath and loosened her shoulder muscles. She rubbed her palms on her pants, cleared her throat, and took a step. "Hold up, I got something to say."

Wyn paused, and both her friends tilted their faces in her direction.

"You were right about the island. I'm sorry," Zita said with sincerity. "I should have taken Andy. He would have been mostly safe. We're cool now, right?"

Andy sputtered, "Mostly safe?" Perhaps realizing how high his voice had risen, he cleared his throat and continued in a lower tone, "I'm tougher and stronger than you, Zita. And though you were a potential gymnast, I was actually on the Olympic judo team the last time around. Well, I was second runner-up in my weight class, but that's close."

The correction shot out of Zita's mouth before she could consider her words. "Judo's not the same. Competition sport is different from actual combat." Realizing she had made things worse, she puffed air out in frustration. "I should not have said that. Can I start again?"

His expression closed. "Probably not, Hagrid. Given your preferred martial art is capoeira, you definitely shouldn't have said that. I've studied ju-jitsu just as you've studied other things."

She held up a hand to forestall additional anger. "My bad. Sorry. Let me clarify. I haven't forgotten bullets bounce off you and you lift thousands of pounds without breaking a sweat. The risk to your identity is why I didn't take you with me. They had cameras. If something happened to your mask or if they got your fingerprints, you and your family would be hosed," Zita explained.

His countenance pensive, he nodded. "But next time, you'll ask, even if they have evil phones and malicious cameras?"

Zita crossed her heart with her fingers. "If I'm going into physical danger, I'll try if there's time. I was right about you flinching, though, and not really liking that sort of thing. I'm sorry. We good?" Hopeful this was over, she held out a fist.

Andy snorted. "Conditional, much?" Despite his words, his body relaxed, and he sounded more amused than not. He smiled. "Fine, that's fair." They bumped fists.

"And?" Wyn prodded her, anger threading through her voice again.

"And what?" Zita asked. "I said you were right and I should've taken Andy to the island. Oh, you mean the museum? That really was a date. Perhaps a picnic stakeout wasn't my best idea, but I didn't think they'd try to rob the place until long after he'd gone."

A line appeared between Wyn's brows, and she pinched the bridge of her nose. She sighed. "What about me?"

Puzzlement was Zita's new best friend. She sweated and searched her memory. *Did I leave something out? She's loca if she thinks I'm taking back what I said about her invading my mind whenever she wants.* "What about you? You were right, I said that. I meant what I said about allowing me privacy in my head though."

Andy's smile vanished.

"I'm crazy if I think—" Wyn halted herself. She took a deep breath, opening the fingers of one hand and pushing it down. "What about asking me to go next time?"

Zita relaxed. She chuckled, shook her head, and reassured her friend with a pat on the arm. "No, don't worry. Of course, I wouldn't do that to you."

Wyn's fists clenched, and her face fell.

Upon seeing that, Zita's smile faded. She frowned and ran a hand over the uneven fuzz of her hair. *Why is this apology not working?*

Next to her, Andy inhaled sharply and winced. "Zita, apologize and tell her, of course, you will," he whispered.

"Don't help her," Wyn hissed.

With a frown, Zita told him, "Why would I lie? Why would I ask her to go somewhere she wouldn't want to go, to do things she's not good at and doesn't want to do?"

"How can you be this dense?" he asked.

"Wait, you want me to ask? Why? You hate violence, have no fight training, and would be in huge danger. That's like..." Zita searched for an appropriate comparison. "You don't bug me to go to your Wicca church or temple or whatever, and I don't nag you to come to Sunday Mass. Neither one of us wants to convert. Why would I make an offer like that?"

"That's different! That's respectful of religious differences," Wyn told her. Her eyes glistened, and she turned away, her shoulders slumping.

Zita bit her lip and swore internally. *I said something wrong. Again.* "You want to come to Mass? Fine, I'd love to have you come. You can sit with me, and I'll introduce you to the priest."

Wyn shook her head. "No! No Mass. Never mind, I see how little you think of me. Why did you even bother to take me with you to kidnap Boris?"

Carajo, is she crying? Zita panicked for a second before she calmed herself. *Deep breaths in and out.* When her breathing was under control, she forced a pleasant tone. "Wait, what? You're not useless. I took you to *question* Boris because I didn't think it would be dangerous and you could find out fast where my brother was being held without hurting anyone. Clearly, I have no idea what I'm saying, or you wouldn't be so upset." She cast around for the right words, seizing on the first ones that came to mind. "Did you change your hair?"

Wyn touched her hair and gaped at her. She sniffed, and her hands flew up in the air. "I surrender! Every conversation goes in circles with you. Are you afraid we'll all leave you if you say something with any depth? Is that what your father did?"

Zita stiffened, and her body tightened, her feet slipping into a defensive stance as if the words had been a physical blow. "Papa would never have left us," she blazed. "Sí, I suck at talking to people. I know this. That's no reason to throw shade at my parents, who did their best. Say what you will about me, but he was a good man! He was killed when I was a kid."

Her friends gaped at her.

Wyn sputtered, "I-I didn't know. You never said..."

"Pues, what kind of conversation is that?" Zita narrowed her eyes at her friend. "When would we have talked about that? When we were teens in the hospital together? How would that have gone? Oh, hey, we might all die from cancer or the experimental therapy or the crappy food here. Speaking of dying, my father was collateral chingado damage in a gun battle between the police and drug runners. Oh, and the police couldn't be bothered to apologize or figure out who shot an unarmed fleeing illegal. So, you going to eat that fine, hospital-grade gelatin? When's the right time to say that sort of thing?"

Andy squeezed her shoulder. His face was a study in sorrow and shadows.

She put her hand on his. "Thanks, mano." Inhaling, she counted seconds before releasing the breath, trying to bring her temper back under control. "Why don't you go make your tea, and I'll shower off this wonderful mud and burnt rubber stench? We can forget about this whole discussion."

Wyn recovered her voice. "I'm sorry for your loss, but that's exactly the sort of thing normal people tell their friends. You needn't engage in hostilities about it. And, by the Goddess, stop trying to divert the conversation. This isn't about your parents. This is about how you don't trust me enough to even hold a meaningful conversation."

Zita held up a hand, her temper reigniting. "Wait, you insult both my parents, and I'm the hostile one for not ignoring it? You've even met my mom. She fed you, talked with you, and even lit candles and prayed for you. That's not right."

"Wait, both your parents?" Wyn said.

"You either assumed that my very Catholic saint of a mother got knocked up three times without getting married or that my father abandoned his wife and three children? How is that not offensive?"

Her friend's mouth was a thin, straight line. "I don't know."

Zita put her hands on her hips. "Well, work it out and handle it. I can't fix your shit for you. Your parents"—*are assholes*— "were awful, but mine weren't. Leave them out of our issues."

Wyn's back was straight and her voice icy. "I'm sorry. My comments have inadvertently disrespected your parents, and you have my apologies. All I wanted was for you to be honest and open with us. Half the time, I need to read your mind to learn anything of substance."

The reminder opened the floodgates. "First, I don't need sympathy or psychoanalysis or whatever you intended. Second, I didn't mention it because I don't dwell on the past. Life can suck, or it can be awesome. You prepare what you can for the tough times because sooner or later, they're gonna happen. In the meantime, you got to reach for the happy. That's my plan, anyway. Last, stay the fuck out of my brain. You wander around in there every time you want to satisfy your curiosity. You were hesitant to read Boris' mind, but you're all over mine like a kid on candy, and you need to quit."

Wyn opened her mouth. "It's not like that."

Zita slashed the air with a finger as she cut off further comments. "It is exactly like that. I'm a person and your friend, not a tourist destination you visit whenever you get bored or don't like my answers. When you couldn't stop it from happening, that was one thing. I was cool with that. It's fine for talking private-like or over distance, whatever. But you have control now, so knock off running around and getting your jollies by sifting through my mind. If you want to ask a question, ask it, and I'll tell you what I want you to know."

"But you never do. I'm not certain you ever will or why I even try," Wyn said, her hazel eyes stormy. She wrapped her arms around herself and whirled out of the room, slamming Zita's bedroom door shut.

Zita swore, reining in her temper again. *Can this get any worse?*

Andy cleared his throat behind her. "Actual love child standing right here. And my dad is Catholic, too." His tone was bland.

Zita ran a hand over her raggedy hair. Teleportation to anywhere else was such a temptation. *This is why I don't have close friends except these two, and I'm not certain how long at least one of those friendships is going to last. It's so much easier when you hang out to do fun stuff and go your separate ways until the next time.* "Mano, I'd bet your dad didn't know about you, or he would have stepped up."

"Mom took years to find and tell him... though truth be told, she didn't look too hard," Andy admitted.

A smile tugged at Zita's mouth. "Your mom's all about walking her own path, preferably with one of those fancy hand-woven runner rugs to precede her, but still. Your dad took responsibility as soon as he found out."

He mumbled agreement, and his shoulders relaxed.

With all sincerity, Zita apologized again. "I wasn't trying to imply anything bad about your parents. Sorry. They rock."

"I'd be surprised if you knew how to imply anything," he replied, a grudging smile peeking out.

She scrunched up her nose and rolled her eyes. "I can be subtle... like when I'm not talking. Or when I'm hiding."

Andy chuckled.

"Mano, seriously, I'm sorry. I wouldn't dis your parents on purpose. You got to clue me in, though, because I'm missing something. Why are you guys so mad at me? Especially Wyn. It's like a bug crawled up her culo and now I can't do anything right." Zita scrubbed a hand over her face.

Sobering, he hid his hands in his pockets. "We had each other's backs in the hospital when we were teens, right?"

She nodded. "You know it," she said.

Andy stared at the rug, then raised his gaze to her chin. "Yeah. You even managed to get that creepy friend of her parents banned from visiting Wyn."

Anger, still simmering from the argument with Wyn, ignited when she remembered that. "Grown man has no right to put his hands on a child like that."

He inclined his head in agreement and continued. "We had good times, but it was years ago. We're all adults now who have to get to know each other all over again. To be blunt, you're not an easy person to be close with. Most of the time when we hung out in quarantine, you wouldn't say anything serious, or you'd go exercise. I'm not certain how much you listened to anything anyone said, either."

"I heard all the important stuff. I did try. Kind of, but sitting around talking—"

"Is sometimes necessary. After our powers manifested and Quentin went missing, you got a pass since we both knew your brothers pretty much raised you. Your mom was always working."

"She's a great mother. Even if she couldn't be there all the time, she did better than most single parents," Zita defended her mother. "I had my coach, too."

Andy's mouth pressed into a thin line. "Until he tossed you to the curb when he found out about the cancer. I've met my share of trainers, and I doubt yours was a nurturer."

Zita snorted at the idea. "As a coach, he kicked major ass. As a person, sober or drunk, he was not a cuddly sort, no. Weakness doesn't win medals. Focus and perseverance do." Spotting wrinkles in her blanket, she reached to straighten it, her fingers itching for the tactile pleasure of the velvet blanket. At the sight of her filthy arm, she withdrew her hand.

He exhaled. "Figured."

"What does this have to do with what I'm doing wrong or why Wyn's upset? That's all the past and not even particularly relevant." To ignore her urge to tidy the bed, she faced him again and tilted her head.

"History shapes the present. You need to open up."

Zita made a rude noise and jiggled her leg, trying to stand still.

Andy rubbed the back of his neck. "Hear me out. Wyn's not like your old coach, is she?"

"Oh, no. She's totally girly and talks about everything and calls eight times a day. Then she wants to drink flowers and talk more. Coach preferred no talking and as little eating as possible. Just practices and obedience." Zita fell silent. Remembering those days, her stomach growled in reflex. *The diet he had wanted me on...*

He nodded. "What do you two have in common?"

She answered on automatic, still distracted by the memory. "We both wanted me to win the gold medal." Frowning, she realized the spots on the rug were blood. *I need to treat those before they set.*

Andy's eyes narrowed, and he shook his head at her. "What do you and Wyn have in common?"

Zita hesitated. "We have a shared past and like doing yoga together." She searched for more similarities. "We're both women, enjoy trying new places, and get along well enough. We have some laughs when I'm not pissing her off."

A half-smile touched his lips. "I'm not certain you really count as female, but I'll give you that one. Do you ever call or text Wyn?"

"Ass." Zita considered the question and shrugged. "No. No need to contact someone who's already blowing up your phone with calls or texts every few hours. Not to mention the surprise visits."

"That is a bit much, but when you do things together, who suggests it?"

"Her. Wait, I asked her to help with Boris. Does that count?"

"No."

She snapped her fingers. "I called her to get her off campus when the squirrel bomber was there. How about that?"

Andy shook his head.

"Oh. It should. Special credit."

He enunciated as if he thought she might miss his words if he didn't. She had to admit it was possible. "Right, so Wyn's putting out all the effort to sustain your friendship. And right now, she's stressed over her aunt and the nursing home, plus whatever the lawsuit is, and the whole life in danger thing."

That caught her attention. Zita's eyes widened. "Her aunt's in a nursing home? The one who took her in when her parents kicked her out?"

He nodded. "Wyn hasn't shared details, though I offered to talk to her about it. She's always idolized you a little, and you're pushing her away when she's stressed."

He's got to be mistaken about her thinking that. Someone as smart and peace-loving as Wyn probably worships at the feet of Einstein and Gandhi, not a failed Olympic athlete who can't even get any hours at work. "Not volunteering things is not the same as pushing people away."

"It is sometimes. Give and take."

Zita rubbed her forehead. "What do I do about Wyn? I want to help her, but everything I say pisses her off."

He paused, then sighed. "Let her cool off, and I'll try to talk to her. Try to be more open next time you're talking. I can't believe I'm asking this but... Remus? Didn't work?"

Zita grimaced. "He's pleasant and a wonderful choice for a girl who's not me... You know, a nice, sweet girl who isn't into outdoor activities, zip lines, or exercise other than running."

Sympathy shone on Andy's face, and he patted her shoulder. "It's okay, Zita. Don't let the Muggles get you down. Maybe next time."

"Most muggers leave me alone. I don't dress like money, and I don't walk like easy prey despite my size," Zita said, frowning. "And don't worry about the Remus thing. I'm glad I asked him out, but it's hardly the first time that some guy and I haven't been a match."

He chuckled. "Muggles... Just, better luck next time, though I'm ecstatic you made it back dressed for once. You want a snack?"

Still digesting the argument, Zita said, "Shower, clean those spots on the rug, then food." *Even if the bloodstains are small, I need to treat them before my brother sees them and freaks.*

Andy nodded. "Sounds like a plan. I'll check on Wyn while you do that."

Chapter Thirteen

The next day, Andy stopped by earlier than usual and brought dinner, perhaps fearing the two women would still be arguing in his absence. Though Wyn was still frosty, she had begun to thaw after yoga and a play session with the cats (which had included Zita as a large, fluffy black cat).

In the hopes of hearing that the police had caught Garm's team, they left the news on during their meal. Zita wanted to switch it off after one segment had covered a spate of crimes by metahumans and ignored all crimes against them, but the other two overruled her. They were still engaged in a friendly debate over the level of bias when they realized the reporter was now interviewing the elderly owner of the third piece of the Key of Hades. When his name and city were given out as part of the segment, all three were horrified. Andy confirmed that a single Web search returned the man's address in a nearby county.

Dinner was abandoned in favor of warning the man in person since a phone call could be more easily ignored.

Mindful of her promise, Zita asked Andy for help, but was unable to convince Wyn to stay home. After donning their disguises, Zita teleported them to the closest webcam, careful to appear on the edges so it would seem as if they might have stepped into the frame while passing by. They walked the rest of the way to the man's estate. Another judicious teleport got all three past the rusty fence, ornate gate, and security cameras without being seen.

Rotting wooden steps, almost invisible beneath multiple years' blanket of leaves, led up a steep hill toward the house. Zita took the steps two at a time, appreciating the uneven widths that added a touch of challenge to it and the rich, molting odors of late summer. Andy and Wyn trailed behind, his progress steady, and Wyn's more halting.

When they arrived at the house, their plan fell to pieces. Zita and Andy reached it first, but Wyn was still the first to speak.

"This is a multimillion-dollar home? After those giant gates, I was expecting turrets or multi-car garages or something. At least a swimming pool. Do we have the right address? Zita, if you made me trudge up those stairs of doom for nothing..."

Andy grumbled. "If a giant rock comes rolling down this hill, I wouldn't be surprised."

For a moment, Zita imagined a huge stone tumbling down the hill, smashing everything in its path. She calculated the possibilities. "If it didn't build up enough speed, it would stop a little into the tree line. Not really a threat even if there was one, other than to one or two of the saplings."

Andy muttered, "Thanks, Indy."

"I use Arca for this shape," Zita said, "Not Indy." She tapped a pointy ear. A half-mask covered the top portion of her face, and she had donned a ratty camouflage top and shorts she usually kept for hunting. Her disguise's long hair fell free over her like a cloak.

He shook his head, rolling his eyes in his domino mask even as his lips curled up. "Not even the classic movies? Your life has been totally deprived, Zita, I mean, Arca." His own disguise consisted of gloves, the mask, and turning his own T-shirt inside out.

"So, is this the place?" Wyn interrupted, staring at the humble dwelling. She had chosen to reuse the illusion of a white blond woman with deep amethyst eyes, clad in a short, glittery dress and a diadem that matched her eyes. Beneath the illusion, she wore a mask and gloves, as well as more practical clothing. She had eschewed a mask in her illusory form.

In front of them, trees dwarfed a small farmhouse, the weathered gray siding overshadowed by the more vibrant browns and greens of the surrounding forest. Overgrown bushes hid most of the two front windows. Zita guessed the whole thing to be two thousand square feet. A handicap van in ubiquitous gold filled the modest carport at the end of the gravel drive. Wrapped in the inoffensive patterned paper she associated with department store wrapping services, a heap of presents stood waist-high by a side door. Other than the gifts, the only sign of money she saw were the high-end security cameras tucked into protected emplacements around the house exterior. *Pity they didn't hire a professional company to install them. They invested in quality cameras, but their placement left gaping blind spots. If it weren't for the need for anonymity, I'd leave Quentin's business number for them.*

The front lawn, such as it was, was littered with odd party detritus. Toppled onto its side, an abandoned and cracked ice sculpture of a man melted slowly in the late-day sun. Bald patches scarred the ground where a table's feet had rested next to the half-liquefied haughty face. A handful of spotless white paper plates and unused clear plastic cups, the fancy ones shaped like martini glasses, lay scattered near the carport. Wheel marks where cars had parked on the grass and under the trees and anywhere with enough room marred the otherwise healthy tangle of weedy grass and unraked leaves. Two enormous evergreens had a portable toilet wedged between them. Bright letters decorating the side announced the rental status of the toilet.

Zita shrugged. *Might as well try to be legal about this.* "We knock. I hope they didn't beat us here." Matching action to words, she walked up and rapped on the door. In case his hearing was poor, she pressed the doorbell as well.

"Let me do the talking, Zita," Wyn said.

Andy hung back.

The door was thrown open by a familiar man whose muscles displayed beneath blue scrubs. Her date from last Friday, Luis, glared at them all with cold eyes. "He's not interested in your party. If you must leave gifts, set them under the carport, and I'll retrieve them when I have a minute." He paused, eyeing the three of them, cracking tattooed knuckles the size of Zita's head. "Boy, are you at the wrong house," he said, looming over them.

Zita blinked and stepped back. She fell into a defensive position for a moment. *If I didn't know Luis was a college boy who went right into nursing school, I'd think he escaped prison yesterday. Didn't know he could front that well or lift his eyes above a girl's chest. They totally should have purchased a better alarm system, though.*

That was your date? I owe you an apology. It might not have been all your fault, just mostly, Andy sent.

Smartass.

Quivering, Wyn glanced at Zita as if seeking reassurance, then stepped forward. Honey and the South sang in her sweet, bell-like voice. "We're sorry to disturb you. May we please speak to Mister Stanley Shivers? It's very important."

Luis seemed satisfied that they were cowed; that or he wanted to avoid having anyone test his tough façade. "No, he's not seeing anyone today. Tomorrow, either. You're trespassing. Get off the property. You have five minutes, and then we call the police." He slammed the door shut.

Wyn blinked at the closed door. "Well, that was unsuccessful."

A click sounded as the door lock engaged.

Zita sighed and gestured for the others to follow her. She withdrew to one of the wooden steps, a location she assumed was in a blind spot and out of camera range. The portable toilet and evergreens provided a screen from the occupants of the house. "How about I take Wyn back, and then I stake it out in animal shape? Andy could hang out deeper in the woods. Sunset's not that far off, and then we can hide closer. We could try breaking in and warning them, but I've been trying to keep everything as legal as possible. In any case, we're in for a long night."

"Maybe Garm won't come." Wyn voiced all their hopes. "And no, I'm not going home."

Andy rubbed the back of his neck. "Can we take that risk with their lives?"

With a shake of her head, Zita replied, "Of course not. Okay, Wyn, you convince them to get to safety and hide their sheath somewhere. Andy, why don't you watch the gate? If Garm and his posse show, knock down a dead tree or something to delay them long enough for us to get Shivers and Luis out. If the cops get here first, warn us so we can all meet and teleport away before we have arrest records. Trespassing is a misdemeanor, but still."

Andy sighed but gave a curt nod. "Can do." He strode down the road.

Wyn moved to the carport and pulled an envelope from one of the presents. "We could slide them a note under their door if they don't want to talk."

"You bring a pen?" Zita asked.

Her friend sniffed. "I brought my bag. I have pens in a wide variety of colors and scents."

A window slid open a crack. "Put that down! Thief!" came an outraged shout from inside.

He's too busy watching us to talk to us? Zita scanned the windows and caught sight of two pairs of eyes.

Wyn spun, setting the paper down. She spread her hands wide and implored, "Listen, we need to talk to you. Criminals are after one of your possessions, and they will come here soon to take it, probably utilizing completely unnecessary force."

"Only trouble I see is you. Get off my property!" came the bellow from inside, followed by a calmer addendum by Luis that the police had been called.

We got company, Andy sent. *The delivery truck they just buzzed in just let out someone. Whoa, that's a tall man, and the wolf is huge. If he eats like Zita but to scale, he had to turn to crime to pay for the mountains of kibble.*

Zita touched Wyn's shoulder. "Say the word, and I'll grab you, the old fart, and Luis and we'll be gone. Once you're safe, I'll come back for Andy and the sheath. I can handle the exposure of my teleportation later." *I heard that, mano, and I'll have you know I have a healthy appetite and high caloric needs. Don't be hating.*

Wyn shivered, bit her lip, then shook her head. "No, I can help. I'll hide or something. You're right, if people know you can do that, they'd shoot you or coerce you or try to make you their favorite drugged research subject."

A massive metallic crash came from farther down the drive.

"Incoming thugs. You get in and hide," Zita said, dragging her friend to the best hiding spot.

Wyn scowled. "It's a porta potty."

Her eyes on the road leading up to the house, Zita replied, "It will muddy or hide your scent, so Garm won't recognize you. Given his hissy fit at your house and the way he clawed up the convenience store security grille, you don't want to be vulnerable around him. If I can keep them facing away from you, I'll tell you. Then you can peek out and put them to sleep, and we can leave them for the cops that way."

Oblivious to their conversation, Andy sent, *I've ridden ponies smaller than that wolf. Seriously, what does he think this is, Twilight? Tall guy attacking me, wolf and woman might be headed your way.*

As she stepped carefully into the stall, Wyn asked. *Why are they walking?*

I stopped their car, Andy replied. *Ah, permanently. It might not work anymore.*

Well, between that and the lady with the shotgun in Alabama, they've got to be running low on giant SUVs at least, Zita mused. She closed the door to the temporary toilet, despite the muffled protest within.

Rushing away from Wyn's hiding place, she picked an old beech tree with numerous wide, crossing branches. She transformed into a turkey vulture. Her clothing fell around her, and she struggled to emerge from her underwear. *I thought I had that figured out. Why didn't my clothes stay on this time? They did at the museum.* With no other options or time, she scooped up her clothing into a wad and lifted it into a fork of her chosen tree. Flapping her powerful wings, she perched on another branch, one thick enough to hold her weight if she had to turn into a jaguar.

Tiffany and Garm crested the steep hill. The woman rode upon the great wolf, her body curling on his back, and fingers caressing the fur behind one ear. He bounded up the hill as if her weight were nothing, his body posture almost jaunty.

When they caught sight of the house, the witch dismounted. Her throaty chuckle and husky murmur to her canine companion had Zita squirming in discomfort as if she spied upon an intimate moment. *It's nice they have each other, but that doesn't give them the right to hurt the old crank inside or Luis,* she reminded herself.

Once again, Tiffany was dressed as if going to a cocktail party rather than committing a crime, the only discordant note a large leather messenger bag draped across her body. Garm, of course, wore fur and four legs.

Wow, Zita thought, *no accounting for taste. I don't know how that can be comfortable for either of them. Wolves are not built to be ridden, but it's not like I haven't seen weirder.*

"Later," Tiffany said, trailing her hand down the fur of his back. "When I am the only eyes to see you upon two legs."

Garm grunted, then sniffed the air, "The pig from the museum yesterday is here somewhere."

All languidness disappeared from Tiffany's body, and she pulled a long, dark bottle from her messenger bag. "Where?"

Zita fluffed her feathers and adjusted her weight. *I hope that's not another bottle of that fire stuff.*

Garm's nose quivered as his head and tail lifted, and he sought the answer. "Close." He zigzagged across the road, little more than a collection of ruts, where patches of gravel made a token effort to tame the churned mud and resilient weeds. The wolf stopped by one of the rotting wooden steps, his ears rising. "Got multiple fresh scents. Lots of people here today, but three strong ones, two female, one male. One is the shifter from the museum. The soap the others used is making my nose burn," he growled.

Even knowing the keenness of a wolf's nose, Zita made a silent protest. *Hey, I showered twice today. At least having Wyn and Andy shower using that stinky soap worked to confuse their scents.*

The wolf's companion nodded and returned the bottle to her bag. "The male must be that fool the others are dispatching. I trust you can handle the other one on your own?"

Andy? Zita's stomach clenched.

Garm huffed, derision in the tone. "If I can't handle one soft female, I wouldn't be an alpha, would I? You get the sheath, I'll handle this."

Approval gleamed in Tiffany's face. With a last stroke of his fur, she turned toward the house.

Andy sent back, sounding distracted, *Busy.*

To Zita's horror, the great wolf lowered his head to follow the trail, stopping by the portable toilet. His ears twitched. "I hear your heart beating, little mouse. You should never have gotten involved." He stretched out his neck to open the door with his mouth.

Zita? What's going on? Wyn sent.

Shifting to her Arca form, Zita said, "Oh, hey, were you looking for me? Were you seriously going to put your mouth on that? I'm over here," She crouched on the tree branch, which creaked beneath her increased weight. Without a conscious decision to use it, her fake Mexican accent was back in her voice.

He whirled to face her, turning his back on Wyn's hiding place.

One down. Time to get the other one before she offs the geezer and his aide. On the bright side, I may not be great at talking, but I'm terrific at annoying. Zita eyed Tiffany's back. "Oye, Tiffy, you want to come talk to your doggie? You would not believe what he wanted to put in his mouth. Then again, maybe you would, all things considered." She cleared her throat and gave a deliberate snicker.

Below her, Garm snarled.

Her back stiffening, Tiffany stopped and pivoted toward Zita. "Queen Halja to you, stupid creature. Show some respect."

Halja? Talk about an interesting choice of mythology. The woman has father issues if she picked that name herself. Wyn's analysis had a distracted tone, one that usually heralded a flood of information.

Not the time for a mythology lesson, Wyn, Zita sent. She decided to draw them out farther, and skittered closer to the tree trunk, crawling to distribute her weight more evenly. "I don't know, Tiffy's got a ring to it, and you need all the help you can get. Anyway, I wanted to tell you not to waste your time. The old fart doesn't have the sheath," she lied. *Move away from the defenseless woman hiding in the porta potty.*

Wyn's mental voice went from thoughtful to alarmed. *What exactly are you doing out there? Are you purposefully trying to get them to attack?*

"Garm, would you?" Tiffany asked. "I need to—" She was interrupted by a bellow from the house. The witch and her wolf both turned their heads to see the source of the noise.

Zita groaned, all her work to keep their attention on her lost.

Under the carport, a raisin of a man, tiny and wrinkled, lifted a bullhorn to his lips. Sunlight gleamed on glasses so thick she was surprised he could hold his head up. "The police have been called. You have until they get here to get off my personal property!"

Hovering beside his employer like a faithful mastiff, Luis crossed his beefy arms, and his face settled into familiar lines. He had worn the same expression on their date when informing her that they were not suited to each other.

Perhaps he means to be intimidating, but it's actually kind of cute, Zita thought. *Ay, caramba. That's something people say when I try the same thing. At least I'm not boring, though.*

"You will give me the Sheath for the Key of Hades immediately," Tiffany demanded. She put her fists on her scrawny hips.

Luis said something softly to the old man, setting a large, gentle hand on one thin shoulder.

His companion shook off the hand and raised the bullhorn again to his lips. "No. Get lost. You want it? You buy it. Unlike you, I don't give anything away for free. And if your dog poops, you'd better pick it up on the way out. If you're a hooker, you can tell whichever one of my idiot relatives who hired you that I'm not interested! If I want to get laid, I'll pick her out myself."

Luis hid his face in both hands for a moment and then massaged his temples. "Mr. Shivers has spoken. Please depart," he finally echoed, before bending down to murmur something to his incensed companion.

Tiffany stiffened, and her hands curled. She stomped toward the carport. It might have been menacing had her impractical stiletto heels not sunken into the mud, requiring her to adopt an odd marching gait; she had to raise each leg up high to release her shoes with each step, an act accompanied by a loud sucking sound as the greedy ground relinquished the shoe. "I am Queen Halja. You will give me what I want or suffer the consequences," she warned as she teetered toward them. "I do not suffer fools or disobedience."

"Call her Tiffy. Everyone does," Zita shouted, desperate to return the attention back to herself and away from the far too frail men in the carport. "And no, she doesn't suffer fools. She sexes them, based on her conversation with the wolf."

Tiffany paused again. Her head turned, giving Zita a silhouette of her face. "Garm, handle it," she said, waving a hand in Zita's direction. Her back rigid, she continued toward the carport, digging through her satchel.

Garm whirled around. With a snarl, his massive paws ate the distance until he stood directly below her tree. He snarled up at her, his eyes deepening to red. "Do not speak of things you are too stupid to comprehend."

Understanding hit. *They're not just sleeping together. It's a real relationship and everything. Is everyone else in the world better at the couples thing than me? So not fair.* Zita's mouth ran wild as she pondered. "Oye, Garm, I didn't realize you and Tiffy were a serious item. I mean, how could I forget that murdering and robbing people is fine, but mentioning the existence of a loving, committed relationship is unforgivable?"

Garm leapt at her, his muscular legs carrying him so close that his jaws scraped at the underside of the limb that was her refuge, almost catching one foot.

Zita yanked her legs up, away from further jumps, and seized the branch overhead. It groaned under her weight, and she abandoned all thought of moving to that branch in her human form. *Of course, I could shift to a talking bird, but they're even less likely to listen to one of those. Let's see, animals that fare well against wolves. She's still moving toward the carport. I have to keep her from hurting them!* Zita inhaled and exhaled to center herself, then ran as far along the branch as she could without it bringing her into Garm's reach. Her bare feet curled, and she blessed all the "wasted" tightrope training she had done. *Not the time to dwell on past boyfriends or family,* she reminded herself.

Heels clicked rapidly on the concrete pad of the carport, then stopped. Tiffany glanced back, a vial raised to her lips and a cork in her hands. She chugged the contents.

When the bough became too narrow and bent too close to the ground, Zita bent her knees and hurled herself through the air, as if catching a trapeze, even throwing in a flip to extend the distance. She hit the ground and rolled, the shock sending pain up her legs, but causing no serious injury. Well aware the wolf had to be ready to spring, she used a bear form and sprinted after Tiffany with a roar. Her ursine speed allowed her to close the distance between them fast, but Garm raced close at her heels. *Whoever made that perfume should be shot. Ugh. Come on, deal with the freaking bear. Turn around and leave the idiots alone.* Some part of her brain was gratified to hear the old man shouting about being carried inside, but most of her attention was on her opponents.

Glass shattered as Tiffany dropped the empty vial and scurried back toward the house.

Zita, should I do something now? Wyn sent.

Thunder rumbled in the distance.

No, stay put and stay safe, Zita sent back, before pain announced that the wolf had caught up to her and bitten her hamstring. She stumbled and whirled with a howl. He had failed to rip it out, but he had done enough damage that she would not run again until healed. Her ursine instincts urged her to rend him to shreds, but she shoved those away, her thoughts whirling. *Knock him out, knock him down, keep him busy. I had hoped disabling Tiffany would get him to take her and run for it. He's too fast, though, and now I have to deal with him first.*

Worry clouded Wyn's voice. *Zita? Are you certain?*

His massive form almost as long as Zita's bear shape, Garm was on her, all fur and fangs and unholy halitosis.

Hide! Zita shouted mentally. With the hope that Wyn would take the hint, she closed off her mind to concentrate on fighting the wolf. She swatted at him in warning.

As she had intended, he fell back, showing his teeth in a snarl. He lunged forward, snapping, and she dodged aside, taking another swipe at him. The tip of her claws hit his face, and he drew back with a yelp. The scent of blood, hers and his mingled, hung in the air.

Garm snarled again and launched himself at her throat.

Animal fights appear to follow the rules of knife fights, and you know how to do that, Zita told herself. *This will hurt, but I can direct the damage to less important places.* She blocked with one arm, taking the brunt of his attack on a meaty portion and hurled him away from her.

Despite his weight, he flew through the air until the porta potty interrupted his flight. Flesh met plastic, and the toilet rocked on its temporary foundations.

Wyn screamed.

He slumped at the base of it for a moment, then rose, shaking his head. The odor of his blood receded, leaving only the scent of Zita's blood and the surrounding forest. A series of sharp snapping sounds came from somewhere out of sight.

Zita's arm dripped blood and sent pain ricocheting through her. She lumbered toward him, her mind spinning. *Carajo. He heals, and I don't. If this goes on too long, he's going to win. I need to get him away from Wyn first, though.* While the wolf still appeared dazed, she attacked, lowering her head and tossing him away from the porta potty. *Por favor, Dios, let him miss her scream.*

Wyn's mental voice shrieked for explanations.

Can't talk. If anyone opens the door, shoot them with magic, Zita sent. She switched to a feral pig, and charged the dazed wolf, her movements hampered by her injured limbs, though adrenaline kept her from feeling most of the pain. A horrendous metal crunch came from nearby.

I don't use that kind of magic, Wyn wailed. *The Wiccan rede—*

Zita collided with the wolf, and he flew a few more feet away. She skidded to a stop and shifted back into a bear. *Make a chingado magic gun. Throw sleep clouds at his face. I really can't talk.*

Wyn sputtered in answer.

This time, Garm was slower to regain his paws. However, he laughed, where before, he had only growled. "Ah, the irony of you going after Halja, when all along, you've been hiding a tender morsel from us. Perhaps we shall see what hostage you have given to fate." His head lowered, and his shoulders rose, ruff rippling upward. "And you don't heal. A poor example of a were, but not without hope. If you run now and leave your pet in the outhouse, perhaps I shall let you live."

Zita swore, which escaped as a rumble deep in her throat, and planted herself between him and the portable toilet. Her ears picked out a creak from behind her, but she did not dare tear her attention from the wolf. *Andy, if you're done, I need backup here*, she sent on the party line. Her mind raced through possibilities. *If he gets here fast, I can catch the wolf, and Andy can hold him while I chase down Tiffany, hopefully before she hurts those men in the house.*

Busy, Andy sent. *Ground trying to eat me, plus painfully bad poetry.*

Sounds like Jen's favorite tricks. Don't let it catch you, Zita answered. She tried to keep her swearing from leaking onto the shared mental link as she tried brainstorming a new plan.

"I'll take that as a no. Pity," Garm said, interpreting her response. "I hate killing a fellow monster if unnecessary. The road to a kingdom is littered with sacrifice, however, especially when it's a realm of powerful beasts. You're certain then?"

With a shake of her heavy head, Zita snorted. *I'm no monster. Perhaps if I were more of one, my friends would be safer.*

Her continued refusal of his offer must have come through, despite her muteness. White teeth gleamed in a sharp-edged smile. "Soft. Shame." He dove at her, pitching to the side at the last minute to go around her toward Wyn's hiding place.

Zita twisted and leapt after him, desperate to keep him away from her friend. She snapped at him, catching a hind leg in her mouth, and ripped, feeling bone and muscle separate. Her stomach heaved, and she fought the urge to gag. Releasing his leg, she spat out the mouthful as fast as possible. *Andy, if you come here, we can switch opponents. I can knock out Jen if you take the wolf.*

Why do you need to tag team? What's going on out there? Wyn sent.

Thunder boomed, this time closer.

Garm yipped and turned to face her, his rear leg hobbled by her bite. He snarled, all amusement gone from his eyes. Instead, they gleamed feral and angry and inhuman.

She pressed her advantage, trying to throw him aside again, but her own damaged limb failed her, and he evaded the move.

Garm wobbled, staring at her and protecting his wounded leg. The blood trailing from his injury slowed.

So unfair. All he has to do is wait until he heals. I can try to lead him away, Zita thought. She feinted.

He dodged, his rear leg giving out, but he recovered before hitting the ground.

She backed up a step or two, trying to lure him from Wyn.

His counterattack came in a flurry of fur and knifelike teeth as he charged, crossing the distance between them at full speed.

She once again blocked, and his teeth tore her biceps before she managed to claw his stomach and get him off her.

The door to the house slammed, and Tiffany stormed out. "Garm, the sheath isn't here," she hissed, throwing another vial against the side of the house. Glass exploded against the weathered siding. To Zita's relief, that bottle must have been empty, as no fire erupted. She caught sight of their tableau. "Aren't you done with that beast yet? Stop playing. I want out of this tacky mess."

Garm circled Zita. "Oh, she's almost done," he assured his companion.

Zita stuck out her tongue at him, turning in a slow circle, keeping most of her attention on him. Her good paw pressed hard above the injury on her other one, hoping to slow the bleeding.

"Not fast enough," Tiffany snapped. She leaned forward and stared. "Why is the toilet glowing with magic? What have you been doing out here? That worthless old man couldn't have resisted my potions, could he?" After raising her arms above her head, she flailed them around as she intoned. Her gestures were two or three times as grandiose as Wyn's, but by now, Zita recognized a spell being cast.

Garm flowed to her side, placing his body between Zita and his girlfriend.

Tiffany finished with a theatrical flourish of the presumably magic twig.

Nothing sparkled, and for a second, Zita thought the spell had fizzled. When she glanced away from Garm again, oily smoke and ooze, darker than the soil or shadows thrown by the trees, pooled near her.

Four blocky figures, like humanoids composed of half-melted wax, coalesced from the puddles. Featureless arms grew claws and grabbed for Zita, who ducked beneath them and rolled out of the way. Her leg complained. She gagged when their sulfuric stench hit.

She shapeshifted back to Arca, one hand still pressing her mangled arm, and then did a partial change to gain gorilla strength. "Seriously? Tiffy, if creating burned, spoiled, meat-pudding monsters is your ability, you got hosed. Speaking of which, your stinky blobby things need baths. They're on par with your boyfriend's atrocious breath and worse than when your lapdog got himself skunked," Zita advised. She sidestepped and ducked as the creatures charged her in unison, careful not to let them surround her. A punch to the head of one, followed by a quick twist and (limping) dance away had her frowning. *They don't seem to feel pain, and I'm losing too much blood.*

"Stop calling me that," Tiffany hissed. "Garm, do something." Two of her blobby creations broke away from Zita and trudged toward the house.

To her dismay, Garm moved to the outhouse and clawed the door open. He laughed and lunged forward, only to bounce off something. He snarled.

Her eyes wide, Wyn stepped from her hiding place, an iridescent soap bubble encasing her entire illusory form. She grasped the amulet at her neck. *What's going on? Oh, those are disgusting.*

Atlas and a gasping Jennifer Stone ran up the hill. For some reason, Jennifer was barefoot, and her companion had a black eye rapidly swelling shut and a limp. "We need to go," Atlas said.

"He's trembling and crushing them, the soft ground gives way, and only the layer of rock remains. Poor rocks, useless locks, mismatched socks," Jennifer said between pants. Her gaze was distant, flat and expressionless, and though her soft voice held torment, her face had little expression.

Tiffany frowned. "What's she babbling about? And where's the car?"

Atlas sighed. "A loss. The engine broke when we hit that guy down there, and the undercarriage snapped when I pushed it over on him. Jen delayed him from coming up here, but he won't stay down long. We need to go and fast."

Garm snapped at Wyn, bouncing off her glimmering bubble again.

"Take the van, then, and let's go," Tiffany ordered.

Atlas grimaced, eyes on the gold van. "Is that the only one here? It's not right taking a handicap vehicle."

"It's breaking, no mistaking, he's going to get us. We need to go, just row, row, row," Jennifer sang. Perhaps because she seemed so confused, Zita ignored her screaming instincts when Jennifer turned lost eyes on her.

Andy! I need to help him, Zita thought, just as something moved behind her. She skipped to the side in time to avoid the blobby creature's swing, but her injured leg sent her down to one knee. She blocked a swipe by the second one with her unhurt arm, the impact jolting through her.

Jennifer gestured. A rock speared up.

When Zita fell backward to escape it, a second broke ground, striking her head and sending her to the dirt. *Andy and Wyn and the others.* She dragged herself up to her knees, trying to ignore the pain and nausea. When she pushed her injured arm the wrong way, however, the increased agony sent her crashing down. The world went black.

Chapter Fourteen

Cool rain drumming on her face awakened her. The first sound a woozy Zita heard was the rumble of an engine as the van exited the carport. Atlas drove again, and Jennifer slumped, eyes shut and drooling, against one of the rear windows. Something glowed at the sleeping woman's throat. Tiffany sat in the passenger seat, window down, fingers tapping staccato impatience. Two blobby creatures guarded Wyn's bubble, but now the (scowling) old man and a battered Luis stood near the toilet as well, with the remaining ooze monsters holding the aide's arms. Her friend's hands flew as she cast some kind of spell.

Garm, strangely, stood by Zita. He was close. Too close. Either he had been talking to her while she'd been unconscious or he had noticed her waking. "No healing factor, but your forms are multiple, and you shapeshift fast enough to be useful. If you survive this, know that the humans brought this on themselves. We monsters are superior, even lesser ones like you, and we have no choice. Perhaps you were fortunate enough to avoid the endless bloodletting of the quarantine vampires, but reconsider your side. Stop holding on to the old and embrace the new if you survive."

She told him what to do with himself, her voice barely more than a whisper.

Atlas honked the horn. Thunder cracked directly above.

The werewolf's tongue lolled from his oversized maw. He leaned in, and heat from his breath washed over her. Unfortunately, so did the rank odor.

Oye, get a breath mint. Did he mistake the porta potty for one?

"No, you're not understanding. The weak deserve to be culled. I repaid my debt to you, so now you're fair game. But, of course, you need an object lesson. Now, where can I find one of those?" His red eyes narrowed, and his shoulders dropped as he gazed beyond her, his tail rising to half-mast. He licked his mouth.

Zita followed his gaze to Wyn, the caretaker, and the elderly man. Her friend's bubble was gone, but so were Tiffany's blobs. Based on the gesturing, Wyn was casting again. She forced the words out. "Dude, I got it. You're evil as fuck. You can leave off kicking puppies and cranky old farts to prove it."

His massive body telegraphed the jump.

Zita shifted into a pig again and knocked him aside before he got close enough to mow down the old man. The resulting pain in her two injured limbs had her stumbling and changing to gorilla to put less weight on her arm. She staggered upright, fighting the urge to vomit.

Garm laughed, and his tongue crept out of his mouth again to lick cruel white teeth. "If you intend to protect the feeble, you'll die with the herd." He turned and ran to the van, leaping through the open side door, to settle behind Tiffany's seat.

In the front passenger seat, Tiffany rummaged through her satchel, the edges of which were just visible from Zita's position, eventually removing a rune-engraved box. Withdrawing the Key from the box, she pointed it at Zita, Wyn, Luis, and Shivers.

Zita blinked, as this was her first chance to see the assembled knife, and Wyn's illusions had lacked much scale. *That thing's practically a short sword.* The reassembled knife was about a foot long, with four to five inches of ornate hilt.

Tiffany smirked. "It's due for a feeding, anyway. I can't wait to see what it can do with a little more power in it. Don't worry, if you don't die immediately, it'll happen eventually. The bleeding can't be stopped."

Muzzle curling away from his teeth, Garm lowered his head and turned away.

To Zita's horror, Wyn still stood by the porta potty. She gestured, and an incandescent soap bubble of magic sprang up around her. The pale illusion her friend wore turned ghostly as Wyn stared at the knife.

With a laugh, Tiffany slashed the air. A whip-like line of crimson-edged shadow lashed outward from the knife in her hand.

Gorillas are too slow. Zita changed to her Arca form. An instant before the trailing edge reached Wyn, she half-sprinted, half-staggered to interpose her body between it and her friend.

The knife's magic hit, and there was nothing to fight.

A sharp, shocking lash on her own chest and arms barely registered. Choking and gasping sounds came from her left, where the elderly man and Luis toppled, scarlet lines appearing on their shoulders and upper arms. Blood poured from the injuries with frightening speed. Wyn's bubble glinted, but she remained standing, uninjured.

"Ni modo," Zita managed before she collapsed, her injuries aggravated by the motion and the most recent insult to her system. She reached out toward the fallen men, but a fetid stench preceded a new pain in her head, and her face met the ground. Decayed leaves and mud filled her mouth, and she spat and sputtered. When she pried her eyes open and rolled to her back, her stomach roiling, a black shape stood over her.

"Pick a side." Garm snarled. "Be buried with honor or die here."

Zita stared up at him, fascinated by the blurry outlines of the world. Waves of agony crashed against her forehead, and she struggled to make the straying words assemble into something understandable. It didn't help that Wyn chanted something nearby. "A side? Beef?" she guessed. "No, change that to venison."

The dark beast paused, and confusion shoved aside anger on his furry face. "What?"

Confident now that she was making the right choice, Zita enunciated, "Venison. My freezer doesn't have room for a cow." She smiled in delight at answering his question.

"Your freezer?" He blinked several times in succession and shook his shaggy head. "No, choose. Our kind or the obsolete. Predators or prey. Those with powers or those without."

Zita frowned. Thought was difficult with her excruciating headache, but it took less time to process his words than before. "I don't eat people, regardless of whether they have powers or hot sauce. No venison?"

Anger won over his confusion, and he growled. "I should weed you from our ranks now."

"No, that's not necessary. I'm gonna run off as soon as the fighting ends and see if I can find my friend to heal me. This is better than the shopping she wanted to do. Not as many dresses. My head's a little fuzzy, but not as fuzzy as you are," Zita confided. Her voice sounded slurred and far away, but she chuckled at her own lame joke. *Andy would be proud.* When that sent a fresh wave of torment through her head, she stopped laughing. "I think it's because my breath's better than yours, even with garlic. Seriously, what have you been eating? Poop?"

With a disgruntled snort, the wolf bolted to the gold van. "Maybe you'll come around if you survive," were his parting words as he leapt inside. Tiffany delicately tapped a button, and the side door of the van began closing.

"But I'm conscious now!" Zita protested. "I think." She pushed herself up, stopping when the urge to retch rose. "Not good," she muttered and lay back down on the squishy ground to try again when the fogginess subsided.

A familiar voice penetrated the fog. "Stop!"

Zita dragged her head up. *Andy?* She squinted to focus.

So filthy that the rain could only trace patterns in the dirt rather than wash him clean, Andy raced up the road. His eyes glowed silver, and a tracery of lightning the same color shimmered down his form like glowing lace. His clothing was ripped and torn, but the only blood Zita smelled was her own.

The van revved its engine and zoomed by, narrowly missing Andy before careening down the long driveway. A flash of black-edged crimson struck out.

With a yelp, Andy skittered back from it. Her friend touched his shoulder, puzzlement in his eyes. No blood dripped from his hand, but beneath his bronze skin, his face was as colorless as if he had been stabbed. He took a few steps toward the vehicle, but then his gaze stopped on Zita, and he ran to her side.

She let her head drop. "Mano, you okay?" Zita croaked, "The old guy and his nurse need help." Her pain receded. A corner of her brain shrieked in warning, but the surcease left her feeling disconnected and floating.

"Bring her here," Wyn said, and the incomprehensible chanting began.

Andy touched a hand to his chest. "Yeah." He lifted Zita, and the movement made her world whirl and spin until she was on the ground again near Wyn and the two injured men.

"The old dude," Zita mumbled, nausea sweeping through her. "Get him first. He's gonna croak." With great difficulty, she turned her head toward Luis and his boss.

Said elderly individual raised his voice in querulous commentary. "I have a name, and I hate it when people are on my personal property, especially if they insist on dying there." He coughed, a rattling sound.

Luis mumbled, alarm in his voice, "Stanley... Mr. Shivers, breathe."

"Don't be ridiculous, Z—Arca," Wyn replied. Muttering to herself, something about weaving and threads, she batted at Andy. Her voice held fear. "Stand near her. It'll be easier. You're all going to be fine."

Zita's eyes drifted shut, and she forced them open again through an effort of will. Rain pelted her abused body. *You guys suck at lying. Don't worry about me. I'm numb anyway. I'll hang on until my turn.* She was too tired to force the words out.

"Don't be an idiot," Andy told her, his voice quivering.

"Jerk face," she mumbled. Moving her head seemed like too much effort, so she just watched.

You're both idiots. Silver-white light trailed from Wyn's hands. She mumbled as she worked, first making a number of gestures, but then she simply rotated her fingers as if balling up something and pulled. The glowing threads dove into the four people in front of her.

Stained with black and red, the silver light uncoiled from Luis and Shivers like thick yarn floating in midair. Another dense stream escaped from Andy, and Zita stared at the even wider branch rising from her chest wound.

Wyn made a gesture as if rolling them up, and all the strands balled up. Silver battered through and encased the black and red, and then the ball dissipated like mist. She exhaled, beginning a familiar chant, this time with an emerald shimmer.

Zita breathed a sigh of relief as her eyes slid closed. She heard Andy swear in the distance as she drifted off into a green-tinged rest.

When she woke, the pain was gone. *What? Garm and Tiffany!* She scrambled to her feet, almost tripping over Wyn, who knelt next to the old man, the glow of her healing spell still active.

"Whoop! There she is," Andy said. "Back in the land of the living, eh?" Despite his words, his faced brightened.

Wyn lifted her head and released her hold on the elderly man. "I'll get the last one now," she said. "Welcome back, Arca. Don't go cracking your skull again anytime soon." She got to her feet and went to Luis. Verdant light sprang up, coiling around him as her healing spell started.

"They're gone then?" Zita asked.

Andy nodded.

She swore and helped the frail centenarian to his feet. Shivers seemed unsteady, so she looped an arm around him and half-carried him to the carved wooden bench by his front door, out of the cold drizzle. Her touch gentle to avoid harming him further, she settled him onto it. "Sit your ass here."

"Thank you," he said. "If you're from that classy monitoring company I pay, they need to work on their customer interaction training, though I would have appreciated the uniform a decade or two ago."

Her body relaxed until his words registered. She glanced down. No clothes, but lots of mud and debris. *Oh, right. My clothes are still in the tree. I really need to figure out how to shift with them.* "No problem. Good thing you hid the sheath."

He cackled. "No, I haven't lived over a hundred years by being a fool. I did what any smart capitalist would do."

Trepidation laced Zita's heart. "You sold it?"

Smile lines deepened on his face, and his deep-set eyes lit above an impressively thick white mustache. "It's at auction. I'm too old for this, and it will earn me a fortune from whoever purchases it. That's why I was inside watching the bidding. That, and I can't abide the vultures waiting for me to die."

Her shoulders tensed again. "Whoever buys it could be in danger. Those crazies who came here tonight will go after the buyer. Who has it now?"

He shrugged. "No idea. The sale's not over yet, and the auction house handles all the petty details. Maybe tonight's visitors will buy it and stop assaulting the elderly. I'll collect the lovely money for it. Based on the bidding, it is one of my better investments in antiquities." The old man laughed, then shivered, goosebumps rising on his arms. He made a request, and Zita stepped into his house to comply.

Andy mused, *I wonder if he swims in all his money?* Mentally, he hummed a jaunty tune.

Andy, please stop. Did you catch any of them? Wyn asked.

His voice darkened, intense dislike chasing around the cheer. *No. Someone thought they'd like to bury me alive, and by the time I got out, the creepy woman got me with the dagger, and Zita was down. They escaped while we were dealing with that. Sorry.*

As she returned with a drink of whiskey (Shivers claimed to "have too short a time left to drink water") her patient had requested and a blanket he had not, Zita stopped dead. *Dios, are you okay? That's Jennifer Stone's favorite trick. I would've dug you out if I had known.*

Oh, Andy, I'm so sorry. That's terrible, Wyn sent. *Zita, can you see if Mr. Shivers will tell us the auction house? It'd help us find the buyer before the others do.*

Andy hovered between the two women as if waiting to be summoned. His water-slicked hair trailed over his domino mask, and he kept his eyes averted from Zita. His mental comment was short. *Being buried alive is high on the list of things I hate now.*

Zita repeated Wyn's question to the old man as she tucked the blanket around him, and he gave her the name of the company that had handled the transaction. He made no protest at her actions, instead, pretending not to scrutinize Wyn chatting with Luis.

"Hey, Arca, try this," Wyn called. She tossed a wad of fabric in Zita's general direction, then turned back to Luis.

Andy snagged it and brought it to her, his eyes averted. After taking it, Zita recognized it as a long shirt. She brushed off as much mud as possible and threw it on. The garment went nearly to her knees. Pulling a twig from her hair and dropping it beside the carport, she checked the centenarian again. She paused, remembering that Hound had said two groups went through Wyn's office. "You might want to hide, at least until the auction's over. There's still one more group that might be coming after the sheath. Can you stay at a relative's house?"

Shivers' chin jutted out, and he sniffed. "Those sycophants? They come to see me on my birthday because they hope to ingratiate themselves with me. Then they expect gratitude for forcing me to endure their reluctant presences while they eat all my cake. Let's not get into the presents they try to bribe me with or the so-called investment advice. Five minutes alone with them is torture. Spending an evening has me contemplating murder. Staying with one the entire night might lead to actual deaths. Hell, they might kill each other first for the chance to grovel."

Despite her attempts to keep a neutral expression, her eyebrows rose. *Wow. I can't even imagine, as annoying as my family can be...* The words slipped out. "Your family's got problems, hombre."

Shivers gave a hoarse chuckle. "Most do. If you're so concerned about me, why don't you stash us in your base of operations? I've seen the movies. Superheroes have bases, halls of do-gooding and so on, where you meet before embarking on missions."

A laugh escaped her. "Like we would have one of those? Do we look like we got that kind of money?"

He ran a disparaging eye over her, then Andy and Wyn. "You and the man do seem low rent." Distant sirens drew closer.

"Exactly." She caught herself. "I mean, no. I mean... Why would we want one?"

The old man rolled his eyes. "So, you can meet somewhere before beginning your latest crusade for justice? The blond could fund it. She's got the trappings of a trophy wife with the jewelry and all."

Zita cut him off before he said more. "Oye, don't be hating on my friend. She likes her sparkles, but she's nobody's plaything." She contemplated his words. "A hideout might make the carpooling easier, but it's not happening. No money, and how do we know some shifty sort wouldn't give the location away?" From what he'd said so far, he qualified as untrustworthy.

As if the elderly man could read her thoughts, a slow smile spread across his face. "What, do you think an ancient relic like me would be a risk?"

I'd rather have a base. A hideout sounds like what eight-year-olds would call their tree fort, though one would be handy, Andy sent. He kept his back turned to the others, watching the woods and driveway.

Zita considered. *A tree fort would be cool.* She nodded, returning her attention to the centenarian. "Absolutely. If you can live to nine hundred or whatever you are, you've got real tricks."

Andy laughed nearby and murmured something to Wyn, who giggled.

Shivers' smile broadened until Zita thought his features would be lost in his wrinkles, and he laughed until he coughed.

At the yowl of approaching sirens and a persistent buzz from the house, Zita addressed the old man again. "You and your friend should check into a hotel and stay there until after this all ends. Don't use your ID or credit cards. Hire somebody to guard you if you're worried about being found, but hopefully, all this will blow over. Upgrade your crap security here, too. Drop a tip to another reporter about your auction. Publicity and all that sells stuff, right?"

He cackled again. "Indeed, it does. I did an interview earlier today to mention the auction and help create a bidding frenzy, but the stupid cow left the auction out of the broadcast. Perhaps your beautiful friend would like to play nurse? Not you."

"Sorry, I'm busy," Andy called out, not bothering to camouflage his eavesdropping.

The old guy harrumphed. "I meant the quiet blond. You're too male, and she's the argumentative type," he said, jerking his thumb toward Zita.

"Weren't you the one complaining about your family agreeing with everything you said and kissing up all the time?" Zita asked as she retrieved her clothes.

"See? Already arguing with me," Shivers said. He grinned at her.

Andy nodded. "Can't debate that description of you, Arca. We should go. The cops are close."

Zita blew air through her teeth. "Ay, caramba, you people. All haters. Take care, old man."

He laughed. "You can call me Stanley, girlie. After all, I have seen you naked already."

When the police pulled up in the carport, sirens raging and lights blazing, she and her friends were gone.

Chapter Fifteen

After teleporting back to her kitchen with her friends, Zita exhaled noisily. The other two stood in place for a moment before they moved, though Wyn let her blond illusion drop.

Wyn drifted over to the dining room table and collapsed into a chair, burying her face in her arms. Her chestnut curls fell forward, screening her face from the others. "I can't believe that just happened." Her shoulders slumped.

Andy shifted from foot to foot. "At least we helped someone," he offered.

After changing back to her natural form, Zita ran a hand over her head, grimacing when her fingers tangled in mud and other things in the short strands. *Ugh. Drink, then shower. I swear I've spent more time in the mud trying to get this knife than a pig in summer,* she thought, while going to the sink and giving her hands a quick scrub. "Andy's right, this once. We saved the old dude and Luis. That should count for something."

"This once? Thanks for the vote of confidence," he said, rolling his eyes. "I'll get Zita's computer and see if I can find out anything about the auction and where the sheath is now." He glanced between the two women and headed down the hallway.

"At least take off your shoes and wash your hands first!" Zita called out.

Wyn moaned and kept her head down, but a sniff leaked out.

Poor Wyn. That was rough, and she seems to be taking it hard. Zita strode across the room and retrieved a pitcher from the fridge, full to the brim with a smoothie Wyn had made earlier. Though her friend had sworn it included healthy "things" (the lack of specificity revealing in and of itself), Zita suspected it was all strawberries and ice cream with a token spinach leaf. However, her parched body screamed for liquid, and any nutrition the drink could offer was a bonus. After pouring herself a couple of servings worth in an oversized cup, she tucked away the pitcher. She took a long pull on the cold, rich liquid and stood by the table. "Going to be okay, Wyn?"

Andy came back in and settled at the table, opening Zita's laptop. The scent of soap rose from his hands as he touched the power button, though a line of dirt delineated where his washing had stopped partway up his forearms. "So, what do you think?" he asked.

"This whole day was a disaster," Wyn moaned.

"Well, it could have gone better," Zita said, sitting down in her favorite glittery chair.

Wyn lifted her head enough to survey Zita with narrowed eyes over her arms. "Could have gone better? Are you trying to be aggravating? You almost died and Garm bit you, plus we would have lost the sheath had it been there."

Zita waved her hand to dismiss it. "You saved me, thank you, and he always bites me. We have yet to fight when he doesn't."

Wyn's head shot up, and she sat up straight. Her hands lowered to the table and clenched into fists, thumbs on the inside. "Wait, you've been bitten multiple times and haven't ever mentioned to us the fact that you might turn into a werewolf?"

Survival instinct kept Zita from correcting Wyn on her finger position, but she made a mental note to help her make a real fist later. *When it's less likely to be used on me.* "Why would I turn into one of those? I'm already a shapeshifter."

"Stand up so I can search your aura for any infection from his magic..." Wyn said. "Being bitten is historically the way to turn into one."

His face unhappy, Andy added, "You should know werewolves don't have a choice about shifting. You've worked so hard for control..."

Obediently, Zita stood, but her eyes kept flicking to Wyn's improperly made fists. "Oh. Well, I don't feel any different."

Rising from her own chair, Wyn circled around her for several long moments before she announced her prognosis. "As usual, you lack any magic whatsoever, but it won't be a full moon for a couple weeks."

"Excellent then, I'm clear. You can always check me closer to the moon, and I'll tell you if I start feeling weird or need a flea dip," Zita said. *You'd think I'd know or have issues changing into anything else if I were just a wolf now. It would suck to give up all my other forms.* She gulped down another mouthful and extended a peace offering. "Did either of you want some of the strawberry drink? I'll get you a glass if you want since I'm up."

Wyn began ranting. "Those monsters almost killed us, you still might turn into a werewolf, and if the sheath had been there, they would have gotten that too! As it was, the Key had these lines of magic between it and everyone it injured, and it was sucking you all dry! Thick, black, nasty ropes gulping down the last of your flickering energy. Your line was thicker than any of the others, maybe because you were so close to death. Even the centenarian had less going to the dagger."

Andy frowned, and his typing halted. "Zita, we need to talk."

"Oh, there's a revelation," Wyn growled. "And Zita, stop with the food already."

Zita lowered herself back into her seat and braced herself. She rested her face in her palm. "Stop eating or stop offering?" One was impossible; the other was rude. Her mother would not approve of either.

That didn't help. Wyn's eyes were so narrow they were mere slits. "Stop offering."

"I can do that." After another deep breath, Zita let her hand drop. *Perhaps I shouldn't have taken them with me. If I keep Wyn and Andy farther away next time, things might go smoother. This fiasco might convince Wyn to stay home, or both of them to give up on the Key thing entirely.* She took another sip, the strawberry and honeyed cream coolness souring in her mouth.

Andy set a hand on Wyn's arm and questioned Zita. "What happened at the house? Before the dagger, I saw that part. When we spar, I can't even touch you when you're in the zone. That wolf shouldn't have been a major problem unless he had super speed, and Wyn should have been able to—"

"Oh, Wyn didn't get a chance. Zita had me hiding in the porta potty the whole fight, and by the time I came out, she was busy dying in a mud puddle," Wyn spat. She shook off Andy's hand, crossed her arms over her chest, and threw herself back into her chair.

Carajo, is this where we get into the emotional post-event argument? If they were alcoholics like my old coach, I could judge their level of upset by the brand of vodka being downed. With exaggerated care, Zita set her cup back on the table and looked at Wyn. "Pues, what did you want me to do? Invite him to kill you or give him tips on the fastest ways to do it? Did you miss the part where he wanted to eat you? And not in a fun way?"

Andy strummed his fingers on the table. His brown eyes considered her, and he pursed his lips. "So, Zita did all the fighting by herself. Did the wolf develop mad skills?"

"No," Zita said, "He was about the same, but he heals, and I don't."

"Then how did you get so hurt this time? Why weren't you in the zone? You almost live up to your own hype when you're really going." His questions shot at her in staccato bursts.

Zita's eyes slid to Wyn, and then she lowered her gaze to the table. She traced a finger over the white-painted wood grain. *What did I do when my coach did this? Talk about improving and mention the next important thing to soften him up. Worth a try.* "I got outnumbered, so clearly I should practice fighting multiple enemies more. The knife must be getting stronger since it now cuts from a distance. We have to find that last piece before Garm and his homicidal girlfriend do."

Wyn sniffed. "Typical distraction move, Zita, bringing up the dagger. I said it would increase exponentially in strength and it has. This isn't about that or why we went there. It's about the debacle we all just participated in."

"If you practice any more, you'll have to invent time travel first," Andy said. "So, were you tanking?"

She nodded. "Sí, I sucked."

He shook his head. "Not what I meant." Andy muttered under his breath, something about newbies. "You were distracted, weren't you?"

Again, Zita tried to keep her eyes from drifting to Wyn and failed. "I'm not letting people get killed if I can help it," she said, snapping each word like a whip.

Following her gaze, Andy inhaled, and sympathy creased his face.

Wyn stood so fast that her chair toppled. "Oh, but it's fine to kill yourself in the process?"

Andy continued on as if Wyn's interjection had not occurred. "And you didn't let Wyn do anything?" He spread his hands out on the table and stared at them.

"She would have gotten hurt," Zita protested.

Her friend arched an eyebrow. "Who ended the fight bleeding out in the dirt? And who emerged unscathed?"

Andy exhaled, puffing out his cheeks. "Wyn, please let me give this a try. Zita, you need to cut out the distractions and focus if you intend to keep going after the Key. Fight to your strengths, instead of trying to play a role you're not suited for." He paused. "You're not able to take hits the way I can, but you dodge better than anyone else I've ever met."

"Remus," Zita interrupted. "He's hard to hit. I haven't tried, but I think you'd have to estimate where he'd be and distract him enough so he wouldn't pay attention until it was too late. Thank you, though."

He sighed. "Right, other than Remus. It's creepy you've already worked out a strategy against a man you dated. I'm assuming you'll go to wherever the auction site or auction winner's home is. If we have to fight there, we're not running a repeat or worse of tonight's show. None of us are going to die, including you."

Zita pressed her lips together. "The knife now cuts multiple people from a distance, and you can't stop the bleeding without magic, so sí, I will do something about it."

Strumming his fingers on the tabletop again, Andy said, "Z, you're a crazy good fighter in human form, but you're hampered against something like a werewolf. When you shapeshift, what do you fight like?"

Well, duh. At least he left out the usual 'for your size' when talking about my fighting prowess, even if it was true. "An animal or a human, depending. Garm's supersized and fast, so I usually go with a bear or feral pig," Zita said. She took another long pull of the drink.

Andy made a discordant noise. "Wrong move." He frowned at her. "What I don't understand is why you're pretending to be a tank when you're clearly a rogue."

"Are you calling me a thief?" Zita's voice was sharp with offense and hurt. *My friends should know me better than that.*

"No, I'm trying to tell you that you're not a brick," he said.

What? Zita frowned, uncertain. *What is he talking about? Fighting is something I've actually trained in.* "Then can you explain that again in English, Spanish, Portuguese, Chinese, or Greek? You know, a language I speak since I doubt you confused me with building materials."

That caught Wyn's attention. "Aren't you working on intermediate Greek?"

Zita shrugged at Wyn. "Must've hit a turning point. I'm fluent now."

Rubbing a hand on his neck, Andy muttered to himself for a minute. "Anyone else in our generation would have understood that. It's harder to explain this without video game analogies than I thought. What I'm asking is why are you fighting like a bear when you're a coyote?"

"No, I'm me," Zita said.

"Now you're just being stubborn," he replied. "Stop hiding behind literalism."

Wyn snorted. "You may as well ask her to design a nuclear missile, Andy. Next up, she'll ask if we want to eat."

Since she had been about to table the discussion in favor of food, her voice sounded defensive, and Zita hated it. *If I go work out, I can avoid all this.* "I'm not hiding. It's selective camouflage."

"Be more selective then. You're fighting all wrong for your power set."

Zita choked on her drink and sputtered. "What? What do you know about fighting as a shapeshifter? You've never fought in your other form. To be honest, it's not really a shape meant for fighting."

He cleared his throat. "That's true, but I have an advantage over you and the creature—"

Irritated on the other shifter's behalf, Zita set her cup down and interrupted. "Garm." *He referred to himself and me as monsters.*

Does he truly see us that way? I can at least make my friends use his name or nickname.

"What?" Andy asked, his eyebrows climbing toward his hairline.

"His name is Garm."

"Does it matter?" Wyn sniffed. "He's a beast. And really, Garm and Halja? How predictable can you get?"

Zita scowled at her friend. "He's an asshole, but still a person. His fighting style is mostly rabid wolf, but when he's not all mad, he gets crafty and sneaky. I haven't ever seen him in any other form."

Andy cleared his throat again. "Right. So, as I was saying, I've got an advantage. Far too much of my pay has gone to comic books and video games, and those have trained me, in theory, on the stuff we're dealing with today. I've read or played endless variations of how to fight effectively as a shapeshifter. So tonight, we'll go somewhere lonely, and you will let loose on me. Switch between forms as fast as you need to instead of sticking with one. If I throw you, shift to a cat, land on your feet, and then change again to something more offensive."

Even though she knew Wyn would wreak horrible vengeance on her for the statement, Zita said, "Cats can be offensive. One of Wyn's barfed on my pillow the other day, and I swear it's because I tossed them off the bed." As if summoned by the mention, Wyn's two Siamese appeared, twining around each other, and stared at Zita. She could have sworn they gloated. Most animals she liked, but those two were uncanny.

Unaware of or ignoring the felines, Andy said, "You can't hurt me. Wyn will throw distractions at you. Pick a place, and we'll all meet there at midnight."

"I'm not getting on that motorcycle with Zita again," Wyn announced, "but other than that, I'm in."

Folding her arms over her chest, Zita said, "Midnight's late."

His voice roughened. "So, we'll all sleep in tomorrow. You'll be fine if you don't get up before the dawn for one day, and it's easier to keep our identities secret if we do this at night. Wear your masks, too. So, Zita, are you in? Or are you going to go cry in your room like a scared little girl and give up? You know, we could all meet tomorrow, give you a makeover, and see if we can find you a big, strong man to keep you safe instead."

"Oh, fighting words, mano. I'll be there. And you better be ready, because I'm going to kick your culo. Find a man to keep me safe, my little brown ass. I don't need nobody to do that," Zita replied. She started to point her finger at him, remembered his aversion to that, and shook her whole hand at him instead.

A fierce smile tugged at the corners of Wyn's lips. "Can we do both? She could use a makeover and a new wardrobe."

"Don't go there," Zita said. She took another fortifying gulp of her drink. *So thirsty. Stupid blood loss. Are you still supporting the effort to get the last piece or am I going in alone?* She took another sip and continued past a sudden lump in her throat, "So after we do the practice, then what? Will they tell us who won the auction if we call and ask?"

Wyn sighed. "Not unless you have an in. My only auctioneer contact doesn't work for the company Shivers mentioned, and since it's a private auction, bids and buyers are all secret. We will have to convince someone with access to break policy and tell us."

Andy grimaced. "That makes it harder, but we need to find that third piece before the wolf." He glanced at Zita and corrected himself. "Before Garm and Halja do. Wyn might be able to charm someone there once we figure out who has access."

We means he's still in, at least. Zita rubbed the back of her head and offered an alternative, her lips tilting into a smile. "Or, we could ask a hacker to find out for us. Jerome might be willing. I'll call him on the throwaway cell he gave me and ask."

Andy nodded.

Wyn frowned. "I could just…"

Zita shook her head. "Don't worry about it. I got this. All you got to do is whip up a magic spell to stop the knife from being able to stab people from a distance. If you can remove the impossible-to-stop bleeding curse, that would be terrific, too, but it becomes less valuable and less of a threat if it can't hurt multiple people at once. I'm guessing breaking the Key won't work given that it's already in pieces and still causing trouble."

Her expression pinched, and Wyn twirled a curl around a finger, stretching it long. "Depends on how the enchantment works. Breaking it might work if it's destroyed the right way. Perhaps a cleansing fire? I haven't been able to study it since they activated the spell. If we go around the existing properties, binding or turning them instead of trying to remove them, that might be easier." Her expression softened as she mused aloud.

Victory! Zita knew better than to wallow in her triumph. "Awesome," she cheered, then bounced out of her seat and to the closet hiding her laundry equipment. Clambering onto the washer, she grabbed an orange floral box from the top shelf. After dismounting with her prize, she padded back to the table and set the box in front of Wyn. "You said something about Wicca and your witchcraft being separate, but connected. In case you need it, here's your special knife."

Her brow wrinkled, Wyn opened the box. Her eyes widened, and she stroked the blade's handle with a finger. "You have my athame? Why did you put it in your sewing kit?"

Zita snorted. "Not mine. That's Quentin's from when he did my gymnastic costumes. I moved his sewing stuff to another container to make room. I don't know if an athame needs a Wicca tabernacle or whatever the witch version is, but that's the closest I had to a special box for it." Uncomfortable, she cleared her throat and rummaged in her fridge. Her voice gruff, she continued, "Figured you'd want it stored somewhere nonviolent and away from the cops who would insist on testing it or mess up the sacredness thing. Anyway, I should finish dinner. Even if I don't dare give blood anymore with the possible superpowers cooties, I think my iron's low."

Withdrawing the blade from the box, Wyn held it reverently. "Thank you. That wasn't necessary, but it was very sweet. It's an important ritual piece, and finding a blade made of silver, or primarily silver, is difficult these days."

Kicking the door shut behind her as she withdrew from the depths of the fridge, triumphant with the chilled remains of dinner, Zita stopped. "Did you say silver?"

"Yes," Wyn said, her voice trailing off. Her eyes lit. "Can I touch you with it? A consecrated silver blade should cause a reaction if you're turning into a werewolf."

"Excellent. Multipurpose then. Go for it." Zita peeked under the cover of her food, idly calculating if she could get another use out of the tinfoil.

"Let me know right away if this hurts." Wyn came over and touched the tip of her athame to Zita's arm, jerking it away so fast she narrowly missed cutting herself.

"Relax. Don't hurt yourself," Zita said. She held out a hand.

Wyn offered her the sacred blade.

Zita put her fingers on the flat of the blade and held it there. Lifting her hand away, she showed her friend the undamaged skin. "See?" She picked up her plate, stripping off the tin foil.

If Andy's relieved smile was the sun breaking through the clouds, Wyn's was a supernova.

As she rinsed the foil, Zita grinned, mischief and amusement warring within her. "Wyn, I need you to figure out how to stick magic on stuff before we go after the sheath." The faucet clunked as she shut off the water.

"Can you be any vaguer?" Andy murmured.

Athame in her hands, Wyn sputtered. "You want something else enchanted? Aren't I already supposed to disenchant the Key and remove the curse properties? If this is about getting you a better climbing backpack again..."

Zita flattened out the tinfoil, setting it beside the sink to dry, the busywork soothing. "Oye, the backpack was a birthday or Christmas present idea, that's all. And no, it's not about that. You got those zip ties back when we hit the drug house. Can you make it so they don't break? It'd be a huge help to have a way to keep Garm out of action that doesn't require anyone dying."

"That's a big ask," her friend said, dubiousness in her tone and face, and she nibbled her lip. "I can try, but a lot depends on how much time we have before we need all these things."

She can do it, then. One more thing out of the way. "Sweet. You can use whatever you want from my spices and crafty stuff. I've got glitter, glue, paracord, and sequins in almost every color."

Warmth leaking from her face, Wyn set the athame back down in the basket and closed the lid in a slow, deliberate motion. "Magic is more than craft supplies and spices."

"Whatever. You do the magic, and then you can read a book or watch your shows the rest of the time." Zita chucked her dinner in the microwave and pushed buttons. "Andy and I will take care of the rest. Mano, we need to figure out an attack plan once we have a location."

An indrawn breath sounded behind her. "Andy, do you mind staying on my sofa in case they come back? I'm going home."

"What? I mean, sure. How about we stay at my place, though? The cops still have yours marked as a crime scene, and my stepmom would love the chance to have a dinner guest for a few nights," Andy said.

In her peripheral vision, Zita caught a flash of color with Wyn's passage into the bedroom and heard things being thrown around.

Andy sidled up next to her, widened his eyes, and nudged Zita. "Go after her and apologize," he whispered.

"For what?" she asked, still trying to figure out what had happened. *I thought we were doing better.* Her microwave beeped, and she turned away to deal with it.

Andy sighed. "Seriously, Z, if I hadn't met your family, I'd swear wolves raised you. You just implied her magic is an amusing little hobby, and she's useless otherwise. Wyn's probably the smartest of the three of us, too."

"That's not what I meant at all," Zita said, setting her plate on the counter. She fisted her hands on her hips. "I know she's smarter than me. We need the magic to take the Key out of commission, and it seems easy for her. I figured she'd appreciate time to herself while we figured out the punchy-kicky stuff she doesn't do."

He shrugged. "I figured, but she doesn't know that."

Zita tapped her fingers on the counter. "Why not?"

Andy sighed and shoved his hands in his pockets. "Maybe I understand how to speak idiot after teaching all those college classes. You need to go apologize before I throw you in there after her."

Wyn stormed back into the room, took one look at the pair of them huddled by the microwave, and snarled. "Don't help her, Andy. Would you please carry my heavier cases for me?" She dropped a small suitcase by the door.

"Somebody's got to assist the poor thing, she's clueless," he protested. Behind the tall brunette's back, he widened his eyes and mouthed, "Apologize." When Wyn turned to glare at him, he stared at the ceiling, his face blank.

"Oye, Wyn, I'm sorry, I didn't—" Zita began.

Wyn shook her head and raised a hand in the air. "Don't. I'm not being completely reasonable, and you'll just make it worse, so I'm leaving."

"You won't be safe! Andy has a job," Zita protested.

"He works at the same university as I do, so I'll go on campus with him. The cats will stay safe with you until this is all over."

"Wyn—"

"Just no, Zita. Not now. I need time to meditate on all this," Wyn said, "Eat your dinner. We'll see you at practice later tonight." She turned and strode back into the bedroom.

Andy trudged after her.

Zita smacked her fist on the counter and swore. She paced the few steps her kitchen allowed, and then stared at her food, appetite gone. Slow and mechanical, she ate. *I still need the calories. I'll try again when she comes out, but maybe distance will help. At least she stayed out of my mind this time.* Her eyes stung. *If dust is getting in my eyes, I'll have to clean, perhaps after a nice long workout. I've been neglecting my aerial practice, and another round on the martial arts dummy never hurts.*

When Wyn flounced out, still unwilling to listen, the food was gone, and the kitchen gleamed.

Andy had followed in silence, but at least he hugged Zita before going.

She had returned it with a punch on the arm. "Keep Wyn safe, sí?"

He nodded and left.

Desperate to stay busy, Zita squared her kitchen towels and caught sight of the floral box. She bustled over, throwing open the lid. "I should put Quentin's things back in now she's taken..." The athame reflected light from the tattered orange lining of the box.

Seizing it, she ran to the door and threw it open. "Wait!"

Wyn and Andy were gone, but one of her neighbors turned in her doorway, saw the athame in Zita's hand, and hurried to get inside. When the door shut behind her, the distinct click of a lock, then the meatier thunk of a deadbolt, followed.

Plastering a smile on her face, Zita lowered the athame. "My friends forgot their cooking knife. I'll just text," she called at the door. Her neighbor did not reply, but Zita doubted she'd get freshly baked cookies again anytime soon.

***

Two days later, as Zita took a few breaths in the relative peace of her bedroom, her eyes fell upon a business card on her desk. Jerome had come through with the information earlier that day.

A quick call updated Andy (and Wyn by extension) since Wyn chose not to speak to her outside of their late-night practice sessions. Although he was rattled from the revelation that the Key's sheath would be at the same museum as his girlfriend's fabric exhibition, he had been happy to report results from the police. They had arrested several members of the humanist group in connection with the theft of Wyn's work machine and connections to the New York incident. The arrests included the leader who had ordered the group to go after the Key. Even better, despite Wyn returning to work, no more stalkers had been spotted. She spent all her time meditating or buried in books, ostensibly researching.

With Andy as an intermediary, they planned to meet in New York before the fabric exhibition. Since Wyn was driving a rental, Zita chose to meet them there. *Far less awkward than a multi-hour car ride with poor Andy stuck as a referee. I still need to figure out how to tell them about the job offer in Brazil.*

She took a deep breath and changed to her Arca form. After retrieving the disposable phone with the blue smiley-face sticker, she flipped it open and stared at it. *This is too important. I'll take any backup I can get. If I'm right about his client, this should give us someone with a clue of what they're doing and less of an inclination to throw fire around. If I'm wrong, worst that can happen is extra police presence.* Clenching the phone and card in her fists, she teleported to the Washington Monument, then dialed Hound's number by the ambient light of the National Mall.

After a short number of rings, Hound answered.

Using her fake Mexican accent, Zita said, "You are the detective seeking Jennifer Stone?" He inhaled sharply. Her ears caught a faint click, as if another line had been picked up or a button pressed.

"I am a detective," he said.

Cautious. I knew I liked him. She picked up the pamphlet. "Right. That sheath her group wants will be part of the 'Revolutions in Materials Engineering' exhibition at the Carter Shuster Museum of Design and Innovation in New York City. Tell your clients. If they can get them, tranquilizer darts and a silver baton would be wise investments."

"Who is this?" Hound asked.

She snorted. *An idiot with more hope than sense.* "Someone who aspires to not getting shot by any lurking professionals. You can tell them that, too."

"How did you get this number?"

"My ears work, and everyone's following the librarian around these days." She hung up, pulled the battery out of the phone, and teleported back to her bedroom.

Chapter Sixteen

The following Wednesday, Andy plowed through the first floor of the museum, towing Zita and Wyn in his buoyant wake. He stopped short and consulted the map they had received with their entrance tickets. Wyn crowded close to peer over his shoulder.

Might as well scream that you've never been here before. With her perfect memory, Wyn shouldn't need to see it again, so she's trying to make a point. Is it just to appear innocent on the cameras? Having scouted out the place the previous night, Zita's eyes skipped over the exhibitions and focused on the people. Additional items had been added since her surreptitious survey of the two-story building, but nothing substantial had changed, and she felt confident she knew the layout. They stood in the long Great Hall that ran most of the length of the first floor. The majority of the marble floor was clear, as it was set up to herd visitors toward a block of elevators, with a gift shop, bathrooms, and small display rooms beckoning on the sides. A large Employees Only area hid a professional catering kitchen, a handful of storerooms, and a pair of offices. Upstairs held the bulk of the displays, including a massive area for the featured exhibits.

"We want the main exhibition area upstairs. This floor is just the gift shop, kid learning center, and permanent displays," Zita told her friends.

Wyn continued to study the map, but Andy nodded and stepped back.

Zita eyed the ornate bank of elevators and the wide, elaborate marble steps with gold-colored handrails. "If you want, the staff area has a stairwell inside it. It'll be less crowded than the elevators or the main steps. Did your girl say where she wanted to meet you?" Zita said. Although they were not the only guests, the turnout for the event was greater than she would have imagined, even though the modern building was nowhere near capacity. She certainly would not have chosen to attend—let alone pay for—the opening of an exhibition of "innovative fabrics" if she hadn't had ulterior motives.

"Brandi said she'd be by the gift shop," Andy replied.

Wyn flicked a chestnut curl over her shoulder and folded up the map, tucking it into her purse. If anyone nearby noticed that the paper should not have fit in the small bag she carried, they neither commented nor stared. "We will take the public elevators," she said, the first words she'd spoken for several blocks.

Sí, still moody. I should have met them here, instead of at the parking garage. At least then I could've snuck in and avoided the fee. As they drifted toward the elevators, Zita waved a hand in the direction of the shop. "Gifts are over there," she said.

"I hope we find the sheath. The spirits have been visiting my dreams almost every night, telling me these people cannot be allowed to use the Key," Wyn fretted softly.

Andy rubbed his eyes. "Funny, I've been dreaming about a woman saying the same thing."

Zita shrugged. "I've had one or two dreams where my subconscious harps on that subject, as if I didn't already know it. It'd be nice if my mind would send me a hot naked guy to ogle during the nagging instead of a church lady with an African accent."

Wyn and Andy froze.

Zita turned and frowned at them. "What? Too real for you?"

"Little round blue hat?" Andy asked.

"She visited you?" Wyn said.

Zita blinked at them. "Yes, how did you guess about the hat?"

Wyn grabbed her arm. "Can you picture her for me?"

The warm touch of party line wound its way through Zita's mind, and she felt her friends waiting. "Sure," she said, visualizing the dream woman.

Air hissed between Wyn's teeth. *Let me show her to Andy.*

After a pause, Andy sent, *That's the same one I saw.*

And she's the spirit who's been warning me. I can understand it cautioning Andy, as his bird form is magical, even if his man form is mundane, but Zita? I've been checking every time I see her for the taint of wolf, but she remains as magical as a pet rock. Disappointment and confusion warred on Wyn's face.

Andy's mental tone was wry. *I'll try to take mundane as a compliment, though I prefer scientifically awesome.*

Zita snorted. Lacking magical talent did not bother her. *Bizarre. What if it's not a spirit and is someone like Wyn with the mind powers?*

Wyn's face grew thoughtful, and she nibbled on her lower lip. *Possible. She could have a form of oneiric telepathy since we only see her in dreams. How would she have found us or discovered what's going on, though?*

Is she a threat to our identities? Zita frowned, watching the crowd around them as if the woman and her hat would materialize.

Clear discomfort came through in Andy's message and in his posture. *Don't know, and really don't like it. What can we do about it?*

I'll work up a dreamcatcher spell or something for you two. Lucid dreaming might allow me to manipulate the dreamscape sufficiently to question her and determine what she is. Wyn wound a curl around her finger. She closed her eyes for a second, and when she opened them again, party line was gone.

By the gift shop, a woman their age lifted her hand, staring at the threesome.

"Dude, is that your lady?" Zita asked, nudging Andy.

He perked up and thrashed his arm in the air as if it were on fire. "That's her!" he said, "That's my Brandi. We'll go grab dinner and meet you guys back here in an hour. Her part of the show begins around then, and afterward, she can talk to you about the clothes, okay?"

Poor guy could use a break from being stuck in the middle of our arguments while we try to find the knife. Zita bit back a laugh and glanced at Wyn, who was also suppressing her mirth. By silent agreement, both women evaluated the girlfriend they had heard about but never met before.

Fidgeting in place, Brandi wore deep magenta lipstick and a matching leather blazer cut to accent curves, of which she had plenty. Beads in crystalline shades, interspersed with little figures, glinted from a million cornrows woven close to her head as she waved and fiddled with the straps of her shoulder bag. Since the odd purse, shaped like a blue phone booth for some reason, matched the blue suede knee-high boots, Zita assumed it was stylish. She couldn't assess her fighting skills until Brandi walked, but she doubted that was important to her friend, given the joy on his face. The man was almost bouncing in his eagerness like a puppy.

Zita smothered a laugh and her eyes met Wyn's. The other woman had a hand in front of her mouth, anger forgotten at the moment.

"Sounds good, mano," Zita said.

Wyn murmured agreement.

He took a step toward his girlfriend and then stopped. Despite his flushed cheeks, his brown eyes were serious. In a soft voice, he asked, "You'll contact me if anything happens?"

"They'd be foolish to do anything with all these people around instead of waiting until later this evening," Wyn reassured him, her voice quiet. She fussed with her pocketbook.

Zita nodded. "I called the museum after Jerome texted that the sheath would be here. Though it sure sounded like they were blowing me off, they might've increased security."

Still, he hesitated. "You're sure?"

"As much as we can be," Zita replied.

Wyn put her hand on Andy's arm and pressed a piece of jewelry into his hand. "Here, take this just in case. Without the actual Key to work with, my options were limited, but I made a charm that should keep you safe from the magic. The dagger will cut like a normal knife if they stab you, but the curse won't take and they can't harm you from a distance." She paused and smiled at him, "Or not cut at all, as the case may be. I've invented a spell that might work if I can get my hands on the sheath, but until then, let's all be safe." She released him.

He flashed a smile at her. "Thanks. Will do." Andy bounded off, tucking the brooch in a jeans pocket.

Smiling, both women watched him go.

Zita blinked, realizing where she had seen Andy's new jewelry before. *Obsidian, a striped stone, amber, and a piece of jade in a circle, bound with wire.* She touched her throat, where a set of smooth, cool beads in a similar circle clung to the inside of her shirt. "Isn't that the pin you insisted I wear on my throat chakram?"

Wyn rolled her eyes but inclined her head. "Chakra, though chakram is almost appropriate for you. I assumed it had the least chance to get destroyed pinned to your clothing rather than around a body part."

"Doesn't he have to wear his there?"

"No, I assumed you might divest yourself of it and wanted to be able to see when you did so. Plus, I assume your throat chakra could use all the assistance it can get, given that it governs communication," Wyn replied, her tone cooling.

Zita rolled her eyes. "Give me a little credit. You said it's protective, plus I like the colors. If it doesn't have to be in that exact spot, though, I'll pin it to my pocket instead, so if someone throat-punches me, I don't have a pointy object at my jugular."

Wyn pressed her lips into a line. "Your mind is disturbing sometimes."

Outside the arty shop, Andy stood close to his girlfriend, smiling, his face and body stance open. He leaned forward.

"I'm glad he has—" Zita began, cutting herself off as she watched Andy's girlfriend turn her head at the last second to redirect his kiss to her cheek. Her smile died. *Brandi's leaning away, and she's not able to meet his eyes. That smile is really fake. Ah, poor guy. I hope I'm wrong because he's so happy to see her. Andy hasn't noticed yet as he's busy being embarrassed by that G-rated display of affection.* She swore under her breath.

Her brows rising, Wyn glared. "Do not swear at me."

"It's not you. It's them. Brandi's going to break up with him," Zita said, nodding toward their friend and his soon-to-be ex. She scowled.

Wyn frowned and turned her attention back to the pair moving to the exit. As they watched, Andy made a shy attempt to take Brandi's hand again, and the woman shifted her purse into that hand. The unhappy lines around her mouth deepening, Wyn's hazel eyes grew distant. "Just because you can't... oh. You're right. She's planning to buy him a drink to assuage her conscience and then use her budding business as an excuse. How did you, of all people, get that before me?"

Zita snorted. *I would love to have been wrong.* "Do you know how many times and different variations I've seen or performed of the 'just not that into you' dance? I suck at being in a relationship, but

I'm an expert at ending one or recognizing when one is ending, however brief it may have been."

Wyn sighed and hugged her bag closer, her eyes wistful. "It's a pity. I had hoped one of us would have a happily ever after..." She straightened her shoulders. "Never mind. At least we have all this interesting material to examine until he requires our consolation."

Zita grunted. *I doubt he's the type to cry on shoulders, but if it keeps her happier to think so, I won't inform her otherwise. If we could find the stupid sheath and go, that'd be even better. Andy may want an intense sparring match to forget his troubles when this is over. I know I do.*

As they went through each exhibit, Wyn insisting on reading every word, her face grew more animated, and she seemed fascinated by everything. Zita only grew more morose when the sheath failed to materialize. After interminable and excruciating inspection of every side room open to the public on the first floor, they finally made it to the second floor. Glass museum cases reflected the ceiling lights, like tiny taunting beacons of tedium along the walls.

Is it possible to pass out from boredom and remain standing up? I think I'm near that, Zita thought as Wyn scrutinized a statue featured at the top of the staircase. Ten feet tall, the marble man was strangely clad in a jaunty plaid toga and a necklace with a dull, thumb-sized brown gem.

Zita twisted to watch the main exhibition area that encompassed most of the second floor. Interrupted by stairs and the wall of elevators at one end, a ring of smaller rooms encircled the large, open area. Across the room from the tourist entrance, a profusion of potted palms and other real tropical plants hid the small employee entrance and stairs behind a discreet screen of vegetation. Each side room represented a concept in materials crafting and textile art, and she had no idea which would be appropriate for the sheath. Wyn seemed determined to view them all, and Zita resigned herself to the possibility they might have to. Choking perfume dominated the softer scents of canapés, cheap white wine, and waxed wooden floors. Bird calls and elevator music played in the background of the murmuring crowd, almost drowning out the sudden rain that darkened the sky and lashed the skylights high above in an unexpected downpour.

Wyn finally moved to the first display case, and Zita continued her perusal of the area. Elongated banners in deep maroon trailed from the ceiling with the names of the innovators honored, and matching cloth covers festooned an assortment of lumpy shapes around the room. From her covert exploration the previous night, she knew the fabric hid dioramas with creepy, headless mannequins in a variety of poses. Brandi's had been one of the more interesting, with a display of plastic pseudo people wearing copies of the outfits Andy had shared, including one with a tennis racket and another with a Styrofoam set of dumbbells.

Almost uniformly black-clad, guests mingled in the room, with only a few standouts daring to wear color, like Zita. The prize for the most color had to go to a woman clad in red from head-to-toe, around whom a constant circle of other guests seemed to revolve.

The scent of aged cheese teased Zita, and she turned toward the tall waitress wending her way through the crowd with a tray held high and the remnants of a military stride. Grateful to see food she recognized, Zita chased after the server, leaving Wyn to her scholarly interests. "Excuse me, Miss?" she called out. *See? Totally being polite and blending into the crowd,* she thought to herself.

Proving her friend eavesdropped again, Wyn replied, *Zita, you're wearing navy pants and a fuchsia top in a crowd wearing mostly black. Additionally, you have a distressing tendency to rock on your feet when you're impatient, which is most of the time. You're not blending in.*

At least I'm trying, she retorted.

Very much so.

Is this because I wouldn't let you pick out my clothes? Zita had to tug the waitress's arm to get her attention. Frizzy red hair hung down in curly bangs over a familiar face. Even beneath a layer of makeup, including weird orange eye shadow, she was recognizable. *Trixie again? She's not with Garm's group, so why is she here?* "Trixie?" she blurted.

The waitress glanced left and tapped the square name badge attached to one tuxedo lapel. In a nasal voice, she replied, "No, my name is Lucy McGillicuddy. Sorry, Miss, I have one of those faces. People mistake me for others all the time." She puckered orangey-scarlet-painted lips and patted her red hair, then proffered the tray to Zita.

What about Trixie? Wyn asked, her mental voice distracted.

Zita frowned. *She's here pretending to be a waitress. Why would she do that?* She reached for one of the tiny bamboo skewers impaling even smaller slivers of cheese, but the tray moved out of reach as the taller woman turned to respond to someone else. Since she could not reach the food without jumping, Zita waited for Trixie to turn back to her. Her foot tapped.

Maybe she lost her job and doesn't want anyone to recognize her? You should understand that. Or it could just be someone who looks similar.

Then why wear different wigs, both here and in Alabama? Given her own financial difficulties, Zita grudgingly acknowledged it was possible. *You could be right, but it's bizarre.* "You do what you need to," she said, giving Trixie a pat on the arm in an attempt to be sympathetic.

Wrinkling her brows, the waitress stared at her and then nodded. "Thanks." She took a cocktail napkin and blotted at the corner of her mouth, dropping it onto her own tray. With a quick quarter turn, she marched off through the crowd, her steps taking on a cadence recognizable from when Miguel and Quentin had returned from their tours overseas.

"Wait! What about my cheese? This is why being supportive never works for me." Zita watched Trixie go. "Whatever her name is, she has military training." She returned her attention to scanning the room for trouble and calculating the probable weight load the banners could carry. *They aren't that different from the silks I use in practice.* Without conscious thought, she moved closer to one of the cloths covering a diorama and stroked the cool, smooth fabric, the slick, tightly woven material slipping between her fingers.

Wyn interrupted her musing when she walked up. "What do you see that's bizarre? Is it the sheath?"

A pair of attractive male waiters hovered near Wyn, both with wine, and one hopeful older man in a business suit examined his thick gold wristwatch ostentatiously when her head turned his way even briefly.

Amusement struck Zita as the orbiting waiters shifted position, mirror images of each other. *They must be in the same acting class.* "Trixie, with her wigs and everything, is what's strange. She's over..." When she turned to point out the erstwhile waitress, Trixie had disappeared into the herd of people. "Lost her." She huffed and let the cloth slip free.

Wyn dismissed her concern, plastering a fake smile on her face. "Whatever, Zita," she said out of the side of her mouth. "Try to seem pleasant and stop fondling the decorative accents. You look like a cranky toddler."

Zita puffed out her cheeks and exhaled. "I'm hungry and bored. Could you bring out that butter container I gave you? I could go for some chicken breast about now."

"Is that what's in there?" Wyn murmured. "If dogs begin following me around, I'll know who to blame. No. We had sandwiches on the walk here, and you should be able to last."

"Fast metabolism, plus I did fly here from Maryland," Zita reminded her friend. After a second to admire the fit forms trapped in the silly tuxedos, she rolled her eyes and strode toward Wyn's pet waiters. Both perked up when Wyn followed, and they saluted by presenting their trays to her for perusal. When Wyn chose a glass from the brown-haired server, the other one tossed too-long bangs out of his eyes and invited Zita to take a glass. "We don't need to see ID." He winked at her, freckles creasing as he grinned.

Zita refrained from telling him her actual age or taking a glass. "I'm totally legal. Do they have real food coming out soon? Something other than booze and jumped up bar food?" she asked.

The freckled one choked on a laugh. "No, Miss, sorry. They bought the package with limited alcohol, hors d'oeuvres, and a dessert. Cream puffs. You'd think they'd spring for more when two famous actresses and Governor Rivera announced they were coming. Wine?" His rich, modulated tones hinted at years of voice lessons.

"Two? I'd say one and a half," his friend said.

"Two reality stars equal one scripted show star," Freckles argued. Another attendee spotted the alcohol and came barreling over.

Zita demurred and thanked the server, stepping back to avoid being run down by the thirsty patron. Spotting an unguarded tray half-hidden by the exuberant foliage in the corner, she headed that direction. *For a crowd of people wearing expensive clothing, they sure have an appetite. I haven't managed to get even one bite to eat.*

The hairs on the back of her neck prickled, and she studied the room again. *The pursuit of snacks can wait.* Finding nothing, she checked above.

Daylight, shaped and focused by fancy skylights to highlight the largest dioramas, faded under the continuing onslaught of the rain. Thanks to the walls extending down around each opening, the tangle of rafters and catwalks themselves were shadowy, the thick beams painted to disappear into the dark roof. Assorted equipment hid along the sides of the ceiling, making her suspect that actual spotlights lurked for when natural light was unavailable or necessity demanded a different placement. *They'll need to turn those on soon if it gets much grayer. Wait, was that motion?* She stopped to focus on it better. *I think someone's up there or their rats have been mating with horses.*

Wyn glided up next to her and touched Zita's arm. Her eyes unfocused and then sharpened. "No one is up there but a lighting technician, and he's not paying attention to anything but his toys. Stop worrying. I think the presentations are commencing. We should gather with the others." She sipped her wine.

Unenthused, Zita grunted, unable to let go of the disquieting sensation of being watched. "Is Andy back yet? Have you seen the sheath?"

Her friend shook her head. "No, I haven't, and no, he needs a moment. Brandi dumped him. He's devastated and asked for privacy."

Zita scanned the area, trying to find the source of her unease. "Figured. Ouch." *Poor Andy. He really cared about her. Perhaps we can find him a new one closer to home once he recovers. Of course, he just got his doctorate, so he may be moving anyway to a real job. Wouldn't be the first time a friend moved away. I still think someone is watching.* She trotted in place and rubbed her arms.

Wyn tilted her head and eyed Zita. "Stop jogging. Fitting in, remember?"

Distracted from her (probably paranoid) speculation, Zita brought herself to a stop. "Brandi didn't do anything mean, did she? Like making him pay the check at a local eatery? Even the homeless around here drink cocktails instead of forties, so that wouldn't be cheap. And Andy makes even less than I do." She paused and corrected herself. "When I can get any hours, that is. At the rate I'm going, I should ask the guy begging out front for money-making tips."

Wyn shook her head. "I didn't pry to find out, but it's doubtful given how guilty she felt when they left."

Zita snorted. "Excellent. I hate it when a date sticks me with the check or makes a scene. The weepy ones are the worst. At least the angry ones you can defend yourself and get in a groin punch if they go after you. They're almost fun. Have you noticed how fast the waiters all walk? Do they need to hold the trays up that high?"

Her friend shuddered. "Your idea of recreation is, as usual, strange and a little scary."

With a shrug, Zita said, "We are who we are. What does it say about you that you're my friend?" She grinned and craned her neck to see if she could spot a waiter with food. *It might be fun to stalk one and grab food when they're distracted.*

Wyn rolled her eyes. "Likely that I'm a masochist. You and your stomach. Here." She shoved her wineglass into Zita's hands. Shielding her actions with her body, she reached into her purse. Her head bent over it as she struggled to get a plastic margarine tub out of the opening. She passed it to Zita.

"You're the best!" Taking it, Zita beamed.

Snapping her bag shut, Wyn nodded. "Yes, and don't you forget it. Now, go hide somewhere with your snack and meet me at Brandi's display as soon as you're done."

With one final upward glance, Zita headed to the leafy corner by the employee stairs. *All those plants should work for camouflage, plus I can see if that tray I saw earlier has anything tasty on it.*

Wyn strolled off into the crowd.

The light in the room dimmed and grayed. Goosebumps prickled along the bare skin of her arms, and an atavistic corner of her brain screamed that something was not right. When the room seemed to contain no more than the displays and gossiping guests she had seen before, she scanned the ceiling again.

She ran a hand through her hair. *I might be paranoid, but I swear I'm being watched.* Zita retreated to a wall where at least she would have cover at her back, unsurprised when the only other wallflower there, a sullen teenage boy who had been half-hidden by the foliage of the decorative plants, peeked at her from the corner of his eyes. He had the height of a basketball player, but none of the musculature. *His gangly frame needs more food and a regular exercise regimen. Perhaps if whoever had purchased him the outfit and the expensive sneakers would feed him, he would be less irritable. Then again, there's an inch showing at his wrists and ankles, so perhaps he's growing faster than they can shovel in the food.* A red tie tilted left and loose around his neck like a crooked noose.

Stop obsessing over nonexistent stalkers and chat with the kid. Wyn scolded mentally. *He's the only one watching you and will likely lose interest past the usual pleasantries. Try not to show off that classy container, too. Aren't you the one who said we should attempt to be inconspicuous?* She angled herself to give Zita a glare before she returned to conversation and her usual serene mask.

Successfully fighting the urge to stick her tongue out at her friend, Zita tried to think of pleasantries. Instead, she blurted, "You forced to come to this too?"

Surprise and something else warred on the kid's face, and he peered at her.

Sorrow, wistfulness, and hunger, she guessed. Zita could relate.

"Yeah," he said at last, "I wouldn't be here if I could help it." His stomach rumbled.

How many of these things has he been hauled to where nobody said boo to him? Pues, he's lucky I'm here to break that pattern. Hope I don't piss him off too much. Sympathetic, she nodded at the boy. "Me, either."

He studied the tips of his shoes. "Yeah," he said. "That's life."

She snorted. "And shit."

A half-grin peeked out, but his eyes never grew any less sad. "Yeah, especially that part." He returned his gaze to the crowd, turning his back to her.

Well, that was awkward. I'll let him wallow for a bit and steer food his way if I ever catch a waiter with appetizers again. Clutching the container to herself, she fell back into a silent survey of the exhibition hall, unable to lose her unease.

Wyn had a few men hovering around her though her personal set of waiters had disappeared. She drifted along the display cases.

The lady in red posed for photographs with a bald guy in a suit that screamed politician, even down to the power tie and requisite hovering sycophants in business dress. His full, magnificent mustache, carefully curled at the ends, twitched as he laughed. *Perhaps one of the stars and the governor that the waiter mentioned?* Other than herself and her youthful companion, everyone seemed to be enjoying the pseudo-party. The kid made eye contact with no one, though she caught his longing look at the trays of canapés.

"Do you think the waiters are deliberately moving too fast so nobody can eat?" she asked.

"Probably," was his glum reply. This time, his attention stayed on the crowd.

Message received. Conversation over. Zita continued toward the abandoned tray and noted with dismay that it had been dumped upside down, spilling aged cheese into the dirt of the plant. A fabric napkin fluttered, one with a smudge of a peculiar shade of lipstick on it. *Trixie dumped her tray.*

Not the most auspicious of portents, Wyn sent back. *Or perhaps, she grew tired of being a waitress.*

Zita scanned the crowd and frowned. *It's not just her. All the attractive waiters are gone, and now, it's just the meaty ones with no experience.*

At the far end of the hall, one of the waiters, this one the epitome of a thug, down to the swagger in his walk and the way he pushed a cart through the crowd to where a cluster of similar waiters, none of them attractive, waited. Alarm thrilled through her, and she abandoned the tray to get to her friend. *Wyn, something's happening.* She was moving toward her friend before she even realized it.

What?

I have no idea, but I think our time is running out to find the sheath quietly. Have you spotted it yet? I think you've done everything but crawl into every display case here.

If it were possible for a mental connection to turn to ice, Wyn did so in her reply. *What a charming description, but no, I haven't seen it yet. I did do a quick walkthrough of all the exhibits on this floor, but I might've missed it.*

As Zita passed the boy, she touched his arm.

He jumped as if she had stabbed him, color draining from his face. "Please don't!"

She released him and pressed her butter container into his hands. "Sorry to startle you. Chicken breast. I gotta go, but you might as well have something." *Whether I'm right or wrong, at least the kid gets some food.*

He stared at her, then nodded.

Only one place left to search then, and our window to do so is closing. "Potty break and I have to pee like a racehorse," Zita sang out as she reached Wyn. She flashed a smile and dragged her unresisting friend away from her circle of admirers and toward the greenery-screened employee stairs.

"Couldn't you come up with a better excuse?" Wyn whispered, her cheeks burning with color. "If you do really need to go that badly, you don't need to announce it. What is it with you associating me with bathrooms, anyway?" She freed herself and frowned, stopping. With a flick of hair over her shoulder, she pasted a bland smile on her face as a couple passed by.

"What? Isn't that the chick excuse to use? The presentations are starting soon, sí? When that happens, the food staff will be all over packing up, retrieving things, and getting ready for an intermission or something. If you—we—are going to search the staff area and not get caught, we should do it when there's a minimal number of people. The alternative is breaking in again after this place closes, and you'll want to do the post-game analysis on Andy's breakup then. Come on." She took hold of her friend's arm and tugged her gently toward the plants.

Wyn nodded. "That makes sense. Wait, what do you mean, again?"

Zita headed toward the stairs, her eyes roving over the area for anyone watching. The closest person to them was the teenager scavenging her snack container, and he was engrossed. She shrugged. "I checked for it last night to avoid this but didn't see it. You'll have to do it."

Wyn stiffened and opened her mouth.

One of the inexperienced, beefy waiters emerged with a tray of wine just as they were about to go down the stairs. "Staff only," he growled. Liquid sloshed over the edges of multiple glasses as he thrust out an arm to bar their progress.

Chapter Seventeen

Zita fought to keep her face blank.

"Oh, my mistake," Wyn cooed, her entire demeanor changing. Her eyelashes fluttered, and one hand touched her heart as she tilted her head and smiled up at the waiter obstructing their path. Her Southern accent thickened until it was almost molasses. "Isn't this the way to the powder room?"

"By the elevators," he growled, but his stance softened beneath her smile.

"Thank you kindly," she said. "We got turned around."

Distracted by the conversation, the teenager glanced over, shoving the container behind his back. After the customary eye-glazed reaction to the sylph beside her, he noticed Zita. His lips twitched into a sly, salacious grin. "Hey. Waiter. Can I get a glass of that booze?" he called out.

The waiter turned toward him and advanced. "Shut up, boy. You don't get to drink."

Zita gave the kid a thumbs up, seized Wyn's arm, and dashed into the stairwell. The surly echo of the boy's riposte to the guard followed them in.

In comparison to the ornate marble steps of the main tourist pathway, the employee stairs were bare cement, empty of ornamentation other than a steel railing, non-slip treads, and tiny circular windows. The two women raced down the stairs, Zita practically dragging Wyn.

At the bottom, they stopped by the door, and Zita set her ear against it. Hearing nothing, she nudged it open and risked a peek both directions. The employee hallway was empty and plain, decorated in the dreary neutral paint found in back service corridors everywhere. Across from them, a gap between double doors offered a glimpse of the storeroom inside. A waitress disappeared around the bend that led to the kitchen. Bright in the dimness, an emergency exit sign burned red at the end of the hall in the opposite direction. Incongruous grinning jack-o-lantern pictures blocked the transom window under the sign, leaving feeble wall sconces as the only light to break the gloom.

Wyn came up behind her. *Ready. I'll follow your lead.*

When it seemed clear, the two women bolted into the storeroom, with Zita easing the doors shut behind them. She slapped off the lights, plunging the room into shadow as the bright fluorescents clicked and died. Hoping to gain better senses and speed their search, she did a partial shift to jaguar. The room brightened with the change, colors shifting to the spectrum she associated with big cats. Dust, straw, and cleansers dominated the scents in the room, with undertones of wine and garbage.

Wyn blinked at her, squinted, and dug into her bag. She pulled a tiny flashlight from her purse and flipped it on. After pulling out a pair of latex gloves, she snapped them on and rummaged in a box.

Out of habit, Zita glanced up for cameras. *None I can see. Didn't notice any last night, either. Sweet.* With the only window high up, storm clouds smothering the sun, and the lights off, the room would be a warren of pooling shadows for normal human eyes. *Nice setup for hiding, not so much for searching.*

She prowled the area, sifting through information. Wall-to-ceiling shelves lined the storeroom, except for the side with a locked and chained loading dock. More shelving stood in rows like a forgotten library of cardboard boxes and crates in a variety of sizes and degradation, with discarded and broken mannequins propped against them at odd intervals. The closest shelves had janitorial supplies. In the center of the room, a rack of clothing loomed over an empty, straw-lined wooden crate, with trays of detritus, used glasses and dirty cocktail napkins, stacked in untidy piles around it. She padded toward the open shipping container, something in the array of scents near it making her uneasy.

Abandoning her box, Wyn moved toward an ancient settee in the far corner of the room.

"Do you see it?" Zita whispered.

Her friend startled and blushed. "What? Oh, the sheath. No. They have books over there. If the sheath's as weak as the original blade, I'd have to be close to see the magic." Her movements exaggerated, she opened a box and peered inside. She closed it and checked the next one. Perhaps coincidentally, her choices took her closer to the stack of books by the sofa.

Zita groaned. "Better hurry then. With any luck, we'll find it fast. That way, you can slip out the emergency exit if any trouble starts and then tell Andy to hurry here."

"What? You don't want me to cower in another restroom?" Wyn said. She whipped out another pair of latex gloves and threw them at Zita.

Oye, her words sound like trouble I don't want to get near. Catching the gloves, Zita eyed the contents of the storeroom. "Okay, you don't have to go, but can you do your magic detecting more quickly? We may not have long before someone comes in for a mop or something."

Color burned in Wyn's cheeks. "One comment and I'm trouble now? Oh, silly me. For a minute, I forgot I'm only here because I'm occasionally useful. You don't trust me. Don't worry, I won't forget again and expect you to actually communicate like a normal human being with me."

"Can you just find the thing and stay out of my mind?" Zita snapped. She pulled on the gloves, the scent of talcum powder and rubber tickling her nose.

Her breath hissing in as if Zita had hit her, Wyn wrapped her arms around her stomach and pressed her lips tight.

As usual, her timing and sense of drama sucks. With a deep breath, Zita started to blow off the statement, but then actually paid attention to her friend.

Body stiff, Wyn lifted her chin, but her shoulders slumped, and her face drew tight in distress. She turned away to poke through another box, sniffing.

Honesty compelled Zita to admit, at least to herself, that if anyone else had put that expression on a friend's face, she would have been furious with them. Andy's advice drifted through her mind. She swallowed a lump in her throat and surrendered to the inevitable, though not without swearing internally. "Sorry. I never said you're useless, and I don't know why you'd think that."

She heard a deep breath followed by a huff. "Let me see... you snuck around to stake out the Alabama museum with Remus."

"To be honest, that was more so you wouldn't bug me about the date," Zita blurted.

Wyn's eyes narrowed, and Zita suspected she had not helped her case. "Oh yes, let's not forget when you allowed Garm to beat you nearly to death rather than ask me to help when I was right there. In the porta potty. Where you told me to stay. In the porta potty. Where I stayed."

This time, Zita could not stop the words from escaping, though she tried to mumble. "You really need to let the toilet thing go."

Other than a glare, Wyn continued as if she had not been interrupted. "How about when you basically patted me on my head and told me to go play with my magic while you and Andy handled the sheath problem? Clearly, you think I'm an idiot and untrustworthy."

Now Zita crossed her arms, though she kept her voice to a whisper. "How can you think I don't trust you? I've been busting my ass getting in fights with assholes over a piece of rusty cutlery on your say-so. Up until Tiffany cut me with the knife, I had to take it on faith you were right. The other day, yes, I messed up with the magic thing. My intention was to allow my stressed friend downtime to relax and do fun things once she finished the spells I requested. It wasn't meant to put you or your magic down. I was trying to spread out the workload." She started to pace along the perimeter of the room, itching to do something. "And for your information, I haven't lied so much as omitted things so you wouldn't worry."

Wyn tilted her head back and closed her eyes. "Zita, how long have you been doing capoeira?"

"Ten years, why?"

Her friend's eyes shot open, and she glared, shaking her finger at Zita. "Don't lie to me. That is impossible since you were in the hospital with me a decade ago."

Her foot tapped as if it had gone mad. Slowly, Zita said, "That was the year I got out of the hospital. The military shipped me to live with my tía in Brazil since Miguel was posted in the Middle East. She started my training as soon as I got there. I was garbage the first few months, but once I got off the barf medication and built a little muscle, I did better."

Wyn stared at her. "But we were on the same meds. I spent the next six months in bed, and it was a year or two before I could do anything without getting winded."

Zita shrugged. "Tía doesn't believe a woman should ever be helpless. She may have pushed, and I don't like to sit still anyway. My brain works better when I'm moving." *And my mouth never says the right thing in any position.* She picked a shelf and began going through a box.

Wyn blinked multiple times and then gave her head a shake. "Pushed. Right. My point was, my magic is like your capoeira. Although you may assume it is simple, it's not. It only appears that way because I've been training and practicing. I've got a related degree. My job lets me research mystical information, and I've been a practitioner and believer for eight years. Plus, my memory is eidetic, and that gives me a boost on rituals. Most of what I've been casting is little spells I've known for years, even if the magic is more immediately effective now than before our powers showed up. It's like... it's like you asked me to analyze complex, unfamiliar technology without any physical samples, come up with a counter to it, invent a few new contraptions as well, and still have time to do my nails."

Nothing in the container bore any resemblance to the sheath. Zita closed it and swallowed the urge to bring up the perfect manicure on Wyn's fingers. "So, what you're saying is you're a badass at magic, but you need more time to do it?"

"No, I'm saying magic is hard and isn't something you just whip up with craft supplies, throw around, and then have time to spend with your feet up." Wyn lifted her chin and clenched her fists as if expecting a fight.

Zita mulled that over as she started another box. "Okay."

Wyn's posture announced the raised voice to come before she even opened her mouth. "That's it? Okay?"

Raising her arms in surrender, Zita lifted a shoulder and let it drop. "What else can I say? I'm not into the magicky woo-woo stuff like you, but I got mad respect for your skills in it. If you say it's hard, then it is, and I'll try to give you more time if I ask for help again. I thought the craft supplies would help because the only spells I've seen you create required half my spice rack."

Wyn said, "And you'll stop charging off on your own like a rhinoceros?"

Activity eased Zita's disquiet as she switched to another box, though her stomach was a cold, hard lump and her shoulders ached with tension. "Claro que sí. I've gotten my culo handed to me for it. I said I'd take Andy when possible and I meant it."

Her friend sniffed. "You'll charge in with him, and he's not a fan of violence. Where's the so-called mad respect in having me hide or stay home?"

Zita closed her eyes for a moment and took a breath. "I've over a decade in martial arts and have been drilling in survival skills since I was a toddler. Andy was an Olympic runner-up in judo, and he's nearly indestructible. Having him along makes sense. As far as taking you, no, I haven't been hauling you into fights. You don't know how to fight, you refuse to learn even self-defense, and you won't use your magic to hurt people. Oye, if there's a spider, you ask me to kill it for you."

"I do not."

"Two weeks ago, the giant killer spider in your bathtub."

Wyn blinked, and roses bloomed in her cheeks. "I forgot about that one. In all fairness, it was gargantuan."

Debate on insects done, Zita continued. "Taking you would get you killed or worse. Can we be done with the subject and move on with the search?" *Please.*

Luck was not with her. To her surprise, her elegant friend snorted in an excellent imitation of a horse as she bent over another carton. "Yes, let's not talk anymore. With you, there's always something else to do first, rather than talking to me. Seeing how long you can hang upside down from a glorified scarf takes priority. You never even gave me a chance to do anything when we were at Shivers' place. Why would I think you would explain that?"

Zita stared at the ground. *Why can't we do something useful?* She shifted her weight from foot to foot and fought down the urge to jog or climb, anything to release the nervous energy building within her. She really didn't want to have this conversation. "I had a friend once. She was brave, clever, and beautiful, but she wasn't a fighter. We used to joke she could talk her way out of anything. People around her wanted to be better just by her example, you know, inspiring and all. Sound familiar?"

Eyes wide, Wyn barely breathed. "Brazil?"

The words were hard to ram past the ball of bile and guilt in her throat. Zita rubbed her eyes. "Yes. When something happened, she stepped up to stop it. I arrived just in time to see them kill her. They didn't talk or give her a chance. Just... dead." Her body gave an involuntary twitch, remembering the gunshot, the splat of brains and blood, and the delayed soft thump of the body falling. The odor of blood and death. Her stomach churned. "Thing is, if she'd waited, I could've done what she tried."

Wyn exhaled. "So, that's why you tried to keep me out of it."

Giving in to her impulses, Zita padded around the room, pushing away the memory. "If it's that important to you, we can figure out how to safely include you more when we have time. Not like now, when we really need to find that sheath before Tiffany and Garm can make the evil knife of evilness more powerful."

"It's not that—well, it is, to an extent, but it's more that you don't trust me enough to tell me anything important or let me help. You don't answer questions, you don't volunteer personal information, and you run off to go fight things with either no warning or worse, a lie about where you're going." Wyn leaned against the shelving, petting a stack of books as if they were cats.

Pausing in her task, Zita stared at her unhappy friend. "Is that what you think? Pues, I prefer to talk about other topics. I don't dwell on things... I'm not..." She huffed out a breath and paced. Quietly. "I can work out. I've been in training my whole life, for one event or another, be it surviving the deportation of my parents or winning the Olympics. For those, I have to be strong and silent and hide weaknesses. None of my classes taught me how to be like you."

"Like me?" Wyn asked.

Zita paced and pitched her voice low in case someone passed by. "You talk to everyone, and everything goes great, even without the powers. Me? Not a clue. When I talk to people, half of them want to pat me on the head and laugh, and the other half get offended. If I'm speaking about a familiar subject, then I do better. Oh, and can't forget that fifteen percent of the guys will miss every word because they're mesmerized by my boobage."

"That's more than one hundred percent, and boobage is still not a word," Wyn said.

Metal scraped in the hall. Wyn dashed to take cover behind the settee. Rushing to the wall, Zita listened to discern if anyone approached their temporary sanctuary. Hearing nothing more than a distant murmur, she continued their conversation. *Might as well get this over with.*

Waving off the correction, Zita's feet moved faster as she thought, though she kept her voice to a whisper. "People are all over the place and never add up to just one hundred percent. It's like when I arm-wrestled Aideen. She picked on you all the time, and I thought giving her a different target would help, but you were all like, 'Don't be so hard on her, she's upset right now.' Fuck that. Emotion is not an excuse to be a bully. I didn't hurt nothing but her pride. She stopped harassing you, so overall, that's a win for me, if you ignore the fact that the rest of you were down on me. I still have no idea what I did wrong, but I'm getting used to that."

Wyn frowned. "How can you not know?"

Zita spread her hands wide. "How can I if you don't tell me? I'm not the mind reader in the room. Best I can do is tell if you're upset by your body language and try to work from there, and that never turns out well. It's like you speak in secret codes, but nobody gave me the key or even a clue as to when you're using it. Do you see my problem here?"

Wyn pursed her lips.

Fighting for words, Zita slashed her hand in the air. "You want me to tell you stuff that it doesn't even occur to me to think about, let alone talk about. No matter my excuses, it's my fault, and I got to work on it. That's not you, it's me." She shook her head slowly and shrugged. The corners of her cheeks twitched into a smile. "If I had a dollar for every time a date said that right before escaping, I could quit my day job. Maybe all my jobs."

A tight smile broke through Wyn's unhappiness. She admitted, "You wouldn't have any money problems from what I've seen and heard. Still, how hard is it to just talk to your friends?"

Her smile fading, Zita scrubbed a hand over her head. "You want my honest feelings now? Fine. I have no idea why we're talking about this when we have creeps to stop, a murder knife to fix, and I guess Andy to help, too. You're always contacting me or with me, but everything I do sets you off, even just getting a snack. It wasn't as often at first, but now you're with me constantly and strung way tight."

"It's never just one snack," Wyn muttered. Her eyes were unfocused, staring at a box.

Zita ignored the aside. "Not only are you always there, but you're also asking me to do things you could do for yourself. Like, why do you always call me to kill the spiders? You don't ask Andy, though he'd be willing. Why aren't you squishing your own chingado bugs? Oye, not only could you do that, but you could convince them to go outdoors and build webs spelling out your name or peace on earth or something. Outside of a physical fight, you can be scary. Plus, you keep dipping into my head and digging around when you won't even skim other people. That there needs to stop. I mean, I'm sorry I'm apparently shit at being communicative, but you got to respect my privacy and stay out of my brain. You're a friend, and I love you and all, but I'm a person, and I deserve privacy and a little space as much as anyone else."

Moisture shimmered in Wyn's eyes. "I suppose I have been clingy."

And cranky. Zita's mouth opened, but she shut it. She had been half-expecting that comment to set off another round of recriminations about how everything was her fault. *I'll take it.*

Wyn lowered her gaze to her hands, and sorrow permeated her scent. The gulp she took before speaking almost drowned out the words that followed. "My personal life has been... My aunt has Alzheimer's, and it would be late-stage if I weren't using my healing spell on her every few weeks. I can't find anything that does more than keep her stable. I can't heal her. I keep trying, and it never lasts. In addition, my parents are suing me for control of her estate, as limited as it is. If they win, I can't afford to keep her in a rest home, let alone the one she likes."

Zita squeezed her friend's shoulder. "That sucks. If you come up with something I can do, let me know. I'd be happy to help, but I can't fix any of those things."

"You did sneak me a card for a lawyer, and he seems competent," Wyn said.

Pointing at her, Zita nodded. "If you can, get him. Miguel set us up on a date, but the lawyer's a total shark and can't handle losing at anything, so that didn't work out. What I don't get, pues, one of the many things I don't understand, is why you're spending all your time hanging out with me, but you're mad at me for most of that."

Her friend bit her lip. "I guess because you always seem to know what you're doing, and I keep thinking you'll find a solution to everything. If there's a problem, you dive in and solve it. When none of us had control over our abilities, you're the one who came up with exercises to handle them and pestered us into doing them. You rescued your brother. When we were teens, you even stopped that man... I don't feel as alone or helpless around you, and sometimes, I touch your mind just to get that feeling." At this point, the waters that had been threatening materialized and poured down her friend's cheeks. Grabbing an actual fabric handkerchief from her purse, Wyn wiped her eyes.

"You're not helpless even without me. That's what I've been trying to tell you," Zita said, working to keep her face stoic and not show any panic at the crying.

A wobbly half-smile peeked through. "The past few days, I've realized you can't solve my problems, and it's not fair of me to expect you to, especially if I don't even tell you what they are. You won't talk to me about anything that matters, either, so I peek, and I've been trying not to, but it's so frustrating..."

Carajo. Tears. Why was it always tears? Maybe we can find a compromise that will help. Zita fidgeted and flicked a glance toward the door. *So far, no one's noticed us in here, but we can't count on that luck to hold.* She gave Wyn a gentle punch on the shoulder. "Oye, we agreed as kids we got each others' backs, and I'm not going back on that. Tell you what, let's make a deal."

Her friend raised her head, eyes silver and brimming.

"You stay out of my head unless it's for vital, silent communication like in emergencies or a really funny joke or free food. If I blow off an important question, not crap like my opinions on your shoes, you say 'new leaf' or something to clue me in that it's serious. I'll reconsider answering you then, but I'm not promising to spill everything. A woman's got to have her secrets, neta? Fair? Also, if I cram my foot in my mouth, let me know instead of getting all upset. I might have a taste for shoe leather and not realize it, but it doesn't have to screw up our friendship."

Wyn nodded, her face lightening.

Zita hardly dared to breathe. "Now, can we be done with the touchy-feely talk and get back to stopping the whole weapon of mass destruction thing?"

Her friend nodded.

"We good now, right?" Zita asked, needing the verification.

"Yes," Wyn replied, "let's find that sheath." A full smile burst through.

¡Gracias a Dios! Zita grinned, and threw her arms around Wyn, giving her a hug, followed by a few pounds on the back. She almost missed the footsteps that stopped outside the door. "Incoming!" She dragged Wyn behind the wooden crate in the center of the room. New information, carried in scents, assailed her, but she had no time to process it.

The two women froze, Wyn whispering a few words under her breath.

A large man stuck his head in. With a growl, he flipped the switch, and the lights buzzed on. The tip of the latest addition to his waiter's uniform, an Uzi, preceded the rest of him into the room. He paced to the other side of the crate and turned in a slow circle.

Zita barely breathed, but her body slid into a crouching defensive position, and her mind raced through ways to take him out.

Wyn trembled and covered her own mouth with her hands. Her presence appeared in the back of Zita's mind.

The armed man stared at them—right through them—and then shook his head. "Must be hearing things," he muttered. He called something into the hall and headed toward the door.

Zita blew air out in a great puff. *You did an illusion? Here I was hoping they'd wait until after the party and all the innocents were gone.*

I can't make us invisible, but I can make us seem like part of the box if we hold still enough. As he turned to leave the storeroom, Wyn tried to peek over the crate, her shoulder hitting a precariously balanced tray of used wine glasses.

Zita lunged and caught the tray, but one glass tipped over the edge and crashed to the ground.

The thug waiter whirled toward where they hid, bringing his weapon down into a firing position.

Swearing mentally, Zita shifted into gorilla. Her ears caught the telltale rip of her clothing, but she had no time to dwell on it.

"Come out now," the man ordered, aiming his gun at the jumble of objects they hid behind. His stance was relaxed and his grip loose; he must have thought he had caught a cowering waiter or guest.

Zita teleported behind him and tapped his shoulder.

He jerked and turned toward her.

She struck him in the jaw and heard bone crack beneath her hairy fist. When his hands rose toward his face in reflex, she batted the gun from them, and then slipped behind him, wrapping her too-long arms around him in a sleeper hold.

He gurgled and kicked, tears streaming from his eyes, and she counted seconds.

Por favor, just pass out already, she thought.

To her relief, he finally lapsed into unconsciousness before her count reached a critical number.

Lifting him, Zita tucked him behind the cart, careful to leave him sitting up so he could breathe even with whatever she had broken. With a quick shift to her Arca form, she whispered, "Can you sleep him? He won't be out long." She stepped back from the unconscious man, remembering the efficiency and undiscriminating nature of that spell.

Wyn nodded, eyes wide. She stared at him from beside Zita, made a few motions, and a pink mist twined around him. His labored breathing eased into something deeper and quieter, if congested. "Sorry," she whispered, "My legs cramped."

Zita shrugged. She stared down at the man. "We'd better hurry with that search. Is Andy on his way?"

"He's distraught and asked me to give him privacy," Wyn hedged.

Rubbing her hands over her face, Zita took a deep breath. "So, I should charge off alone?"

"No! He's just so depressed. I wanted to give him time to grieve."

Straw from the wooden crate crunched underfoot. "He'll have to fight now, grieve later. Museum security does not generally carry around Uzis, so Garm and Tiffany must be making their move. Andy asked to be told and will be even more upset if we don't call him in on this, especially if anyone dies." *Like you or me.* Zita sniffed, then realized what the tangled aromas on the box meant.

Wyn nodded. "Point made. I'll start talking to him. Now what?"

Zita prowled to the front of the container and dug through it, unsurprised when her fingers touched a rough, crumpled cardboard box that rattled when she pulled it out. Opening it, a cool, smooth metal object fell into her hand. She showed it to her friend. "Garm and Atlas are already here, and they brought a lot of guns. Their scents are all over this box. If Tiffany or Jennifer came, they didn't handle the box. This must have been a staging area. If you want, I can unlock the loading dock, and you can run to safety. I'll keep hunting for the sheath on my own."

"I'm surprised you bothered to tell me instead of just shoving me out the door or into another bathroom. I refuse to go to the toilet again," Wyn said.

Zita snickered and grinned. "That'll be awkward at work and parties." She moved the sleeping man behind the carton, gentle to avoid waking him.

Her friend protested, "That's not what I meant!"

"Then you should say what you mean when you talk," Zita teased. "Seriously, I'll try not to coddle you as much if that's what you want, but I'm not promising to stop protecting you."

"It's what I want."

The lights went out.

"What was it you were saying about bad portents earlier?" After a partial shift to jaguar, Zita snuck to the storeroom door and listened while her friend remained by the unconscious man. Nudging it open, she checked both directions. Her improved night vision came in handy as none of the bulbs along the walls remained lit.

Watery sunlight escaped the pouring rain to skirt the edges of the pumpkins blocking the windows by the door. The bouncing movement of headlamps splashed light on the chairs and a small table set up by the emergency exit, currently occupied by two more armed faux waiters. A blank television occupied the table. The men seemed more engrossed in their card game than in watching the hall. Another headlamp bounced and disappeared as a third man disappeared around the bend that led to the kitchen.

She shared the information. *It's easy to locate them when they've all got lights on their heads. The television must be the security camera feed to the outside, but it's dead now.* Withdrawing back into the room, Zita poked Wyn's arm. "How fast are you with that sleep spell? Think you can put those guys by the door out? By the way, you should put on a disguise."

With a shimmer, Wyn disappeared, and the icy, foreign form of her illusion stood in her place. "I've only ever done one guy at a time," she whispered, "though I suppose I could try two or three."

Zita snickered before she could stop herself. "Though I'm sure lots of men would be willing to help you expand your sexual horizons, I asked about putting them to sleep."

Wyn frowned at her for a second, and then giggled, quickly putting her hand to her mouth as she tried to smother a laugh.

They grinned at each other like idiots, then tiptoed to the door again.

As Zita stretched out her hand to open the door, Wyn cleared her throat softly. "By the way, are you aware you're naked again? Unless you're going to use your impressive endowment as a distraction measure, you may wish to don apparel before continuing today's crazed plans. I picked up your clothing remains and put them in my purse." Her flashlight clicked and went out.

Zita glanced down and sighed. *I had hoped at least my underwear would survive. Should have packed more clothing.* "No, I'm not planning on using the girls as a weapon." She trudged over to the rack of samples and whipped through it. *Everything's meant for tall, skinny types like Wyn. My arms, chest, and shoulders would split most of this crap. Momentito, what's that?* Catching a flash of dull purple, almost lost amid the brighter hues, she seized a set of familiar sports apparel.

"Is that Brandi's sportswear?" Wyn asked. Digging into her purse, she pulled out a spare mask and the brooch.

Ruefully, Zita said, "Nothing else will fit." She threw on the sportswear, then accepted the mask and brooch from Wyn. The borrowed close-cut garments fit just as well as the set at home. *I have to admit the hussy makes a nice set of clothes, even if she has the terrible taste to kick Andy to the curb.* Dressed, she pinned the brooch inside her pocket and crept to the door again. "Let's go for the guys by the exit first. You do your sleepy-time spell. Once they're out, I'll shut down the alarms on the door, and we can use it to help people escape."

Wyn bit her lip but inclined her head. "I'll try."

With a roll of her eyes, Zita elbowed her friend. "Are you forgetting the dealers in the meth house a few weeks ago? Maybe you thought your spell was going from guy to guy, but Andy and I were standing nearby and almost took a nap, too. You got this, and your magic means fewer people get hurt."

Wyn took a deep breath and nodded.

"Great. Make yourself look like the guy we knocked out until we get close enough for you to cast."

Wyn's illusion shimmered, and the beefy waiter replaced the slim blonde, an uncertain expression on his face. Dragging her feet, she moved to the door. In an unsteady baritone, she said, "It's really dark. I might need to get closer to see them well enough to use the spell."

Zita took a deep breath. *Trust. Yeah. Hopefully, none of the guards will notice their friend swings his hips like a chick now.* "I'll sneak along, and if they seem too interested in you, I'll jump them. You cast. If you put me to sleep, wake me up."

The two women pushed open one door just enough to slip out and begin a slow walk toward the men at the emergency exit. When a familiar mist settled over the guards, and their bodies slumped, Zita gave her friend a gentle punch in the arm. "Knew you could do two at once, even without alcohol. Stay put while I check them."

With a tap on her necklace, Wyn changed to her favored illusion of the blond in the sparkly dress. She made a face at Zita, but the grimace included a small smile.

Zita grinned, checked behind them, and then ran to the sleepers. She emptied the guns of ammunition, including the chambers, and searched the men for additional weapons. Once that was done, she resisted the urge to put them in silly poses, and instead gently tweaked their posture so they would seem inattentive from a distance rather than unconscious. She unlocked and unchained the door, also disabling the door alarm while there.

Her friend stood staring, eyes unfocused, at the men.

"Wyn?" Zita whispered and nudged her.

With a jerk, Wyn's face cleared and she turned to Zita. "Oh, yes. Sorry. I was thinking. I was going to create illusions of us escaping outside. However, my illusions will wink out when I can't see them anymore. If the police have men surrounding the building, they'll notice when two running women suddenly disappear in front of them."

Zita paused and nodded. "Understood. So, we'll skip that illusion and figure out a good lie to tell the cops later if necessary.

Let's get you searching again, and I'll finish scouting to see what
Garm's people are up to." After a glance had determined the second
storage area was empty except for an unconscious woman, she left
Wyn there so her friend could tend to the injured and search for
the sheath.

Most of the rooms she checked were empty, save for the last
one near the exit, an office where a sweaty senior citizen in a
ticket-taker's uniform hid under his desk, his balding head
bleeding, and a cash register sagging open nearby.

She squatted next to him. "You hanging in there? Hombre, if
you want, you can escape out the emergency exit right now. Or you
can try to wait until we've cleared the rest of the crazies out."

He nodded but refused to come out from under his desk.

The crazy patter of his heart and dilated pupils worried Zita. *I
got another victim with a head wound in the office by the exit door,
probable concussion and his pulse is all over. Apparently, Garm and
company can't resist adding a little attempted murder to their big heist.*

*I'll be there when I can. The woman we found has a spinal fracture,
and it takes longer to heal bone.* Wyn's tone held that distracted note
that made Zita wonder if she would need to remind her friend
about the old man again later.

Zita patted the ticket-taker's foot, the only reachable part of
him. "You know what? You stay put, and I'll send medical help in a
minute, and then you can run off." She left the office and headed
to the area she had saved for last—the kitchen.

Chapter Eighteen

Zita peered around the edge of the open kitchen doorway, keeping low. White walls constrained what seemed like endless stainless-steel tables, counters, and shelving above a bland beige tile floor. Burning food—her brain cataloged it as bacon, chicken, and Heaven—begged her nose for help, and one or more mechanical timers buzzed repetitively. A disorderly collection of used trays, plates, and serving tools loomed on one long table. Along another table, three trays held tiny cream puffs, with a remaining empty tray waiting in front of the ovens.

Two armed men, tall and muscular, compared wine bottles and snickered. An Uzi hung from a strap on one man's shoulder, and the other had a semiautomatic pistol in a hip carry. In addition to headlamps, they had procured camp lanterns somewhere and were using them to light the windowless room.

Their posture, or lack thereof, plus the unprofessional way they're handling the whole thing explains why nobody's noticed the sleeping guards yet. Definitely no military experience in either of them. Still, they've got size and weapons on their side. This is a lot of guards for a quick search, smash, and grab operation.

Her eyes drifted over the flat black of unused stoves to the fridge and freezer of her dreams, giant industrial walk-ins, when she saw a flash of red in the fridge window. *Wait. What?* Zita shifted position and glimpsed someone inside the closed fridge, a person who glared through the square window, eyes fierce and a bit insane. *Trixie? They must have shut the legitimate staff in the fridge. Well, at least they're not slaughtering everyone in their path. Carajo, does this mean they're doing the whole hostage thing?* Focusing, she sent, *Wyn, I've got two in need of a snooze fest here. Take a left out of the storage room. Their debate over the wine won't last forever, so hurry.*

Coming, but I can't stay. You said the ticket-taker needs healing. Wyn scurried up beside her. While it took a minute and some backpedaling to catch one man who had escaped the initial cloud and advanced on them, her spell put both men to sleep.

Trixie pounded on the window.

Zita nodded to the woman in the fridge and held up a finger. "Can you get my phone out?" After a quick partial shift to gorilla for the strength, she moved the unconscious men to a wine cart in the corner.

Wyn pressed the disposable phone into her hand.

Zita hesitated and then inhaled deeply. *Trust.* "Thanks, can you tie them up? I would, but I might wake them."

With a smile blossoming, Wyn trussed the kitchen guards in discarded aprons.

Zita opened as many locks on the fridge as possible. Once she had undone a slide-bolt, she heard a clunk from inside, and the door opened, spilling a crowd of waiters and white-clad kitchen staff. A handful had injuries. *It's like a creepy clown-car fridge. How many people did they have crammed in there?* "The back emergency exit is unlocked. Hurry up and go," she urged them. A few shoved by her, but the rest seemed to need a minute to mill in confusion. Just in case, she unlocked and opened the walk-in freezer, but it was empty.

Backing into an untenanted corner as she watched the discombobulated staff filter out, Zita punched a programmed number and whispered into her phone when a masculine voice answered. "Remus?"

"Yes, who is this?"

"It's Arca."

His voice grew more distant, and she was sorry for it. Well, somewhat. *He had been boring on their date, other than during the fighting at the end.* "Oh? Listen, I'm pretty busy..."

Zita rolled her eyes and made a shooing gesture at a dazed-looking waiter nearby. "I'm not asking you out this time. Your message after the last date was clear. Oye, those thieves we ran into at the museum? They've turned all terrorist and have holed up in the Carter Shuster Museum of Design and Innovation in New York City. They've locked all the doors with chains. Can you run here and help me get people out?"

He swore in Spanish. "I can get there, but what do you expect me to do?"

"I'll unlock the doors, and you help people escape. If they're taking hostages, they could have over a hundred cooped up here— I haven't finished scouting to know. I'm sure a SWAT team will come busting in soon, but the fewer captives the thieves have, the better."

"How do I get in?" Keys tapped in the background; she hoped that meant Remus was searching for the address.

Zita did a quick calculation. "Use the last door on the eastern side of the building, the unlocked one with the pumpkins hanging up in the window above it. I'm in a kitchen near there. If you see the police, tell them about the unlocked entrance so they don't blow down walls and accidentally hurt anyone."

"Right, give me a minute." More clicking.

She hadn't expected that request from him. "You need more time? Did you sprain your ankle?"

His tone sharpened. "Have to wait for the computer to give me the map to get there. My internet's slow."

"Oh, yeah, waiting for that sucks. See you soon," she said, closing the phone.

Wyn materialized next to her. "Done?"

Zita fought the urge to check the knots on the sleepers, and instead pasted a smile on her face. "Sweet. Can you take this?" She passed Wyn the phone and remembered the old ticket-taker. She sent Wyn to tend his wounds and convince him to leave.

Corralling the stragglers in the kitchen, Zita urged them to leave. "Go and keep it down. Don't stop in any rooms. Don't go up the stairs. The building's still full of terrorists. We only cleared this section so far. Tell the cops not to shoot us. Just hurry!" While they stampeded in slow motion toward the exit, she dialed off the ovens, shut off the timers, and then took out the ruined canapés with a pair of discarded potholders. She dropped them on an empty counter and watched acrid smoke rise from them. *Far too many buildings have caught on fire around me the last few months. Let's not add another.*

Her Lucy nametag askew, Trixie ministered to one of the waiters, the freckled one from earlier, who held a bloodied white towel to his head. She was in full doctor mode, issuing orders in an authoritative voice nothing like the nasal drawl she had affected earlier. As another waiter assisted Freckles toward the door, she barked a final warning after him. "Don't forget what I said about scarring!"

He nodded and straggled out with the last of the crowd. Trixie started to follow, but Zita bolted over and touched her sleeve before the doctor could leave. "You. Red."

"Me?" Trixie said, her mouth in an "O" and adenoidal voice back in full force. "What about me?" She patted her hair.

Before Zita could say anything else, the double doors to the main hall banged open. Atlas ducked as he stepped through the doors, his oversized frame blocking the doorway. He wore no headlamp. "Her Majesty, the pain in my ass, wants to know why we're not getting check-ins. We've got two men missing, a bear barricading a room with a group of tourists, a hostage exchange going down to get electricity back on and evening news coverage, and you can't be bothered to check in on schedule? What happened?" His litany of complaints stopped as his eyes fell on Zita and Trixie.

Zita swore internally. *They've got hostages, more than we found in the cold storage units, and a bear?*

The pseudo-redhead was grinning for some reason.

He eyed the two sleeping men piled on top of the wine cart.

With a hum, the lights all sprang to brilliant life.

Blinking her eyes rapidly to adjust to the renewed lighting, Zita stepped in front of the unconscious men, smiled, and shrugged. *If moving puts a counter between Atlas and me, all the better. Run, Trixie.* She spread her hands wide. "Minor wine problem. Everything's fine. We're fine. We're all just fine right now, thanks. How are you?" Rocking onto the balls of her feet, her body balanced for combat. *First I talk, and then they attack me. People are so unreasonable.*

He blinked and held his position. "Huh. Thought you were dead."

Her eyes ticked over him, noting his lack of a weapon, even the ankle sheath he'd used before. "My health plan can't be beat. No gun?"

A small smile came to his lips. "Hard to find one that fits comfortably." Atlas held up an immense hand in explanation.

From the doorway opposite, Trixie shook her head so violently that her wig tilted to the side. She straightened her bouffant. "That's not how it goes. You two should start over. He needs to say his first line again, and then you need to mention the slight weapons malfunction before you start in on all the fines." Her voice was back to normal again.

"What are you talking about?" Zita asked, glancing at Trixie before returning her attention to Atlas.

"The chat you're having with Darth Humongous over there? Oh, never mind. This is a boring conversation anyway," Trixie complained. "Great, now you've got me doing it." Her reflection in a stainless-steel stockpot pouted.

A tiny mechanical squawk interrupted. Atlas pinched the bridge of his nose, his mouth turning downward, and his whole body radiating his uneasiness. After removing a Bluetooth earpiece, he dropped it into his pocket. He cracked his knuckles and lumbered toward Zita. "Guess this explains why nobody's answering their radios here. Nothing personal, but I can't let you keep up the comedy routine. Apparently, we have a schedule to keep."

"Run!" Zita commanded the other woman. She seized a wine bottle.

"I dunno. I feel lucky. Comedy is my thing," Trixie said, apropos of nothing. "All of the wine is terrible, by the way."

Atlas lunged.

Zita jumped onto a nearby counter and smacked him on the head with the wine bottle. It broke, spilling liquid down his face and sending the scent of alcohol throughout the room.

Shaking his head like a dog, the man swept out a long arm to seize her.

Somewhere nearby, Trixie said, "See? Even the bottles are cheap."

Slashing at Atlas' hand with the broken bottle, Zita was unsurprised when the glass shattered at the contact with his arm, and he gained only a minor gash. She vaulted to the next counter, her mind whirling. *So, he's extra tough, but not invulnerable. No real training. Based on how he ruined the hose in Alabama, he's got unnatural strength, too. Maybe I can lead him into one of the walk-ins long enough for Wyn to put him to sleep? Large animals are out. No room to maneuver.*

"You know," Atlas said, "If you'd let me hit you just once, you can go down and stay there. The others might not notice you if you were already out of the way. You might survive that way, unlike if they use that awful knife on you." He swiped at her again.

Zita ran along the top of the counter, seizing a huge stockpot, and then leapt up. She slammed the pot down over his head, and then kicked the side of it hard enough to send him staggering sideways. Bouncing off the counter, she ran by the ovens, hoping to lure him closer to the fridge. She would have replied, but had no breath to spare.

"Go for the frying pan next!" Trixie cheered, rattling something.

Atlas stumbled against the counter and pulled the pot off his head. "Nobody wants to be reasonable," he mourned as he continued to follow her.

Is one of my plans actually working? Zita donned potholders and let him get closer. She seized the pan of still-smoking hors d'oeuvres and swung it at him. Blackened appetizers flew.

He caught the edges of the tray and tore it away from her. With a yelp, he dropped it, shaking his burned hands.

The pan clattered to the floor.

"Food fight!" came the cheerful suggestion from behind her.

Zita took another step backward, hot food squishing and searing the bottom of her foot before she kicked the appetizer off. *Pan comido,* she thought. *Trixie's loca, though.*

A butcher knife flew by her.

Atlas ducked.

The butcher knife stuck in a cabinet and quivered.

Zita frowned. "Wait. How is that happening? Those aren't balanced for throwing, and they shouldn't stick in the cabinet."

Another chef's knife flew by, striking Atlas in the shoulder. "Comedy is an art. One should never listen to the critics or hecklers," Trixie said, the words almost unintelligible beneath wild chortling.

Pulling out the knife with a wince and letting it fall, Atlas seized the end of a steel table and heaved it into the air. He took a step back, holding it like a shield. The table's length nearly matched his height, providing him almost full cover.

Another blade planted itself in the steel, followed by... a camp lantern? It flickered and died upon impact, sending bits of plastic flying.

At Zita's glance, Trixie shrugged, her eyes still gleaming. "They didn't bring the full set of knives." She cackled.

Atlas tossed aside the table and sprang at Trixie.

Trixie rolled out of the way, letting his charge pass by and into the hall. "Neener."

He turned around. His hands were red and puffy, his shoulder bled, and one of his eyes was swollen. Wordlessly, he went after Trixie again.

Zita positioned herself in front of the walk-in fridge. "Hey, you want to hide from her over here with me? I'll only kick your ass a little," she called out to him.

Trixie seized another plate and chucked it at him. It bounced off, hit a wall, and broke. She backed up in the wrong direction, toward the corner that held the sleeping men, and tripped over a foot. She stumbled.

Atlas raised a foot to stomp on her.

Putting her full weight and enhanced strength into it, Zita executed a modified rasteira de costa, the spinning back kick sweeping the ankle of his supporting leg from under him. He fell backward, and Zita danced out of the way before he could land on her.

Back on her feet, Trixie scooted out around him and ran past Zita.

Her escape blocked Zita, now armed with a pair of skillets, from reaching Atlas before he stood again.

The giant punched at Zita, a quick jab followed by a right cross. Both missed.

A fluffy pie sailed through the air and splattered all over his face, blinding him, followed in rapid succession by another pie that splashed squishy coolness all over his injured shoulder and Zita's left side. The scent of coconut made her stomach rumble.

Weirdest fight ever, Zita thought, leaping up to smash her pans over both of his ears. She slid a little in spilled cream and filling but managed to keep her feet.

Already wiping pie off his face, he reeled under her assault, slipped, and fell. His head banged against the industrial stove, and he landed on the ground. Blood trickled out of a gash in his scalp.

Zita swore. *Wyn? Going to need you back in the kitchen.*

"You're welcome for rescuing you," Trixie said, spinning a third pie on her finger like a basketball trick.

"Back at you. I was going to lure him into the fridge and shut him in there until we could put him to sleep like those guys," Zita said, pointing her thumb at the two thugs dozing in the corner and tied up with aprons. "I wouldn't leave him in there to asphyxiate. Where did you get those pies from, anyway? I don't know how I missed that. All I saw were the little cream puffs." She gestured toward the empty trays where the desserts had been and scowled. "I thought..."

Still cradling the remaining pastry, Trixie seemed nonplussed as she walked over to peer at the giant. "Oh. I just thought you were incompetent when you didn't kill him. Turns out you're an idealist. Who knew? I thought those were all extinct," she said, turning to face Zita.

"Seriously, where did you get the pies from—Look out!" Zita shouted and knocked Trixie out of the way of Atlas' sloppy lunge.

Groggy from his earlier fall, he continued a few steps past her.

Zita spun to gather momentum and booted him in the back. This time when he fell, he caught himself on the fridge doorway. With a wince, Zita slammed the heavy walk-in door on his head and hands until he collapsed. "Dude. Stay down."

This time, he did not get back up.

Trixie frowned. "Guess the party's over, and I didn't even get to play Spin the Bottle." She stepped around Atlas and retrieved a handgun from one of the men in the corner. She checked the magazine and the chamber, keeping the muzzle pointed down. "I'll shoot them."

"No, no murdering," Zita said. "I don't know why everyone's so hot to kill, but no."

Wyn ran in. "Sorry it took so long. Murders?"

Trixie smiled, tucked her newly acquired weapon into her cummerbund, and ran a finger through the pie she held. She licked it. "Mm, coconut cream pie. You see this one?" she asked Wyn, pointing to Zita. "She's a crazy woman. No deaths on a battlefield, indeed. You take care." She sauntered by Wyn and handed her the dessert. "I'll be on my way, then. I need to see a bear about a man."

Wyn's mouth opened and closed as she stared at the departing Trixie, destroyed kitchen, Zita, and the man at her feet.

"Need a sleep spell on this guy and a heal. Maybe. He's tough, but he should've gotten back up by now, and I think I broke his fingers," Zita said. She shifted fully to a gorilla and heaved Atlas' bulk to prop him up in the back corner of the fridge. *His reasons for participating in this are a mystery to me, but there's no reason to risk him choking or encourage hypothermia.*

Her friend's eyes were very wide as she set down the pie. "What is all over you?" She chanted, pink mist rising around Atlas.

The air snapped, and Remus appeared. "I'm here. You have no idea how irritating it is waiting for a computer and getting lost at high speed. Also, were you aware the police are everywhere outside? What am I doing?" he said, and then he did a double-take at the scene before him.

Zita hooted. *Claro que sí, the hot guy arrives when the fighting's over, and I am a mess. At least the pie smells delicious.* She shifted back to Arca and regarded him. "Keep the doors unlocked, and if you're willing, disarm anyone who tries to shoot at the escapees. I'll send everyone I can your way, then see if I can free anyone on the upper floor. They have people shut up in more side rooms based on what the huge dude in the corner said. Come find me, my friend here, or a skinny guy in a mask if you need help." *Assuming Andy finds a mask and shows up soon, that is. I hope the police don't have him.*

"I have a name. Call me Muse," Wyn said, flashing a smile at the man, her healing magic sparkling around her hands as she tended Atlas.

Remus grinned back, though his wavered. "Pleased. I'm Remus."

Muse? Shoving her worry about Andy and curiosity about Wyn's alias aside, Zita continued, "If you want, you can tell the cops that the thieves have a weapon that can kill or injure a room of people all at once. It looks like a short sword. We're hoping to disable that." She grabbed a white rag from a pile of clean ones and mopped pie off herself. *Still wearing clothing. Awesome.*

He nodded slowly.

"You want a mask?" Zita paused in her efforts to clean herself off.

Remus bowed his head, his voice strangled. "No. All I'm doing is holding a door open and maybe collecting guns."

Wyn cleared her throat and rose. "Actually, if you would reconnoiter the building and tell us where everyone is, it would help. Especially if you see these." She held out her hand, and illusions of the Key floated above it.

Zita raised her hands. "Your decision. Be safe. When the cops take over, feel free to run off. My friends and I'll be out of here once they're in command."

He frowned at her. "I'll scout. You won't change your mind about being more open about your identity or your abilities? It would help with the police..."

Wyn closed her fingers, and her illusion disappeared.

Zita shook her head. "No, and I assume you're not budging, either. I'm also going to be punching people since I can't disarm them as easily as you can. So, in the interest of avoiding assault charges..."

He nodded. The air cracked twice, and he gave them a brief summary of the positions of the invaders. "I'll just go help the elderly man in that one office leave, since he's getting ready to run for it on his own."

"Thanks," Zita said. As he walked away, she admired the view. *Even if it's not going to work out between us, he's still lovely eye candy.*

Zita, really? Wyn sent. *Just when I thought you were starting to act like an adult, you get distracted by a man's rear end.*

Andy announced his presence. *I can see you added me to party line just in time for another conversation I'd prefer to miss. Is the emergency over?*

Zita relaxed a little. If he was complaining about their conversation, he wasn't in police custody. *What? You need to enjoy the natural wonders of the world when you have a chance. Don't be haters. I'll watch Garm's group to see if they find the sheath while Wyn searches for it down here. If I see the sheath, I'll grab it.*

Chapter Nineteen

Even transformed into a fluffy black cat, scouting the building was a challenge for Zita, despite the intelligence Remus had supplied. The public area of the first floor had held more goons with guns, with a pair at each building entrance. The weapons were a mix of cheap semiautomatic pistols and Uzis. As she watched, a pregnant woman and two other hostages were shoved out the front door by a few other guards, who then slammed the door shut and bolted it. *Gesture of good will for a hostage negotiator?* A handful of people were locked into one room, presumably the ones guarded by a bear, a fact she surmised by the growls audible even through the walls and the thick scent of ursine anger. A guard shifted uneasily outside that door. After a brief struggle with herself, she sent that information to Wyn, managing to not instruct her to hide, in the spirit of their new pact. Despite her unhappiness when her friend indicated she would put them to sleep and continue with the search for the sheath, Zita left the guards alone. She snuck back up the employee stairs to check the status of the main exhibition hall, her mask bouncing on its string around her neck.

To her surprise, the invaders had made themselves comfortable and were almost relaxed. Lit by a spotlight, a wheeled office chair sat atop a platform in solitary splendor, the diorama that had been there before cast to the floor. Tiffany twirled a microphone from that seat and surveyed her temporary domain, a tiny earpiece decorating one ear. A white phone, one of the giant rectangular models, sat on the floor by her seat, alongside a bulging leather knapsack. Two sneering men with handguns revolved around her makeshift dais. The whole room was fetid with sweat, fear, and sour wine.

At the base of the platform, four guests stood, guarded by two men. The selected hostages, their hands tied behind their backs, included the mustached politician, the lady in red, the grizzled businessman who had so admired Wyn, and a stunning, too-thin teenage girl. Additional guards in tuxedos stood at both the employee and public entrances to the room, many with familiar faces. *That explains why half the waitstaff sucked.*

Along one wall, all the remaining museum employees and visitors sat on the floor, bound hand and foot. Although fewer men watched over more people, those guards carried Uzis. A gunman and a familiar teenage boy wove through those prisoners. The youth held an overflowing red velvet bag and took jewelry, phones, and wallets from the tied people.

When the gangling youth went to remove a shiny watch from the wrist of one prisoner, the man lashed out with his feet, forcing the kid to skitter back.

Zita bit back a mew of protest.

The gunman smacked the prisoner in the head with the butt of his pistol before kicking the man in the stomach a few times once he was down. Putting the gun away, he said something.

Sweating and ashen, the lanky teen resumed collecting valuables.

Tiffany cleared her throat and raised a microphone to her lips. "Just a reminder, we control this building right now, and your continued existence relies on your cooperation. Now, your future overlords require funds to continue their work, so when our volunteer comes around, allow him access to your valuables. Gauche, I know, but the others really wanted to start with the classics. Once you have deposited your former belongings, you will get to enjoy a little movie. Do be civilized. If you'd rather be rude, we will make an example of you." Her gaze swept over the hall, and she gave a tight smile at the battered man, her eerie eyes glinting in the spotlights.

A flash of midnight fur revealed Garm, gliding from one side room to the next.

Zita exhaled and made a mental note to move before he got near her hiding place beneath an exuberant black and green elephant ear plant.

Escorted by the silent gunman, the teen trudged over and placed the bag in a pile of similar bags. "That's all of them," he said, his head hanging low. Even with feline hearing, his words were barely audible.

"Don't talk to me. Go stand back where you were," Tiffany snapped at him. She made an imperious gesture in the air and brought the microphone to her lips. "Ladies and gentlemen, we will begin our presentation now."

The boy curled up at the foot of the dais platform, as far away from Tiffany as possible. He stared down at his feet, his shoulders slumped.

An enormous screen descended from the ceiling, just behind Tiffany, the whir of motors cutting through the constant soft rustle of furtive movement and whispers. Once it had clicked into position, it lit with a video. The lights in the room dimmed. With the storm clouds overhead smothering the sunlight, the entire room became a dusky cave, lit primarily by the massive monitor, Tiffany's personal spotlight, and emergency exit signs.

On screen, a muscled blond man wearing a crown sat upon a seat draped in fur and prattled, his magnified voice crashing through the exhibition hall. Zita caught enough to understand he was explaining his own superiority and stopped listening. Behind him, a solid row of people waited in matching uniforms, all at attention like soldiers for review. Only one person lacked the costume the others wore other than the spokesman—Jennifer Stone slumped in her own smaller throne, a dainty golden coronet askew on her head. Her focus on a book, she paid no attention to anything else, including her own personal disarray; her clothing was crumpled, her brown hair disordered, and her shoes were missing. The woman tapped a pencil against her chin before stowing it behind her ear. Even when the enthroned man tossed a casual lightning bolt that boomed and crackled at a volume that made Zita's sensitive ears ache, the act only won a faint frown and a mutter from Jennifer.

Must be some crossword puzzle she's got going on. Zita turned her attention back to the room. With amusement, she watched Tiffany roll her chair a few feet so she would appear to be seated beside the crowned man. The sheath was not visible, so Tiffany and her cronies must not have found it, either. *The show seems important to them. Perhaps I can delay it long enough for the cops to free the hostages. They've got to have a geek working around here for her microphone and the movie or streaming video or whatever.* She wracked her memory, and finally remembered the small booth above the main area, accessible only by ladder and filled with mysterious blinky equipment. A quick check confirmed the ladder was missing.

Slinking to the edge of the plants, Zita changed to her favorite owl form, a South American Horned Owl. After flying to the ceiling, she landed on one of the narrow catwalks leading to the booth. Other than the ambient illumination from below and the faltering sunlight that escaped the skylights, the rafters had no lights or rails. She switched to Arca and then did a partial shift to gain jaguar traits. Inky darkness gave way to mere shadow. Metal beams and the occasional catwalk crisscrossed at irregular intervals, with the paths barely wider than the supports. When she straightened up, she stopped for a moment and plucked at the

Spandex-like fabric covering her. *Excellent! I kept my clothes again. Shame my shoes didn't come along.* She pulled up her mask from around her neck, settling it over her eyes.

One careful foot ahead of another, she padded along the cold metal catwalk, most of her attention on the situation below.

Shapes played upon the huge screen, unrecognizable from her angle. A bombastic voice boomed out from the speakers set nearby, explaining the role of humanity under the God Kings. Having abandoned her perch, Tiffany stood next to her dais, pouring a vial of liquid into Garm's massive maw, one hand cupping his snout. When it was gone, she corked it and returned it to her oversized purse, even as he pawed at his nose and shook his head.

Must taste awful, whatever it is, Zita thought.

An additional shake of the wolf's head revealed another earpiece, similar to the ones worn by Tiffany and Atlas. The witch and wolf exchanged a few words, then he darted down the main stairs.

Garm incoming, main stairs, Zita warned Wyn.

Understood, Wyn sent back, her mental tone distracted.

Concern distracting her, Zita couldn't help but ask. *Andy, you coming or what?*

Irritation laced his reply. *The cops have a solid cordon around the building. I'm trying to get in without getting shot by the SWAT team or letting people notice the man wearing a ninja mask and gloves. I can't switch forms without losing my clothes and damaging buildings.*

Yeah, I already destroyed one set, but the current ones have lasted through two major shapeshifts... wait. The only times I've gotten to keep my clothes after a shift up in size, I was wearing Brandi's experimental sportswear. Maybe it's not my doing. Something to practice later.

Andy agreed, his tone distant.

Oblivious to Zita overhead, Tiffany strolled over to dig through the bulky bag next to her chair. She removed what appeared to be an extended family-size ketchup container bursting with brown liquid. Dismounting from her dais, she walked out past the inner group of hostages. A spotlight clung to her as she dripped the thick sludge of the bottle onto the floor. Her two bruisers, bodyguards, trailed behind, one on either side of the growing line of darkness.

A glint of reflected light in the darkness alerted Zita, and she dropped into a crouch, her instincts screaming. She inspected the area methodically until she caught sight of a hard, streamlined form, a long gun nestled in his arms and braced on a tripod, almost invisible at the crossing of two major beams. The muzzle pointed at her, as did the goggles that hid the part of his face left uncovered by a mask. *Not good, but he hasn't shot me yet.* She sniffed, opening her mouth to allow the flavors of the air to flow into her, nodding when she caught the faintest traces of a scent she recognized.

"Oye, Freelance," she called softly toward him. "Should have known you would be up here. I was hoping you would come."

He returned no response, not that she had expected one.

"Look, we could have an undoubtedly awesome and dangerous fight up here, jumping from beam to beam and almost falling and chasing each other around—Pues, that sounds like fun other than the probable death part of it—but I got a different proposition for you." She offered him a bright smile, straightened, and took two steps toward him. To show she was unarmed, she spread her hands wide and turned from side to side. Brandi's athletic wear was form-fitting enough to make it obvious she carried nothing but Wyn's brooch in her pocket.

Did his head tilt a little? At any rate, she chose to interpret the lack of gunfire as interest. "I don't suppose you want to tell me why you're here tonight? I somehow doubt you're into fabrics of the new millennium. We might not have conflicting goals." She pushed her long hair over her shoulder, the string of her mask tangling with her fingers, and sent up a prayer of thanks for keeping her clothing on. A lifetime in locker rooms might have stripped her of any false modesty, but nudity around Freelance bothered her on a visceral level. *Nature gave him plenty of advantages, so I don't need to grant him any more,* she thought, eyeing him.

Once again, he chose not to speak.

"Fine, then. I'm guessing that you're not working for those idiots below. You seem like a hands-on type. If you were, you would have come in hard and silent and left after doing the job right instead of creating an evil circus." Zita's mind wandered, or rather, her libido did, and she gave herself a mental shake. *Don't think about it, Zita, don't… Oye. Stop thinking about how he must have a perfect body encased in all that black fabric and what I'm pretty certain is a fitted bulletproof vest. Wish I knew where he shops, too.*

She cleared her throat and swallowed, her mouth suddenly dry. "You weren't working with the thieves at the museum, or more people would be dead. So, someone else is paying you, because being professional and all, you don't do freebies. You were quite clear about that in our previous encounters. Is the reward for Jennifer Stone what you're after? All I want out of this is to stop people from stealing a chingado sheath or killing anyone in their big, dramatic, evil coming-out party. I know that'd help you. You got something I need. We can help each out here."

He paused. The gun lowered a millimeter. Some might have argued it did not waver, but Zita was determined to be an optimist. *Might as well die happy.*

"If you're after Jennifer Stone, that is."

This time, she got a reply. "Perhaps."

Zita resisted the urge to cheer at having made him speak, but she felt her smile widen. "You can't see it because of the angle up here, but she's with the dude doing all the blabbing in the video below. He farts lightning and calls himself Zeiss, or something like the rifle scope. She's sitting behind him on a smaller chair. It might be a throne, but it just looks uncomfortable to me."

"Zeus."

She pointed a finger at him and nodded. "That's him. Tall, blond, and stuck on himself. So, you want Jennifer, right?"

The gun dipped. His head inclined.

"Great. You need her defender and keeper then." She considered what she had seen of Atlas. "He's squeamish, too, so he's not buying into the whole world-domination-by-any-means-necessary garbage, either. Those jumped-up thugs down there need Atlas to handle Jennifer—she's unpredictable as you may have noticed, and he seems to be her nursemaid."

"Atlas?"

Oddly enough, winning a few words from him made her almost giddy with victory. "Yes. He's here. You planning to kill him?"

A shake of the head.

Zita risked a peek to assess the situation below. Little had changed while the video played. *How long is that, anyway? Is their plan to bore people to death? If that's all they want to do, I won't have to intervene further before SWAT busts in.*

The men with guns stood in various indifferent poses. Tiffany had finished creating a massive dark circle on the floor and consulted her phone as she drew four equidistant smaller circles along the edges of the circle.

Magic stuff. Bad. Very bad. Zita sped up, her words tumbling over themselves. "Great, we can work together then. In return, you don't kill anyone, and you help me out if you see a chance to do so. Absolutely no murdering. Oh, and if the morons brought a bomb, you disarm it." *That is why I tipped off Hound, after all. I only know of two bomb experts, and I'm not bringing my brother to a possible terrorist event.*

Freelance gazed at her for a silent moment that stretched for a seeming eternity. Finally, he gave a brusque nod. With a move that seemed as natural as breathing for him, he swung his long gun to his back and picked up his tripod.

Zita released a breath she had not realized she was holding. "Let your team know not to go after my friends or me, too."

He paused, still in a crouch. "Team?" came the mechanical voice.

Zita waved her hand at the mass of people below. "The woman and the driver of the white truck. I'm assuming they're here somewhere as they keep popping up when you and I meet. I've got people helping, too, but none of them kill, so you guys will be safe from us."

He rose and strode away.

"Wait!" she hissed, "I have a plan!" *Or will have a plan. Any second now. I had hoped to find the sheath before anything happened. Failing that, before the NYC SWAT team broke in to end the hostage situation.* Her attention snagged on the grapple gun and then on the derriere next to it. *Mmm. Nice culo. Sweet toy, too.*

Freelance paused, and his head turned.

To stall (and because if she succeeded, she'd center a plan around it), she asked, "Can I use your grapple gun?"

"No."

She drummed her fingers on her hips. Discovering a glob of yellow filling, she tried to discreetly wipe it off. It fell in a messy splash to the catwalk, splattering her feet. *As always, I am awesome and classy.* "Going to need a minute to make a new plan then." Zita sighed. "Fine. Atlas is the eight-foot-tall guy tied up in the refrigerator in the kitchen with a few other thugs. He's asleep but will wake if you shake him a little. Shake, not shoot, mind you."

Her soon-to-be accomplice gazed at her without comment.

"What? I could have held that information until later, but it's a"—she thought frantically— "gesture of trust and goodwill and all. Don't hurt my friends. One of them can remove the curse if any of your group gets hit by the magic knife. My friends are a ghostly woman in a shiny dress and impractical shoes, a pretty pouty man who is helping people sneak out of the building, and eventually a guy in a ninja mask and gloves. Who should I tell them to expect?"

He failed to answer.

She waved a hand, impatient. "I'm trying to avoid friendly fire, here."

"Big man, naked. Strawberry-blonde woman, waitress outfit," he said.

Theory confirmed. The pickup truck driver is the large man with an amazingly loud snore we saw during Quentin's rescue. Go team me! Zita smiled. "See? Not so hard." She touched a hand to the side of her head, pretending to use an earpiece, and mentally shouted. *Hey, Wyn!*

Do you have to shout? Wyn complained. *Party line's up. I haven't seen Trixie since she wandered off earlier, and Remus is appearing and disappearing. I'm in the middle of something.*

Andy chimed in. *I'm doing my Zita impersonation and skulking on a rooftop two or three buildings away. Still trying to figure out how to get in.*

Zita did her best to lower the mental volume, now that she knew her friends were listening. Moving her lips without letting any words escape, she sent, *A large, naked man and Trixie are coming to take Atlas off your hands. We're teaming up with Ninja SWAT Man and his peeps. I've asked them not to hurt us. You want to stay in there or get out while you can? Garm's searching for the sheath, and Tiffany's drawing magic pictures here.* She checked below.

Tiffany had paused, one hand in her bag and the other touching her ear. The teenage boy slumped further as if he'd like to disappear completely. The witch stalked over to him and yanked him to his feet. She shoved him toward the stairs and barked, "Run!" He took off with the loping pace of someone whose coordination has not caught up to his size. Tiffany resumed digging through her bag.

Andy's mental voice interrupted. *Wait, your imaginary sniper friend is here?*

Freelance is not my friend. He's a temporary ally and very much not imaginary. Zita turned to consider the man in question, but he was gone. *I think. He just disappeared again.* She put her hands on her hips and turned a slow circle, scanning for him.

Wyn's tone was dubious when she joined in. *You've named him now too? I've got a spell up in the room to avoid being noticed since Garm almost caught me a few minutes ago.*

Your illusion doesn't hide your scent, and Tiffany made Garm drink something from a bottle before he ran off.

Are you saying I stink? Wyn replied. *May I remind you which of us is redolent of coconut cream pie?* Despite her jocular words, worry emanated from her.

A smile flirted with Zita's lips. *No, I'm saying he has a nose, and he's not afraid to use it. Mano, you going to be here soon?* Zita checked below again. The evil witch was now chalking squiggly shapes on the floor. A pain thumped against the inside of her head, and Zita raised a hand to her temple, her vision blurring for a second. After she had blinked a few times, the pain disappeared, and she stared down. *Tiffany's writing on the floor, stuff about Hades and power. Can't quite make out what she's trying to say.*

Trying, Andy sent. *The New York Police Department has the museum sewed up tight.*

Spell symbolism does not always require complete sentences. Give me a moment, Wyn sent.

Although her words were inaudible at the distance, Tiffany ordered her men to do something, and they dragged the special hostages behind her. After baring her teeth at the crowd in a cruel mockery of a smile, Tiffany paused in one spot, checked a compass, and pointed. The politician was herded to that position. She repeated her actions until each of the four prisoners was corralled into one of the small circles. Once sitting, their feet were bound. In the center of the room above the witch's head, the video continued to play, with the blond man admiring his own voice and megalomaniacal ambitions to godhood at length.

Even though she had the suspicion she already knew the answer, Zita sent, *Wyn? They're pushing hostages into positions on a giant rune-inscribed circle and Tiffany's fondling the knife. You guys will get up here soon, right?* Once again, she fought her instincts to elbow the person standing too close as her vision abruptly doubled.

A minute later, as Tiffany chalked another rune, the sensation disappeared.

Panic vibrated through Wyn's mental voice as she struggled to remain calm. *If my hypothesis is correct, that circle protects the people inside it. It also amplifies the blade's abilities, perhaps even by an order of magnitude, and collects power resulting from use of the Key. It'll go further and cut deeper, and then those deaths will fuel some kind of magical battery.*

Zita's stomach clenched, and she rubbed her midsection as if that would dislodge the boulder sitting there. *So, she can hurt everyone in the building even if they're not in the same room? Do you have one of those no-cut charms you made Andy and me?*

Wyn was silent a beat. *Without further study, I can't be certain, but it might be everyone outside that circle within a few city blocks. And no, I didn't have time. I can use my shield to protect myself from magic, but I can't cast anything else if I'm doing that. As much as I hate to add to the bad news, Garm has the sheath. Right after I found it, Garm headed my direction, so I hid it up high to keep him away from it. Then I hid in a closet filled with strong, smelly cleansers. He managed to sniff out the sheath anyway, and I couldn't stop him, or he would have gotten me, too.*

Andy beat Zita to swearing over the mental link. *I can't tell where to go from outside.*

It's the only room with skylights, Zita sent, once she finished her own cursing. Bile burned bitter and acrid in her throat. *See if you*

*can do a roof access door. Wyn, you had no choice. Can you sleep Garm
and get the sheath back? Or can Remus get it for you? He's probably
done everything up to and including his taxes by now.*

Wyn's mental voice carried a touch of asperity. *I informed
Remus, and he ran out to consult with the police. The wolf moves too
fast for me to use my sleep spell on him, and that adolescent you fussed
over earlier took the sheath and ran off.*

Zita took a deep breath. "Right. The spell they're setting up can
wipe out blocks or more, and they've got the third piece. We can't
afford to let the cops handle them." Whether or not anyone heard
her soft words, she didn't know, but she hoped her temporary ally
understood, wherever he was. She looked down.

The teenager cringed before Tiffany, the sheath held out like
an offering.

Her smile triumphant, the witch snatched it.

Retreating to his spot at the base of her platform, the boy
wrapped his arms over his head. He rocked in place.

Tiffany rushed to her chair and pulled the knife's fancy box out
of the leather rucksack. When one of her men tapped her arm, she
almost stabbed him.

He murmured and nodded toward the doorway.

The witch's countenance lightened when she saw two nervous
men carrying cameras and one man with a light on a stand, escorted
by another waiter with an Uzi. A light blinked on one of the
cameras.

After a few imperious words, one of Tiffany's bodyguards
walked over and brought the camera crew within the circle. He
remained by their side, while the other guard dropped back to the
stairs.

Tiffany studied the lines of the circle after their passage, and
then touched her earpiece, murmuring something into it. She
reclaimed her microphone and smirked. "Finally. Ladies and

gentlemen, your sacrifice will not be forgotten." Dropping it, she began to chant, raising the knife and sheath over her head.

The boy whimpered and curled up tighter.

"Carajo." Zita recognized her cue when she saw it.

Chapter Twenty

After a second to sort through animals, Zita chose one and threw herself off the catwalk, shifting to a Blakiston's fish owl. Her brown speckled form nearly invisible in the dim room, she arrowed toward the items Tiffany held upraised on the platform below. She spread her wings wide to slow her descent and seize the sheath, not wanting to risk an accidental cut from the knife.

What's going on? I can feel magic building, and it's not a nice spell, Wyn sent.

One of the guards shouted and pulled a gun faster than Zita would have thought possible.

Zita banked hard to the side.

He fired.

The shot missed, but it cost Zita her opportunity to seize the sheath.

Surprised, Tiffany stopped her spell and held the Key of Hades close. Her gaze darted to the side as if waiting for something.

Shapeshifting back to Arca, Zita landed on the platform, absorbing the impact with a roll that ended next to Tiffany. Before the startled witch could react, Zita sprang up, hit the witch hard with a rapid cotovelada to one arm, and then followed up with another elbow strike to the opposite arm.

Under her attack, the witch squawked and dropped both the knife and the sheath.

Zita kicked the sheath deeper into the exhibition hall and then somersaulted off the dais to avoid the bodyguard's swing. She reached for the knife handle as she passed, but missed.

With a shrug of well-built shoulders, Tiffany's remaining bodyguard hopped down after her. From the slow stroll and casual swagger in his muscled form, he was assuming she would be an easy target.

She ran around and vaulted back up onto the platform. Leapfrogging over the witch, Zita went for the knife, but it was gone.

The teenager peeked over the edge of the platform and then ducked back down. *Yeah, go back into the fetal curl, kid.*

The bodyguard altered course to amble after her, flexing his large hands.

Her mind whirled, and Zita shifted to take on jaguar traits. The enormous hall brightened, and scents rose to prominence. Acrid old blood and sulfur and a sweet floral perfume... oleander? *From where?* She sniffed and dodged another blow by the persistent bodyguard. *Circle has poison in it.*

Magic's no longer building, but it's still active, Wyn replied. *Don't touch the spell circle.*

Tiffany screeched behind her. "Someone find the sheath now and kill that bitch! Shoot her!"

"Oye, given you're the one sleeping with the wolfman, is that really what you want to call me? Just saying. Also, you're right next to me. If they fire at me, they'll hit you," Zita managed to squeeze out as she lunged at the bodyguard, feinting as if she was going for his face.

Tiffany snarled. Zita's words must have penetrated her thick skull, because she whirled toward the bulk of her men and announced, "Guard the exits. If anyone tries to leave, shoot them." She singled out the bodyguard who was already stalking Zita. "You, take care of this nuisance! Everyone else, find the Key and give it back to me!"

Good thing I'm going to cheat against him. In the meantime, let's try a wild shot to distract her. Aloud, Zita said, "So, answer a question for me. If the knife already hurts multiple people at one time from a distance, what does adding the sheath do?"

Smoothing her hair, Tiffany stepped aside to allow her bodyguard to pass. To Zita's surprise, she answered the question. "It opens the doors of godhood to the wielder once enough sacrifices have been gathered." She bared her white teeth in a mockery of a grin at the hostages. Gasps and a few sobs rose from the crowd.

One of the camera crew stepped toward the platform while the other two shifted uncomfortably.

The bodyguard next to him backhanded him.

The cameraman stopped.

Tapping a finger against her pursed lips, Zita translated for the people gathered. "So, what I'm hearing is that you don't know. Also, you don't care if you lose all your men in the process because if you use the knife on these people, you'll hit your own guys, too. Way to cheap out on paychecks." She scanned the area. *Where were the knife and sheath?*

The bodyguard who had been advancing on Zita paused and stared at his boss for a minute.

Her superior expression fading, Tiffany pointed at Zita.

Shuddering as if emerging from a dream, her guard advanced on Zita again.

As her eyes swept the room for the knife, she sent, *Where you at, Andy?*

Coming, he sent.

The bodyguard swung again. His face darkened when she escaped the blow.

Zita feinted, pretending to miss, dancing until she stood next to Tiffany again.

The witch was chanting again.

Pausing over Tiffany's bag, Zita twisted and seized the chair instead. *If that bag is full of that napalm-like stuff, I'm not dumping it on anyone.* Holding the chair, she swung it at the man following her.

He caught it, ripped it from her hands, and then smashed it down at her.

Zita somersaulted to the side, falling into her ginga. When the chair broke in half and the wooden dais cracked under the hit, she revised her opinion of the guards. *No wonder he's so sloppy. He's extra strong, maybe has better senses since he noticed me as a bird. Can't tell if he's any tougher than usual, so hitting him as anything where I can't judge the strength of the hit is out. Pues, he still fights like a thug.* She danced backward. Scooping up part of the chair that had skittered across the platform toward her, she threw it hard at the spell-casting witch.

It hit Tiffany's back, making her shriek, ending the chant, and knocking her to her knees.

Tossing aside his half of the broken chair, her opponent grunted as he struck out again, his whole body pivoting to put his strength behind a massive punch.

She dodged below his blow, and the powerful punch whistled by overhead. Zita struck his solar plexus with an elbow strike and danced out of the way.

Air expelled from his lungs with a whoosh, and he coughed, dazed.

Stronger than average, but not that much tougher. Right. While he recovered, Zita spun forward in a martelo rotado and kicked him. She pulled her hit a little, blessing all the years of sparring experience.

Even dazed, his head jerked, and her instep connected with his jaw with a crunch.

He stumbled back and fell off the dais, where he lay gasping, blood trailing from his mouth. One hand went to his face, and he spat out a tooth.

After vaulting down behind him, Zita seized his pistol and threw it out of the circle. Using a foot, she pushed him onto his stomach so he wouldn't choke.

The guard groaned and struggled to sit, one hand cradling his injury. He glared at her.

Zita grabbed the closest half of the chair, the lower part with the wheels. With all her strength, she shoved it hard. The broken chair zoomed by the bodyguard, missing him by several feet.

Almost unintelligible with his injury, the bodyguard managed a sneer. "You missed."

Scarlet light flared up as the wheels of the chair hit the circle, and it tipped over, rolling through the black gunk and smearing runes.

I don't feel the massive spell anymore, Wyn sent.

"Did I?" Zita said to the guard, relief forcing her to grin.

Tiffany snarled again. She raised the knife, which had made its way back into her hand while Zita had been occupied with the bodyguard.

Carajo. She got it first.

Although several feet separated them, Tiffany stabbed at Zita. Crimson-edged darkness whipped from the edge of the blade and slashed through the air toward Zita.

Heat poured from Zita's pocket, and she felt a round shape burning against her leg for a few seconds until the light of the knife's curse died. Behind her, she heard screaming, and a guttural sound. Fear clutched at her, and she turned. The already injured bodyguard was down, this time gripping a long gash in his leg and swearing at his employer. Beyond him, a section of the crowd and some of the other guards moaned and clutched injuries. *I hate that knife so bad. Those poor people. Wyn, she got a bunch of people with the Key.*

Her friend's tone was grave. *Coming. Removing the curse may take several tries if she hit too many more people. The four of you last time were pretty tough.*

One of the skylights shattered overhead. Several people screamed. Rain slapped her with cold as a dark shape hurtled in with a high-pitched screech, landing on his feet and falling to one knee. Spidery breaks in the stone spread from his feet.

Zita blinked. *Andy?*

An improvised mask hid the newcomer's face, but the long braid and form matched that of her friend. Pellets of glass rained down around him as he steadied himself with one hand, and the other closed into a fist. His head snapped up to scan the room. He rose. Then... he giggled.

Definitely him. Andy's here, and he's forgotten how to use a door, Zita sent.

Breathless even mentally, Wyn sent, *I'm on my way. Sending the guards along the way to sleep. Garm's tied up with some bear.*

Zita ran toward Tiffany and slammed a strike into the witch's forearm, forcing her to drop the knife. She seized the weapon and backed away.

Based on her imprecations, Tiffany was more angry than frightened. "Guards, protect me!" she ordered. She rubbed at her scrawny arm, muttering to herself.

Andy turned his gaze toward Zita, and she was relieved to see the sparks around his eyes sinking into his skin. If he shifted to his jet-sized bird form inside the building, the museum wouldn't last. He stood. "Holy... I think I just did a superhero landing. How cool is that?" Andy's voice climbed in pitch in his excitement.

Maintenance is going to hate you for that skylight, especially since the entire east side of the building is unlocked. The circle stinks of blood and poison so be careful not to touch it, Zita sent. "Excellent.

You finally showed up, mano," she said. "You want to help out? I got places to be. Garm's running around, probably randomly eating people. I blame whoever went for the cheap appetizer package instead of a full buffet with a meat carving station or two." She could practically hear Tiffany's blood pressure rising with each word, so drew out her conversation with her friend. She held the evil knife gingerly as her mind raced, trying to figure out where to put it.

Tiffany made a few small, sharp gestures that seemed to cut the air.

Behind Andy, the remaining bodyguard moved to leave the cameramen.

The lighting guy smashed him with his stand. When the bodyguard attempted to stand, the lighting guy cracked him in the head again with his own gun.

The bodyguard fell.

Well, I guess that answers the question about whether or not the cops sent in a ringer with the cameras. Zita ran to interrupt the spellcaster.

With a triumphant shout, Tiffany finished her incantation and four of the ominous blobby humanoids she had summoned before appeared around her. "Kill her," she hissed to them. The handful of captives who had been slinking toward the lines of the circle drew back as the disgusting things moved.

"I was in a hurry and didn't think the cops would let a costumed vigilante through. You know they're here, right? Oh, eww, what are the those?" Andy jerked his chin at Tiffany's creations. His discomfort welled up in the shared mental link, but his voice remained steady, and his mask hid his expression. Blue nitrile gloves covered his arms to his elbows.

Zita inhaled, deciphering scents. *I can smell food grease and soap from your hands, despite the distance. Some dishwasher's going to be upset his work gear's missing.* The sulfuric scent of Tiffany's creations drew closer, and she focused on modulating her breathing. "Tiffy here enjoys making monsters. They're like mud pies, but less inspiring. Didn't you see them before?"

"They got dispelled before I got up to the house, remember?" Andy said.

"They're demons," Tiffany shrieked. "Someone kill this woman!"

Tapping her foot, Zita dropped into a ginga, dancing away from the sludge creatures. "I'm just keeping it real, Tiffy. Don't hate the messenger of truth."

Tiffany grabbed a dull brown amulet around her neck, her mismatched eyes narrow and accusing. "I won't put up with your nonsense anymore, even if I have to take care of you myself." She began to chant again. Two bright spots of red stood out on her milk-pale skin.

Andy inclined his head as he intercepted one of Tiffany's creations. "Classic villain line. I didn't think anyone actually talked like that."

"Also, she's rude, and from me, that's saying something," Zita said. As Tiffany's arms lifted dramatically into the air, Zita smacked the witch in the back of the head. While she inwardly cringed at striking someone physically weaker, she had no intention of allowing her to cast another spell or of dropping the Key.

Tiffany stumbled forward and screeched as if Zita had set her on fire, her chant broken.

"Oh, please. That was totally a gentle, openhanded slap such as might be delivered from a dying parent to a naughty child. Not at all the boot to the head you deserve," Zita said, delaying. "Mano, I need a boost. Would you?"

Andy stepped forward, punching one of the so-called demons. The force of his hit sprayed the slimy matter of the creature all over, and the remains of it collapsed into an inky ooze at his feet. "Sure. One down. It's like punching flubber."

"Why would you punch flubber? And what is that, anyway?" Dodging one of the creatures, Zita ran toward him.

Andy shrugged and stepped over the remains of the destroyed creature. He cupped his hands outward and bent his knees. "It's a non-Newtonian fluid. Maybe I'll search the Web for the recipe for you later."

Using him as a springboard, Zita leapt, Key clutched in one hand, and seized the long edge of a maroon banner. Twining her legs around it, she climbed upward until she was halfway up. The fabric strained but held under her grasp, and for once, she was grateful for her small size.

"Flubber is typically water, glue, and Borax," Wyn called out, her pale, shimmering illusion emerging from the plants screening the employee stairs. "Ugh, those things again?" She paused and made a few gestures as she passed by an unconscious, snoring man with an Uzi.

Andy smashed another of Tiffany's creations.

Tiffany clutched at her ugly necklace and mouthed something, doubtless obscenities.

Threading the knife through the fabric like a needle into a pincushion, Zita was relieved to see that it did not have any apparent magical properties against nylon.

The remaining blobby monsters melted just as Andy swung at one.

"Aww," he said.

Wyn sniffed and walked toward the platform. She stepped delicately over the edge of the ruined circle, her eyes flicking over the symbols. Her mouth tilted upward at the sight of the overturned chair. Pausing, she rubbed the broken chair over one rune. "Nasty thing," she said.

Up on the platform, Tiffany let out a triumphant shout, and a low, grinding sound began.

"Oh, that sounds bad," Zita said. From her swaying vantage point, she scanned the room, seeking the source. Most of the guards on the periphery were down, though she had not seen who or what had accomplished that. She suspected most of them had fallen victim to Wyn's pink mist. The crowd, half of which bled freely, struggled against their bonds. Of the four special victims that Tiffany had selected for her circle, only the mustached politician bled. His swarthy skin had blanched of color.

A heavy crack split the air and then another. As a sickly, lime-green glow lit the unattractive amulet around his neck, a twin to Tiffany's, the kilt-clad statue tore his feet free of his pedestal and moved in thunderous steps toward the center of the room and Zita's friends.

Chapter Twenty-One

Flooring groaned as the marble monolith proceeded toward the platform Tiffany had claimed. Instead of going around displays, he simply plowed through them. Styrofoam, plastic, and wood crunched and snapped under his heavy tread. All four hostages tied within the circle cried out and struggled. Wyn made a squeak of protest and Andy winced.

Zita's fingers clenched the banner she clung to, bunching up the silky fabric. She relaxed her grip and checked to ensure she had not loosened the Key. It seemed held fast. "Get the hostages to safety," she shouted. With a deep breath, she released the fabric and dropped, shifting to a fish owl again. *If there's a next time, I'm going to knock that witch, Tiffany, unconscious, no matter how wimpy she seems.*

As if woken by her cry, her friends began moving again.

"Don't touch the lines. The magic's gone, but they might be poisonous," Wyn called out, her attention flicking between the hostages and the inexorable approach of the stone man.

Andy ran over, picked up the injured politician in his arms, and jogged to the other hostages, setting the man down. "Take care of Tiffany! I'll move the others, then smash it."

On the dais, Tiffany cackled. Her eerie eyes glinted as she surveyed the stone monolith. "Boy, fetch my Garm to me," she ordered the hapless teen. Any hesitation she had shown earlier evaporated, and her stride held only arrogance as she retrieved her messenger bag. Glancing up, she barked an order at her statue. "Tear down the banners. Kill anyone who gets in your way."

Eyes huge, the teen uncurled. Zita had almost forgotten he was there.

The statue stopped, turned, and ripped down a banner.

Zita landed and shifted back to her Arca form. Her head turned to the kid, and she pursed her lips. Her stomach churned at his hopeless expression. *Nothing I can do for him now,* she thought. *Should I feel sorry he's under Tiffany's command or annoyed he's giving up? Maybe she has a hold on him, perhaps even blackmail? It sure isn't love. Okay, let's take her down before she can get her paws on the Key.* She vaulted onto the dais and advanced on the witch.

"Do not make me tell you again, Janus," Tiffany said, her attention focused on digging through her bag. Perhaps sensing Zita behind her, she whirled, clutching a black stick.

Better a twig than the napalm, I suppose, Zita thought.

Ashen, the teen—Janus—gave a quick nod and ripped a glowing hole in the air. Another incandescent circle opened by the stairs. He dove through, materializing at the other end, and then raced down the stairs.

Raising the stick in her hand, Tiffany laughed. Electricity crackled as she aimed it at Zita with a theatrical flourish.

Warned by the telegraphed movement, Zita dodged, dropping to the platform.

The lightning bolt seared the air overhead, close enough to make the fine hair on her arms rise and her ears pop from the pressure. Her eyes watered from the brilliance of the nearby discharge.

Wyn shrieked.

Zita spun around, rolling onto her feet and balancing to defend from whatever new attack threatened.

Andy stood, his back to her. He patted as much of his back as he could reach, now bare as the entire rear of his shirt was missing from neck to waist. Jagged black edges marred what little fabric was left, and his hair tie smoldered, but his long black hair and bronze skin seemed untouched. He turned to stare at Tiffany, his eyes blinking repeatedly behind his untouched mask, as he pulled his braid to his front and pinched out the tiny fire in a deliberate motion. Behind him, the lady in the red dress stared, her mouth agape.

Zita gasped. "Mano?"

"Tickled," Andy assured her.

Tiffany howled. She raised the sparking and fizzing twig.

"Oh no. That's not gonna happen again!" Zita sprinted to the witch and struck her arm before she could shoot again. When the weapon fell, she snagged it.

"Over here," Wyn called. She held up her hands.

Zita tossed the stick to Wyn, not bothering to see if her friend caught it or not. She seized Tiffany's bag. Glass clunked, and liquid sloshed like a warning. "You lost your toys for that."

Tiffany made a grab for it but failed when Zita elbowed her aside.

Hugging the bag close to keep the contents from being jarred, Zita carried it off the platform and handed it to Wyn. "She doesn't need these, either," she said.

"Forget the banners, kill them!" Tiffany shrieked.

Her statue stopped, fabric in hand, lowered his arm, and plodded toward the nearest person. In this case, Andy.

He ran toward the moving statue. "I'll get it." Andy's foot slipped, and glass crunched as he ran. He slowed, finally stopping, and stared at the glittering debris.

The statue took a swing at Andy.

Absently, he caught the fist and held it, still staring at the floor. While he may have been talking to himself, his words carried. "I can't just hit the statue or stone shrapnel will spray out over the crowd. What... Oh." He glanced up at the marble monolith as if startled to find it there.

It tried to pull its hand away and brought the other around.

Andy flinched but caught the second hand. Grinding sounds emerged from where he held the stone man and exerted pressure on the marble. Tiny particles, like sand, dripped from his hands, and he flexed his shoulders.

The statue crashed backward to the floor, tile cracking under its weight. Both arms now ended in stumps.

Her face angry, Tiffany raised her arms to begin casting again.

Zita paid little attention to her words, instead seizing Tiffany's arms and holding them behind her back. "No more mud monsters today."

Tiffany struggled but lacked the physical strength to free her arms. She began prattling about how her talismans were masterpieces and how no one could use them but her. Her volume rose as her indignation grew.

Unfortunately, Zita couldn't tie her up while pinning her arms. She tuned the angry witch out. "Can I get rope or duct tape and a gag? Especially the gag part. I'll settle for a sock, preferably a dirty one."

Withdrawing a pen from her purse, Wyn scribbled on the wand. She bit her lip and seemed to ignore Zita.

Did you get her monologuing? You did! Good going, Z, especially since you have no clue what I'm referencing, Andy sent from where he watched over the statue. *I'm not certain why I wasn't shoved across the room by that thing. I should revisit Farnswaggle's theorems to figure out the physics.*

It's like they can't help but try to talk me to death. Squirrel King and Sobek did it, too. This group had a whole video or something that they were subjecting their captives to prior to the planned mass

murder. That's inhumane. Wyn, you going to help me here or what?
she sent.

The statue rocked from side to side like an upended tortoise, arms thunking and hammering against the tile as it struggled to rise without hands.

Wyn tucked away her pen. "Ahem. If you're quite done, Tiffany? Arca, please let her go and move away."

Zita released the witch and hopped off the platform.

"Queen Halja," Tiffany insisted, rubbing at her wrists.

Wyn shrugged. "Just so you know, your wand is an apprentice or junior journeyman's work. You've gotten this rune wrong, and the positions of these two reversed. It's amazing it functioned at all. I fixed it, though. See?" Holding out the stick, she sent a slim bolt of lightning at the other witch, who collapsed in a heap. She let the wand slip from her fingers into Tiffany's bag of evil magic and wiped her fingers on her skirt. "Ugh, she used blood magic. I'm going to need a bath."

Zita blinked down at the prone Tiffany. "Is she?"

Wyn sniffed. "Just unconscious. Who do you think I am?"

"The biggest witch in the room?" Zita said. She grinned at her friend.

Wyn rolled her eyes, but her lips curled upward, and her tone was light. "Do restrain her before she awakens."

Zita nodded. "I'll just disarm her first," she said, and then carried out a ruthless search. Tiffany carried no conventional weapons. Mindful of her own brooch, Zita removed all jewelry just in case, including a necklace that held a ring and a handcuff key.

Wyn received those as well.

Zita untied the lady in red and used that rope on Halja. "Let me know if any of the jewelry's magic. I think I got it all," she said as she bound Tiffany's wrists.

"No more magic on her. She's not inherently magical." After flicking through the small pile, Wyn touched the amulet and the handcuff key with one finger. "Just these." Her eyes met Zita's.

I'm not asking why someone would enchant a handcuff key.

Wyn giggled, covering her mouth with a hand. "Takes all kinds?" *Then I won't tell you.*

Zita snickered. *Thanks.*

Andy sighed and opened his hands, dropping clouds of white dust. He strode forward to meet the moving statue again as it managed to bring itself to its knees.

"You better believe it," Zita said. Tiffany was just beginning to stir, her eyelids fluttering. "Is it possible to cast without using gestures?"

Wyn nodded. "Depends on the magic system in use. Most often, the motions grant focus... never mind. Just, yes."

"That's all I needed." Zita ripped a strip of fabric off a nearby display cloth and gagged Tiffany. "There you go, Tiffers. All set."

That earned her a round of muffled exclamations from their captive. Zita patted her on the head and turned back to her friend.

Wyn set down the bag and turned her attention to the moaning, bleeding crowd along the wall. Her face seemed torn between sympathy and panic.

With a loud pop that had everyone but the animated statue wincing, Remus appeared next to Zita. "We have a problem."

"More than we already had?" Zita asked, nodding at the statue and the injured.

Remus paused and gave the statue a nervous glance. "A giant black wolf has cornered a grizzly and some people in one of the rooms downstairs. I'm not certain what else to do."

In her mind, Zita swore. Aloud, she said, "I need to go handle him."

Wyn nodded. "And I need to help the people here. There're so many injured, though."

"I got the statue," Andy called, catching his opponent's club-arm in his hand. He must have squeezed because when he opened his hand again, only dust and pebbles remained. "It's going to take a while to do without anyone getting hurt though."

Zita patted Wyn's shoulder. "You can do it. Biggest witch, remember?"

Another round of muffled exclamations came from the bound witch.

"Hush, Tiffy, the grown-ups are talking," Zita chided, letting her hand drop. She remembered her backup plan and faced her friend again. "Oh, and I meant to tell you. In case you needed it, I brought you something. It's in the plastic bag I gave you back at the car along with my chicken so you could keep everything safe in your purse."

A prolonged grinding sound announced Andy's occupation behind her.

Wyn raised an eyebrow. "What's in your bag? Isn't that just replacement clothes and maybe another snack?" After a few graceful gestures and a now-familiar chant, pink smoke twined around Tiffany. The evil witch slumped, eyes closing.

If I say those words, can I put people to sleep without resorting to reciting IRS regulations? Never mind, no time for that. Zita squashed the errant question. "Uh, no. The chicken was it for snacks. I brought your knife, with towels wrapped around it for safety, and a spare mask or two."

Joy lit Wyn's face. "You brought my athame?" *No, you lack any magical ability whatsoever.*

"It's silver. If Garm gets back in here first, you can defend yourself." *Well, I'll always have the tax code.*

A corner of Wyn's lips tilted up. "Not with my sacred instrument, but you may have solved another problem. Go. The crowd will be up and around soon." She dug in her bag and reverently withdrew the towel-wrapped knife. Her smile serene,

Wyn pulled a pair of zip ties out as well and tossed them at Zita. "Only ones I finished enchanting."

Zita snatched them and waved. "Thanks." She paused, uncertain what to say.

"We're good," Wyn assured her. She glanced toward where Andy and the statue grappled. "The amulet it's wearing is magic. If you destroy that, you might break the spell on the statue," she called out.

"What do you want me to do?" Remus asked.

Running toward the main stairs, Zita called back, "Find the sheath and the knife and take them to..."

"Muse," Wyn called.

You picked a name? I still need to do that, Andy complained mentally.

"Right, her," Zita said. She jogged down the stairs, toward the roaring audible now that she was away from Andy's slow pulverization of the marble.

Garm stood in the Great Hall, facing one of the side rooms. He crouched, ears flat, with his shoulders and ruff hunched high above his head. He lunged, snapping his great jaws. His eyes never left those of his opponent.

His move almost got his nose clawed off by the swipe of a massive brown paw. A huge bear blocked the doorway to the room. *Remus was wrong. That's a Kodiak. He's too large to be a grizzly, and his coat has orange in it. Por supuesto, Garm's oversized for the breed he most closely resembles.*

The eyes of the wolf and bear were locked on each other. *Ah. Apparently, peeing rights take priority over surviving a mass murder spell.* A flicker of movement behind a gift shop display caught her eye, and she identified it as the teenager, Janus. When he glanced at her, she jerked her head in the direction of the door.

Janus gave the door a glance filled with a desperate longing. His eyes darted toward Garm, and then he shook himself and ducked down.

With a frown, Zita shoved the long, heavy hair of her disguise over her shoulder and turned her attention back to the monster wolf. *Not going to deal with Janus now. I need to keep Garm away from the people the bear is guarding and any cops who come in.*

Blood splatters and a tiny earpiece lay on the floor near Garm, suggesting that the stand-off had been going on for a while, and explaining why he had not come upstairs sooner. Her nose sorted through the scents. *Male bear, overtones of burgers... is that the bear from the island? He's either got the ability to self-heal like Garm, or he's much better at fighting in bear form than I am. Probably both.*

Garm prowled backward, taking a few steps either direction. His eyes never strayed from the bear, and his tail stuck out straight behind him.

Zita suppressed the urge to pull the wolf's tail. "Dudes. We got to stop running into each other like this. And seriously, dominance battles now? What are you, twelve?" she called out. She tossed her zip ties to the side and flexed her shoulders.

Garm whirled around.

"Made you look," she taunted. "Bear wins."

From his position in the doorway, the bear chuffed, and his nose twitched in her direction.

"If you're the bear from before, nice to see you again. If you're not with this loser, feel free to get a move on. As for you, Garm, I hope you've brushed your teeth since we last met." She affected a nonchalance she didn't feel, though she shifted her weight to be ready to fight.

As Garm stalked on four enormous paws toward her, Zita inhaled deeply. She exhaled a slow, deliberate breath, and sought her focus. For a second, she wavered, wanting to check on her friends above, but she made herself concentrate.

He circled. Fur bristled in his ruff and along his spine, and his ears laid back. "You survived. Surprising. I would take the credit, but your scent bears no werewolf strength yet, and you do not grovel before your alpha. The infection should have changed you by now. Are you ready to admit you're one of the monsters and embrace it? Stop all this foolish protection of the humans."

His body language is more like a real wolf than before. Not mad enough yet though to stop thinking, but I bet I can annoy him into it soon. She started her ginga, relaxing into the familiar footwork. For her, it was a moving meditation, the sort she did best. Her breathing evened into the regular pattern, and she let her mouth fly. "Unlike you, I'm full up on self-esteem and all that New Age-y crap. I'm not about to hide behind some lame excuse of being a beast for my bad choices. I own them. If you don't got the huevos to say the same, you need to do work on yourself. Just saying." She waved dismissively and backed away from the bear's doorway.

Garm leapt at her, his powerful legs launching his great bulk farther than he should have been able to move. His jaws opened, showing endless rows of white teeth.

Of course, she had fought him before and expected the move. Zita flipped to the side at the last second, spinning her body to gain momentum for a kick. The wash of his incredibly foul breath and a splatter of warm saliva hit her, and she grimaced, even as her foot connected hard to one ear. "That's disgusting. Please brush your teeth if you're going to keep fighting today," she said, cartwheeling away. "I'll wait. Really, hombre."

He snarled and shook his head.

"Seriously, you kiss your woman with that mouth? You keep that up, she's going to leave your hairy ass. Then again, she did try her mass murder spell with you outside the circle, so maybe she thought a more permanent end would work," she goaded.

He paused, jaw working without sound, and finally said, "Then I would be collateral damage and proud to be so for her." Garm lunged again, lupine jaws wide.

This time, she did not wait for his attack, though his words made her frown. Dodging his snapping jaws with a twist of her hips, she spun onto his back, letting her full weight crash against his withers. She might be smaller, but even huge wolves were not built to have a sudden weight fall on their shoulders.

His legs gave beneath him, and he howled.

Rolling off before he could trap her leg beneath his bulk, Zita kicked the back of his head twice before resuming her ginga. "You're not much of a ride," she said, letting the movement bring her breathing back under control. She thought she heard a snicker and the movement of feet toward the kitchen, but kept her attention on Garm.

When he snarled again, his words were near-unintelligible, and his eyes glowed a bloody crimson. "You will die." He staggered to his feet.

She shrugged and lured him backward, away from the doorway where the bear guided hostages toward freedom. "Good thing I went to Confession on Saturday then, neta?"

From somewhere above, a single shot rang out, followed by an enormous crashing sound. Both Zita and the wolf froze for a second as flakes of the ceiling drifted down around them.

Statue down, Andy reported. *NYPD must have a really good rooftop sniper who shot its amulet.*

"That was my friends finishing the statue," she explained. "Halja's all tied up and gagged, or I'm certain she'd be shouting at them again." *Might have been Freelance.*

Garm charged at her again, intelligence gone from his eyes.

She calculated the arc of his flight and threw herself forward at the right moment, shifting down in size into a porcupine. Zita raised her quills as she passed under him, rolling out in a spiky ball on the other side.

He yelped and fell away to the side. His wounds were already healing, but he curled around his stomach, where several long quills protruded.

Zita changed shape to a polar bear, spread her arms, and threw her massive form on him. Her weight forced him almost flat and the quills deeper into his flesh. From beneath her, she heard a muffled yowl, and she set her mouth by his neck, growling a warning. She slammed her paws down on his front limbs to avoid any clawing.

His body froze beneath her for all of a second, and then the tension left his body. A derisive laugh had escaped him before he convulsed. His front legs slipped from her grasp, the flesh and bone bulging and contorting grotesquely beneath her. His breath gurgled in his throat, and he quivered all over.

Carajo, if he shifts back to human while I'm like this I'll crush him, Zita thought, horrified, and eased some of her weight off him.

With a half-swallowed whimper, Garm flung her the rest of the way off.

Zita shifted shape again, this time in midair, to a fluffy cat. She twisted and bounced off a wall, landing on her feet. Borrowing a move from Wyn's pets, she turned her back on him and purred, smirking over her shoulder at him. She flicked the tip of her tail at him to add to his irritation. *Sí, that is the cat version of the finger I just gave you, Steroid Dog.*

Garm rose to two giant, hairy feet in an obscene seven-foot-tall mix of man and wolf, body still stretching and reshaping itself. His head bulged upward and then settled into place. It cracked. The embedded quills were gone, as was any damage they had done. "Deny the monster now."

Knowing he would be unable to resist, she ran toward the entrance door, stealing glances behind her.

He took a few steps toward her, a long string of drool emerging from a jaw unnaturally distending by an excess of teeth. His whole body still swelled and twisted as it settled into the new shape, slowing him. He snarled and crouched.

She whirled around at the massive entrance doors as if stymied, and shifted to Arca. "Oye, your new look's not working for me, especially without pants."

Garm snarled and broke, sprinting toward her in an uneven run marred by his still-twisting legs.

Zita transformed to a cheetah and charged at him. Her speed accelerated exponentially, and an instant before they collided, she shifted into a rhino, turning her head away so her horn would not spear him. *Colossal for a wolf he might be, but I'm heavier and have more momentum.*

Bone cracked as he was thrown to the side.

Zita had to continue a few more steps before skidding her enormous bulk to a stop on the slippery tile. She spun to assess her opponent, grunting with the effort.

Garm slumped on the ground. His breath rattled in his throat, and one monstrous arm hung useless at his side. The metallic scent of his blood flooded the hall.

After shifting to Arca, she said, "I'm really sorry about the pain. And hombre, you are not collateral damage. Nobody deserves that." She ran and scooped up the enchanted zip ties.

Garm's body convulsed, and he cried out as he healed.

Zita slammed his hand-paws into the ties and secured them.

As she reached for his rear paws, Remus appeared with a pop. "Incoming SWAT. They didn't want to wait any longer."

Chingado police. Zita slapped the remaining tie on Garm's legs.

She sprinted up the stairs toward her friends.

Andy met her halfway down, worry on his face.

"Cops," she said. At a noise behind her, she glanced back in time to see Janus roll Garm through an incandescent hole. Zita swore.

The kid darted a frightened glance at her, then dove in. The hole closed behind them.

Unable to do more, she ran up the stairs, arriving at the top in time to see Wyn take the Key and place it into the sheath. Black and silver light flared.

Involuntarily, Zita raised a hand to protect her eyes as a protest sprang to her lips. She braced herself, but nothing happened. After a second, she lowered her arms and peeked.

Beside her, Remus and Andy lowered their arms as well.

Wyn raised her head and smiled as she set the reassembled Key of Hades on the battered platform. "It's still magic, but it can only stab the old-fashioned way now, and the bleeding curse shouldn't happen."

"Cops are in," Zita blurted as she ran toward Wyn, Andy at her heels. "We're going to have to use our last-resort escape plan."

Wyn frowned. "I hate that plan. I abhor every single part of it." Still, she picked up the mangled remains of one of the maroon drop cloths and walked to Andy.

He picked her up, and Wyn draped the cloth over herself. Bending at the knees, he leapt up, his strength carrying the pair of them up onto the catwalk. Andy jumped again, out through the hole in the skylight. Behind him, the creaking walkway shuddered and broke, one end hanging down.

"If you want to run, now's the time, Remus. Catch you later in a totally friend-zone way," Zita said. She shifted into a golden eagle and soared up, but not before she heard the handsome man's muttered reply.

"Not if I see you first."

Chapter Twenty-Two

The next night, as Zita snuck through the university building, her first clue that she was not alone was an angry feminine shout and the scent of sweet and sour pork, fried rice, and garlic. Her stomach gave a wistful growl of appreciation even as she hurried to hide in the graduate student warren. Once again, she wore her tired black workout gear and a mask, and both helped her take cover in one of the cubicles.

Another outraged shriek echoed in the room, and Zita fell into a defensive stance before the words registered.

"I can't believe my own teammate fragged me. Rat bastard. You guys watch my gear? I'll get there from regen as soon as I can."

After ensuring her mask was on straight, she padded toward the sound.

Illumination poured from dual screens, shining on the form of a woman sitting in front of them. Her back was to Zita, but the weird blue phone booth purse hanging on the back of the chair and soft click of hair beads suggested who remained so late.

So much for leaving it all on her desk. Don't graduate students sleep? I've dodged more people here than I've ever seen at night in any other building. Pues, I can keep sneaking, or I can brazen it out. Given the way my plans have gone lately, I'll go direct. Shaking out her shoulders, Zita sauntered through the dark office and knocked on the metal section of a partition.

"What? I'm working, mostly," Brandi said, spinning around in her chair and confirming Zita's guess to her identity. A headset sat over her rumpled hair, a microphone curving toward her mouth. Tiny round glasses perched on her nose and reflected light from the screens. Behind her, a decrepit workstation buzzed and displayed a page with a single line of text. Ice melted in a giant cup of fluorescent blue liquid. Next to it, a jumble of food cartons framed a sleek laptop with a separate keyboard that glowed neon rainbow colors. The laptop had the pixelated image of a mostly-naked muscled creature in a bikini stomping through a forest. Somewhere in the wilderness of computer gear, multiple fans whirred. Defensiveness converted to crankiness as she registered the mask on Zita's face.

"You're the one from the convention who stole my clothes!" she accused. "Do you know how few samples I have? If you're here for more, I don't keep them in this location."

Zita shook her head and held out the stack of washed, folded clothing. Though her preference would have been to set them down on the desk, every inch was occupied by the litter of equipment, food, and scribbled-on papers, inches deep in some spots. Her fingers itched to tidy it, but she squashed the impulse. "No, had to clean them. They work good," she said, the cheesy Mexican accent thick. *She saw my real form at the museum, so best to keep up the Mexican charade. Andy doesn't go for stupid chicks, even if she doesn't recognize a good, albeit geeky, man when she has one.*

Eyes narrowing, Brandi snatched the clothing and held it against her chest. "I've called security. You need to leave."

Zita gave her credit for lying with a straight face. She shrugged and set out her lure. It had taken hours of testing, but she had discovered that the trick to keeping her clothes after shifting was to wear Brandi's experimental outfits. "Whatever. You may want to know that your fabric works extra good for people with powers.

Get that on the market, and you've got guaranteed customers once people figure it out. Of course, some might suspect you've got special abilities yourself, so you can decide if you want to publicize that aspect."

Excitement sparked in Brandi's eyes, and she tore her headset off. "It did? What did it do? Can you describe it in detail? That data would be invaluable to my research."

Zita cocked her head to the side. "In addition to having the best moisture-wicking and breathability I've ever seen, you can press the torn edges together while wearing it and the fabric heals even if big chunks are missing. For shapeshifters, it transforms with you instead of turning into fabric shreds, and anything in your pockets comes along, too. I could do more testing with it, maybe get some of my friends in, too, if you want to make a deal." She kept the last sentence nonchalant as if the offer were an afterthought, rather than a practiced line.

Brandi's eyes shone. "Oh, that would be fab! I mean, it's totally nonstandard but who cares?" She paused, and wariness pushed away some of her joy. "Wait, what do you want in return?"

With a shrug, Zita relaxed as her nerves eased. Bargaining was familiar. "Freebies for me and the test subjects, including masks and gloves. I can get you at least three or four more people with powers who'd try it, and one's got access to a whole network of supers."

Brandi pursed her lips, lipstick long since chewed off, and nodded. "You can have four outfits and masks, but I want more than shapeshifters."

Zita suppressed a smile. *I had intended to give one to Remus anyway. We might not work out as a couple, but his business plan did not include flashing customers from what I recall of it. Understandable, if a pity, and I definitely owe him one or two.* "I can do that, but no promises that you'll get any samples back. A list of any specifics you want tested would be okay, provided it's on paper."

The other woman nodded and rubbed her hands together. "Done!" The abandoned headset squawked, and the creature onscreen began bleeding as a monstrous spider attacked. Brandi turned and swore. "Wait, let me clear this up, and then you can give me a number to text once I have your samples. I have that many in storage for the outfits. Gloves and masks will take longer."

"Bueno. Get your stuff together and call this number." Zita freed a Post-It from a plastic dinosaur and scribbled Remus' number on it. She withdrew during Brandi's preoccupation with the game. *No need to tempt fate by staying longer than necessary.*

Since she had time to kill, Zita texted Remus to let him know about the clothing, then spent an enjoyable hour or two exploring the area and mapping out possible buildings for future climbs.

***

When Zita finally teleported to her dark bedroom, it was close to midnight. A sliver of light sneaking through a gap in the jungle print curtains shed enough illumination to move through the room and pull her phone from her drawer.

She thumbed it on and stared at it. After a moment's pause, she pressed a number on speed dial and shifted to her own form.

"What's wrong?" Wyn said on the other end. "Are you hurt again? Goddess, not that squirrel bomber again..."

Zita grumped. "What, I can't call without something being wrong? I'm being social and all. You said you'd have trouble sleeping tonight after spending the night in a strange hotel and then driving from New York back to Maryland."

The phone line was empty for a moment, and Zita felt a pang of guilt. Perhaps she *had* been coasting on the bonds of their friendship if Wyn expected her to only call in emergencies. She peeled off her mask.

"No, of course not," Wyn answered. Curiosity and suspicion warred in her voice.

Zita set the mask aside. "So, why weren't we in the building when all the action went down?"

Resignation reverberated in Wyn's voice. "Yes, of course, we need to get our excuses straight."

"I was thinking we could claim to have hidden in the staff bathrooms," she teased, unable to resist.

"Not the bathroom again!" Wyn said. At Zita's snicker, her friend paused. "Are you kidding me?"

Swallowing down her laugh, Zita answered. "Little bit. That was my second choice, but I thought I'd present it first, knowing how you felt about that. My favorite is that we missed all the action because we left to find Andy. That work for you?"

"Much better. He took too long to come back from dinner," Wyn said.

"Speaking of Andy, how is he? He rode back from New York with you, right?"

Wyn sighed. "He had me pull over at a rest stop and said he'd get himself home. He needed air time."

She knew what that meant. "Brutal. So not taking the whole Brandi thing well?" Zita grimaced and stared at the ceiling.

"No."

Zita voiced her sincere hope. "Pues, he just needs time."

"Perhaps. You realize this is an instance when a friend would console him?"

What, get him into another fight? I can do that, but maybe he'd like to hibernate and process before people jump all over him insisting he lighten up. Finally, Zita said, "Give him a recovery period before you go messing around in his life. He's private, you know."

"True. Fine. If he needs us..."

"We go kick his butt until he's better, duh."

"Very well. Oh, I meant to ask if you heard the latest on that museum incident?" Wyn said.

Zita paused, trepidation fluttering in her stomach. "No."

Her friend giggled. "They got a lot of video from the museum. I haven't caught up on all the media about it, but the NYPD and federal courts are arguing over who gets to charge Tiffany and her minions first. They're being held in a federal prison until then. With the support of some humans-first groups, one or two outlets tried to play off the museum as superpowered gang warfare. They hurt their own cause when supporters got caught breaking into the police station to steal evidence. In contrast, Remus and New York Governor Rivera supported a different interpretation where the second group were Good Samaritans trying to stop the terrorists and rescue the hostages. It helps that every station is running interviews with Remus since he's terribly photogenic."

"That's true, especially in the tight running clothes."

Wyn chuckled and continued, her voice taking on a teasing tone. "Isn't that all he wears these days? Local DC vigilante Arca has been upgraded from a naked teenage gangbanger to an exotic dancer and person of interest in the event."

Tension eased in Zita's shoulders, and she snickered. "Stripper? Where do they come up with this stuff? Can't Arca just be a Good Samaritan? She was even mostly dressed this time."

She couldn't see Wyn, but she imagined her friend shrugging. "Nudity sells better. Apparently, Arca and Mano, who may or may not be her brother, take orders from the brilliant, gorgeous, and talented witch Muse."

Zita made a face, then snickered. "Did they actually describe Muse like that?"

A sniff preceded Wyn's answer, the primness of her tone ruined by the giggle at the end. "I may have extrapolated that part."

Zita laughed.

Static crackled over the line as both women fell silent.

With a deep sigh, Zita extended an invitation. "Andy and I are doing the Water Balloon Death Run 3000 this weekend, right? Now, I know you wouldn't be interested in running it—"

"Who says? I jog," Wyn protested. Indignation sang in her voice.

Zita plowed on. "It's a five-kilometer obstacle-course run, most of which will be through mud." She straightened the plush softness of the blanket on her bed, her fingers caressing the fabric. *Shower and then bed,* she promised herself.

Her voice less sure, Wyn answered, "Kilometers? That's only two miles, right? I can jog that, easy."

After a few years doing taxes, metric conversion was easy. "Three-point-one miles, roughly," Zita said, "You could, but it's an obstacle course where you have to climb walls and swim through mud pits and stuff. Event workers and fans throw water balloons at you for part of it, too, plus the traps. Our team is full because it's sponsored by a charity, but you could run it solo if you wanted to pay the cash."

Her friend's voice deflated. "That sounds painful and messy. You're right, it's not my thing."

Zita stared at her ancient wooden desk. Her darkened laptop hummed atop it, still on from when she had used it to teleport earlier. *If she says yes, food budget's wiped for the week.* "Well, I thought you might enjoy watching the race. Afterward, you, me, and Andy could meet up for dinner. The other two men on our team are newlyweds and too googly-eyed over each other to join us."

"Wait," Wyn paused. "Do spectators get to pitch water balloons at the runners?"

A smile tugged at Zita's mouth. *I wondered if she would catch that.* "Sí, and I figure I owe you a couple of free shots, but I'm not promising to let them hit."

"Text me the details, and I'll be there," Wyn promised. "I'll pick a restaurant that serves meat for afterward. I know how sad salad makes you after a serious workout."

"Great. No place too fancy since we'll be filthy. See you then," Zita said, setting down the phone. Squaring her shoulders, she stretched and took off her shoes and socks. A light caught her eye. *Didn't I turn off everything before I left?* After a minute, she realized her air conditioning was turned down as well, making the place frigid compared to her usual settings. She did a partial shift to gain jaguar traits and loosened her shoulders. A sniff with her heightened senses revealed nothing out of the ordinary. Despite her suspicion that she knew who was there, she grabbed a Taser from the box in her closet and padded on silent, bare feet toward the kitchen. The range's light glowed, and soft, even breathing told her the story.

Oh, mano, she thought, catching sight of her brother.

Quentin lay curled on her futon, grimacing even as he slept. His face angled toward the light, revealing tiny lines radiating from his mouth that never showed when he was awake. He smelled of sweat and cheap perfume. In easy reach, his gun rested on the floor beneath him.

Not like I can judge, given the knives I have concealed in my bedframe. Zita crept to the door and set the deadbolts. Keeping her motions quiet, she scooped up the blanket Quentin had kicked off and covered him again. He drew his legs up further, if that were possible, and pulled the blanket to cover his neck.

Nurturing isn't one of my strengths, but at least I'll be here. Looking for work, but here. She took a deep breath, squared her shoulders, and went back to her bedroom to turn down the job offer in Brazil.

Spanish and Portuguese Glossary

These are definitions of the words as Zita uses them in the book, and may not include all possible variations. The Spanish is primarily Mexican in usage and slang. Needless to say, anything marked with "Vulgar" should not be used in polite company.

adiós: Spanish. Goodbye.

alambres: Spanish. Chopped meat and a combination of vegetables, cheese, etc., usually cooked on a skewer.

arca: Spanish. A chest or ark. Zita originally used it referring to Noah's ark in *Super*.

arroz con frijoles. Spanish. Rice and beans.

ay: Spanish. An interjection indicating sorrow or regret. Similar to "Oh."

brigadeiros: Portuguese. Truffle-like Brazilian chocolates.

bueno: Spanish. Good.

capoeira: Portuguese. A fast, fluid Brazilian martial art known for its acrobatic and dance-like kicks, spins and other techniques.

carajo: Spanish. Shit. Vulgar.

caramba: Spanish. A mild interjection of surprise or dismay.

chingado: Spanish. Fucked or fucking. This has other meanings as well, but this is how Zita generally uses it. Vulgar.

claro que sí: Spanish. Of course.

comprendo: Spanish. I understand.

cotovelada: Portuguese. A capoeira elbow strike from outside to inside.

de verdad: Spanish. Really.

Dios: Spanish. God.

favela: Portuguese. Historically low-income urban areas in Brazil.

finalmente: Spanish. Finally.

ginga: Portuguese. The most basic capoeira footwork, a moving fight stance.

gracias: Spanish. Thank you.

gracias a Dios: Spanish. Thank God or Thanks be to God.

guapo: Spanish. Handsome.

hermano: Spanish. Brother.

hombre: Spanish. Man.

horchata: Spanish. A chilled, sweetened drink made with grains or nuts. The version Zita makes is a rice milk with cinnamon and vanilla.

huevos: Spanish. Testicles. Literally "eggs." Vulgar.

idiota: Spanish. Idiot.

loco/loca: Spanish. Crazy man or woman.

mano: Spanish. Bro. Abbreviated form of "hermano" as Zita uses it. Mano also means hand.

martelo rotado: Portuguese. A capoeira move that combines a spin with a high kick using the instep of the foot, typically targeting the head. Similar to a 540 or "tornado kick" used by other martial arts.

momentito: Spanish. Just a moment.

neta: Spanish. Really, for real, you know.

ni modo: Spanish. Interjection. No way.

no hay bronca: Spanish. No problem.

no importa: Spanish. It doesn't matter.

no lo creo: Spanish. I don't believe it.

oye: Spanish. An interjection that can be used as hey, listen, or yo.

pan comido: Spanish. Piece of cake, literally "eaten cake."

papi chulo: Spanish. Hot guy.

pendejo: Spanish. A jerk or asshole. Vulgar.

pues: Spanish. An interjection, equivalent of well, then, or since.

qué lástima: Spanish. What a shame.

quizás: Spanish. Maybe or perhaps.

rasteira de costa: Portuguese. A spinning back kick performed close to the ground as a low sweeping move. The goal is to hit an attacker's ankle and cause them to fall.

roda: Portuguese. Literally, a circle. This is a gathering where participants play capoeira (and music) in a circle (hence the name) against each other.

sí: Spanish. Yes.

tía: Spanish. Aunt.

From the Author

Thank you for reading!

Please consider leaving reviews for any books you've enjoyed. Reviews assist other readers in finding books and let authors know what they've done right (or wrong).

For the latest on past and future releases, monthly chatter, free short stories, and the occasional other freebie, subscribe to the newsletter on my website, www.karendiem.com. You can also use the website to contact me, browse free content, or find me on social media sites (Twitter, Facebook, etc.). Since I'd hate to read the same stuff everywhere, I do try to post different information in each place. New release notices are the exception and go everywhere.

Arca Chronology

See my website for the most up-to-date list.
Super
Washout (Short Story)
Octopus (Short Story)
Human
Tourists (Short Story)
Power (Upcoming)
Pie (Upcoming Short Story)

Made in the USA
Lexington, KY
28 May 2019